Edmund Gosse

The Naturalist of the Sea-Shore

The Life of Philip Henry Gosse

Edmund Gosse

The Naturalist of the Sea-Shore
The Life of Philip Henry Gosse

ISBN/EAN: 9783337415990

Printed in Europe, USA, Canada, Australia, Japan

Cover: Foto ©Raphael Reischuk / pixelio.de

More available books at **www.hansebooks.com**

HE NATURALIST OF
THE SEA-SHORE,

THE LIFE OF
PHILIP HENRY GOSSE

BY HIS SON

EDMUND GO[SSE]

HON. M.A. OF TRINITY COL[LEGE]

LONDON
WILLIAM HEINEMANN
1896

TO

EDWIN RAY LANKESTER, F.R.S., LL.D.,

JODRELL PROFESSOR OF ZOOLOGY AND COMPARATIVE ANATOMY
IN UNIVERSITY COLLEGE, LONDON,
AND HONORARY FELLOW OF EXETER COLLEGE, OXFORD.

DEAR LANKESTER,

No one who reads this book will require to be told that there were many points of vital importance upon which your convictions and those of the subject of this biography were diametrically opposed. Yet you respected him and he admired you, and of all our friends you were the earliest to urge me to undertake this labour of love. I desire to inscribe your name on this first page of my book, not merely because of those pleasant relations which have so long existed between your family and mine, but as a hint to such readers as may come to the perusal of it with opinions strongly biassed in one direction or in another, that it is wise to "condemn not all things in the Council of Trent, nor approve all in the Synod of Dort." You, at least, in reading this life of your old acquaintance, will be pleased where you can share his beliefs, and interested in the attitude of his mind where you wholly disagree with him.

Believe me to be

Yours very sincerely,

EDMUND GOSSE.

October, 1890.

PREFACE.

ALTHOUGH my father never made any direct reference to
the subject, the condition of his papers left us without
doubt that he had contemplated the probability of the
publication of a memoir. We found that he had arranged his diaries, notes, and correspondence in strict
order, and as though with a view to their use as bio-
graphical material. In 1868 he became greatly interested
in all that reminded him of his early life. He paid a visit
to the haunts of his childhood, he wrote to such persons as
were likely to recall the events in which he was interested,
and he amassed a great quantity of anecdotes and memoranda. As is usually the case with the autobiographies
of elderly persons, his interest in the task dwindled when
he had passed the period of childhood ; but it did not
quite cease until it had reached the point where existing
letters, and an unbroken series of diaries, took up and
completed the tale. The biographer, therefore, has had
the rather unusual good fortune of being evenly supplied
with material, and of having no gaps to leap over.

The subject of this memoir was a man of very singular
character. He was less in sympathy with the literary and
scientific movement of our age than, perhaps, any writer
or observer of equal distinction. It was very curious that
a man should write a long series of popular books, and

should add in many directions to the sum of exact knowledge, and at the same time have so little in common with
his contemporaries as my father had. I hope that in the
course of this narrative the salient points of a remarkable
mental constitution, of a peculiarly isolated mind, will be
found to have been so illuminated as to permit the reader
to form for himself a portrait of the man. I have not concealed or manipulated any of his peculiarities. My only
endeavour has been to present my father as he was, and in
so doing I have felt sure of his own approval. He utterly
despised that species of modern biography which depicts
what was a human being as though transformed into the
tinted wax of a hairdresser's block. He used to speak
with strong contempt of " goody-goody lives of good m e n.'
He was careless of opinion, and he lived rigidly up to a
private standard of his own. I have taken it to be the
truest piety to represent him exactly as I knew him and
have found him.

For various statements in the earlier pages I am
indebted to the still unpublished autobiography of my
grandfather, Mr. Thomas Gosse, and to the memory of my
venerable uncle, Mr. William Gosse. Among those whom
I have to thank for their kindness in helping me to produce this volume, I must mention two friends in particular,
Mr. Francis Darwin, F.R.S., who has allowed me to print
a number of very interesting letters from his father ; and
Mr. Arthur E. Shipley, Fellow of Christ's College, Cam-
bridge, who has very kindly revised the zoological
portions of the text.

CONTENTS.

CHAP.		PAGE
I.	CHILDHOOD (1810–1827)	1
II.	NEWFOUNDLAND (1827, 1828)	30
III.	NEWFOUNDLAND (1828–1835)	61
IV.	CANADA (1835–1838)	89
V.	ALABAMA (1838)	110
VI.	LITERARY STRUGGLES (1839–1844)	149
VII.	JAMAICA (1844–1846)	180
VIII.	LITERARY WORK IN LONDON (1846–1851)	206
IX.	WORK AT THE SEASHORE (1852–1856)	235
X.	LITERARY WORK IN DEVONSHIRE (1857–1864)	271
XI.	LAST YEARS (1864–1888)	306
XII.	GENERAL CHARACTERISTICS	324
	APPENDIX I.	353
	APPENDIX II.	375

THE LIFE OF
PHILIP HENRY GOSSE, F.R.S.

CHAPTER I.

CHILDHOOD.

1810–1827.

EARLY in the spring of 1807 a middle-aged gentleman arrived in Worcester by the Bath coach, and proceeded to modest lodgings, where he was already well known and highly respected. He was a man of a somewhat rueful countenance, whose well-made, thread-bare clothes indicated at the same time a certain past quality and an obvious state of present impecuniosity. He was tall and thin, his hair was prematurely whitening above a dark complexion, and his grave and gentle features very rarely relaxed into a smile. The simple wallet which comprised all his worldly possessions contained, beside his slender store of clothes and necessaries, little except a Bible, and a Theocritus in Greek, which never quitted him, but formed, at the darkest moments of his career, a gate of instant exit from the hard facts of life into an idyllic world of glowing pastoral antiquity. His one other and most indispensable companion was a box, containing colours, a bundle of five brushes, and some leaves of ivory, for he was a perambulating miniature-painter.

This was Mr. Thomas Gosse, father of the subject and grandfather of the writer of the present memoir.   Born in 1765, he had been the eleventh of the twelve children of William Gosse, a wealthy cloth manufacturer of Ringwood, in Hampshire.   The family had been leading citizens of that town, and had always been engaged in the same industry since the reign of Charles II., legend attributing to the race a French origin, and an advent into England at the Restoration.   The name appears to have no direct or recent relation with Goss, a frequent name in the west of England ; but to mark kinship with the southern French family, from which Étienne Gosse, the author of *Le Médisant*, sprang at the close of the eighteenth century. Mr. William Gosse had been not a little of a local magnate, and had served, by virtue of some Welsh estates, as High Sheriff of Radnorshire.   But the earliest introduction of machinery had struck heavily at the woollen manufacture, and he died in 1784, at the age of seventy, an impoverished though not a ruined man.

Of the divided remnant of the father's fortune, Thomas Gosse had, by 1807, long spent the last penny of his trifling share.   He had been trained, at his own passionate request, to be an artist, had worked at the schools of the Royal Academy under Sir Joshua Reynolds, and for twenty years had lived precariously as a mezzotint engraver, first under Anker Smith, A.R.A., then under William Ward, A.R.A., and at length independently. But he had no push in him, no ambition, and no energy. He was of a solitary and retiring disposition, and incapable of any business exertion.   At last, in the summer of 1803, he had ceased to follow engraving.   The fashion for mezzotints was everywhere on the decline, and their place was being taken by the highly finished miniatures on ivory of which Cosway had been the most famous executant in the previous generation. The fashion had now filtered down to the lower middle class, and it was become the practice for artists not of the highest rank to go round the country from town to town, staying long enough in each place to paint the heads of such clients as they met with. Thomas Gosse, who had worked under Edward Penny, R.A., had preserved something of the dry manner of that pupil of Hudson's, but had learned from his own long practice in mezzotint engraving to draw with accuracy. Never inspired or in any way first-rate, his miniatures are nevertheless fairly accomplished, and the best of them possess a certain delicate charm of colour. But he had no introductions, he shrank with extreme timidity from any advertisement of himself, and during the first years of his new profession he sank lower and lower into the depths of genteel poverty. When he entered Worcester in 1807, the fortunes of the gentle, melancholy, unupbraiding man were at their nadir. He was in his forty-third year, and he was ready to despair of life.

In his perambulations he had several times visited the city of Worcester, for which he professed a special partiality. His particular patrons and friends were a Mr. and Mrs. Green, people of wealth and education, at whose table the miniature-painter, with his tags of Theocritus and his Parson Adams' manner, was always welcome. On this occasion he met for the first time a fresh inmate of their establishment, a Miss Hannah Best, a very handsome and powerfully built girl of twenty-six, who occupied an ambiguous position, half lady's-maid, half companion, in the Green household. The fact was that she had run away from her own home to escape the tyranny of her mother.

Her father, Philip Best, of Titton Brook, near Stourport, was a yeoman, who cultivated his paternal acres, and added to his income occasionally by working for hire under neighbouring farmers. His wife, the mother of Hannah Best, was a virago of a bygone type. She was a thorough shrew, who kept her children, and for that matter her husband, in wholesome awe of her tongue and hand. Even when her daughters were grown women, Mrs. Best would scruple not, when her temper was aroused, to whip off her high-heeled shoe and apply personal chastisement in no perfunctory fashion. It was while smarting under one of these humiliating inflictions that Hannah Best had fled to an asylum in the house of Mrs. Green, in Worcester.

The beauty, the strength, the pastoral richness of the nature of Hannah Best produced an instant and extra-ordinary effect on Thomas Gosse. She was one of his Sicilian shepherdesses come to life again. Theocritus him-self seemed to have prophesied of this beautiful child of a race of neatherds. Like another daughter of Polybotas, she had but just come from piping to the reapers on the Titton farm. He fell violently in love, for the first time in his life. Hannah Best, when he proposed, was startled and repelled. This grey and withered man, who never smiled, without fortune, without prospects—what sort of husband was that for her? But Mr. and Mrs. Green, glad perhaps to have an embarrassing knot thus opportunely cut, presented other views of the matter to her. He was a gentleman and a man of education, such as Hannah could not hope otherwise to secure ; he was a man of pure conduct and pious habits ; he would doubtless thrive when once her strength of purpose and practical good sense should supply a backbone to his character. Not enthusi-astically, she consented to marry him, and after a fashion she learned to love him. Love or no love, she made for nearly forty years an ideal mainstay and central standard of his family life. They were married at the parish church of St. Nicholas, in the city of Worcester, on July 15, 1807.

He had taken to a nomadic life, and where he wandered she was bound to wander. They began a desperate flight from town to town, equalled only in discomfort by the hurried and incessant pilgrimages of the parents of Laurence Sterne. The first movement was to Gloucester, where no one could be found to sit for a portrait. In a panic, the couple presently fled to Bristol, where they lodged for a few months, near the Hot Wells, Thomas Gosse painting "valetudinary" and other ladies and teaching drawing with tolerable success. On April 24, 1808, a son, William, who still survives, was born to them in Bristol. After shifting out to Clifton, and then in again to Bristol itself, they came to the conclusion that business was exhausted in that neighbourhood, and in January, 1810, shifted again, this time back to Worcester; thence to Upton-on-Severn, thence to Evesham, and back once more to Worcester, just in time for the auspicious incident to take place of which the previous lines are but the necessary prologue.

PHILIP HENRY GOSSE, the second child of Thomas and Hannah Gosse, was born in lodgings over the shop of Mr. Garner, the shoemaker, in High Street, Worcester, on April 6, 1810. Short rest was given to the unfortunate mother, for in July the family, now four in number, made yet another migration, this time to Coventry, where they took lodgings in West Orchard. For some months Coventry proved to be a capital centre, and Mr. Gosse had plenty of business, but in December of the same year they were off again, and now to Leicester. Mrs. Gosse, however, was by this time weary of such an aimless life, such incessant pitching of the tent a day's march further on. She swept aside the objections of her husband's gentility, and determined to see whether she could not bring grist to the mill. While Mr. Gosse was away painting his portraits, she obtained permission to turn the front room of their lodgings into a shop. She was "at the expense of a large and finely sashed bow-window," and this she stocked with groceries. The consequence was that, when her husband made his next proposal that, as usual, they should move on, she declined to leave Leicester, and allowed him to start on a professional tour through the east of England alone. She was, however, in spite of her energy, unskilled in the arts of shopkeeping, and when he returned, she easily agreed to make one more flitting—as far as she was concerned, the final one.

Three of Thomas Gosse's elder sisters had married well, and were all domiciled at Poole, in Dorsetshire. In the autumn of 1811 he went thither to visit them, and was struck by the advantages that might accrue from settling in the neighbourhood of these three well-to-do establishments. His visit to Poole, moreover, was attended by the exhibition in the heavens of a comet of unusual splendour, and this imposing spectacle impressed his wife as an omen of favourable import. Thomas Gosse passed the winter in visiting his three sisters in turn, was encouraged by them all to come to reside in Dorset, and in May, 1812, returned to Leicester to prepare for the final flitting. The family set out by stages in the coach, their furniture following them by waggon. They spent a few days at Titton Brook with the grand-parents, and on this occasion my father formed his earliest durable recollection of a scene. He was two years and one month old at the time, and his record of the fact may be given as the first example of the astonishing power of memory which was to accompany him through life. "I was in my mother's arms," he wrote in a memorandum dated 1868, "at the bottom of the front garden [at Titton], where it was divided by a hedge from the road. There came by a team of oxen or horses, driven by a peasant who guided them by his voice :—'Gee, Captain! Wo, Merryman!' These two names I vividly recollect, and the whole scene." He never again visited Titton Brook, and it is certain that no portion of the impression could be derived from later knowledge. Travelling by Birmingham and Salisbury, the Gosses came, in June, 1812, to Poole, and settled in furnished lodgings in the Old Orchard.

The borough and county of the borough of Poole, to give it its full honours, possessed in those days a population of about six thousand souls. It was a prosperous little town, whose good streets, sufficiently broad and well paved, were lined with solid and comfortable red-brick houses. The upper part of the borough was clean, the sandy soil on which it was built aiding a rapid drainage after rain. The lower streets, such as the sea end of Lagland and Fish Streets, the Strand, and the lanes abutting on the Quay, were filthy enough ; while the nose was certainly not regaled by the reeking odours of the Quay itself, with its stores and piles of salt cod, its ranges of barrels of train oil, its rope and tar and turpentine, and its well-stocked shambles for fresh fish, sometimes too obviously in the act of becoming stale fish. Yet, among seaport towns, its character was one of exceptional sweetness and cleanliness. And here, though the memory is one of some years' later date, I may print my father's impression of the Poole of his early childhood :—

"The Quay, with its shipping and sailors ; their songs, "and cries of 'Heave with a will, yoho !' the busy mer-

"chants bustling to and fro; fishermen and boatmen
"and hoymen in their sou'westers, guernsey frocks, and
"loose trousers ; countrymen, young bumpkins in smocks,
"seeking to be shipped as 'youngsters' for Newfound-
"land ; rows of casks redolent of train oil ; Dobell, the
"gauger, moving among them, rod in hand ; customs-
"officers and tide-waiters taking notes ; piles of salt fish
"loading ; packages of dry goods being shipped ; coal
"cargoes discharging ; dogs in scores ; idle boys larking
"about or mounting the rigging,—among them Bill
"Goodwin displaying his agility and hardihood on the
"very truck of some tall brig ;—all this makes a lively
"picture in my memory, while the church bells, a full
"peal of eight, are ringing merrily. The Poole men
"gloried somewhat in this peal ; and one of the low inns
"frequented by sailors, in one of the lanes opening on
"the Quay, had for its sign the Eight Bells duly depicted
"in full.

"Owing to the immense area of mud in Poole Harbour,
"dry at low water, and treacherously covered at high,
"leaving only narrow and winding channels of water
"deep enough for shipping to traverse, skilled pilots
"were indispensable for every vessel arriving or sailing.
"From our upper windows in Skinner Street, we could
"see the vessels pursuing their course along Main
"Channel, now approaching Lilliput, then turning and
"apparently coasting under the sand-banks of North
"Haven. Pilots, fishermen, boatmen of various grades,
"a loose-trousered, guernsey-frocked sou'westered race,
"were always lounging about the Quay."

Such was in 1812, and such continued to be for the next
twelve years, the background to the domestic fortunes of
the Gosses. Thomas Gosse presently departed, in his
customary nomadic way, and spent the winter at Yeovil,

in Somerset. Before leaving his wife and children, he took the house, No. 1, Skinner Street, which is mentioned in the above quotation. The sisters-in-law helped with the furnishing, and life promised to be far more pleasant with Hannah Gosse than ever before; but the protection of these relations was tempered by a kind of conscious condescension, and Thomas was not allowed to forget that he had been guilty of a mésalliance. I have heard my grandmother describe how deep an impression was made upon her by the loneliness of her first winter in Poole. She was timid and not a little inclined to superstition, and she had newly come into what seemed to her a large house, with not a soul to relieve her nocturnal solitude, except her two sleeping babies. She used to keep them in a crib in the parlour till she went to bed, as some feeble company. These painful feelings were much increased by a terrifying circumstance, which was never satisfactorily accounted for. There was no shutter to the back-parlour window, and late one dark evening, in the depth of the winter of 1812, one of the bottom panes was suddenly smashed, by no apparent cause. Perhaps a cat had lost his footing on the tiles, and, pitching on the sill, had rebounded against the glass. But it was the last straw that broke my poor grandmother's philosophy.

Partly to increase her income, partly to lose this dreadful sense of loneliness, Mrs. Gosse let some of her rooms as lodgings. They were taken by two ladies of the name of Bird, whose occupation was that of teaching a mysterious art known as " Poonah painting " in private, but on their printed advertisement described as "Oriental tinting." A good many young ladies came to learn; but the fair professors affected great secrecy in their process, and bound their pupils by a solemn pledge to keep the secret of "the Indian formulas." This greatly stimulated Mrs. Gosse's curiosity, and when, long afterwards, the ladies left, she tried to worm out the secrets of the art by pumping the servant-maid. All that that poor oracle could tell, however, was that she had been frequently sent to the chemist's for "million;" this the united brains of the family translated into "vermilion," and it was felt that a considerable discovery had been made.

Immediately after the family had removed into Skinner Street, Philip was seized with a serious attack of water on the brain, and for a while his life hung on an even balance. His subsequent health does not seem to have been impaired and through life, in spite of frequent temporary disorders, he enjoyed a very tough and elastic constitution. He acquired the rudiments of book-learning from a venerable dame, called "Ma'am Sly," who taught babies their alphabet in a little alley leading out of Skinner Street. To her he went at three years old, to be out of harm's way. A little later, he began to suffer from a phenomenon which would perhaps not be worth recording if it had not shown, in our family, a hereditary recurrence, having tormented the early childhood of my grandfather and also of myself. My father has thus described it:

"I suffered when I was about five years old from some
"strange indescribable dreams, which were repeated
"quite frequently. It was as if space was occupied with
"a multitude of concentric circles, the outer ones im-
"measurably vast, I myself being the common centre.
"They seemed to revolve and converge upon me, causing
"a most painful sensation of dread. I do not know that
"I had heard, and I was too young to have read, the
"description of Ezekiel's 'dreadful wheels.'"

At the age of four, the instinct of the future naturalist was first aroused, as in later years he was fond of repeating, by a vision which imprinted itself upon his memory with perfect clearness. Being alone in the Springwell Fields, from amidst the tall ripening wheat he saw rise, close to the footpath, and within a few yards of him, a large white grallatorial bird, which he was afterwards sure was the great white heron, or else the stork ; both of them, even in 1814, very rare English birds. In the next winter, between his fourth and fifth years, the child observed, with much interest, a robin, sitting day after day, pouring forth his cheery song from the corner brick of the summit of the parlour-chimney in Skinner Street, right above the yard, in which the delighted Philip stood watching him. Of his slightly later inclinations towards natural history, a note of his own shall speak more fully :—

"My love for natural history was very early "awakened. In Mr. Brown's library was a complete " series of *Encyclopædia Perthensis*, of which father also "possessed the first seven volumes. For some time " I was accustomed to call this *Encyclopædia Parenthesis*. " Well, the plates of animals in this work, poor as they " were, John and I were never tired of studying, and in "later years of copying. But at Uncle Gosse's I had " the opportunity of looking over the *Cyclopædia* " *Pantologia*, which, though a work of inferior value, had "much more pretentious figures of animals, nicely "coloured. Aunt Bell and Cousin Salter both cultivated "natural history, and when I found any specimen that "appeared to me curious, or beautiful, or strange, I "would take it to Aunt Bell, with confidence that I "should learn something of its history from her. I "learned something of the metamorphosis of insects " from her, though I do not recollect actually rearing any "caterpillars except that of the gooseberry or magpie " moth (*Abraxas grossulariata*). I used not unfrequently "to find the pretty ermine moths (both the buff and

" the white) under the window ledges, and once we
" found on the doorstep a very large moth with light
" brown deflected wings, which Aunt Bell took for her
" cabinet. I presume it was one of the eggers. A
" little later I found, at very low springtides, around
" Poole quays, the common forms of *Actinia mesem-*
" *bryanthemum*, but I think no other species of sea-
" anemone. Aunt Bell taught me their name of
" *Actinia*, and suggested that I should keep them alive
" in a vessel of sea-water. I recollect finding a very
" showy specimen of the strawberry variety, round by
" Oakley's Quay. It was too much trouble to get fresh
" sea-water, and there was nothing known in those days
" of aquarian philosophy, so the poor things were kept
" involved in their mucus until the water stank and they
" had to be thrown away. I well recollect them stand-
" ing in jugs of sea-water in the kitchen window."

To " Aunt Bell," then, belongs the distinction of having
been the first person to suggest the preservation of living
animals in aquaria of sea-water. This was Susan, the
fourth and by far the most intellectual of the children of
William Gosse; she was remarkable for her gracious
sentimental manners, and for a devotion to science, then so
rare in a woman as to be almost unique. She had been born
in 1752, had in 1788 married Mr. Bell, a surgeon of Poole,
and was the mother of Thomas Bell, afterwards an F.R.S.
and a distinguished zoologist. From this cousin my
father in later life received much sympathy, but they did
not meet in the youth of the latter. Thomas Bell was
eighteen years my father's senior, and left Poole for Guy's
Hospital in 1813. At home in Skinner Street, the early
partiality for animals was not welcomed so warmly as by
Aunt Bell :—

" Constitution Hill, not quite two miles from Poole, on

"the Ringwood Road, was the limit of my walking in
"this direction, but here, scrambling up a gravelly cliff
"on the left, on a broad expanse of heath, with a fine
"view on all sides, one day in summer, probably in
"1819 or '20, we caught some beautiful green lizards,
"which I incline, from recent evidence, to believe were
"the true *Lacerta viridis* of continental Europe, not-
"withstanding what Thomas Bell says in his 'British
"Reptiles.' William brought them home in his hand-
"kerchief; but on showing our treasures to mother,
"she was terribly frightened, supposing them to be
"venomous. She ordered us to kill the 'nasty things,'
"which of course we immediately did, though with great
"regret, on the pebbles in front of the house.

If Mrs. Gosse lacked a due appreciation of reptiles, she
was none the less an admirable mother. Her life was by
no means an easy one. The peculiarity of her husband's
profession made him absent from home for ten or eleven
months of every year, and during his prolonged journeys
all the responsibility fell upon her. The income of the
family was extremely restricted, yet she contrived all
through the anxious period of their childhood to bring up
three sons and one daughter in what they were able to
look back upon as a "reputable subgentility;" she took
care that they were always clean in person and neat in cloth-
ing, sufficiently fed and decently educated. Mr. Gosse's
earnings were not very considerable, were so irregular that
they could not be depended upon, and were to a large
degree expended by himself in his ceaseless wanderings.
But his wife had an abhorrence and terror of debt, and
rarely indeed was the rent not paid on the very day it
was due. To secure this, the greatest frugality and
industry were required, and ceaseless exercise of ingenuity.

Between Mrs. Gosse and her husband there was an ever-widening alienation, arising from their wholly different habits of thought and life. Each respected the other, but the peculiarities and weaknesses of the painter jarred more and more on the narrow sympathies and practical energy of his wife. It was an unceasing matter of dispute between them that my grandfather was always scribbling. For, in truth, he was a most voluminous writer, producing volumes upon volumes of manuscripts, which he was always endeavouring, and always vainly, to palm off upon the publishers. His works were varied enough—tales, dialogues, allegories, philosophical treatises, in verse as well as in prose. He completed two epic poems, if not more; *The English Crew wintering in Spitzbergen* and *The Attempts of the Cainite Giants to re-conquer Paradise* still languish in the family possession. Mr. Thomas Gosse is perhaps unique as a very voluminous author who never contrived to publish a line. My grandmother, soon perceiving that all this writing brought no grist to the mill, and even interfered with the painting of miniatures, which was fairly lucrative, waged incessant and ruthless war against it, scrupled not to style it "that cursèd writin'," and scolded him whenever she found him at it. Many years after, when Philip was in the stream of successful literary life, and indeed supporting both parents in their old age by his pen, the war still continued. Grandfather would meekly object, "But there's Philip; he writes books; you don't find fault with *him !*" "Philip! no, his books bring in bread-and-cheese for you and me! When did your writings ever bring in anything?" And the meek author of the *Cainite Giants* would fall back on his favourite ejaculation, "Pooh! my dear!" and let the discussion drop.

Like all prudent housewives, Mrs. Gosse had a strong aversion to tramps. Her husband, on the contrary, was as easy a prey to them as the great Bishop Butler was, and squandered his halfpence on their ill-desert. Once, when the family was at dinner, a beggar strolled to the door; the maid came in and told the tale. My grandmother refused—"Nothing for him!" But grandfather's soft compassionate heart stayed the denial. "Oh yes! here's a halfpenny for the poor man." The beggar who, through the open parlour-door, had heard all, shouted in, as he took the copper, "God bless the man,—but not the woman!"

Thomas Gosse was a great reader, especially of poetry, but his wife had no approval for this exercise either. In later years the children often recalled how he would, while engaged in finishing a miniature in the back parlour, lay down his brush and take up a volume of verse, till, on hearing Mrs. Gosse's footstep in the passage, he would hastily whip it under his little green-baize desk and set to work on the ivory. My father well remembered the borrowing of Scott's *Lady of the Lake* and the *Lord of the Isles* in their original quartos, and especially, about 1816, the arrival of a batch of Byron's *Tales*, then quite new, and in particular *The Siege of Corinth.* These my grandfather read and re-read with an evident delight, to the great curiosity of his little second son, in whom the literary instinct was already faintly awakened; but the pleasure was confined to himself as a matter of course, since Mrs. Gosse, from her absolute ignorance of books, could not have appreciated or even comprehended it.

When the miniature-painter was expected home from one of his journeys, his little sons, evening after evening in summer-time, would go up to the Angel Inn in the Market Place, and wait on the pavement till the Salisbury coach came rumbling in. The particular day of his coming was never announced, and the children would be often disappointed, till at length one evening they would see the white hair, the strange costume, the familiar tall thin figure on the box. The dress in which he would reappear was ever a subject of speculation. Once he arrived in yellow-topped boots and nankeen small-clothes; another time in a cut-away, snuff-coloured coat; and once in leather breeches. Expostulation on these occasions was thrown away; his unfailing resource under my grandmother's sarcasm was, " Pooh! the tailor told me it was proper for me to have!" His copious head of hair had grown pure silver before he was fifty, and was extremely becoming. In spite of the beautiful and venerable appearance with which nature had supplied him, he nourished a guilty hankering after a brown wig. My grandmother had long suspected the existence of such a piece of goods, but he had never had the temerity to produce it at home. At last, however, when Philip was thirteen or fourteen years of age, the old gentleman came home from his travels daringly adorned with the lovely snuff-coloured peruke. My grandmother was no palterer. Her first salute was to snatch it off his head, and to whip it into the fire, where the possessor was fain ruefully to watch it frizzle and consume.

Mr. Thomas Gosse had collected a considerable mass of miscellaneous literary information, and his son afterwards often regretted that he so seldom felt drawn to impart it to his children. The memory of his second son would certainly have borne away the greater portion of any instruction so given, and as a very extraordinary instance of the child's retentive power, I may mention the following fact:—My father happened once to relate to me a conversation he had with his father about the year 1823—that is to say, nearly half a century previously—in the course of which Mr. Thomas Gosse had quoted a stanza of a poem on the Norman Conquest, in which there were many Saxonisms. This stanza my father had never heard a second time, had never met with in any book, and yet remembered so perfectly that I, happening to recollect the source, begged him (in 1869) to write it down. He did so literally as follows :—

> " With thilka force he hit him to the ground,
>   And was demaising how to take his life ;
> When from behind he gat a treach'rous wound,
>   Given by De Torcy with a stabbing knife.
> O treach'rous Normans ! if such acts ye do,
> The conquer'd may claim victory of you."

The passage comes from the twenty-eighth stanza of Chatterton's *Battle of Hastings No.* 1, and the divergencies are so extremely slight and unimportant that they merely add to the impression of the extraordinary tenacity of a memory which could retain these words from childhood to old age after only hearing them once recited.

In a paper which has been printed since his death,[1] my father has described the schooling which he enjoyed in Poole. After having imbibed a slender stream of tuition successively from Ma'am Sly, and from a slightly more advanced Ma'am Drew, at the age of eight he joined his elder brother at the school of one Charles Sells, whose establishment was at that time the best day school in Poole. While he was there, Mrs. Gosse " would sometimes, for economy, keep us at home a quarter to carry on our studies in the back garret by ourselves. We were indus-trious, and mother was on the keen look-out, and we did not miss much." It was before this, in 1815, that Philip began to form a friendship which lasted, with only one momentary interruption, until adolescence and the un-timely death of his friend. John Hammond Brown was the nephew of a widow lady, a Mrs. Josiah Brown, who

---

[1] "A Country Day School Seventy Years Ago," in *Longman's Magazine* for March, 1889.

lodged in the Skinner Street house in succession to the fair professors of the mystery of Poonah-painting. The two little boys, who were identical in age, and who shared several peculiarities of temperament which were not found in any of their playmates, immediately became and remained inseparable companions from morning to night. My father has recorded, " My tastes were always literary. As early as I can recollect, a book had at any time more attraction for me than any game of play. And my plays were quiet; I always preferred my single playmate, John Brown, to many." In another note I find this statement enlarged :—

"From infancy my tastes were bookish. I can recall "myself, when a very tiny boy, stretched at full length "on the hearth-rug before the parlour fire, reading with "eager delight some childish book ; and this as an "ordinary habit. The earliest books I read were, I "think, *London Cries*, *The History of Little Jack*, and "*Prince Leboo*. Old Mrs. Thompson, our former land-"lady, gave me a Sparrman's *Travels in South Africa* "*and the East Indies*. This became one of my most "valued books, yet, owing to my morbid bashfulness, I "could not be persuaded to formally thank the old lady "for her gift. *Robinson Crusoe* was an early delight, of "course, and *Pilgrim's Progress* another. This latter "I knew nearly by heart when I was ten or twelve years "old. It was the first part only that we had. "Christiania's adventures I did not know until long "after, and when I came to read them they never "possessed for me the same charm as Christian's. I "could not persuade myself that they were genuine."

The first break in the monotony of the child's life occurred when he was nine years old. For seven years Mrs. Gosse had not seen her parents, and in order that she might go to Titton, it was necessary first of all to find a place where she could leave her children. They were accordingly boarded at the house of a farmer in the village of Canford Parva, a mile from Wimborne. This was the first experience of the country, or of anything but the tarry quays of Poole, which the children had enjoyed. My father's memory of it was very vivid, but it was divided between the meadows and the orchards, on one hand, and a store of the highly coloured romances, by Miss Porter and Lady Morgan, which had just come into fashion, and had found their way down into a cupboard of the Dorset farmhouse. It was here, moreover, that he read *Father Clement*, and formed, at the tender age of nine, the basis of that violent prejudice against the Roman Catholic faith and practice which he retained all through life. At Canford Magna there was a nunnery, and the precocious little Protestant shuddered in passing it, with a vague notion of the terrible practices which, no doubt, were the occupation of its inmates.

It is pleasanter, and more agreeably characteristic, to note that the event which, above all others, illuminated the visit to Canford Parva was the discovery of a kingfisher's nest. Just beyond the farm, a short and narrow lane ran down to a bend of the river Stour. In this lane there was a low gravelly cliff over a horse-pond. From a hole in this cliff the child used to watch the brilliant little gem fly out many times a day, and as often return ; while, by going a few rods further, the bird could be seen coursing to and fro over the breadth of the river, sitting on the low horizontal branches, or swooping down for fish. The child was already naturalist enough fully to appreciate the interest of this incident. The visit to Canford Parva was the only stay in a rural English district which my father enjoyed until, in middle life, he came to reside in Devonshire.

Next year, in July, 1820, the boys had another brief outing, this time by sea to Swanage. It was haymaking time, and they were playing in the hayfield, whence the crop was being carried until pretty late in the evening. It was quite dark, when Philip found, moving rapidly through the short mown grass, already wet with dew, a half-grown conger eel, though the field was a long way, perhaps half a mile, from the seashore. The incident was a decidedly curious one; though far from unprecedented, and, in fact, mentioned by Yarrell as having occurred within his experience. About the end of this same year, Poole, like other country towns, was almost universally illuminated on occasion of the termination of the trial of Queen Caroline in accordance with popular sympathy. The house of the Gosses became, on this occasion, the cynosure of Skinner Street, for while neighbours were content with a candle or two in each window, the Gosse boys adorned their front with heads and figures borrowed from out of the paternal portfolio—the queen at full length, a dark bandit who did duty for "Non mi ricordo" Majocchi, a priest, a scaramouch, and other vaguely effective personalities, handsomely illuminated from behind.

The first incident which could be called a landmark in this uneventful career was the departure of the elder brother to make his way in the world. Early in 1822, William, being fourteen years old, sailed from Poole for service in the firm of his uncle, in the port of Carbonear, Newfoundland. Philip accompanied him on board the ship, returning in the pilot's boat, and William's last act was to tie a comforter round his brother's throat just as the latter was leaving the ship. This mark of brotherly care would bring tears into the younger boy's eyes for months afterwards, whenever he thought of it. It appears that the departure of William drew more attention to Philip, whose curious cleverness in certain un-familiar directions began from this time to be more and more a subject of local talk. In spite of his mother's absence of education, she knew the value of book-learning, and the aptitude which her second son showed induced her to make peculiar sacrifices for his advantage. She was determined to give him a chance of acquiring some knowledge of Latin, and in January, 1823, she contrived to get him admitted into the well-known school at Blandford. Of his brief stay in this school not many memorials exist. But one anecdote may not be thought too trivial to relate, because it illustrates the early development of the boy's independent curiosity in all matters connected with literature :—

"One day, when we boys were out walking on the "Wimborne Road, and had just come to the opening "of Snow's Folly and Hanger Down, an elderly "gentleman with a long beard met us, and gathering the "elder boys around him, began to question us about "learning. He pulled an Eton Latin Grammar from "his pocket, and turning to the example '——nec hujus "'existimo, qui me pili æstimat,' asked us to explain "it. Several, in an instant, *construed* it, correctly enough, "'Nor do I regard him this, who esteems me not a hair.' "'Yes,' said our bearded friend, 'that is the translation, "'but I want the meaning ; what is meant by *this ?*' "All were dumb, till I, whose curiosity had long before "been exercised on this very point, having guessed out "for myself, unaided, the solution, snapped my fingers at "the word '*this*,' as I repeated it to him. He immedi-"ately approved my answer, and praised me before the "others as ' a thinker.'"

When my father, however, in later years was desired to recall the incidents of this part of his boyish life, he was apt to recollect more clearly when the narcissus bloomed in fields beside the Stour, and where yellow frogs of an uncommon marking were to be found, than what boys more usually remember. Yet he never failed highly to appreciate the education which he received during these months, the only classical training which he ever enjoyed. His favourite walk was over the race-down to Tarrant Monkton, along the course of that primitive telegraph, on the six-shutter principle, which had been opened by Government to connect London with Weymouth in the course of the Napoleonic wars. Of the working of this line of telegraph, a picturesque account is given in Mr. Hardy's admirable Dorset novel, *The Trumpet Major.* In summer my father used to wander off, across Lord Portman's park, to the bend in the river just below Stourpaine, where the "clotes," the water-lilies, grow thickest; and in after years, looking back on these childish excursions, he used to repeat with peculiar gusto those exquisite lines of William Barnes'—

> " Wi' eärms a-spreadèn, an' cheäks a-blowèn,
>> How proud wer I when I vu'st could zwim
>> Athirt the pleäce where thou bist a-growèn,
>> Wi' thy long more vrom the bottom dim ;
>>> While cows, knee-high, O,
>>> In brook, wer nigh, O,
>> Where thou dost float, goolden zummer clote ! "

The inseparable John Brown had accompanied his friend to Blandford, and these two were sufficient unto themselves throughout their school-days there. My father, at no time of life much given to promiscuous cordiality, does not seem to have formed lasting acquaintanceships with any of his Blandford schoolfellows. John Brown and he continued their zoological studies with unabated ardour, and at this time began to make coloured drawings of animals with great assiduity. In 1824 Wombwell's travelling menagerie arrived at Blandford. The two young naturalists were excessively interested in a canvas painting on the booth, which advertised an animal unknown to either of them by name or figure. This was "The Fierce Nondescript, never before seen in this Country alive." John Brown, to allay his feverish curiosity, contrived overnight an interview with the attendant, who confessed that the Nondescript was also sometimes known by the less mysterious name of the tortoiseshell hyena. This, on the following day, was found to be the case, and the boys had the delight of seeing the South African hyena or Cape hunting-dog (*Lycaon pictus*), now familiar to English sightseers, but in those days a quadruped never before secured by any travelling menagerie.

Philip was at Blandford until the end of the first term of 1824. He acquired during his one full year at Blandford a good fundamental knowledge of Latin and the elements of Greek, being well grounded in the grammar of the former language. His vocabulary in Latin was not extensive; he had read but few authors, and only Virgil at all thoroughly, yet he had secured an acquaintance with the language which was of great service to him in later life, and which he steadily increased until quite recent years. Like all boys who are destined to be men of letters, he began to versify, and such specimens of his early rhymes as have been preserved from his Blandford days show that he was beginning to secure facility in the arrangement of phrases. The expense of keeping him at boarding-school now became more than the household at Poole could sustain any longer, and he came home early in his fifteenth year. For the next twelvemonth he continued his studies as well as he could with none, or with at best very inadequate local help.

At fifteen Philip Gosse was a broad-shouldered, healthy

boy, short for his age, with a profusion of straight dark-brown hair on his head, and a dark complexion which he inherited from his father. He describes himself at that age as "a burly lad, tolerably educated, pretty well read, fairly well behaved, habitually truthful, modest, obedient, timid, shy, studious, ingenuous." It was time for him to begin bread-winning, but what was to be done with him? Poole was a town of merchants. His brother William had entered life in a merchant's counting-house; why should not he? His parents had kind and influential friends, and one of them spoke to Mr. Garland, the much-respected head of a large mercantile house in the Newfoundland trade. There was a junior place vacant in his Poole business, and he sent permission for Philip to call on him. Accordingly, Mrs. Gosse took him to the office, where the kind and genial old gentleman readily offered to engage the boy as a junior clerk, at a salary of £20 per annum to begin with. This, of course, would not pay for his food, yet it was better than lying idle, and there were hopes that it might lead to something better. The proposal was thankfully accepted.

The counting-house of Messrs. George Garland and Sons was a spacious old-fashioned apartment, adapted from a sort of corridor in the rambling family mansion. The whole of one side, except an area at the doors which was shut off by a rail, was occupied by three ample desks, which looked down into the back-yard. The first of these desks was occupied by Mr. Edward Lisby, chief clerk, a spruce little man of about twenty-three. The second was assigned to young Gosse, and the third remained untenanted. Each clerk was ensconced in a den, since each several desk was surrounded by a dark wainscot wall, around the summit of which ran a set of turned rails. Mr. Lisby was very silent; the new clerk was very shy; and a portentous hush, broken only by the squeaking of pens, was accustomed to reign in that solemn apartment. There was not nearly work enough to keep the boy employed, and he enjoyed a great deal of leisure. The time he spent at Mr. Garland's office was very pleasant. The further end of the counting-house was occupied by an antique bookcase, in which were many old books and a few new ones. There was an extensive series of the *Gentleman's Magazine*, and another of the *Town and Country Magazine ;* and these the boy read with great avidity. But, far more important to record, it was in this bookcase that Philip discovered a volume which exercised, as he has said, "a more powerful fascination upon me than anything which I had ever read." This was the first edition of Byron's *Lara*, the issue of 1814, with Roger's *Jacqueline* printed at the end of it. To the close of his days my father used to avow, with rising heat, that it was most impertinent of Rogers to pour out his warm water by the side of Byron's wine. *Lara* he had till now, in 1825, never even heard of, but as he read and re-read, devouring the romantic poem with an absorbing interest which obliterated the world about him, almost the entire book imprinted itself upon his memory, and remained there indelibly impressed. The reading of *Lara*, he says, " was an era to me ; for it was the dawning of Poetry on my imagination. It appeared to me that I had acquired a new sense. Before this I had, of course, read some poetry, many standard pieces of the eighteenth century, including something of Cowper, Thomson, and Shenstone ; but Shakespeare, Milton, and Dryden I knew only by the extracts in my school-books, and of the modern sensational school nothing at all." About the same time, the two volumes of Wordsworth's *Lyrical Ballads* came into his hands, and caused him great pleasure, tame, however, it must be confessed, in comparison with his ecstatic enjoyment of Byron's tale.

There was in the office bookcase a copy of Scarron's *Roman Comique* in English, and the broad humour of this farcical classic delighted the boy amazingly, although its coarseness a little shocked him. He enjoyed it infinitely more than *Don Quixote*, which he had read a short time before. "Perhaps my boyish mind," he says, "could not appreciate the polished wit and satire of Cervantes so well as the broad grins and buffoonery of Scarron." But *Don Quixote* was a book to which he retained through life an inexplicable aversion. Another novel in the office book-case was the immortal *Joseph Andrews*, with which he was so greatly charmed that, on a second perusal, he could not refrain from taking it home to read aloud in the evenings for the delectation of his mother and his sister. The rough expressions which he had not observed as he read the book to himself, however, became painfully patent when propounded openly by the fireside, and he found, what others have discovered before and since, that *Joseph Andrews*, noble as it is, is one of the male children of the Muses ; he had to make an excuse and leave the tale half told. Among other literary stores laid up in this delight-ful bookcase were the "Peter Porcupine" pamphlets of William Cobbett, and these, when everything else was exhausted, were waded through for lack of better reading in many unoccupied hours.

John Brown remained at school in Blandford until mid-summer, 1825, when the friends were once more reunited in Poole. He was presently put into a counting-house on the Quay, and after office-hours, which closed at five in each case, the two lads were always together. They read and studied science together, tried their hands at music, and stained their clothes with chemicals, on one occasion coming near to a public scandal with the unparalleled success of an artificial volcano. A large room at the top of the house now occupied by John Brown's mother they turned into a studio and workroom. John was mechanical, Philip inclined to the arts, both were equally bookish. One experiment of theirs mildly foreshadowed a famous invention of our own day. Philip contrived to make an acoustic tube of the rain-spout that led from a gutter within the parapet of his mother's house all down the front of the house to the street, and into this sort of speaking-tube, the speaker being concealed close beneath the roof, he used to breathe prophetic utterances, which rose as if from the pavement, to the alarm of mystified passersby. But the serious amusement or main studious entertainment of the boys was zoology. From every available source they added to their knowledge of natural history, eagerly reading up for the dimensions, colours, postures, and habits generally of the principal quadrupeds and birds. This, with incessant copying of cuts and plates of animals, could not fail to give them both a solid substratum of zoological knowledge.

At sixteen they were children still, unsophisticated, bashful, and ignorant of the world, far more interested in such a show as Sir Ashton Lever's travelling exhibition of natural history than in any public events or local politics. It was the collection which I have just mentioned which first awakened in Philip Gosse one of the master passions of his life, a love of exotic lepidoptera. The Lever Museum contained one of the grand silver-blue butterflies of South America,—it was probably *Morpho Menelaus*—and this created an extraordinary longing in the boy's heart to go out and capture such imperial creatures for himself. It was outside this show that was exhibited the portrait of a mermaid, " radiant in feminine loveliness and piscine scaliness." But the boy had studied his zoology with far too much care to be deceived for one moment by the real object, a shrivelled and blackened little thing composed by the ingenuity of some rascally Japanese fisherman out of the head and shoulders of a monkey and the body and tail of a salmon. It was in the year 1826 that Philip made his first *début* in the world of letters, in a very humble way. He composed a little article on "The Mouse a Lover of Music," and sent it to the editor of the *Youth's Magazine*. It was usual, in those days, to get the local M.P., so far as his good nature extended, to frank your letters, and the boy appeared early at the door of Mr. Lester, the member for Poole. He had addressed the envelope to the publishers, "Messrs. Hamilton, Adams, and Co.;" the footman, as he took it in, misread the "Messrs." for "Miss," and benevolently smiling, rallied the lad on its being "for his young lady." The member franked it, however, and in due time, to the inexpressible joy of its author, "The Mouse a Lover of Music" appeared, signed Φιλιπ, in the pages of the *Youth's Magazine*.

One day, in 1826, he had a narrow escape from death by drowning. Standing at the edge of the quay just behind his employers' business premises, he suddenly slipped down between the quay and one of Garlands' brigs which was anchored there. By an extraordinary good fortune he fell astride a spar which happened to be lashed alongside at that point, acting as a "fender," and he was hoisted up again, jarred and terrified, but unhurt, having escaped the death of a rat by a mere hand-breadth. A further stage in his imaginative susceptibility was marked this year by his enjoyment of Campbell's *Last Man*, then recently published in the *New Monthly Magazine*. He thought it very noble, as indeed it is, but in making copies of it for his friends he must needs, an infant Bentley, be tampering with the text, and, in his remarkable revision, a line—

"The aggregate of woe,"

takes the place of Campbell's (truly rather feeble)

"That shall no longer flow !"

Employment at the Garlands' office came to a natural end towards the close of 1826, when they found they had no further use for a junior clerk. Mrs. Gosse became anxious once more, and was constantly urging Philip to "show himself about on the Quay," that the sight of him might keep him in the mind of mercantile acquaintances. But he had no liking for the babel of the Quay, and after going thither he used immediately to take himself off over the ferry to Ham, where he would sit for hours in one of the vessels building in the shipwrights' yards, reading some book which he had brought in his pocket. Friends, however, would appear to have noticed him as he strolled across, or else their memories needed no such refreshing, for at length, as the spring of 1827 came on, the firm of Messrs. Harrison, Slade, and Co. offered the lad employment as a clerk in their counting-house at the port of Carbonear, in Newfoundland. He dreaded expatriation, and this proposal did not meet with his wishes; his mother, however, promptly vetoed all objection on his part, and he presently signed an agreement to go out for six years to the American counting-house, on a very small salary. On Sunday morning, April 22, 1827, as the bells were ringing the people of Poole to church, having a few days before completed his seventeenth year, Philip Gosse, with a very heavy heart, slipped down the harbour in a boat and climbed on board the brig *Carbonear*, which was lying at Stakes ready to get under way for Newfoundland.

CHAPTER II.

NEWFOUNDLAND.

1827, 1828.

THE brig *Carbonear*, on which Philip Gosse sailed away for the New World, was a poor tub of a craft. Her sailing powers were limited; the voyagers suffered from a large proportion of westerly winds; and the voyage extended over not fewer than forty-six days. The prevalence of fine warm weather, however, the pleasant society on board, together with the rare faculty of observation which the boy possessed, and could now exercise on so novel a field as the ocean, prevented his feeling the inordinate length of the voyage to be at all tedious. Beside the captain and mate, there were three other passengers—Luke Thomas, a lad two years younger than Gosse; a Mr. Phippard, sailmaker to the firm; and Mr. Oehlenschläger, a German gentleman from Hamburg, now going out to establish a mercantile connection in St. John's. The grown-up people behaved with great cordiality to the two lads, and they formed a lively party around the cabin-table. Philip's sense of depression at parting from home was very transient. As soon as he grew accustomed to the sickening motion of the sea, his pleasures began. He soon learned to mount the rigging, and to take up a pleasant station in the maintop, delighting to sit and read there, in the warm sunshine, with all the turmoil of the ship far below him. Of course, the first time that he essayed this feat he had to pay his footing, for one of the sailors swarmed up after him, and tied his legs with an end of spun-yarn in the rigging, until he promised to stand treat with a quart of rum.

He soon found that he could write and even draw without any difficulty on board, in fair weather ; and so he went on with the literary work which had beguiled his young ambition at Poole, a volume of Quadrupeds, copied and described from various books in his possession. This was good practice, though not in any sense an original exercise; he kept hard at it, however, and it was finished in time to be sent home on the first returning vessel from Carbonear. More important, as a work of self-education for the future naturalist, was a copious journal kept for the delectation of the loved ones at home, mainly devoted to the birds and animals seen or conjectured on the voyage, and illustrated by coloured drawings of everything that seemed paintable, such as whales spouting ; porpoises leaping and plunging ; petrels, boatswain-birds, "hog-downs," and other birds ; Portuguese men-o'-war (*Physalia*), of which curious and gorgeous beings they encountered several ; icebergs ; Cape St. Francis from seaward, and the like. All this, though the adventures which were chronicled were small and trite, was excellent exercise both for pencil and pen. It was while on the Atlantic that the lad found himself, almost suddenly, to have acquired the art of finishing a drawing—of "working-up," as it was termed in the profession of miniature-painting.

During this voyage, Philip Gosse scrupulously obeyed what had been his mother's final injunction, that he should read his Bible daily. No one else in the ship had culti-vated the same habit, and, as there was no opportunity for retirement, and as the lad was obliged to brave publicity, it was not altogether easy to persevere. His young shipmate, Luke Thomas, looked upon the practice with stern disapproval, and took an opportunity of advising him "to get rid of that sort of thing, as that wouldn't do for Newfoundland." At no period of his life, however, was my father affected in the slightest degree by considerations of this sort. His conscience was a law to him, and a law that he was prepared to obey in face of an army of ridicule drawn up in line of battle. At this time, he was far from having accepted the vigorous forms of religious belief which he adopted later on. He was not, as he would afterwards have put it, "converted;" he was as other light-hearted boys are, but with the addition of an inflexible determination to do what was right, and in particular what he had promised to carry out, however unpleasant the performance might prove to be. This was a personal characteristic with him, and one which will be found to have coloured his whole career. In an age which has mainly valued and cultivated breadth of religious feeling, he was almost physiologically predisposed to depth, even at the risk of narrowness.

At length, on the morning of Wednesday, June 6, 1827, a long line of dim blue, ending in a point, was visible on the western horizon,—Newfoundland apparent at last, in the form of Cape St. Francis, the eastern boundary of Conception Bay, to which the brig was bound. All that day the promontory continued to occupy the same position, for there was very little wind. A noble iceberg of vast dimensions was also in view; and this, while they were gazing at it, majestically shifted its balance, and turned about one-third over, causing an immense turmoil of water and a swell that was felt for a long time afterwards. To the impatient and imaginative lad, fretting for the conquest of a new continent, this iceberg seemed no inappropriate sentinel to guard the approach to those cold shores. Next morning Cape St. Francis lay behind them, and the ship was bowling along with a fair breeze into the ample and beautiful Bay of Conception. The town of Carbonear (the third in size in the colony, being exceeded only by St. John's and by Harbour Grace) lay near the head of the long gulf. Philip was agreeably surprised by the first sight of the town from on board.' It was a much more considerable place than he had expected to find. The number, respectability, and continuity of the houses ; the crowd of shipping, including a fleet of about seventy schooners just about to start for Labrador ; the small boats hurrying to and fro ; the multitude of cries at sea and movement on the shore ;—all these made up a scene very different from the desolation which, in his uninformed fancy, the lad had imagined of Newfoundland. It was early summer, too ; fields and gardens and potato-patches mapped out the sides of the hills which formed an amphitheatre around the long lake-like harbour, and verdure was smiling everywhere up to the very edge of the universal dark environment of pine woods.

Among the first of those who came out in boats to welcome the new-coming ship from England was William Gosse, who, in his fraternal anxiety, had kindly drawn up a code of regulations for his brother's behaviour in matters of deportment and etiquette. Philip was unsophisticated as well as unaffected ; he took this odd attention in the spirit in which it was tendered, and endeavoured scrupulously to observe the judicious precepts of his nineteen years old brother. The presence of the Labrador fleet was disturbing, and until these vessels were gone, he was put, for a week or two, under the storekeeper, Mr. Apsey. But as soon as the Labrador men had sailed away, he took up his permanent place in the counting-house. This office was pleasantly situated in the midst of a large garden, in front of the dwelling-house of the firm, the resident member of which was a Mr. Elson. Of the four clerks, the third was William Charles St. John, a lad of about twenty years of age, a native of the neighbouring town of Harbour Grace, where his parents resided. His father, Mr. Oliver St. John, belonged to a Protestant Tipperary family, which claimed relationship alike with Cromwell and with Lord Bolingbroke. As the young St. John was destined for many years to be my father's most intimate friend, I will now transcribe his portrait as I find it recorded among my father's notes :—

"Charley was a youth of manly height, with features "of the Grecian type, exquisitely chiselled, formed in a "very aristocratic mould, to which an aquiline nose of "unusual dimensions gave character. A mouth of "feminine smallness ; a finely cut chin ; a lofty forehead ; "dark eyes and hair, the latter copious, and rather "crisp than lank, completed the physiognomy of my "new acquaintance, which was continually animated "and lighted up by arch smiles, and by the frolic wit "and merry repartee which his prolific brain was "constantly forging. I saw in him a new type of "character ; he was a fair sample of the Irish youth at "his best. Sarcastic and keen, ready in reply, un-"abashed, prompt to throw back a Roland for every "Oliver, full of fun and frolic, as ready at a practical as "at a verbal joke, possessing a strong perception of the "ludicrous side of everything, cool and self-possessed, "already a well-furnished man of the world, St. John "presented as great a contrast as can well be imagined "to me. I was thoroughly a greenhorn ; fresh from my "Puritan home and companionships ; utterly ignorant of "the world ; raw, awkward, and unsophisticated ; simple

"in countenance as unsuspicious in mind;—the very
"quaintness of the costume in which I had been sent
"forth from the parental nest told what a yokel I was.
"A surtout coat of snuff-brown hue, reaching to my
"ankles, and made out of a worn great-coat of my
"uncle Gosse's which had been given to mother,
"enveloped my somewhat sturdy body; for I was

"' Totus, teres, atque rotundus;'

"while my intellectual region rejoiced in the protection
"of a *white* hat (forsooth!) somewhat battered in sides
"and crown, and manifestly the worse for wear. Such
"was I in outward guise: the idea of a witticism or
"repartee, made hot. on the occasion, had never entered
"my noddle; but then, had I not in my chest those
"manuscript pages of stale jests, which I had toilfully
"copied out of the *Joe Miller*, with which I expected to
"take captive the laugh of the office? What wonder
"that I became immediately the butt of so keen an
"archer as St. John, the inviting centre about which the
"flashes of his sparkling wit constantly coruscated
"until at length, by the very inhalation of the
"atmosphere, I learned gradually to play the same
"game, and to pay him back with his own weapons?

"Intellectually I think we were pretty much on a
"par. We were both readers, but possibly I had read
"more books than he; I had learned Latin at school, he
"French; my slight knowledge of natural history was
"balanced by his acquaintance with chemistry, mainly
"acquired from Parkes's *Chemical Catechism*, which I
"had been used to see at John Brown's. But then he
"was a poet; at least, he had the art of versification,
"which, however, he chiefly exercised in semi-doggerel
"Hudibrastic satirical pieces. A poem of his was extant
"when I came, on the Methodist Missionary Meeting

"of the preceding autumn—a merry lampoon on the
"preachers, and most of the people of the place, on the
"occasion of their gathering. It was very smart and
"telling, and entertained us greatly. His favourite poet
"was Pope, whose *Essay on Man* he was continually
"citing, perhaps because it was dedicated to St. John, its
"opening lines running—

> "' Awake, my St. John, leave all meaner things
> To low ambition, and the pride of Kings.'

"The philosophy of this poem, such as it is, formed
"another of our staple subjects of discussion. His mode
"of thinking was somewhat loose, dashy, indefinite ;
"mine, on the other hand, precise, microscopic, according
"to rule. Withal, he was lithe and active in bodily
"exercises, a skilful and much-admired skater, a
"vigorous swimmer, a good leaper and runner. He
"possessed, too, an inexhaustible fund of good humour ;
"was a jovial boon-companion on occasion ; and, to
"crown all, a great favourite with the ladies, being hand-
"some, gallant, attentive, with a fluent flattering tongue,
"ready wit, and a good store of frivolous conversation,
"the small-talk which is the spice of life and means
"nothing."

William Charles St. John and Philip Henry Gosse not
only became knit in a warm friendship which lasted until
circumstances drew them apart, but the former had very
much to do in moulding the far from susceptible mind of
the latter. At least, their two minds grew very steadily
together, in the daily, hourly, momentary companionship of
several years of budding manhood. The two friends walked
together, read together, discussed and disputed together,
on every imaginable subject ; in the office they joked
together, and spent their spare moments in a never-ending
series of intellectual combats, so that the counting-house

became the arena of constant mental gladiatorship between these ardent and vigorous young intelligences. "Whatever of humour or wit in conversation I possess," my father has written ; "whatever of logical precision of thought ; whatever of readiness of speech or power in debate, I largely owe to those years of merry companionship." St. John went to Boston, U.S.A., where he died on March 13, 1874.

The establishment of Mr. Elson in Carbonear was composed of two contiguous buildings—the upper house, where the family resided, and where the head of the firm slept ; and the lower house, where all the clerks slept and boarded, and where Mr. Elson took his meals with them, spending the day from breakfast-time till about eleven o'clock at night. The lower house, a large but low structure of wood, was old and ramshackled ; the only ornament on its rude colonial front, opposite the counting-house, was an antique sundial. Immediately before this façade, and running along its entire extent, was a raised platform of boards, known as "the gallery," so old and rotten that in a year or two it was cleared away and replaced by a walk of hard gravel. On this platform it was usual for the officials to assemble, as well as all those captains of ships in port who were free of Mr. Elson's table, at one o'clock, when a bell aloft was rung as the signal for dinner. Here they would form in knots, conversing, until the man-cook appeared at the door and announced that Mr. Elson was served. The bedrooms of the clerks were barns of places, destitute of carpet or curtain, the unpainted deal of the walls and floors being black with age. Whatever bedding was required was supplied from the shop, without any supervision from Mr. Elson, and the young fellows took care to sleep warm enough. They made their own beds, and did for themselves whatever service was needed, sweeping each the floor of his room, and performing his ablutions at a sink at the end of the gallery.

For Sundays there were three places of religious assembly : firstly, the Roman Catholic chapel, attended by the great mass of the working population, as also by Mrs. Elson and her daughters; secondly, the Established Church, a small edifice ministered to by the Rev. John Burt, who came over for the purpose from his own parish of Harbour Grace, of which he was the incumbent ; and, thirdly, the Methodist chapel, which rivalled the Catholic chapel in the number of its attendants. Mr. Elson was a Freethinker, and attended no religious service. On the first Sunday afternoon at Carbonear, Philip Gosse, feeling much at a loss for occupation, went boldly into the parlour and asked Mr. Elson to lend him a book. He was very kind, entered into conversation with the lad regarding recent literature, and lent him at once two works which were still fresh to the world of readers, *The Fortunes of Nigel* and the first series of the collected *Essays of Elia*. As at home in England, so even in Newfoundland, in that fortunate age for authors, there was a book-club in every town of any consequence. Of the Carbonear book-club Mr. Elson was the president and librarian, and the books were kept in a closet to which the clerks, most of whom were members of the club, had free access at breakfast-time and on Sundays. New books were bought but once a year, when a solemn meeting of members was held in the parlour, and the purchase of volumes was voted. The choice was mainly left to Mr. Elson himself. Of course there was the usual large pro-portion of novels, of which Gosse became a great devourer. Most of Scott's, Bulwer's, Cooper's, Galt's, and the *O'Hara* series were to be found at Carbonear within a year of their publication in London. Biography, poetry, travels, and even science were very fairly represented, and the basis of a sound knowledge of contemporary literature could be, and was, formed in this remote harbour of Newfoundland. It would be interesting to know whether, in the course of sixty years, the colonial standard of civilization has risen or fallen, and whether the clerks of the Carbonear of to-day know their Stevenson and their Haggard as well as my father and his colleagues knew their Bulwer and their Banim. At this point I may quote an amusing letter from the late Mr. W. C. St. John to my father, dated May 25, 1868, but referring to events of the year 1827—

"One of my first experiences with the 'old white hat'
"was an evening's walk on that most delectable of all
"turnpikes, Carbonear beach, when the surf-worn stones
"spread themselves out so invitingly to one, like your-
"self, but recently recovered from rheumatism in the
"feet. Bad as is my memory, I remember the heads of
"our confabulation. You told me about your school
"curriculum under one Charles Henry Sells (I think),
"and of a further polishing-off under a Unitarian minis-
"ter. You had begun the French, and had made some
"considerable progress in Latin. As I knew nothing
"of the latter myself, I felt flattered that I should have
"a classical scholar for my companion, and wasn't at all
"unwilling that the street passengers should hear us
"*conversing* in an unknown tongue. So I asked you to
"repeat some Latin verses, which you did very readily,
"ever and anon, however, stopping to rub your toe or
"ankle, as those outlying members would receive damage
"from the treacherous stones. Your favourite poet
"appeared to be Virgil; and I hear you now going
"measuredly and with admirable *ore rotundo* and em-
"phasis over the old Roman's 'Bucolic'—

"'Sicelides Musæ, paullo majora canamus :
Non om—— [oh ! psha ! my toe ! hop, hop, hop]

> Non omnes arbusta [ankle turns : limp, limp]
> Non omnes arbusta juvant, humil—— [psha !]
> .   .   .   .   .   humilesque myricæ ;
> Si canimus silvas, silvæ sint Consule dignæ !'

"The last line was brought out with great oratorical
"power, as being 'eminently beautiful;' to which I
"assented *without hesitation*—requesting you, over and
"over, to repeat it, perhaps half a dozen times before we
"reached the bridge ; and always with an eye to have
"you spouting the incomprehensible language just as
"somebody—it might be only Johnny Dunn the cooper
"—was passing. But the naughty beach-stones sadly
"disturbed my calculations, and the audience was sure
"to pass in the midst of a parenthesis ; thereby render-
"ing the limping sufferer anything but an object of envy
"or admiration. I have picked up a little Latin since ;
"and many and many a time have those lines recurred
"to me,—with all their concomitants of 'psha ! O dear !'
"etc., etc., as well as the glowing expression of counte-
"nance at the inimitable—

> "'.   .   .   silvæ sint Consule dignæ.'

"On this memorable occasion you discovered that I
"knew a little about French, and had dabbled somewhat
"in chemistry, and you were prepared to assure Pack's
"chaps that I wasn't such an ignoramus as they took
"me to be.* I think it was this evening that, on our
"return to our chambers, you produced a voluminous
"compilation of Joe Miller anecdotes in manuscript,
"many of which you read to me, taking care to look
"grave on reaching *the point*, lest it should be thought
"(as I took it) that you knew no better than to laugh
"at your own (compiled) jokes !"

---

* "The fact was 'Pack's chaps' were very much in awe of my friend's wit
and powers of sarcasm. For his candle was not hid under a bushel."

Another walk which Gosse took with St. John at a very early period may be recalled, because it gave occasion for one of those burlesque poems of the latter which, if not quite up to the highest level, was quite good enough to gain for "Charley" St. John a local reputation as a dangerously gifted poet. The laugh was raised at Gosse's expense, and it is the butt himself who has preserved the ditty. On one of those June evenings the two friends, having sauntered through the long town until they had passed the contiguous houses, had protracted their ramble to the very lonely lane near Burnt Head, known as Rocky Drong. This "drong," or lane, was reputed to be haunted. It was now ten o'clock at night, when, turning round in this desolate and gloomy locality, Gosse saw ahead what seemed a dim female figure in white, afterwards ignominiously identified as "one of Dicky the Bird's nieces coming up from the 'landwash' with a 'turn' of sand for her mother's kitchen floor." The young naturalist from Poole endured and quite failed to conceal a paroxysm of terror, and got home in an exhausted condition. Two days afterwards, Charley St. John produced at the office a piece of foolscap, from which he proceeded to read to a delighted audience the following doggerel effusion, the only surviving text of which is, I regret to say, imperfect :—

> . . . The other night
> The moon it shone, not very bright,
> When lo ! in *Rocky Drong* appear'd
> A form that made poor GOSSE afeard,
> It seem'd to wear a woman's clothes,
> A horse's head, a buck-goat's nose ;
> And with a deep and hollow moan,
> It thus addressed the Latin drone—
> "Young Man, I'm happy for to say
> That long in *Poole* you did not stay ;
> For to your house that very night,
> The Devil claim'd you as his right.

> A Parson who was right at hand,
> Told him you'd gone to Newfoundland."
> "Indeed!" says Bell,[1] "when did he go?
> For he's deserted, you must know.
> But morrow-morning I shall post
> On every wall his bloody ghost,
> And, in a fiery placard, speak
> The following words, in broken Greek :—
>
> ' *Notice.*
>
> ' Deserted from old BEELZEBUB,
> ' Two nights ago, PHIL GOSSE, my cub.
> ' Had on, when left, an old white hat,
> ' A brown surtout, choke full of fat,
> ' A [half-line missing], and in his box
> ' Were two old books by Doctor Watts,
> ' One sermon by Durant, and, dang 'ee,
> ' A book of riddles from his granny.
> ' Whoever harbours this my man,
> ' Let him beware ! his hide I'll tan !' "

One of the public characteristics of Newfoundland life of which Gosse became earliest aware was the growing jealousy of the Irish element in the population. The lad quickly took the tone of the Saxon and purely colonial minority among whom he had been thrown. A special nuisance of the town of Carbonear was the abundance of mongrel curs in the streets; and one day, when young Gosse had strolled down to Harbour Rock (an elevated spot about half-way down the port, which formed a very general resort as a terminus to a moderate walk), in company with his brother William, two or three of the ships' captains, and some clerks of various firms, he committed an indiscretion which left a strong impression on his memory. One of his companions was a very gentleman-like young fellow, called Moore, book-keeper to one of the

---

[1] Beelzebub.

smaller firms. A captain asked Gosse how he liked New-foundland ; safe, as he thought, with none but colonists, he replied smartly, " I see little in it, except dogs and Irishmen." The silence that followed, where he had expected approving laughter, told him that something was wrong. At length his brother said, " Do you not know that Mr. Moore is an Irishman ? " Philip Gosse was immediately extremely abashed ; but Moore replied, with great good humour, " There's no offence ; I am an Ulsterman, and love the Papist Irish no better than the rest of you." The southern Irish were not slow, of course, to observe the feeling of which this conversation was an example. They immensely preponderated in numbers, and they already formed an anti-English party in Newfoundland, the rancour of which was an inconvenience, if not a danger to the colony. My father says, in one of his manuscript notes—

" There existed in Newfoundland in 1827, among the " Protestant population of the island, an habitual dread " of the Irish as a class, which was more oppressively " felt than openly expressed, and there was customary " an habitual caution in conversation, to avoid any " unguarded expression which might be laid hold of by " their jealous enmity. It was very largely this dread " which impelled me to forsake Newfoundland, as a " residence, in 1835 ; and I recollect saying to my " friends the Jaqueses, ' that when we got to Canada, we " ' might climb to the top of the tallest tree in the forest, " ' and shout " Irishman ! " at the top of our voice, without " ' fear.' "

Gosse's first summer in Newfoundland was one of much freedom. Mr. Elson, not having seen his English partners for several years, took a holiday in the mother-country, and Newall, the easy-going book-keeper, ruled at Carbonear as his *locum tenens.* Besides this, the summer was always a light time. The fleet of schooners sailed for Labrador in the middle of June, and from that time till the end of October, when the crews had to be paid off and all accounts settled, there was very little to be done in the counting-house. Fortunately the brief summer of Newfoundland is a very delightful one. Of the winter pleasures of Carbonear I may well permit my father to speak for himself, nor interrupt the unaffected chronicle of his earliest loves :—

"Parties were frequent, but they were almost always "'balls.' The clerks of the different mercantile firms, "were of course in demand, as being almost the only "young chaps with the least pretensions to a genteel "appearance. Jane Elson one day sent me a note, inviting "me to a forthcoming 'ball.' I had never danced in "my life, and so was compelled to decline. Her note "began, 'Dear Henry ;' and I thought it was the proper "thing, in replying, to begin mine with 'Dear Jane.' "Having my note in my pocket, I gave it to her, as "I met her and Mary in the lane, just below the plat-"form. Lush, who had seen the action, benevolently "took me aside, and told me that 'it was not etiquette, "'to write a note to a lady, and deliver it myself;' at "which I again felt much ashamed. This ignorance of "the art of dancing caused me to refuse all the parties, "and very much isolated me from the female society of "the place. I do not doubt that this was really very "much for my good, and preserved me from a good deal "of frivolity ; but I rebelled in spirit at it, and mur-"mured at the 'Puritan prejudices' of my parents, which "had not allowed me to be taught the elegant accom-"plishment, which every Irish lad and girl acquires, as it "were, instinctively. I supposed it was absolutely im-"possible to join these parties without having been "taught ; though, in truth, such movements as sufficed

"for those simple hops would have been readily ac-
"quired in an evening or two's observation, under the
"willing tuition of any of the merry girls. William,
"indeed, as I afterwards found, went to them, and ac-
"quitted himself *comme il faut;* though he had no more
"learned than I had. However, I believe I had some-
"what of the 'Puritan prejudice' myself; at least,
"conscience was uneasy on the point, as I had been
"used to hear balls classed with the theatre.

"My familiarities with the Elsons never proceeded
"farther than a making of childish signals with my
"candle at night. My bedroom window looked across
"the meadow towards the Upper House, in front of
"which was the bedroom window of the girls. We
"used to signal to each other, holding the candle in the
"various panes of the window, in turn, in response to
"each other. There was no ulterior meaning attached
"to the movements; it was mere child's play. They
"certainly began it, for I am sure I should not have
"ventured on such a liberty myself. Apsey, however,
"took greater freedoms, for if he were on the platform
"waiting for dinner, when they happened to be coming
"down the meadows to go into the town, he would way-
"lay them at the end of the platform (which they were
"obliged to cross) and not suffer them to pass, till each
"had paid him the toll of a kiss. It was readily yielded;
"and though they affected to frown, and said, 'Mr.
"'Apsey is such a tease,' they were evidently not much
"discomposed, and bore him no malice, being of a for-
"giving disposition. The toll was taken with full
"publicity, in presence of us all, some of whom envied
"him his impudence and success.

"In truth, Jane Elson became the unconscious object
"of my first boyish love. Before the autumn of this

"first season had yielded to winter, I loved Jane with
"a deep and passionate love,—all the deeper because I
"kept the secret close locked in my own bosom.

> "'He never told his love;
> But let concealment, like a worm i' the bud,
> Feed on his damask cheek.'

"The chaps in the office used to rally me about Mary,
"who was indeed much the prettier and more vivacious
"of the two, and I never undeceived them; but Jane
"was my flame. One night I awoke from a dream, in
"which she had appeared endowed with a beauty quite
"unearthly, and as it were angelic; so utterly unde-
"scribable, and indeed inconceivable, that on waking
"I could only recall the general impression, every effort
"to reproduce the details of her beauty being vain.
"They were not so much gone from memory, as from
"the possibility of imagining. There was in truth no
"great resemblance in the radiant vision to Jane's
"homely face and person; and yet I intuitively knew it
"to be her.

"My unconquerable bashfulness precluded my ever
"hinting my love to Jane. A year or two afterwards,
"I was at a 'ball' at Newell's, the only one which I ever
"attended, and the Elson girls were there. It was cus-
"tomary for the fellows each to escort a lady home:
"I asked Jane to allow me the honour. She took my
"arm; and there, under the moon, we walked for full
"half a mile, and not a word—literally, not a single
"word—broke the awful silence! I felt the awkward-
"ness most painfully; but the more I sought something
"to say, the more my tongue seemed tied to the roof of
"my mouth.

"This boyish passion gradually wore out: I think all
"traces of it had ceased long before I visited England

"in 1832. About a year after that Jane married a
"young merchant of St. John's, named Wood; and
"Mary accepted one of the small merchants of Car-
"bonear, one Tom Gamble, in June, 1836."

What society Carbonear possessed was mainly to be
met with in the houses of the planters, several of whom
were wealthy and hospitable. The name "planter" needs
explanation. It had no connection with the cultivation of
the soil, although doubtless inherited from colonies where
it had that meaning. In Newfoundland the word de-
signated a man who owned a schooner, in which he pro-
secuted one or both of the two fisheries of the colony,
that for seals in spring and that for cod in winter. In
Carbonear, a town of some two thousand five hundred
inhabitants in 1828, there were about seventy planters,
whose dealings were distributed amongst the mercantile
houses of the place. Of these, about twenty-five were
fitted out by the firm in which my father was a clerk, that
of Messrs. Slade, Elson, and Co. In general, business was
carried on upon the following terms. The mercantile firm,
having a house in England as well as one in Newfoundland, imported into the island, from various ports of Europe
and America, all supplies needful for local consumption
and for the prosecution of the fisheries, the colony itself
producing no provisions except fish, fresh meat, oats, and
a few vegetables. The planter was supplied by his merchant, and always on credit, with everything requisite, the
whole produce of his voyage being bound to be delivered
to the house. The planter shipped a crew, averaging
about eighteen hands to each schooner, who (in the seal-
fishery) claimed one-half of the gross produce to be divided
among them; the other half going to the owner, who in
most instances commanded his own vessel. The names
of the crew having been registered at the counting-house,

each man was allowed to take up goods on the credit of the voyage, to a certain amount, perhaps one-third, or even one-half, of his probable earnings. The clerks were the judges of the amount. For these goods both planter and crew applied at the office, in order, and received tickets, or "notes," for the several articles. In the busy season the registering of these notes, delivering the goods, and entering the transactions in the books would occupy the whole staff until late into the night.

In his *Introduction to Zoology* (i. 110) my father has given the details of the seal-fishery, on which, as he was never personally cognizant of them, I need not dwell. But the preparation of the seal-fleet for starting was the busiest time of the year to him, the North Shore, and particularly Carbonear, being, from the 1st to the 17th of March, all alive with a very active, noisy, rude, and exacting population. During this fortnight, life was a purgatory for the clerks, who were besieged from morning till night by these vociferous and fragrant fellows. By St. Patrick's Day, however, it was a point of honour for all the sealers to have sailed, and thence, until the middle of April, when the more fortunate schooners began to return, the counting-house kept a sort of holiday. Then, once more, a press of work set in. The seal-pelts brought home were delivered in tale, all the accounts incurred had to be settled, and amounts due to the successful crews to be paid them. This had to be done partly in cash—the Spanish dollar of four shillings and twopence sterling passing for five shillings—and partly in goods, which involved more "notes." The planters' accounts, too, had to be squared and the profit or loss on the voyage of each determined.

By this time May would be far advanced, and now all was hurry, almost exactly a repetition of the scenes in March ; on this occasion, the cod-fishery being prepared for. The same schooners, commanded by the same skippers, but with newly selected crews, were fitted out on exactly the same system of credit as before, with the same bustle. By the middle of June, all had sailed for Labrador, where they remained, catching and curing fish, until October, when they brought their produce back. This interval was nearly a four months' holiday for the clerks, and in the most delightful part of the year. The work in the office was then little more than routine—the copying of letters, keeping the goods' accounts of such residents as dealt at Mr. Elson's stores, despatching two or three vessels to England with the seal oil of the spring collection, and the business connected with what was called the Shore fishery.

In the coves round about, and especially along the "North Shore"—that is, the coast of Conception Bay which stretched from Carbonear to Point Baccalao, an iron-bound, precipitous shore, much indented with small inlets, but containing no harbours for ships—along this North Shore, there resided a hardy population, mainly English and Protestant, who possessed no schooners, but held small sailing-boats, with which, mostly by families, they pursued the cod-fishery in the bay. The fish they took were commonly of larger size, were better cured, and commanded a higher price than the Labrador produce, but the quantity of it was strictly limited. Many of the North Shore men were tall, well-made, handsome fellows, singularly simple and guileless, with a marked aversion and dread of the Irish population of the harbours, to whom their peculiarities of idiom and manners afforded objects of current ribaldry. In the spring, as they had no resources at home, these mild giants shipped with the planters for the ice, and during the noisy first fortnight of March, when the crews "came to collar," as their arrival was called, the port was resounding every night with shouts and cries and responses, bandied from vessel to vessel, nicknames, ribald jokes, and opprobrious epithets showered on the inoffensive heads of the poor meek men from the North Shore. Their dialect was peculiar. It sounded particularly strange in the ears of the Irish, although it was really equally diverse from that of any English peasantry. One of its traits was an inability to pronounce the *th*, which became *t* or *d*. Most of them were Wesleyans, and it was amusing to hear them fervently singing hymns in their odd language :—

> " De ting my God dut hate,
> Dat I no more may do."

With these simple folk the summer business of the counting-house was mainly occupied, they bringing their little boat-loads of excellent fish, according as it was cured, with such subordinate matters as fresh salmon for the house-table, and various delicious berries. Of these latter the Newfoundland summer produces a considerable variety, as cranberries, whortleberries, and the exquisitely delicate cloudberry (*Rubus chamæmorus*), locally known as "bake-apples." These were always saleable, and sometimes, though not often, the North Shore men would bring a carcase of reindeer venison, nearly as large as a cow—an excellent and savoury meat. Such minute transactions as these, however, hardly broke the office holiday, and altogether the work of these four summer months would have been by no means oppressive, if performed in one.

In October the harbour gradually filled again, and as the 31st of that month was the terminus of every engagement, no sooner did that much-hated and dreaded day arrive, than the counting-house was beset by the clamorous rogues, a dozen or more crowding in at once into the office, all shouting, swearing, and wrangling together, dirty and greasy, redolent with a commingled fragrance of fish, oil, rum, and tobacco—one calling Heaven to witness in the richest Milesian accents that a certain pair of hose charged in his account never went upon *his* legs, showing the said legs at the same time, as a patent proof that he had no such stockings four months before; another affecting great indignation, because the usual charge of one shilling has been made for "hospital;" another finding the balance of cash due to him rather less than his vivid imagination has anticipated, and romping and tearing about, swearing that he will not touch the dirty money, that the clerks may keep it, that he doesn't care two pins for the clerks, but presently cooling down, pocketing the cash, and signing his beautiful autograph in the receipt-book. The hottest part of this settling business did not last through November; at least, the crews, the roughest utter *plebs*, were pretty well done with by the end of that month. But as the year drew near its close, books had to be wound up, long planters' accounts to be copied, ample inventories of all stock in the various stores and shops to be taken and copied, various statements to be drawn up for transmission to England, long letters to be transcribed, and general arrears in many branches to be made up. The winter business, therefore, was long and pretty arduous.

The prices charged on account varied little; in general they were about double what they cost in England; that is to say nominally, but the difference between sterling and currency must be borne in mind. To residents in the town, who paid cash over the counter, prices were considerably less. The clerks had all their goods charged to them at the actual invoice prices, to which twenty-five per cent. was then added, and all the cash they had drawn was, at settling time, turned into sterling, and the difference allowed to them. The wages Philip Gosse received were small, but then board and lodging were provided. Washing, however, he had to pay himself, and the following anecdote may be permitted to illustrate the system and his personal economy :—

"It must have been in the summer of 1829 that I had "been a little exceeding my income, and Mr. Elson had "evidently his eye on my account. One little item "brought matters to a crisis. There suddenly appeared "in the ledger against my name, '2 ozs. Cinnamon, 1s.' "This I had got at the shop, to chew, as a little luxury ; "but the skipper noticed it, and, *suo more*, said nothing "to me, but gave orders to Lush that Philip Gosse must "have nothing more without a note from him. Soon after "this, my laundress applied to me—through her usual "messenger, a buxom daughter—for some goods on "account, for which I, suspecting nothing, gave her a "note in my own hand. This note was dishonoured ; "and a few days later, old Mrs. Rowe herself applies to "Mr. E., who comes with her into the office. It so "happened that I did not recognize her, having generally "done business with one or other of her daughters, and "I took no heed whatever to what she and Mr. E. were "talking about, the chief of the discussion having doubt-"less passed before they entered the office. Mr. E. at "length gave her the note she asked in my name, and "she went out looking daggers at me as she passed. "The skipper presently retired also, saying not a word "to me ; and not till then did I, through St. John's "raillery, who had from the first apprehended the state "of affairs, know what had transpired. Both Durell and "he had wondered at my coolness and nonchalance, "which was now explained. Thenceforward I was more "economical ; and my disbursements, which had not

"*greatly* exceeded my earnings, at length were overtaken
"by them, and all was right again. It was a lesson I
"never forgot."

The remainder of this chapter shall be formed of a
variety of desultory scraps, referring mainly to the years
1827 and 1828, which I find in my father's handwriting.
They have never before been printed, and they may serve
to complete the picture of his first years in Newfoundland :—

"During the first summer, while the skipper (our
"representative for the modern term 'governor') was in
"England, the dwelling-house had a narrow escape from
"fire. I was standing alone at the office window which
"looked up to the house, just after dinner one day,
"watching a vivid thunderstorm. Suddenly I saw what
"appeared exactly as if a cannon had been fired directly
"out of the house chimney. This was the lightning
"flash, which struck the house, attracted by an iron
"fender, which was set on end in the fireplace of the
"best bedroom. I saw the wide column of intense
"flame; the apparent direction, which suggested the
"resemblance to a cannon fired *out of* the chimney, was
"of course, an illusion of my senses. The report, too,
"was the short ear-piercing crack of a great gun when
"fired close by you; nothing like ordinary thunder.
"There was now a general rush to the house. Newell
"and Captain Andrews had been cosily sitting before
"the empty fireplace in the parlour, each smoking his
"long pipe after dinner, while the glass of grog was in
"one case standing on the hob, in the other in the
"owner's hand. The two sitters had been in a moment
"jerked half round, though unhurt; the glasses dashed
"down, much row and terror caused, but wondrously
"little damage. The electric course could be distinctly

"traced along the bell-wire half round the room, to the
"door opposite. The wire had been melted here and
"there ; the gilding on the frames of two pictures
"on the wall had contracted into transverse bands, alter-
"nating with bands of black destitute of gold ; the door
"had been thrown off its hinges, though these were
"unusually massive ; and a few other freaks of this
"playful character had sated the lightning's ire.

  " St. John thus recalls to my memory one result of this
"storm : 'Do you recollect Newell's account of that
"'event (the thunderbolt?) in his letter to Poole? We
"'amused ourselves with its diction, counting the
"'prodigious number of was-es crowded into the
"'sentences. "I was," and "he was," and "it was," etc.,
"'without end. I think you copied the letter, and fairly
"'foamed with laughter ;—bad boys as we were!'

  "My friend John Brown wrote me, *I think*, but one
"letter. I left him ill of consumption ; and the summer
"had scarcely set in, when he died at home in Poole. The
"death of my early friend did not affect my feelings in
"any appreciable degree. It seemed as if I had forgotten
"him. I was much ashamed of this, and, I may say,
"even shocked ; but, as it was, new scenes, new friend-
"ships, had come in, and, what was perhaps more to
"the point, I had, since I parted from him, brief as the
"period really was, changed from the boy into the *man*.
"Thus there seemed a great chasm between my present
"feelings, aspirations, and habits of thought, and those
"of only a few months before ; and it had so happened
"that this physical transition had been exactly coin-
"cident with the change of place and circumstances.
"John Brown seemed to belong to another era, which
"had faded away. It was true, in more than one sense,
"that I had migrated to 'The New World.'

"Charley would occasionally invite me to accompany
"him over to Harbour Grace, about three miles distant,
"to spend the evening with his family, sleep with him,
"and return to business next morning. His parents
"were a venerable pair of the *ancien régime;* all their
"manners and their furniture told of high breeding and
"'blue blood.' There was a vast oil painting, covering
"nearly one wall of the dining-room, such as we
"occasionally see in old mansions, representing a great
"spread of fruit, and a peacock, in all the dimensions and
"all the splendour of life. Charley had two sisters—
"Hannah, a sweet, sunny girl, with bright eyes and
"auburn hair ; Charlotte (Lotty), a little deformed, very
"gentle, but retiring, and less attractive. Both were
"very sweet, amiable girls.

"One day (I think within my first year), having
"occasion to go over to Harbour Grace, I borrowed a
"horse to do the journey *en cavalier.* I think this was
"the first time I had ever crossed a horse's back, unless
"it was in going with my cousins Kemp from Holme to
"Corfe Castle, and then I had not attempted more than
"a walk. Now, however, I was more ambitious ; and
"as my steed broke into a gentle trot, I jerked from
"side to side in a style quite edifying and novel to any
"passing pedestrians, no doubt; for I had no notion of
"holding with my knees. The success of the experi-
"ment did not encourage me to repeat it, and I didn't
"know how to ride till I learned in Jamaica, in 1845.

"The facilities for reading afforded by the library
"I eagerly availed myself of, particularly in novels, of
"which I presently became a great devourer. Several
"of Scott's, several of Bulwer's, of D'Israeli's, I read ; but
"the American tales of Cooper, and the Irish series
"published under the *nom de guerre* of ' The O'Hara

"Family,' were the prime favourites. As an example
"of the absorption of interest with which I entered into
"these imaginary scenes, I remember that on one
"occasion this autumn (1827), I was sitting in my bed-
"room late at night, finishing a novel, and when I had
"done, it was some minutes before I could at all recall
"where I was, or my circumstances. At another time,
"I actually read through two of the three volumes of a
"novel at one sitting.

  "It was, if I am not mistaken, in *The Collegians,**
"one of the O'Hara tales, that I met with the following
"sentence :—'If time be rightly defined as " a succession
"'"of ideas," then to him whose mind holds but one
"'abiding idea, there is no time.' This definition struck
"me forcibly at the time; and all through life I have
"recurred to it, ever and anon, when I have read the
"ordinary confused definitions of time, in which the
"motions of the heavenly bodies are prominently
"mentioned. There are indeed the *measures* of time ;
"but the essence of time is something quite distinct
"from its admeasurement. The sentence I have just
"quoted formed the basis of many a discussion between
"St. John and me; and we speculated much upon
"eternity, as if its essence precluded succession. We
"talked too of God, as the schoolmen had done long
"before us ; assuming that to Him there was no succes-
"sion, but one abiding *now.*

  "The year 1827 closed, and I knew by experience
"what a Newfoundland winter was. It was by no
"means unbearable. The thermometer very rarely
"descends below zero more than once or twice in the
"season ; snow sets in generally by the end of Sep-

---

* By Gerald Griffin.

"tember, and by the middle of November it has be-
"come permanent till April. However, the weather is
"generally fine ; we in the office kept good fires, took
"daily walks to the great gun upon Harbour Rock, or
"in some other direction, and contrived to enjoy our-
"selves. Mr. Elson had returned in October and
"resumed his wonted authority, and Newell had sunk
"to mere book-keeper again. It was, I think, in this
"winter that St. John urged me to write a novel. I at
"length complied ; and taking down a quire of foolscap,
"began the adventures of one Edwin Something, 'a youth
"' about eighteen,' who 'dropped a tear over the ship's
"' side' as he left his native country. I passed my hero
"through sundry scenes, and, among the rest, into a sea-
"fight with a Tunis corsair, in which, I said, 'the Turks
"' remained masters of the field.' There was no attempt
"at fine writing ; it was all very simple, and all very
"brief ; for I finished off my story in some three or four
"pages. St. John read it very seriously, and mercifully
"restricted his criticism to the expression 'field,' in the
"sentence above cited, which, he said, as the subject was
"a *sea*-fight, was hardly *comme il faut*. He did not
"laugh at me ; but I had sense enough to know that it
"was a very poor affair, and did not preserve it.

"In the spring of 1828, when the vessels began to
"return from the ice, I was sent to the oil-stage to take
"count of the seal-pelts delivered. The stage was a
"long projecting wharf, roofed and inclosed, carried out
"over the sea upon piles driven into the bottom. I take
"my place, pencil and paper in hand, at the open end of
"this stage, seated on an inverted tub. Before me is a
"wide hand-barrow. A boat loaded to the water's edge
"with seal-pelts is being slowly pulled from one of the
"schooners by a noisy crew, mostly Irish. As soon as

"she arrives at the wharf, two or three scramble up, and
"the rest, remaining in the boat, begin to throw the
"heavy pelts of greasy bloody fat up on the floor of the
"stage. At the same time one of the crew that has
"climbed up begins to lay them one by one, fur down-
"ward, on the barrow ; singing out, as he lays down
"each, 'One—two—three—four—tally,' I at each one
"making a mark on my paper. Five pelts make a
"barrow-load, and instead of the word 'five,' the word
"'tally' is used, for then I am to make a diagonal line
"across the four marks, and this formula is called 'a
"tally.' Immediately the word 'tally' is uttered by the
"loader, which is always with a loud emphasis, I also
"say 'tally;' and then two labourers catch up the
"barrow, and carry it into the recesses of the stage for
"the pelts to be skinned ; a second barrow meanwhile
"receiving its tally in exactly the same manner, while
"my marking goes on, but on the opposite side of the
"basal line ; so that the record assumes a form which
"represents fifty pelts. This is very easily counted,
"while mistake is almost impossible. I forgot to say
"that one of the more responsible hands, perhaps the
"mate, also stands by, and keeps a like tally with mine,
"on behalf of the owner and crew.

"Of course this was by no means so pleasant an
"employment as that I had been used to in the warmth
"and comfort and congenial company of the counting-
"house. The dirty, brawling vulgar fellows crowding
"around, uttering their low witless jokes, or cursing
"and swearing, or abusing others, or bragging their
"achievements ; the filth everywhere ; the rancid grease,
"which could not fail to be absorbed by my shoes and
"scattered over my clothes ; so that whenever, at bell-
"ringing or in evening, I essayed to join my companions,

" the plain-spoken rogues would welcome me with—
" 'Oh, Gosse, pray don't come very near ! you stink so
" 'of seal-oil !' then, at times, the bitter cold of winter,
" not yet yielding to spring, the snowy gales driving in
" on me, and blowing up through the corduroy poles
" which made the floor ;—all this made me heartily glad
" when the last schooner was discharged, and I was
" again free to take my place with my fellows.

" I picked up, however, during this occupation, a good
" deal of interesting information. I became familiar with
" the different species of seals ; learned much of their
" habits and natural history, and of the adventures of the
" hunters ; and formed a pretty graphic and correct
" idea of the circumstances of the voyage, and scenes at
" the ice. A good deal of this I embodied in a journal,
" which I had continued to keep ever since I parted from
" home, sending it consecutively to mother, as book after
" book became filled. The one I now transmitted was
" embellished, as I well recollect, with a coloured frontis-
" piece, of full sheet size, folded so as to correspond with
" the leaves of the book. This represented an animated
" scene at the ice, in which several schooners were
" moored and several boats' crews were scattered about,
" with their gaffs and guns, pursuing the young seals ;
" others pelting them, and others dragging their loads of
" pelts to their boats. Though destitute of all artistic
" power, it was a valuable picture ; for it represented,
" with vividness and truth, a scene which then had
" never been adequately described in print, certainly
" never depicted. I am sorry to say that this, with all
" the other records of those times and scenes, has long
" been utterly and unaccountably lost ; no trace having
" been preserved, except in fading memory, of what I
" took so much pains to perpetuate. Many shiftings of

"homes have occurred, and 'three removes are as bad
"'as a fire.'

" I have already alluded to my painful susceptibility
"to ghostly fears. In my imagination, a skeleton, or
"even a corpse, was nearly the same thing as a ghost.
"This spring, the body of a drowned sailor was picked
"up in the harbour, and laid under a shed on our
"premises, covered with a sail, till it could be buried.
"My morbid curiosity impelled me to look on it; and
"Captain Stevens turned back the sail, to show me the
"face. The corpse had evidently lain long in the water,
" so that only the greenish-white bones were left—at least,
"in the parts not protected by the clothes. I felt a
"great awe and revulsion as I looked at it; and the
"grim grinning skull haunted my dreams, and would
"suddenly come up before my eyes, when alone in the
"dark, for months. It was the first time I had ever
" beheld the relics of poor deceased humanity.

" Among the numerous scraps which had lain, from
"time immemorial, in my father's great portfolio, there
" was an engraving by Bartolozzi, in his peculiar manner
" imitating red chalk. It was a Venus bathing, after
" Cipriani,—a most exquisite thing. This I had taken
"possession of, and had brought to Newfoundland.
"There was a servant girl, named Mary March, living
"in one of the houses near our premises, whom I used
"to see occasionally, as she came with her pitcher to
"fetch water from the clear cold brook that ran along
"at the end of our platform. Mary was quite a toast
"among our chaps—a pleasant, smiling, perfectly modest
" girl ; but what attracted my eager interest was that her
" face was the exact counterpart of that of my most
" lovely Venus of Bartolozzi's."

CHAPTER III.

1828–1835.

EARLY in August, 1828, Philip Gosse was sent for by Mr. Elson, and told that he must get himself ready to go and take his place in the office at St. Mary's. This he knew of only as an obscure, semi-barbarous settlement on the south coast of Newfoundland, where, as the clerks had gathered, the firm had just purchased an old establishment. The young man's heart sank within him as this command was delivered to him in Mr. Elson's dry, short, peremptory manner. Remonstrance, of course, was out of the question, but it seemed an exile to the antipodes, to be severed from all his pleasant companions and environment, to be shut up in an out-of-the-world hole, for an indefinite period, since no hint was given of any term to this banishment. He could only bow in silence, and rush down to the counting-house, there to pour forth his sorrows to his sympathizing fellows, not without tears.

The *Plover*, a schooner recently purchased by Mr. Elson, was being sent round with a cargo of supplies. On board this vessel Gosse sailed a few days later, enveloped, as the ship ran down the coast, in a dense sea-fog, raw, damp, cold, and miserable. On the second day he saw a curious phenomenon, which roused him a little out of his depression. Mounting the rigging some twenty feet or so above the sea-level, he found himself in bright sunshine, with the fog spread below him, like a plain of cotton. On this surface his shadow was projected, the head surrounded, at some distance, by a circling halo of rainbow colours. This is the rare Arctic appearance known as the fog-bow, or fog-circle. On the third morning, still sailing in blind fog, the vessel got into the harbour of St. Mary's. It proved a dreary, desolate place indeed. There were perhaps three or four hundred inhabitants, almost all of the fisherman or labourer class, and for the most part Irish. There were two mercantile establishments—the principal, which the Carbonear firm had recently purchased ; and another, of much humbler pretensions, kept by a genial, jovial, twinkling little old Englishman, named William Phippard, who also filled the office of stipendiary magistrate. The manager of Elson's was one John W. Martin, a Poole man, the son of a certain Mr. Martin who was a little fat man, with a merry laugh and a loud chirping voice, a jest ever on his lips, as he bustled hither and thither, who had been in Gosse's boyhood one of the familiar objects of Poole life. There was nothing genial about his son, John W. Martin, however ; consequential and bumptious in his deportment, he enjoyed wielding his rod of authority, and soon began to make his new clerk feel it. At the first meal young Gosse ate with his new chief, the latter took his intellectual measure. Gosse asked if there were any Indians in the neighbourhood. "What! you mean," said Martin, "the abo—abo—abo—reeginees ?" affecting learning, but pronouncing the awful word with the greatest difficulty. Martin began at once to bore the young man with constant petty tyrannies, which, after the liberty to which he had become accustomed at Carbonear, were very galling. One day on the wharf, among the labourers, where Gosse was doing some duty or other, Martin took offence, and said, " You shan't be called *Mr.* Gosse any more ; you shall be called plain Philip." The lad was very timid ; but on this occasion he thought he saw his advantage in the manager's own overweening sense of dignity, and he pertly replied, " Very well ; and I'll call you plain John," which shut his mouth and stopped that move, while the labourers grinned approval.

On Sundays only Philip Gosse was his own master at St. Mary's. Sometimes, while the summer lasted, he took an exploring walk on this day. But though the scenery seaward was grand, it was not attractive ; the land was a treeless waste, and the young man had no companion to interchange a word with. He therefore soon took to the habit of going round the. beach to Phippard's immediately after breakfast, spending the whole day there, and returning to his solitary bedroom at night. Phippard had two daughters—one married to an Englishman named Coles, who commanded a little coasting craft, and who lived in the house ; the other a pretty girl, named Emma, who insensibly became the young clerk's closest friend and principal companion. The Elson stores and wharf had the reputation of being haunted. The Irish servants told of strange lights seen and unaccountable noises heard there at night, although there was insinuated, on sunshiny mornings, a sly suspicion that the demon was one Ned Toole, a faithful servitor and confidential factotum of Martin's. It was quite salutary that such a superstition should prevail ; a ghost is an excellent watch-dog. Martin affected to despise the belief, but secretly nourished it notwithstanding. Gosse's bedroom was over the office, and between it and the other inhabited rooms there was a large unoccupied chamber called the fur-room. The house did a good deal of business in valuable furs— beaver, otter, fox, and musquash—and the whole room was hung round with dry skins, received from the trappers, awaiting shipment. It was important that this very costly property should be protected, and so—this fur-room was haunted. The maid-servants recounted to the young clerk a harrowing tale of an incident which had happened before he came. One night one of them told Martin that conversation was heard in the house, but no one could say whence the voices came. He listened, and heard the sound as of a man's grave tones, rather subdued, and occasionally intermitted. After a while it was concluded that it was the ghost in the fur-room. Martin, therefore, with a theatrical air of devilry, took a cocked pistol in each hand, marched upstairs—the timid women crouching at his back with a candle—and, throwing open the door of the fur-room, authoritatively asked, " Who's there ? " Nothing, however, was heard or seen ; nor was any explanation of the mystery attained. But one of the girls quietly said, at the close, that she thought it was only the buzz of a blue-bottle fly !

There can be no question that his timidity was increased, and his dislike of company which he was not certain would be congenial deepened, by Philip Gosse's dreary experiences at St. Mary's. One thing he learned which was afterwards useful to him, book-keeping by double entry, both in principal and in practice. He sat all day at the desk, mostly alone ; but the work was not nearly sufficient to fill the time, there was no literature in the place, and he was hard set for occupation. His love of animals was known, however, and the good-natured fellows in the port would bring him oddities. One day a fisherman brought him a pretty bird, of dense, soft, spotless white plumage, calling it a sea-pigeon. It was a kittiwake gull in remarkably fine condition ; as Philip was holding it in his hands, gazing on it with admiration, it suddenly darted its long sharp beak up one of his nostrils, bringing down a pouring stream of blood. With such poor incidents as these, 1828 passed gloomily and drearily away. But one morning, soon after the new year had opened, Martin at breakfast electrified Gosse by the announcement that he was going to send the latter to Carbonear. The lad was to travel on foot across the country, trackless and buried deep in snow. Philip thought not for an instant, however, of danger or labour, in the joy of getting back to companionship and home. Old Joe Byrne, a trapper and furrier, familiar with the interior—a worthy, simple old fellow, and quite a character—was to be his pilot, and to carry his little kit, his chest remaining to be sent round the coast by the first spring schooner.

Accordingly, the next day, they left in a small boat, and were rowed up the bay, to its extreme point, where Colinet river enters. Here was Joe's house, and here Philip Gosse remained for one day as his guest, regaled with delicious beaver meat. He declared to the end of his life that no flesh was so exquisite as the hind quarters of beaver roasted. An old Irish farmer was living near, whose English was imperfect. He came in to speed the travelling party, and wishing to describe the abundance of ptarmigan in the interior, he assured them that "you will see a thousand partridge, and she will look you right in the face." After a last revel on the delicious tail of the beaver, late in the afternoon Joe and Philip Gosse started to walk to Carbonear, striking due north for the head-waters of Trinity Bay, some sixteen or seventeen miles distant in a direct line. Just before nightfall they arrived at a little "tilt," or rude hut, of Joe's, made in his pursuit of fur animals. Here they soon built up a good fire and prepared their evening meal, falling asleep at last in a fog of pungent wood-smoke.

The second day was far more laborious. In many places the snow was several feet deep ; the foot on being set down would sink to mid-thigh, and had to be slowly and painfully dragged out for the next step. Seven hours' hard walking only accomplished, by Joe's estimate, five miles. The over-exertion produced symptoms of distress in the physical frame of the young man, and he was utterly exhausted when they reached a second and much poorer tilt. They were now about half-way across the isthmus. The third day was more pleasant. The weather was fine, the snow tolerably firm, and the elasticity of youth began to respond to the necessity. A remarkable characteristic of the interior of Newfoundland is a multitude of lakes or ponds, mere dilatations of the rivers and rivulets ; they occur in succession, like links of a chain, or like beads on a string. These were now hard frozen and snow-covered ; but their perfect level, and the comparative thinness of the wind-swept snow upon them, induced the old trapper to select these expansions of Rocky River and its tributaries wherever their course would admit. Some of the larger ponds were several miles in length, and were often studded with islets clothed with lofty hard-woods, such as birch and witch-hazel, forms of vegetation not met with near the coast. This country the young man pictured as probably full of beauty and variety in summer.

Old Joe was communicative, and in his capacity of furrier and trapper his experience was interesting. He pointed out some large rounded masses of snow at the head of one lake, which, he said, covered a beaver-house whence he had drawn many beavers. In other places he pointed out otter (or, as he pronounced it, "author") slides, always on the steep slope of the bank, where the water, even throughout the winter, remained unfrozen. "These slides," says my father, "were as smooth and slippery as glass, caused by the otters sliding on them in play, in the following manner :—Several of these amusing creatures combine to select a suitable spot. Then each in succession, lying flat on his belly, from the top of the bank slides swiftly down over the snow, and plunges into the water. The others follow, while he crawls up the bank at some distance, and running round to the sliding-place, takes his turn again to perform the same evolution as before. The wet running from their bodies freezes on the surface of the slide, and so the snow becomes a smooth gutter of ice. This sport the old trapper had frequently seen continued with the utmost eagerness, and with every demonstration of delight, for hours together." It reminds one of tobogganing, although the attitude is not quite the same. My father used to say that he knew no other example of adult quadrupeds doing so human a thing as joining in a regular set and ordained game.

They had made fair progress in this third day, and at its end, as there were no more hospitable tilts, they were fain to bivouac under the skies. Old Joe, however, was equal to the emergency. With the axe that he carried at his belt, he promptly felled a number of trees in a spruce wood, causing them so to fall as that their branches and leafy tops should form a dense wall of foliage around an open area, within which he lighted an immense blazing fire, feeding it with the trunks, which he cut into logs, and piled up in store sufficient for the whole night, before he ceased labour. Next morning they trudged on again, and while this fourth day was still early, they arrived at the sea in Trinity Bay. The long narrow inlet at the head was frozen over, and they walked down it. The ice was solid enough, but fresh water had flowed over it, flooding the whole to the depth of about a foot. This also had frozen over during the night, but so thinly as to bear the pressure of the foot for only an instant. As soon as the weight of the body came, down went the foot through to the ice below. Trudging thus through freezing water, while the edge of the thin surface-ice cut the skin at every step, and this for a distance of two miles, proved the most trying incident of the whole journey ; but the sense of having reached the northern coast sustained them. A mile or two now brought them to the point whence they had again to strike across country to Conception Bay. The distance was still about a dozen miles, but along a regular beaten track, and they did it jauntily. Near nightfall they reached the head of Spaniard's Bay, and presently walked into the familiar streets of the town of Harbour Grace, where, at the house of his friend Charley St. John, Gosse parted from his trapper pilot, and received a cordial greeting from the whole of the affectionate St. John family. A letter from Mr. St. John takes up the tale. " Have you forgotten," he says forty years later (1868), " the night when, on your return from St. Mary's to Carbonear, you stopped at my father's, and when I kept you awake until near daybreak relating what had occurred during your absence, till my father had to tap at the partition to stop our clacking and laughing ? And how, when you went over next day, the lads were disappointed at finding their bottled ale all fizzled down flat and stale ? " Very shortly after this, W. C. St. John married, under somewhat romantic circumstances, and thenceforward began to run over to Harbour Grace for two or three nights of each week, returning to the office in the early morning. Still, he was not quite the same to his friends as before, and the marriage of a clerk without special consent was not looked upon with favour. Mr. Elson, after a time, intimated that St. John must seek some other employment, and in the autumn of 1830 he ceased to be one of the circle at Carbonear.

It was in the winter of that year that Philip Gosse became consumed with a passion for poetry, a return to the feeling roused three years before by the reading of *Lara.* He began to devour all the verse that was to be discovered in Carbonear, and to form a manuscript selection of the pieces which struck him as being the best, an anthology which he patiently continued to form until 1834. This collection, in two volumes, is now in my possession, and testifies to the refined, but, of course, somewhat conventional taste, of the lad. Much reading of poetry inevitably leads to the writing of it, and Philip wrote the words " Sprigs of Laurel " on the title-page of a blank volume which it was his intention to fill with lyrics of his own. He achieved a " Song to Poland," some scriptural pieces inspired by Byron, a blank-verse address to Spring, and then the laurel grove withered up and budded no more. His genius was not for poetry. Music followed in the wake of verse ; a *furore* for making musical instruments seized the clerks. Under the tuition of a Mr. Twohig, a carpenter, my father constructed in 1831 an Æolian harp and a violin, neither of which was unsatisfactory. In the same summer he taught himself to swim.

Up to this time the record of my father's life has been the chronicle of a child, although by the close of the season he was actually well advanced in his twenty-second year. In reality, however, he was extremely young, unformed, without definition of character, without distinct aim of any kind, and lacking, too, the ordinary buoyancy of early manhood. He was suspended, as it were, between the artlessness of childhood and the finished shape which his maturity was to adopt. This is probably no rare phenomenon in the youth of men born to be remarkable, and yet placed in circumstances which arrest rather than advance their development. In glancing over my father's diaries and notes,

I find no difficulty in perceiving that the year 1832 was in several respects the most remarkable in his life. In it he commenced that serious and decisive devotion to scientific natural history which henceforward was his central occupation. In it he first, as he himself put it forty years later, "definitely and solemnly yielded himself to God; and began that course heavenward, which, through many deviations and many haltings and many falls, I have been enabled to pursue, on the whole steadfastly, until now." It was in this year also that, after five years' absence in Newfoundland, he once more visited his parents and his native country. This, however, was but a trifling matter in comparison with the great importance of the change which turned the soft and molluscous temperament of the youth into the vertebrate character of the man. In 1832 Philip Gosse, suddenly and consciously, became a naturalist and a Christian. On the former subject he must now speak for himself:—

"The 5th of May was one of the main pivots of life
"to me. The Wesleyan minister, Rev. Richard Knight,
"was selling some of his spare books by auction. I was
"there, and bought Kaumacher's edition of Adams's
"*Essays on the Microscope*, a quarto which I still
"possess. The plan of this work had led the author to
"treat largely of insects, and to give minute instructions
"for their collection and preservation. I was delighted
"with my prize; it just condensed and focussed the
"wandering rays of science that were kindling in my
"mind, and I enthusiastically resolved forthwith to collect
"insects. At first I proposed only to include the more
"handsome butterflies and moths and the larger beetles, of
"which barren Newfoundland yielded a poor store indeed;
"but not knowing how to make a limit, I presently
"enlarged my plan, and commenced as an entomologist

"in earnest. The *Sirex gigas*, which I had taken in
" 1829, was still lying on the sash of the parlour window ;
"with this I began my collection.   On the 6th of June
"I took, on a currant bush in the garden, a very fine
"specimen of a very fine butterfly, the Camberwell
"Beauty (*Vanessa Antiopa*), of which, strange to say, I
"never saw another example while I remained in the
."island.

   "Owing to the long continuance of the Arctic ice on
"the coast, the spring of 1832 was unprecedentedly late ;
"so that my collection had not gone beyond a few
"minute and inconspicuous insects, before I sailed for
"England.

   "The preface to my *Entomological Journal*, from which
"I gather the above particulars, ends with these pro-
"'phetic sentences : 'I cannot conclude . . . without
"'noticing the superintending Providence, that, without
"'our forethought, often causes the most important
"'events of our life to originate in some trifling and
"'apparently accidental circumstance—to be, like our
"'own huge globe, "hung upon nothing"! After years
"'only can decide how much of that happiness which
"'chequers my earthly existence may have depended
"'on the laying out of ten shillings at a book sale.'"
The arrival of the spring vessels from Poole had announced the serious illness of Philip's only sister, Elizabeth,
but he had not felt any special alarm, until in the beginning of June news came that her life was in danger, and
that she wished to see her absent brothers once more.
Philip Gosse immediately took in the letter to Mr. Elson,
who, in the kindest manner, said that he should go home
by the next ship, which was to sail in a few weeks. It
had been distinctly stipulated that this privilege should
be given to the lad during his apprenticeship, and five out

of the six years had now expired. The anticipation of the death of one so beloved as Elizabeth, and the tedium of waiting for the opportunity to visit her, produced a peculiar effect on the young man's mind. As has already been shown, he was by temperament grave and somewhat Puritanical. His giddiest flights of spirit had not raised him to the customary altitude of innocent youthful behaviour, and nothing was lacking but such an incident as the illness of Elizabeth to develop in him the sternest forms of religious self-devotion. He shall himself describe the course of events in his spiritual nature, and I am the more ready to print his exact words, because their tenour is very unusual, and far enough removed from the conventional language of modern religious life :—

"My prominent thought in this crisis was legal. I "wanted the Almighty to be my Friend; to go to Him "in my need. I knew He required me to be holy. He "had said, 'My son, give Me thy heart.' I closed with "Him, not hypocritically, but sincerely; intending "henceforth to live a new, a holy life; to please and "serve God. I knew nothing of my own weakness, or "of the power of sin. I cannot say that I was born "again as yet; but a work was commenced which was "preparatory to, and which culminated in, regeneration. "I came at once to God, with much confidence, as a "hearer of prayer, and He graciously honoured my faith, "imperfect as it was.

"As illustrating the tenderness of conscience then "induced, I recollect the following incident :—The use of "profane language, so common around me, I had always "avoided, until the last twelvemonth or so, when I had "been gradually sliding into it. One day, some week "or two after my exercise with God, I was alone in the "office, when some agreeable occupation or other was

"suddenly interrupted by work sent down from Mr.
"Elson. In the irritation of the moment, I muttered
"'Damn it!' not audibly, but to myself. Instantly my
"conscience was smitten; I confessed my sin before
"God, and never again fell into that transgression."

On July 10, 1832, he sailed from Carbonear, in the brig
Convivial, for Poole. The skipper, Captain Compton, was
the most gentleman-like of the Elson captains, a man of
immense bulk, genial and agreeable in manners, and he
made the voyage a very pleasing one. Philip kept a
journal of this expedition, which still exists and bears
witness to his increased power of observation and description. On August 6 the young naturalist, who was now
within sight of the coasts of Devon and Dorset, had the
satisfaction of observing one of the rarest visitors to our
shores, the white whale, or *Beluga*. Late in the evening
of the same day he stepped on Poole Quay, and five
minutes brought him to the familiar house in Skinner
Street. As he knocked at the door, his heart was in his
mouth, for he knew not what tidings awaited him. His
brother answered his knock. "Oh," Philip said, as he
grasped his hand, "is all well?" for he could not speak
the name of Elizabeth. "Yes," was the reply, "*very* well!"
and the new-comer felt a load lifted from him. Though
still weak, Elizabeth was fast recovering, and had been
removed to lodgings at Parkstone, in company with her
mother, for purer air.

Little did Philip sleep that night. Awake in conversation until past midnight, he was up at four o'clock next
morning, and sallied forth, armed with pill-boxes, ready
for the capture of any unlucky insect desirous to experience
the benefits of early rising. During the voyage home his
dreams had been nightly running in the pursuit of insects
over the flowery meadows of Dorset. At length it was a

reality. He was in a humour to be pleased with every-thing ; but even if it had not been so, the morning was so fresh and bracing, the hedges so thickly green, and the flowers so sweet after the harsh uplands of Newfoundland, that he could not fail of an ecstasy. In later life my father constantly recalled that delightful morning, which appears to have singularly and deeply moved him with its beauty· "I was brimful of happiness," he said in a letter of a year later (November 16, 1833). "The beautiful and luxuriant hedgerows ; the mossy, gnarled oaks ; the fields ; the flowers ; the pretty warbling birds ; the blue sky and bright sun ; the dancing butterflies ; but, above all, the unwonted freedom from a load of anxiety ;—altogether it seemed to my en-chanted senses, just come from dreary Newfoundland, that I was in Paradise. How I love to recall every little incident connected with that first morning excursion !—the poor brown cranefly, which was the first English insect I caught ; the little grey moth under the oaks at the end of the last field ; the meadow where the *Satyridæ* were sport-ing on the sunny bank ; the heavy fat *Musca* in Heckford-field hedge, which I in my ignorance called a *Bombylius*, and the consequent display of entomological lore mani-fested all that day by the family, who frequently repeated the sounding words 'Bombylius bee-fly.'"

The mother and sister soon returned from Parkstone, and the circle around the table in Skinner Street was once more complete. Philip did not stray three miles from Poole during the whole of his visit. He found little changed in Poole during his five years' absence. "Our lane," which had been a *cul-de-sac*, was now a thoroughfare, by the turning of the old gardens at the end into new streets, and there was a new Public Library built at the bottom of High Street. Of this Philip was made free, and there he read a good deal. His time was largely spent in entomological excursions, and he threw himself into scientific study with extreme ardour and singleness of purpose. He found an occasional companion in his cousin, Tom Salter, an ardent young botanist, and he discovered that, in a young man named Samuel Harrison, Poole now possessed a local entomologist. With this latter Gosse agreed to correspond and exchange duplicates when he returned to Newfoundland, and these pledges were faithfully kept. Harrison was the son of the most influential member of the firm, and probably his friendship with Philip Gosse gave the latter a sort of status with Mr. Elson and the captains, and invested his pursuit of insects with a certain consideration. From this time forth, my father's zoological proclivities were matters of notoriety, but he does not seem to have met with any of the ridicule which so unusual an employment of his leisure might be presumed to bring upon him in a society like that of Carbonear.

On September 20, 1832 ("the day before Sir Walter Scott died," as he notes in his diary), my father's brief but pleasant sojourn in England ended. He sailed with the *Convivial*, on her return to Carbonear. He kept no notes of this voyage, which was both tempestuous and long, for they did not arrive until the 1st of November. Late as it was in the season, and the Arctic winter already setting in, he did what he could in collection and in study. Of course, he met with many difficulties, of which his personal isolation from all scientific sympathy was perhaps the greatest, but by degrees many of them were surmounted, and he learned much in the best and hardest school, that of actual observation. He carefully recorded every fact which appeared to be of importance, a habit which proved of the highest value. He thus became, not merely an assiduous collector of insects, but a scientific naturalist. Immediately after his return from Poole he began to keep a methodical meteorological journal ; recording the temperature thrice a day by a thermometer hung outside the office window, and, after a few months, recording the weather also. These records were regularly published every week in *The Conception Bay Mercury*, and were the earliest meteorological notes which were issued by any Newfoundland newspaper.

Philip Gosse now held the second place in the office. His standing duty was to take a duplicate copy of the ledger, in three volumes, for transmission to the firm at Poole. This was easy work, for he estimated that he could have completed it, in a steady effort, within three months, and that without any distressing fatigue. There was additional work, such as occasional copying of letters and routine jobs ; and in the times of pressure—as in the outfits for the ice and for Labrador, and in the settlement of accounts—he bore his part. None the less, he enjoyed an easy time and plenty of leisure. Early in 1833, under the influence of the then much-admired apocalyptical romances of the Rev. George Croly, Philip Gosse achieved rather a long poem, *The Restoration of Israel*, which is scarcely likely ever to be printed. His main and most absorbing occupation, however, was from this time forth natural history, and, for the present, entomology in particular. I have before me a large collection of letters written by Philip Gosse at this period, to his family and to Samuel Harrison in Poole, and to W. C. St. John in Harbour Grace. They breathe the full professional ardour of the collector ; they supply scarcely any facts concerning the life of the writer, but chronicle with an almost passionate eagerness the daily history of his discoveries and experiments. With the sudden development of intellect and conscience which I have described as taking place in 1832, there came the conscious pleasure in perception, and the conscious power to give it literary expression. From the letters before me I will give one or two examples. On January 12, 1833, he describes to Sam Harrison an incident of his late return voyage to Newfoundland :—

"Our passage to this country was long and rough, "and towards the latter part very cold and uncomfort- "able. An odd circumstance happened while I was on "board; one of the men coming up from the half-deck "found sticking on to his trousers a living animal, which "the mate brought down to me, that it might have the "benefit of my scientific lore. The crew, not being much "versed in zoology, could not tell what to make of it, he "said, for 'it did not seem to be a jackass, nor a tomtit, "'nor, in short, any of that specie.' After sagely gazing "at the creature awhile, I pronounced it to be a *scorpion.* "It was about two inches long, of a light-brown colour ; "when we would touch it, it would instantly turn the "point of its sting towards the place, as if in defence, "but did not attempt to run. However, we soon put an "end to its career by popping it into a little drop of "Jamaica, and the fellow is now in the possession of "your humble servant, snugly lying at the bottom of a "phial bottle. The wonder is where or how it could "have come on board, for they are never found in Eng- "land. I think it must have been in the ship ever since "she took a cargo of bark in Italy last winter.".

To the same correspondent he says, on May 25—and in this passage I seem to detect for the first time the complete accent of that peculiar felicity in description which was eventually to make him famous :—

"Of all the sights I have witnessed since I began the "study of this delightful science, none has charmed me "more than one I observed this morning. On opening "my breeding-box, I saw a small fly with four wings

"just at the moment it cleared itself of the *puparium*.
"The wings were white, thick, and rumpled ; the body
"slender, and about three-eighths of an inch in length.
"I took it gently out and watched its proceedings. It
"first bent its long antennæ under the breast, and then
"curved the abdomen, in which position it remained. It
"was some time before I could perceive any change in
"the wings, but at last they began to increase, and in
"about an hour they were at the full size, though they
"did not attain their markings and spots till two or
"three hours. I now discovered that it is a lace-winged
"fly (*Hemerobius*), the first of the genus I have ever seen ;
"and I cannot sufficiently admire the beauty and delicacy
"of the ample wings, the gracefulness of the little head,
"and the *lady-like* appearance of the whole insect. I
"know not from what pupa it could have come (for
"though it was evolved the moment I first saw it, yet I
"was so taken up with the fly that I neglected to observe
"the pupa-case, and afterwards I could not find it), unless,
"which I think probable, it was from one of those little
"silky cocoons, on the inner surface of willow bark, which
"I found on the 19th of March, and which I took for
"weevils ! However, I shall soon ascertain, for I have
"more of them."

Another fragment of this copious correspondence may
be given, from a letter of June 21, 1833, as an example of
Newfoundland landscape :—

"Before six this morning, I was on the shore of Little
"Beaver Pond, where I stood for a few moments in mere
"admiration of the day and quiet beauty of the scene.
"The black, calm pond was sleeping below me, reflecting
"from its unruffled surface every tree and bush of the
"towering hill above, as in a perfect mirror. Stretching
"away to the east were other ponds, embosomed in the

"mountains, while further on in the same direction,
"between two distant peaks, the ocean, with the golden
"sun above it, flashed forth in dazzling splendour. The
"low, unvarying, somewhat mournful note of the snipes
"on the opposite hill, and, as one would occasionally fly
"across the water, the short, quick flapping of his wings,
"seemed rather to increase than to diminish the general
"feeling of repose. The air seemed (perhaps from its
"extreme calmness) to have an extraordinary power of
"conveying sounds, for I could with perfect ease keep up
"a conversation with Sprague on the other side (not less
"than one-eighth of a mile off), without raising the voice
"above the pitch used in ordinary discourse."

The entomological work done in 1833 and the personal record of it are so profuse, that the biographer is inclined to wonder where the duties of the counting-house came in. But Mr. Elson was spending the summer in England, which gave a little more leisure than usual, and the young man became a kind of interesting local celebrity. The sons of Mr. Elson had a pleasure-boat of their own, the *Red Rover*, and she was placed at Philip Gosse's service for visiting the islands. One of the captains, Mr. Hampton, became an enthusiastic pupil of the young naturalist, and collected ardently for him in southern ports of Europe and Africa. Even the townspeople vied with one another to be on the watch for strange-looking insects "for Gosse's collection." His desk in the counting-house stood against one of the windows, and in the window-sill, close to his right hand, he kept his card-covered tumblers, in which he watched the development and transformation of many species while at his work. Mr. Elson never made the slightest objection to this, and from these simple apparatus many a fact was learned. In the summer of 1833 he began, under the title of *Entomologia Terræ-novæ*, to fill a volume with drawings of great scientific accuracy. Some of the figures were magnified, and for this purpose he had brought with him from Poole two lenses, which he contrived to mount very decently in bone, securing the substance from the dinner-table, and grinding and shaping it wholly by himself. The lens itself was neatly set in putty; and this rough but sufficient instrument was the only microscope which he was able to procure for many years. It rendered him an immense amount of service in his investigations. He also made a scale for his own use, out of an old tooth-brush handle; graduating it on one side to tenths, and on the other side to twelfths, of an inch; and this, in contempt of all modern improvements, he continued to use until the year of his death. His journal for 1833 closes with the following remarks :—

"*December* 31.—One year of my entomological "researches in this country has passed away. It has "been to me a pleasant and a profitable one; for, though "I have not been so successful as I anticipated in the "capture of insects, I have gained a good stock of "valuable scientific information, as well from books as "from my own observations. The season has been, from "its shortness and the general coldness of the weather, "particularly unfavourable to the pursuits of the ento- "mologist; several species of insects which I have "noticed in former years have been either very scarce "or altogether wanting. I have not seen a single "specimen of the large swallow-tailed butterflies this "year, nor heard of one, though some years I have "observed one yellow species in considerable numbers. "The Camberwell Beauty, too, I have not met with. "The claims of business, moreover, have prevented me "from giving so much time and attention to science as

"I could have wished, so that, considering my oppor-
"tunities, I have no reason to complain of want of
"success. Besides the specimens which I have already
"sent, and those which I have to send, to England, I
"have collected in the different orders as follows :—
"*Coleoptera*, 102 species ; *Hemiptera*, 29 ; *Lepidoptera*, 70
"(15 butterflies and 55 moths); *Neuroptera*, 43 ; *Hymen-*
"*optera*, 69 ; and *Diptera*, 75, making a total of 388
"species, not including the foreign insects received from
"Spain. . . . I enter upon the coming year with un-
"abated ardour, and with sanguine expectations, trusting
"that, if I am spared, it will prove still more successful
"and profitable than the past."

The year 1833 closed socially for Newfoundland in ominous thunders. Ever since the colonial legislation had been granted, the Irish party had been striving to gain a monopoly of political power. Party spirit ran high ; Protestants went in mortal fear, for the Irish everywhere vastly outnumbered them, and threatening glances and muttering words beset the minority. One St. John's newspaper, *The Public Ledger*, was on the Protestant side, and was edited by a young man of much spirit, Henry Winton, a friend of my father's. He advocated the colonial cause with wit and courage, and was in con-sequence greatly hated. He was, in the course of this winter, round in the Bay, collecting his accounts, when one night, walking alone from Carbonear to Harbour Grace, he was suddenly seized in a lonely spot by a set of fellows, who pinioned him, while one of their party cut off both his ears. This outrage created an immense sensation, and caused a sort of terror among the loyalists. A perfunctory inquiry was made, but the Irish influence prevented it from being carried far. It was soon known that the mutilation was the act of a Dr. Molloy, a surgeon of Carbonear, with whom the clerks at Elson's were well acquainted ; but he escaped all punishment. The state of things which prevailed at that time in Newfoundland was a direct reflection of the condition of Ireland, at that moment swayed by the oratory of Daniel O'Connell. Large contributions were being sent home from the colony to swell "the O'Connell thribbit," as it was called ; and Newfoundland was fast becoming a most unpleasant place to live in.

The year 1834 passed, almost without incident, in absorbing attention to natural history. To understand the difficulties under which Philip Gosse laboured, it must be borne in mind that no one in Newfoundland had ever attempted to study its entomology before ; that there were no museums, no cabinets to refer to for identification, in the whole colony—no list of native insects ; that the young man was entirely self-taught ; that he was poor, and could not buy what, in fact, did not exist if he had had the money. In October, 1834, Captain Hampton brought back for him, from Hamburg, a cabinet for insects which had been made there by Gosse's order and strictly according to his written directions. This was three feet high, three feet long, two feet wide, with twelve drawers, and folding doors. It was ill planned ; the drawers were not corked, and therefore the specimens had to be pinned into the wood, which was deal throughout ; the substance was but slight, and when he came to travel, he found it very unsatisfactory. However, it served its turn, and Gosse was too good a workman to grumble at his tools. His only written guide was the system of terse, highly condensed, intensely technical generic characters out of Linnæus's *Systema Naturæ,* as printed in the article "Entomology" in Tegg's *London Encyclopædia.* These characters he copied out, and they were of great value. He studied them most intently ; was often puzzled, discouraged, but ever returned to the attack. He made many mistakes, which experience gradually corrected. The want of books cast him the more upon nature, and so he struggled on, constantly increasing his acquaintance with actual facts, and laying a solid basis for book-knowledge whenever it might fall in his path.

All this time, the religious fervour to which allusion has already been made continued to keep pace with the scientific. Philip Gosse joined the Wesleyan Society, being led in that particular direction mainly by two new friends, G. E. Jaques and his wife, the former a colonist settled in the town of Carbonear, the latter an English lady. He presently became very intimate with them, spending his Sundays at their house, and frequently his week evenings. This friendship, to which reference will often be made in these pages, lasted more than forty years, and it should be noted here that it was mainly owing to the influence of this estimable couple that my father adopted a view of his duty to his fellows which henceforward, though in a fluctuating degree, never left him, and which towards the close of his life became paramount, namely, his belief that it was proper to exclude from his companionship all those whose opinions on religious matters did not coincide with his own. That I know this to have been the result of intense conscientiousness and a conviction that his duty lay in such isolation, must not induce me to pretend that the effects of it were not in many ways deplorable, or that it did not narrow, more than any other of his characteristics, the range of his sympathy and usefulness. He, however, of course, thought otherwise. He wrote, long afterwards, " My friendship with the Jaqueses was very helpful to my spiritual life. It alienated me more and more from the companionship of the unconverted young men of the place; it was a marked commencement of that course of decided separateness from the world, which I have sought to maintain ever since."

Although his religious practice then, as ever afterwards, was rigid and Puritanic to an unusual degree, he had a seventeenth-century freshness in mingling the human mood with the Divine. In letters of this period I find, side by side with outpourings of devotion and aspirations after godliness, quaint passages of simple humour. Philip Gosse took his place in the singing gallery at the Wesleyan Chapel, where his brother William led the instrumental part with the first violin. "Other chaps," he remarks, "and a few ladies swell the choir." One evening in the week they met to practise in the gallery, and on a single occasion, at least, he records that they all walked to Harbour Rock, a commanding eminence overlooking the port of Carbonear, and clustering there, sang a hymn under the summer stars before they separated. Two other of Elson's clerks, who had become "serious," in like manner attached themselves to the choir of the Established Church, and practised there in the evenings. Gosse would often join them, and the party would go home together. The old parish clerk, one Loader, was a character. He kept a school, but was quite illiterate. His office, of course, made incumbent upon him a zealous Protestantism. He would come to the counting-house, and glancing up at the Roman Catholic chapel, with a patronising smile on the clerks, would talk of "the misguided papishes, ye know!" One stormy Sunday the clergyman had not ventured over from Harbour Grace, and Loader thought it a fine chance for his own ministrations. He ran over to his house, close by, and returning with a book, mounted the pulpit, and read a flaring red-hot sermon of denunciatory character against popery : "Then there was Hildebrand, or, more properly speaking, Firebrand," etc., etc.—the whole read out in a miserable, limping style, but with thumping emphasis on the more incisive passages. Sad to say, in spite of his orthodoxy, poor Loader was a confirmed drunkard. One Saturday night, as my father and his colleagues were coming home from their several choir-practice, the snow being deep, they saw a dark object lying across the ditch. They went to it, and, behold! it was Loader, fallen helplessly on his front, happily in such a manner that his face hung over the ditch. "Why, Mr. Loader, is this you? What's the matter?" "Let me alone!" "Can we help you, Mr. Loader? You mustn't lie here, you know, Mr. Loader!" "Go along, ye imperdent fellers! Can't you see I'm a—looking—for—something? G'long!" They managed, however, to drag him to his own door, much against his will, he protesting to the very last that he had been "looking for something."

Philip Gosse's indentured engagement with the firm had expired in the spring of 1833. Since then he had remained on, with no expressed agreement, as copyer, receiving a small salary, besides board and lodging. Hitherto he had formed no plans for the future. In the autumn of 1834, his friends Mr. and Mrs. Jaques, their mercantile business in Carbonear not being very successful, were turning their eyes towards Upper Canada as a residence. They had met with some flaming accounts of the fertility of the regions around Lake Huron, and of the certainty of success being attained in agriculture by emigrants settling there. They determined to remove thither and begin life anew as farmers in a Western forest. Philip Gosse's intimacy with them had by this time become very close. He could not support the notion of parting with them ; and, moreover, the social gloom which hung over Newfoundland in consequence of the ever-increasing rancour of the Irish, was making the colony extremely

distasteful to him.   He, also, was fired by the highly
coloured reports of the emigration advertisements, and
thought that, as he was young and strong, he was sure to
make a capable farmer.   Then, too, there was the charm
of the unknown ; of life under totally new conditions ;
the romance of what was then the Far West, of the boundless primeval forests.

These are the only motives confessed in his letters of the
time, but under and behind all these there was another
unuttered even to himself, but stronger than all.   He had
pretty well exhausted the entomology of Newfoundland.
It was a cold, barren, unproductive region.   He longed to
try a new field.   One of the numerous works they read
that winter—for they all three eagerly devoured everything
about Canada that they could find—was a pleasant volume
of gossip by a lady, in which she enthusiastically and in
much detail, although unscientifically, described the insects
and familiar flowers of Upper Canada.   The account was
attractive enough to fire the young naturalist's imagination,
and thenceforth the time seemed long till he could wield
his butterfly-net in the forests of Acadia.

The vigorous faith with which he calculated on success
may be gathered from an extract from a letter to his
younger brother, dated December 1, 1834 :—

"Now I have a serious proposal to make to you, which
"I hope and ardently trust will meet not only your
"approval, but your warm co-operation.   I ask by this
"opportunity mother, father, and Elizabeth to come out
"to me at Canada, not *immediately*, but *in a year or two*,
"when I have, by God's blessing, got up a home on my
"estate for them to come to.   My plans I detail in my
"letters to them, and if they accede to my requests
"you must stay and bring them out.   But if they think
"the undertaking too great, please let me know whether

"*you* will be willing to cast in *your* lot with us. We
" would have all things common ; we could entomologize
" together in the noble forest, and, in the peaceful and
" happy pursuits of agriculture, forget the toils and
" anxieties of commerce.* Not that our lives will be
" idle, for we shall have to work with our own hands,
" but there will be the pleasing and stirring consciousness
" that our labour is for ourselves, and not for an unkind,
" ungrateful master. The land where I go is exceeding
" fertile and productive, and, with little more than half
" the toil necessary on an English farm, it will yield not
" only the necessaries, but even the luxuries of life. I
" want you to bring no money with you ; *yourself* I
" desire. . . . I shall not leave this country until the
" middle of May. I take for granted that you will join
" me ; do not let me be disappointed. Well then, this
" ensuing summer do all you can in procuring insects for
" your cabinet, even of those which you have already, as
" it will probably be your last opportunity of ever get-
" ting English insects. If you have not time to set
" them, never mind, only pin them ; it is not of the least
" consequence, as I can do them again at any length of
" time, and however dry they may have got. . . . Mr.
" and Mrs. Jaques know that I am inviting you to join
" us, and they earnestly desire you to come. I have
" learned to stuff birds, and there are beauties in Canada.
" We could make a nice museum."

It was the old story, the familiar and pathetic optimism
of the emigrant, but that they had to comprehend from
sad experience. For the moment, everything favoured the

---

* All this unconscious Fourierism curiously foreshadows the coming co-opera-
tive projects in America. What my father proposed in 1834 was attempted
at Fruitlands by Alcott in 1839, and carried out, after a fashion, at Brook Farm
in 1840.

scheme.   In the spring of 1835 Philip Gosse received replies.   His brother ardently responded ; but the rest of the family had no such enthusiasm, and not only refused to join the farm colony, but sought strongly to dissuade Philip from what they did not scruple to stigmatize as madness.   He was not dissuaded, however, and continued to elaborate the plans by which, with his slender savings, he meant to buy a hundred acres of virgin soil.   He spent pretty nearly all his evenings with the Jaqueses, eagerly reading every scrap of information about Canada, forming plans, and discussing prospects.   One evening, on coming home, as Mr. Elson had not quitted the parlour, Philip Gosse went in and abruptly announced his intention of leaving.   It happened to be a severely cold night, the effect of which was to benumb his organs of speech, and he spoke abruptly, with a stumbling thickness of pronunciation.   Mr. Elson made no remark, received the notice with coldness, offered no remonstrance, and expressed no sorrow at parting, nor any allusion to his eight years' service.   It is possible that, from Mr. Elson's point of view, Gosse, with all his foreign interests, had ceased to be a valuable or even an endurable occupant of the counting-house, conscientious as he intended to be.   After the friendly relations which had existed between them, it was none the less unfortunate that master and man should part on terms so far from cordial on either side.   But Philip Gosse had unconsciously grown too large a bird for the little nest at Carbonear.

CHAPTER IV.

CANADA.

1835–1838.

ON Midsummer Day, 1835, Philip Gosse took a final farewell of the little town which had been his home for eight years, and set off, full of sanguine anticipations, for a new life of liberty and enterprise. He walked from Carbonear to Harbour Grace, where the *Camilla* was lying, and went on board of her to sleep that night, to be joined next morning by Mr. and Mrs. Jaques. In the course of this, his last walk in Newfoundland, he saw in flight what all those years he had been looking for in vain—a specimen of the large yellow swallow-tail butterfly. He gave chase to it at once, and, after a long run, succeeded in capturing it easily with his hat, for it was very fearless. In the evening a boy brought out to the vessel for him a large cockroach, of a kind not native to North America, which he had picked up in the streets, dropped perhaps out of some cargo of sugar. This quaint species of tribute was his last gift from Newfoundland, a country in which he was destined never to set foot again. He took on board a variety of chrysalides, caterpillars, and eggs, the premature transformation of some of which gave him a great deal of anxiety. How completely he was absorbed in his duties as the nurse of these insects may be amusingly gathered from his diary, in which, for instance, in turning for some information regarding that important day on which he landed in the new country of his adoption, I find these words and no others :—

"*July* 15.—As I this day arrived at Quebec, I pro-"cured some lettuce for my caterpillars, which they ate "greedily."

The voyage from Harbour Grace to Quebec, a comparatively short distance on the map, proved an intolerably tedious one, from lack of wind. In the St. Lawrence the strong ebb tide continually carried them back during the night, running down with such force that it was impossible to stem it without a strong breeze up. The only resource was to cast anchor during the ebb and take advantage of the flood tide, which runs upward five hours in every twelve. They suffered from want of fresh food, and it was annoying to their appetites to pass close to little wooded islands stocked with ostentatious rabbits, and have no chance of rabbit-pie. On the nineteenth day they landed for ten minutes on Grosse Island, where the quarantine establishment was, and this was an agreeable refreshment. At length their impatience was rewarded, and they penetrated to the very heart of that land of promise from which they anticipated so much. They saw it in a golden light, and in these words, which betray his enthusiasm, Philip Gosse described his approach in a letter home :—

" On Wednesday last, as we were favoured with a fair "wind, we weighed and set sail very early, proceeding "along the fertile and well-cultivated Isle of Orleans, "which, as well as the south bank of the river, was "smiling in luxuriance and loveliness. When we had "passed the end of Orleans we opened the noble "Cataract of Montmorenci, a vast volume of foaming "waters rushing over a cliff of immense height. We "now came in sight of the city of Quebec, which being

"on the side of a hill, and gradually rising, like the seats
"of a theatre, from the lower town on the water-side to
"the upper town, and on to the lofty heights of Abra-
"ham, far exceeded in grandeur even my raised antici-
"pations. When the officers of quarantine had visited
"us we went on shore and took lodgings. In the
"evening we enjoyed a pleasant walk to the Heights."

They had intended to settle, as has already been said, in
the London district of Canada, on the shores of Lake
Huron. But already, at their first arrival, their hopes
were dashed. Those in Quebec who knew the interior,
and who were sympathetic with their inexperience, gave
an account of that country which was very different from
the roseate descriptions of the advertisements. At all
events, said these new friends, decide nothing until you
have at least seen the eastern townships of the Lower
Province. Thither accordingly, after four days spent in
Quebec, they all proceeded in an open carriage, and visited
a partially cleared farm in the township of Compton.
This they agreed to buy, and ten days later they all came
back to Quebec. This excursion, taken in the height of
summer and when everything looked its very best, was
admirably fitted to confirm the party of settlers in their
conviction that they had found a land flowing with the
milk and honey of prosperity. The profusion of butterflies, which of course he could not stop to catch, dazzled
Philip Gosse's imagination, so that the important matter
of selecting a scene of residence and occupation *for life*,
since that was their intention, never once arrested his
serious thought. He wrote long afterwards, in reference
to this settlement at Compton, "I felt and acted as if
butterfly-catching had been the one great business of life."

They immediately removed from Quebec, with their
slender store of goods, to Compton, and took possession of

their farm. The village was on the river Coatacook, a tributary of the St. Francis, in the county of Sherbrooke, very near the angle formed by a line drawn south from Quebec and one drawn east from Montreal. It was thirteen miles distant from the town of Sherbrooke, and about twenty from the frontier of the state of Vermont, U.S.A. What the farm consisted of, and what their labour in it, may be plainly seen, though still through somewhat rose-coloured spectacles, in the following extract from a letter written November 4, 1835, to his friend, Dr. P. E. Molloy, in Montreal :—

"I like my location here very much ; it seems the "general opinion that our farm was a bargain :—one "hundred and ten acres of land (forty-five cleared), a "frame-house, a log-house, a frame-barn, young orchard, "four tons of hay, etc., for £100—£50 in hand, the "remainder in two annual instalments. It is a pic- "turesque-looking place, containing hill and dale, hard "and soft wood, and streams of water. The first thing "I did was to cut the hay which was on *my* allotment. "This I did by hired labour ; I *made* it chiefly myself. "I then ploughed a field of about six acres, except "three-quarters of an acre, which was done by hired "labour. I found ploughing rather different from book- "keeping, but not near so difficult nor so laborious as "I had expected. Since then I have been collecting "stones from the fields, which are very numerous in "some parts, and dragging them off. I have had about "six acres of wild land (from which the heavy timber "had been cut before) cleared of logs and bushes, and "am getting them ploughed ; though I intend trying to "do part of this myself. My intended next year's crops "will be as follows:—Three acres wheat; three acres oats; "one acre peas ; two acres turnips ; three acres potatoes ;

"perhaps one acre buckwheat; eight acres grass; and
"four acres pasture. Sometimes at first, when weary
"with labour, and finding things rather awkward, I was
"inclined to discontent; but *that* soon wore off: the
"thought of projected improvements and anticipated
"returns, together with the beauty of the country and
"freedom from the bustle of the counting-house, have
"dispelled the gloom, and I am now as merry as a
"cricket all day long. I have made successful applica-
"tion for the conducting of one of the Government
"schools through the winter, say four months, at the
"rate of £3 per month, besides board. This will help
"my finances, though I am not *compelled* to have recourse
"to it, having still a few pounds in my pocket-book.

"You ask if we have to work *severely :* I think I may
"say no; our labour is occasionally *hard*, but not *severe*—
"not nearly so hard to learn as I anticipated. As our
"minds were set on the Upper Province, it is hard to
"draw a comparison between our expectations and the
"realization, as it is so *different* from our anticipations;
"but I think I may say we are not disappointed. On
"no account would I change my acres for my place at
"Slade, Elson, and Co.'s desk. Society here is almost
"wholly 'Yankee.' Their manners are far too forward
"and intruding for our English notions, still *all* are not
"so; there are some very agreeable and good neighbours.
"I much regret that you did not come here to reside the
"winter. Pardon me for saying you could have boarded
"much more cheaply in the village than I take for
"granted you would in a city like Montreal, and perhaps
"realize nearly as much practice. We shall eagerly look
"forward to the promised pleasure of seeing you in the
"spring, if all be well. I think you will find it advan-
"tageous to cultivate a small farm in addition to your

"professional pursuits: suppose it were only twenty "acres, it would materially aid your domestic economy.

"And now, as you have 'drawn me out' by asking "about entomology, pardon me if I mount my hobby "for a few moments. Since my arrival, I have enriched "my cabinet with a great number of new and splendid "insects; indeed, to a naturalist, this country holds out "a charming field of exploration in all branches of "natural history. My agricultural labours are not so "severe or so engrossing as to prevent my having some "time to devote to the pursuit of my interesting science, "of which I do not fail to avail myself. When I was "in Quebec, I made the acquaintance of one or two "members of the Literary and Historical Society, who "introduced me to their museum, and promised to pro- "pose me as a corresponding member. (A correspond- "ing member must be a non-resident, and *pays no fees.*) "I have written to Quebec since I have been here, but "have received no answer, so I suppose the promise has "been forgotten. Perhaps you have become acquainted "with some of the members of the Natural History "Society of Montreal; if so, would you be kind enough "to inquire if a person residing here could be admitted "as a corresponding member, and if so, what qualifica- "tions would be required, what fees, etc.? I have col- "lected many duplicate specimens of insects which I "had intended for the museum at Quebec, but if they "would be received at Montreal, I should prefer sending "them there. Perhaps it would not be troubling you "too much, to ask if there are at present any entomo- "logical members, and whether they are *scientific.* I "should like very much to have some scientific friend "in this country, with whom I could correspond. I "hope you will excuse my boldness in asking so many

"favours at once, especially as I have not had the hap-
"piness of being able to confer any."

In addition to what is said above, it may be explained
that the hundred and ten acres which formed the farm
were divided by the high-road into two portions. The one
consisting of fifty acres, but having a frame dwelling-house
and barn, fell to Mr. Jaques ; the western section, of sixty
acres, having a log-hut, an apple-orchard, a young maple-
sugary, and four tons of hay, Philip Gosse took for his.
This statement, however, gives much too favourable a
notion of the enterprise. Only about a third of the acreage
was cleared and in cultivation, and the whole farm,
although originally of good land, was sadly neglected and
exhausted by the miserable husbandry of its former pos-
sessors. The new tenant bought a horse and a cow,
stabling them in the log-hut. His first labour was to get
in his hay, and then he undertook to plough about five
acres, himself both holding and driving. He got three
acres more cleared of bushes and underwood, and ploughed,
by hired labour. These eight acres were all his tillage
land at first, and he divided them, as he had proposed,
between wheat, barley, peas, and potatoes. In all the
farm work he was quite unaided by the Jaqueses, the
notion of all toiling together, in an atmosphere of refined
intelligence, for a common purse, having broken down at
the first moment. The two laborious little farms had to
be worked independently, and Philip Gosse paid a modest
sum as a boarded lodger. In August they got into their
house, and one of Gosse's earliest acts was to paint the
outside of it with a mixture of skim milk and powdered lime.

The Jaqueses, in particular, were soon disillusioned. Mrs.
Jaques, who had been brought up as a lady, and who was
then nursing a baby, found it almost intolerably irksome
to carry out the entire labour of the house herself, but they

could afford no servant. The two men, also, found the practical drudgery of the farm work very different from the idyllic occupation which it had seemed in fancy, and through the pleasant telescopes of hope and romance. Their hands grew blistered with the axe and the plough ; their backs ached with the unwonted stooping and straining ; no intellectual companionships brightened their evening hours ; their neighbours, few and far between, were vulgar and sordid, sharp and mean ; they saw no books, save those they had brought with them. So far as my father was concerned, this painful isolation from the outer world of man, though disagreeable, was not harmful. It thrust him more and more on the society of nature. Entomology had been his pastime ; it was now his only resource, and what had been a condiment and the salt of life grew now to be its very pabulum. The toil at the plough was harsh and exhausting, but not nearly enough so to dim his intellectual curiosity. His mind, the tendency of which was always to flow in a deep and narrow channel, concentrated all its forces in the prosecution of zoological research. In summer, as soon as his labour in the fields was over, he would instantly sally back to the margins of the forest, insect-net in hand, all fatigue forgotten in one flapping of a purple wing. His entomological journals, continued throughout the whole of his residence in Canada, are a memorial of his unflagging industry and success in the pursuit of science. It was these journals which later on formed the basis of his first published volume, *The Canadian Naturalist* of 1840.

The toil would have been less difficult to endure, if the returns had been commensurate. But in these, as in almost everything else (except the butterflies), the emigrants were grievously disappointed. Their neighbours described their first season as abnormally unpropitious ; frosts came unusually early in 1836, so that the unripe corn-crops were frozen and spoiled. From whatever cause it might be, and penuriously as they lived, they presently found that they were not making both ends meet. Existing as they did in wretched poverty, it was depressing to find that, even so, their toil was insufficient to maintain them. They soon became convinced that they had made a serious mistake in swerving from their original intention of choosing the Upper Province, but still more in buying a wasted and exhausted farm. It is true that about half of Philip Gosse's acres were as yet virgin forest, which he might have reclaimed and cultivated. But they consisted, for the most part, of "black timber"—that is to say, the species of pine, spruce, and fir which indicate low and swampy soil, unfit for ploughing. Perhaps if he had more perseverance, or a little capital, he might have turned this into meadow. But his personal strength and skill were not equal to the huge effort of clearing forest-land, and he soon ceased to have the power to hire even the poorest labour. He was accustomed, long afterwards, to reflect with bitterness on what he might have done if they had kept to their plans, and struck for the shores of Lake Huron. But bearing in mind the conditions of the experiment, I cannot feel that the result would have been much better. No doubt the land they could have bought in the North-west would have been far more fertile than at Compton, but it was clothed with heavier timber, which they would have been obliged to fell even before they could build a hut to cover their heads. The labour would have been far more severe, the life even more recluse and savage. But the real fact is that my father had no natural gift for agriculture ; he was not one of Emerson's "doctors of land, skilled in turning a swamp or a sandbank into a fruitful field." The thoughts that came to him at the plough were dry thoughts ; there was no fresh flavour of the earth about them. If it had not been for the blessed insects he must have died of ennui.

It was not, however, for a long while that Philip Gosse realized his disappointment. The rose-colour was in no hurry to rub off. In September, 1835, he writes home to a friend in Poole, relapsing into the old familiar vernacular, " I am now become such a farmer that I believe I could smack a whip with ere a chap in the county o' Dorset." He was full of enthusiasm for the natural beauties of the Canadian autumn. In the same letter he writes : " The trees are now beginning to fade in leaf, which causes the forest to assume a most splendid appearance. The foliage is of the most gorgeous hues ; the brilliant rich crimson of the maple, the yellow of the elm, the orange and scarlet of other trees, set off by the fine dark green of the beech and the nearly black of the cedars and pines, give a beauty, a splendour, to the landscape which cannot be conceived by those who have not seen it." The following extract is from a letter to his father, dated June 11, 1836 :—

" I have to work with my own hands. To be sure, I " have not felled many trees yet, except for fuel ; nor is " it necessary, as I have several large fields which have " been many years in cultivation. However, if you could " peep at me, you would haply see me at the tail of the " plough, bawling at the top of my voice to the horses ; " or casting the seed into the ground ; or mowing the " seedy grass ; or pitching the sun-dried hay to the top " of the cart. The country is a lovely one, especially " at this most charming season—*formosissimus annus*— " when the ground is covered with grass and flowers, and " the woods adorned with masses of the richest foliage, " enlivened by birds of sweet song and gay plumage. I " have seen the beautiful *Tanagra rubra*, with his coat

"of brilliant scarlet and deep-bluish wings and tail. The
"ruby-throated humming-bird, too, begins to appear,
"with its loud hum as it sucks the nectar of some
"syngenesious flower, its fine eyes darting hither and
"thither, its wings invisible from their rapid vibration,
"and its throat glowing in the sun like a flame of fire.
"Then the woodpeckers, with their caps of deep scarlet;
"the pine grosbeak, with its pink and crimson plumage;
"and others, *quos nunc*, etc. You asked me if I had shot
"any turkeys or deer; you know not how good a shot
"I am. I have shot at a squirrel three times successively,
"without doing him any 'bodily harm,' without even
"the satisfaction of the Irish sportsman who made the
"bird 'lave that, any way;' for the squirrel would not
"leave the tree, but continued chattering and scolding
"me all the time. However, wild turkey is not found
"east of Lake Erie. Deer come round in the winter,
"and sometimes get into our fields, and eat the standing
"corn in autumn; I have seen some that were shot by
"a neighbour, but they were does and had no horns.
"They looked much like our fallow deer, but larger.
"The reindeer or caribou, as it is called, and the moose
"occasionally, but rarely, are taken. I have seen a few
"Indians, belonging to the St. Francis tribe: some of
"them encamped within a few miles of us last winter;
"but they are a poor, debased, broken, half-civilized
"people, not the lordly savage, the red man of the far
"West; not such as Logan or Metacom of Pokanoket."
He was not, however, entirely thrown upon nature for
intellectual resources at Compton. Teachers of the township schools, which were held in the winter, were in demand,
and he found no difficulty in obtaining an engagement for
the dead months of each of the three seasons he resided
in Canada. The teacher received free board and £10 for

the season of twelve weeks, which Philip Gosse found a very timely alleviation of his expenses, though the occupation was unpleasing to his taste and irksome to his rapid habit of mind. But the ever-present stimulus of scientific investigation kept up his spirits, and there began to grow up within him a new sensation, the definite ambition to gain scientific and literary distinction. The first encouragement from without which came to him in his career, the earliest welcome from the academic world, arrived in the early spring of 1836, in the modest shape of a corresponding membership of the Literary and Historical Society of Quebec. This was quickly followed by a similar compliment from the Natural History Society of Montreal. These elections, indeed, conferred in themselves no great honour, for these institutions, in those early colonial days, were still in their boyhood, and too inexperienced to be critical in their selection. It was none the less a great gratification to the young man. He contributed papers to the *Transactions* of either society, sending to Montreal a *Lepidoptera Comptoniensa* and to Quebec an essay on *The Temperature of Newfoundland* and *Notes on the Comparative Forwardness of the Spring in Newfoundland and Canada.* He also sent to the new museum at Montreal a collection of the lepidoptera of Compton. All the while he was keeping his copious daily journal of observations, a diary which lies before me now, and from which I extract one day's record as a sample of the rest :—

" *August* 10, [1835].—I took a walk before breakfast " to a maple-wood, where I spent a few hours very " pleasantly. There was one large but quite decayed " tree, whose trunk was pierced with very many holes, " and in almost every hole were the remains of a *Sirex*, " almost gone to dust—a large species somewhat " resembling *Sirex gigas.* There were also remnants of

"many beetles, among which was a *Buprestis*, like one I
"caught at Three Rivers, and several bright red beetles
"new to me, which have some characters of *Lucanus*.
"There were many oval cases, as large as pigeons' eggs,
"containing *exuviæ* of some beetle, and in one I found a
"*Scarabæus*, as that of 8th inst., complete though decayed.
"In another rotten tree I found several *Juli*, some of
"which were of gigantic size. While in the wood, I
"heard a loud hum, and looking round saw what I took
"to be a large insect, but viewing it more intently, I
"saw it was a humming-bird of an olive colour, poising
"itself before some tubular flowers, and inserting its bill
"for an instant, then whisking to another like lightning ;
"while I stood motionless, it came and sucked flowers
"within a yard of me, but on the least motion was off
"to a distance. I saw the star crane-fly of Newfound-
"land. On coming home I found to my sorrow that,
"having put the large chafer of yesterday into my store-
"box, pinned but not dead, he had got his pin out of
"the cork, and had been amusing himself during my
"absence, carrying his pin about the box and biting
"other insects. He has spoiled a pearl-border fritillary,
"a tiger-moth, and, what I regret most of all, he has bitten
"two of the wings off the great *Hemerobius* of 30th ult."
During the winter of 1835-36, he made his first serious
attempt at book-making, *The Entomology of Newfoundland.* The manuscript is still in existence, for, though he
completed it, he made no attempt to find a publisher for it.
Indeed, his lack of systematic knowledge, and of the then
present condition of zoology, rendered it probably what
would have been considered by London *savants* as unfit
for publication, although the amount of actual observation
recorded at first hand, occasional anecdotes, and descriptions
of habitats around Carbonear constitute a store from

which, to this day, a more orderly work on the insects of Newfoundland might, no doubt, with great propriety be enriched. The main value of this lengthy production was the familiarity with the use of the pen which it supplied. It is a main feat for an unfledged author when he succeeds in setting *Explicit* at the bottom of a body of manuscript. He has learned the lesson of literary life, not to grow weary of well-doing. The unlucky *Entomology of New-foundland* was a mere preamble to a far more important occupation, that of collecting materials for a work, the pecuniary success of which was to be an epoch in my father's life, and to make him an author by profession. This was his *Canadian Naturalist.* " The whole plan of this work occurred to me," he says in a letter of 1840, " and was at once sketched in my mind, one day as I was walking up to Tilden's, the road that led along from my maple grove westward through the woods. It was a lovely spring day, the 11th of May, 1837, the day before my brother arrived. I had a large amount of material already in my entomological journal, and thenceforward I kept my eyes always wide open for every other branch of natural history. It was Sir Humphrey Davy's *Salmonia ; or Days of Fly-Fishing,* that formed my model for the dialogue. The work remains a vivid picture of what chiefly engaged my thoughts during my three Canadian years." He ceased, with this wider ambition, to be merely an entomologist ; he became a naturalist in the broader and fuller sense.

During the first eighteen months his letters home were still sanguine, and, despite the discomforts and limitations of the life at Compton, he continued to urge the members of his family to join him. In May, 1837, in fact, his younger brother came, but stayed only six months, and returned, bitterly disenchanted, to England. I do not, indeed, find it quite easy to comprehend my father's condition of mind throughout this year. He continues, in spite of all disappointment, to importune his father, mother, and sister to "be ready to come out and live under the protection of my wing," and talks, so late as the autumn of 1837, of having "some idea of getting out the materials of a house in the following winter, to be erected in the south-west corner of my Leghorn Field." Yet he had already, in July of the same year, advertised his farm at Compton for sale, not failing to mention in the terms his "garden of rare exotic flowers;" for he had enclosed a corner opposite the house, and had cultivated with success the seeds and plants which his brother had brought from Poole, and others that he had collected from friends around. As this season closed in, and his crops, which he had sanguinely persuaded himself were better than those of his neighbours, proved to be lamentable failures, his thoughts, unwillingly at first, but soon more and more, began to turn to some other scene and some other occupation for the living which seemed to be obstinately denied to him in Canada. The disastrous visit of his brother was the last straw, and the back of his optimism was broken at length. During the autumn he was vexed and disturbed by having to appear in court to give evidence in a criminal case against one of his few neighbours ; and for some weeks he was laid up with acute rheumatism. On November 4, 1837, he wrote a very melancholy letter to his sister Elizabeth, and, after upbraiding and yet excusing himself for having induced his brother to make so untoward an expedition, he continues—

"For myself, I have lately been somewhat brought "down by sickness : nothing very alarming, but sufficient "to disable me in a great degree from labour; in conse-"quence of which I have become very backward in my

" work, such as getting in my crops and ploughing. I
" believe my complaint to be an attack of rheumatism,
" brought on by a chill taken during a day's work in the
" field amidst heavy rain. Besides this, however, which
" was trifling, though painful, I have suffered from a
" general debility of body, with a depression of mind,
" from which I am not yet freed, though I am recovering.
" Could any employment be obtained at home? I am
" tired of more than ten years' exile, far from friends and
" kindred. I have been thinking that I might do well
" by establishing a school in Poole, or in some of the
" neighbouring towns. Is there any opening? Would
" a school at Parkstone do? I should be very glad if
" you would let me know by the first spring vessel. If
" you give me any encouragement, I will endeavour to
" sell my farm, and, please God, embark for Poole next
" fall. I believe I am competent to take a respectable
" academy, teaching all the ordinary branches of
" education, mathematics, book-keeping, Latin, and the
" rudiments of Greek and navigation. I should be glad
" of a change of food, for I live on buckwheat and pig's-
" meat."

About the same time he urged a former Newfoundland companion, who had just got a clerk's situation in
Philadelphia, to inquire what chances there were for
him in that city, either mercantile or scholastic. And
in the ensuing winter he had made up his mind; for he
wrote to this same friend on February 5, 1838, as
follows :—

" My purpose is to sell my farm at any sacrifice, and
" take the first opportunity of the Hudson navigation to
" proceed south. My eye is towards Georgia or South
" Carolina, as I understand persons of education are in
" demand there, both in mercantile and academical

"situations. I believe, however, that I shall take
"Philadelphia in my course, and if anything can be
"done there, I shall not proceed further."

This scheme soon ripened into accomplishment, and on
March 22, 1838, having realized the farm and stock as
best he could, he left Canada for the United States, his
friend Jaques driving him in his waggon as far as Burlington, on Lake Champlain.

This is the moment, perhaps, briefly to recapitulate the
results of the three years which had elapsed since he left
Newfoundland. As a monetary speculation, he had done
deplorably. He was twenty-eight years of age, and he was
not possessed, when all his property was told, of so many
pounds. By his change from Carbonear he had greatly
increased his toil ; he had lived much more meanly and on
a coarser fare, had been more poorly clad, and had suffered
in general health. To set against all these losses there
were two or three considerations. The mercantile house
which he had left in Newfoundland had, during these three
years, rapidly fallen into grave difficulties, and had broken
up, the clerks being dispersed to seek fresh employment.
The state of society in the colony had by this time, through
the ever-increasing turbulence and lawlessness of the Irish
population, become almost unbearable for Protestants.
But the great, the only, counterbalance to the wretched
disappointments and privations of these years in Canada
was the constant advance in scientific knowledge and range
of mental vision, which was checked, if at all, only during
the physical trouble of the last six months.

From the distressing correspondence of this period, with
its patient record of poverty, fatigue, and deferred hope,
I turn gladly to the professional journals, with their
unflagging note of triumph, and I permit myself one more
extract. It is not thrilling, perhaps, but I take it as an

example of that extraordinary power of retaining the results
of minute observation which made my father unique
among the naturalists of his time, and to find a parallel to
which it was then necessary to go back to Gilbert White of
Selborne :—

"On September 5, 1837, I and my brother visited the
"Bois Brulè. We went up by Bradley's Brook, and on
"the bank I found a new thistle, with crenated leaves.
"The first quarter of a mile lay through a very rough
"slash, where we had to climb over the fallen trees and
"through the limbs ; and, to make it worse, these were
"concealed by the tall wickup * plants with which the
"ground was absolutely covered, and as the seed-pods were
"just bursting, every movement dispersed clouds of the
"light cottony down, which getting into our mouths and
"nostrils, caused us great inconvenience. Presently we
"descended the steep bank, and walked, or rather
"scrambled, up the rocky bed of the stream by means
"of the stones which were above water, though, as they
"were wet and slimy, we occasionally wetted our feet.
"Thus we went on, sometimes in the stream, sometimes
"among the alders and underwood on the banks, for
"about a mile and a half. I met with many specimens of
"fruits and seeds which I had not [found] before, espe-
"cially the orange cup-flower, the handsome scarlet fruits
"of the white and the red death, bright blue berries, etc.
"In pressing through the brush, I got my clothes be-
"daubed with a nasty substance, which I discovered to
"proceed from thousands of the *Aphis lanigera*, which
"I had crushed. They were so thickly clustered round
"the alder branches as to make a solid mass, half an
"inch thick, covered with ragged filaments of white

* Or " wickaby," the leather-plant (*Dirca palustris*), a shrub common in
the Canadian woods, and covered in spring with small yellow blossoms.

"down. The insects were much larger than most of the
"genus, and of a lead-grey colour.

"We were getting nearly tired of the ruggedness of
"our path, when we suddenly came upon a new and
"very good bridge across the brook, made of sound logs,
"which connected a good broad bridle-path, from which
"the fallen logs, etc., had been cleared away, and which
"had been used for the purpose of drawing out mill logs.
"As its course seemed to be nearly parallel with that of
"the brook (about south-west), we preferred pursuing it,
"as being much more pleasant and more easy of travel.
"The sides of the road were lined with the stumps of
"large spruces and hemlocks which had been felled the
"previous winter, and the road itself was strewn with
"the chips of the axe-men. The course lying through
"a cedar swamp, the ground was mossy, and in some
"places wet; here the scarlet stoneberry (*Cornus
"Canadensis*) was abundant, as well as the berries
"mentioned before. The former was ripe, and we ate
"very many ; they are farinaceous and rather agreeable.
"We followed this path till it appeared almost intermi-
"nable, though its tedious uniformity made it seem
"longer than it really was, as I suppose we did not walk
"more than a mile and a half on it, when I saw by the
"increasing light that we were approaching a large
"opening.

"We now pressed on and found that we had reached
"the Brulè, which was not a clearing, as I had expected,
"but covered with stunted and ragged spruce, from
"eight to twelve feet high, exactly resembling the small
"woods of Newfoundland on the borders of the large
"marshes. I found also the same plants, which I now
"saw for the first time in Canada. The ground was
"covered with the same spongy moss, with shrubs of

"Indian tea (*Ledum latif.*), gould (*Kalmia glauca* and
"*K. angustif.*), and other Newfoundland plants, and, above
"all, numbers of that curious plant, the Indian cup or
"pitcher plant (*Sarracenia*), in flower, the leaves being
"all full of water. I brought home specimens as well
"of other curious flowers. The road merely touched
"the edge of the Brulè, and went straight on, entering
"the tall woods on the other side, emerging as I under-
"stand on the Hatley road, about a mile or two further.
"We went a little way into the Brulè to see if there was
"any clearing, but could perceive no change in the
"ugly, dead, half-burnt spruce, and therefore returned.
"This singular piece of ground consists of some
"thousands of acres, and is said to owe its origin to the
"beavers, which were formerly numerous, damming up
"the streams, which, spreading over the flat land, killed
"the growing timber. It is a resort of wolves and other
"wild animals, though we perceived no sign of life in
"the stillness which pervaded the solitude ; nor indeed
"in all the journey, with the exception of one or two
"little birds which were not near enough to identify, and
"a few insignificant insects in the forest.

" Having satisfied our curiosity, we began to return as
"we came, until we arrived at the bridge, when, instead of
"retracing the course of the stream, we crossed the bridge,
"and continued to pursue the road, which for some dis-
"tance led us through towering spruces and hemlocks
"as before. On a sudden we found the sides lined with
"young maple, birch, beech, etc., which met overhead
"at the height of about twelve feet, forming a very
"perfect continued Gothic arch, or rather a long series of
"arches. This long green avenue was the most pleasant
"part of our walk, and the more so as it was quite
"unexpected. We presently opened upon a large field

"which had been just mown, but which I had never
"before seen, nor could I recognize any of the objects
"which I saw.   There appeared to be no outlet through
"the woods by which it seemed to be environed.   There
"was the skeleton of an old log-house, without a roof, in
"one part, and a portion of the field was planted with
"potatoes.   We at length saw a path through these
"potatoes, and we walked on till, coming to the brow of
"a hill, we perceived the river, with Smith's mills, and
"the rest of that neighbourhood.   The road appeared to
"lead out towards Mr. Bostwick's, but we took a short
"cut, and came by the back of Webster's barn, and so
"by Bradley's mill, and home.   I forgot to observe that
"we were much surprised in going up the brook, about
"a mile up, at coming upon a ruined building, which had
"been erected over the stream, of which the timbers were
"fallen down, and some of them carried some distance
"downwards by the freshets.   I supposed it must have
"been a mill, but wondered at its situation so far from
"any road.   I have since been informed that it was a
"sawmill, which was built by Messrs. S. and D. Spafford,
"and that there was a good road to it, which went
"through P. O. Barker's south-west field ; but being now
"overrun with bushes, it escaped our notice.   The mill
"has been disused near twenty years."

CHAPTER V.

ALABAMA.

1838.

THE only piece of valuable property which Philip Gosse took with him from Canada was the cabinet of insects which he had had made years before in Hamburg, and which was now tightly stocked with the selected species of six years' incessant labour. The space in it was so limited that he had been fain to use not merely the usual floor of each drawer, but the tops as well, and even the sides. As has been said, the thing had been a cheap affair at first, and none of the drawers being lined with cork, the pins which fastened the insects had to be insecurely thrust into the deal wood itself. He had scarcely started from Compton on Mr. Jaques's light travelling waggon when he began to suffer from a mental agony which can scarcely be exaggerated. His poor shaky cabinet, with its frail contents, jolting over the hard-frozen roads, rough and destitute of snow, began more and more to give forth a rustling and faintly metallic sound which told him only too clearly that the pins were coming loose; and soon he sat there, in a condition of misery beyond speech or tears, the witness of a catastrophe which he was absolutely powerless to avert, watching in a wretched patience the cabinet, in which the delicate captures of his last years were being ground to dust.

His was a temperament which could not, however, for any length of time be depressed. After three years of confinement to a dreary Canadian township, he was now seeing the world again, and, what was important, going southwards, to warmth and sunlight. As they drove through the numerous villages of Vermont, he was captivated by the pretty, neat, and trim houses of wood, brightly painted, and as different as possible from the gaunt log-houses of Compton. In the woods he saw for the first time glades full of the paper-birch (Mr. Lowell's "birch, most shy and ladylike of trees"), with its dead-white bark, so unlike the glossy and silky surface of the common birch. One night they heard "from the most sombre and gloomy recesses of the black-timbered forest the tinkle of the saw-whetter. The unexpectedness of the sound struck me forcibly, and, cold as it was, I stopped the horse for some time to listen to it. In the darkness and silence of midnight the regularly recurring sound, proceeding too from so gloomy a spot, had an effect on my mind, solemn and almost unearthly, yet not unmixed with pleasure. Perhaps the mystery hanging about the origin of the sound tended to increase the effect. It is like the measured tinkle of a cow-bell, or regular strokes upon a piece of iron quickly repeated." It is supposed that the saw-whetter is a bird, but I believe that the author of this sound, familiar to New England woodsmen, has never been positively identified.

Late on the third day the travellers reached Burlington. The vast and frozen lake, a huge expanse of snow, crossed in every direction by dirty sledge and sleigh tracks, was dreary and uninteresting. Jaques immediately returned, and Philip Gosse was left in this remote Yankee town, without a single acquaintance in the wide world, and utterly depressed in spirits. The same night, since there was nothing to tempt him to stay at Burlington, he took his place in the stage-coach, a rough sort of leathern diligence, which carried a third seat hung transversely between the front and back seats. A middle-aged woman occupied one seat, and Gosse the other, and thus they spent the night, swinging dully along the frozen road without a word passing between them. In the middle of the night, at some village where the concern changed horses, Philip Gosse got out for some refreshment; dizzy with broken sleep, he laid his purse down on the bar counter, with seven dollars in it, and stumbled back to the coach without perceiving his loss. The uncouth stage-coach disgorged him at Albany in the quiet of an early Sunday morning. He instantly embarked on the steamer, and was running all that day down the beautiful ranges of the Hudson. But curiosity was almost as dead in him as hope. He spoke to no one on board, he formed no plans and took no observations; only at the Palisades he woke up to some perception of the noble precipices under which they were passing. He had not even the wretched excitement of examining the shattered contents of his insect cabinet, for the stage-coach had peremptorily refused to take that piece of furniture on board, and it had been left at Burlington.

In the evening he reached New York, landed on a crowded wharf, and in Liberty Street, the nearest thoroughfare, sought out a sordid hole, in which he took one night's lodging and shelter for his boxes. He made no attempt to explore New York. His slender pittance was fast melting away, and he had many a league to traverse yet before he could hope, in ever so slight a measure, to recruit it. In the morning, therefore, without going up a single street, he steamed across the broad Hudson, and took the railway, the first he had ever seen, across the flat sands of New Jersey. Before noon on March 26, he had crossed the Delaware and had set foot in Philadelphia.

In the Quaker city he had an old friend, one of his former fellow-clerks at Carbonear, Mr. W. F. Lush, settled in the office of the American Colonization Society. This young man carried him off to his own boarding-house, where Gosse also took lodgings, and stayed very pleasantly for above three weeks. In this establishment were several other young fellows, comrades of Lush's, who received the new-comer agreeably. The long solitary years in Canada, however, had set an indelible mark on the face and manners of the naturalist. He found it impossible to join in their gaiety of conversation, and they asked Lush privately if " Gosse was a minister," being struck with his fluent gravity in monologue and lack of capacity for small-talk. It was in Philadelphia that he first enjoyed the sympathy and help of genuine men of science. At the museum in Chestnut Street, he met Mr. Titian R. Peale, a local zoological artist of considerable eminence, who charmed him at once, and surprised him by his deferential civility and his instinctive recognition of this grim-featured, unknown youth as one destined to be "somebody." Mr. Peale was just then starting as the artist of an exploring expedition to the South Seas, under Lieutenant Charles Wilkes, and he was particularly interested in the exquisite drawings of insects which Philip Gosse had brought from Canada. A more distinguished man of science was Professor Thomas Nuttal, the botanist, whom he discovered in the herbarium of the Academy of Natural Science. In his diary my father calls him "venerable," although he was little more than fifty at the time. By Professor Nuttal's invitation, he attended an evening meeting of the society, and met many of the American *savants*. The distinguished Philadelphian zoologist, Dr. Joseph Leidy, then a boy of

I

sixteen, tells me that he recollects my father on one of these occasions—a proof that his personality, unknown as he had been, awakened some general attention. The society and its visitors sat around a table in the great hall of the museum, candles dimly and ineffectually lighting up the space. In the gallery, just above their heads, sat the skeleton of a murderer, riding the skeleton of a horse, the steed galloping, and the ghastly rider flourishing his up-lifted hand with an air of great hilarity. Part of the social entertainment consisted in looking over some fine coloured plates of American fishes, just out; among which Gosse recognized, with interest, the large, richly coloured sculpen (*Cottus*), so common in the clear water round the wharves of Carbonear.

It seems to have been suggested to him by one of the *savants* of Philadelphia that he would find a useful field for his energy in the state of Alabama; and this gentle-man—Mr. Timothy A. Conrad, the conchologist—was so kind as to give him an introduction to a friend of his at Claiborne, which afterwards proved useful. On Sundays, while he was in Philadelphia, he went to the Dutch Reformed Church, in Sassafras and Crown Streets. There was no pulpit there, but a wide raised platform with chairs. The Rev. George Washington Bethune, an eloquent and genial man, who died much lamented in 1862, walked to and fro as he discoursed, in the manner since adopted by Mr. Spurgeon. But Gosse's thoughts in Philadelphia were almost exclusively occupied with the memories of Alex-ander Wilson, that greatest of ornithologists. Wilson was at that time his main object of enthusiastic admiration, and he occupied himself in visiting every spot which bore reminiscences of the noble naturalist. Here was his residence; in yonder house he "kept school;" here were the birds which his own hands had shot and skinned;

here were the very scenes described in his delightful volumes; and the young man made conscientious pilgrimages to the meadows below the city, to the marshy flats of the Schuylkill, to the rushy and half-submerged islets of the Delaware, to Thompson's Point, the former residence of the night-heron or qua-bird, and to the notorious Pea Patch, resort of crows in multitudes. He found an old man who had personally known the ornithologist, although Wilson had at that time been dead twenty-three years; but although Wilson had been a constant visitor at his house, the old man could relate little about him that was characteristic. One thing he said was sufficiently memorable. "Wilson and I," he said, "were always disputing about the sparrows. He would have it that the sparrows here were different from those in the old country. I knew well enough they were just the same, but I could not persuade him of it." It is scarcely necessary to say that the American sparrow is wholly distinct from the English.

The delay in the hospitable city of Philadelphia was, however, not altogether the result of his admiration for the museums or pleasure in the associations of the past. It was due to the difficulty he found in obtaining transit to the South. At length he engaged a passage in the *White Oak*, a small schooner bound to the port of Mobile. He sailed on April 18, and the voyage, a very picturesque and interesting one, occupied nearly a month. They were two days getting down to the Delaware Bay, for they were constantly running aground on the spits and banks which lay under the mirror-like surface of the river. At last, after loitering in the mean fishing village of Delaware City, they were off down to the ocean. It was exceedingly cold, although they were in the latitude of Lisbon, and ice a quarter of an inch thick formed on deck. At first,

Philip Gosse was very miserable. He was the only pas-
senger, and the skipper was a churlish, illiterate fellow,
with a crew of the same stamp as himself. The fact that
Gosse was a "Britisher" was quite enough to warrant
them in the perpetration of a score of petty incivilities, just
short of actual insult. "The conversation," he says, "was
of the lowest sort, and it was not the smallest infliction
that every night I was compelled to hear, as I lay in
my wretched berth, the interchange of obscene narratives
between the skipper and his mate, before I could close my
eyes in sleep. Dirt, dirt, was the rule everywhere ; dirt in
the cabin, dirt in the caboose, dirt in the water-cask ; dirt
doubly begrimed on the tablecloth, on the cups and
glasses, the dishes and plates that served the food ; while
the boy who filled the double office of cook and waiter
was the very impersonation of dirt." The cabin was a
filthy hole, hardly large enough to stand up in, redolent
of tar, grease, fusty clothes, mouldy biscuit, and a score of
other unendurable odours combined, such as only those
can imagine who have been the tenants of a small trading
craft. The single berth on either side "in dimensions and
appearance resembled a dog-kennel more than anything
else, the state of the blankets being, thanks to the grave-
like darkness of the hole, but partially revealed, to sight at
least." The only resource was to eat with as little thought
as possible, to see as little as possible, and to be on deck
as much as possible, and this last habit was furthered by
the glorious weather which set in soon after they were
well out to sea.

For the first few days he was horribly sick, and spent
the time in his little, close, dirty cabin, with nothing to
relieve the tedium of the voyage. But on the 24th he
came on deck to find that they were in the latitude of
Savannah, and had entered the Gulf Stream. He fished

up some of the gulf-weed and amused himself with examining it :—

"Many of the stems and berries were covered with a
"thin tissue of coral, like a very minute network ; many
"small barnacles (*Lepas*) were about it ; some shrimps
"of an olive colour with bright violet spots ; small crabs,
"about half an inch wide, yellow, with dark-brown spots
"and mottlings, one with the fore-half of the shell white ;
"some small univalve shells, and some curious, soft,
"leathery things, almost shapeless. I put all the animals
"I could collect into water, and watched their motions.
"One of the small shrimps swam near a crab, which
"instantly seized it with his claw. With this he held it
"firmly, while with the other claw he proceeded very
"deliberately to pick off small portions of the shrimp,
"beginning at the head, which he put into his mouth.
"He continued to do this, maugre the struggles of the
"shrimp, sometimes shifting it from one claw to the
"other, until he had finished ; he picked off all the
"members of the head, and the legs, before he began to
"eat the body, chewing every morsel very slowly, and
"seeming to enjoy it with great gusto ; when only the
"tail was left, he examined it carefully, then rejected it,
"throwing it from him with a sudden jerk."

Within a week after the sharp frosts already mentioned, the vertical rays of the sun were making the deck almost too hot to touch. But to one who had languished so long in sub-arctic climates, this was a blessed change. On they swept through the meadow-like Gulf Stream, ploughing their noiseless way through the yellow strings of sargasso-weed, or accompanied by splendid creatures unknown to the colder waters of the North. Rudder-fish, with pale spots, would pass in and out beneath the stern ; a shoal of porpoises would come leaping round the bows, in the coolness of the moonlight, and start off again together into the darkness. A shark would play about the ship, with its beautiful little attendant, the purple-bodied pilot-fish. The exquisite coryphenes, or sailor's dolphins, were the ship's constant companions, their backs now of the deepest azure, almost black, and then suddenly, with a writhe, flashing with silver or gleaming with mother-of-pearl, lounging through the water with so indolent an air that to harpoon them seemed child's play. One of the crew, however, trying this easy task, fell off the taffrail with a splash.

On May 1 they caught the welcome trade-wind blowing from the east, and this fresh breeze carried them cheerily in sight of the West Indies. They rapidly passed the southern point of Abaco, one of the Bahamas, and Gosse saw for the first time on its precipitous shores the fan-like leaves of the palm tree. While in sight of Abaco two beautiful sloops of war passed them, beating out, and a little schooner, all of which hoisted the British flag at the gaff-end. It was three years since the exile had seen this pleasant sight, and he hailed with deep emotion the colours of that " meteor flag " which has " braved a thousand years the battle and the breeze." Next day the *White Oak* had an excellent run, and rushing before the freshening trade, threaded an archipelago of those countless " kays," or inlets, which animate the Florida Reef. " The water on this reef," says the journal, "is very shoal, which is strongly indicated by its colour ; instead of the deep-blue tint which marks the ocean, the water here is of a bright pea-green, and the shallower the water, the paler is the tint. To me it is very pleasing to peer down into the depths below, especially in the clear water of these southern seas, and look at the many-coloured bottom,— sometimes a bright pearly sand, spotted with shells and corals, then a large patch of brown rock, whose gaping clefts and fissures are but half hidden by the waving tangles of purple weed, where multitudes of shapeless creatures revel and riot undisturbed." Almost through one day their course bore them through a fleet of "Portuguese men-of-war," those exquisite mimic vessels, with their sapphire hulls and pale pink sails, whose magic navigation seems made to conduct some fairy queen of the tropics through the foam of perilous seas to her haven in an island of pearl.

All these glorious sights in halcyon weather did not, however, last long. The ship was already within sight of the last kay of the long reef, when a violent storm of rain and a westerly gale came on. They were glad to drop anchor at once between Cayo Boca and Cayo Marquess, two green little islands of palm trees and sand. The crew set themselves to fish in the rain, and soon pulled out of the water plentiful fishes of the most extraordinary harlequin colours, vermilion-gilled, amber-banded, striped like a zebra but with violet, or streaked with fantastic forked lightnings of pink and silver. Next morning, May 5, broke in radiant sunshine, and as the wind continued foul, the captain proposed to go ashore and take a peep at Cayo Boca, a suggestion which Philip Gosse warmly seconded. The sailors rowed for a long white spit of sand, and the naturalist leaped ashore, and rushed into the bushes brandishing his insect-net. He expected to find this first specimen of West Indian vegetation studded with brilliant tropical insects, but he was disappointed. The bushes had thick saline leaves, and insects were very rare. Gosse presently turned back to the shore, and found the corals and madrepores more interesting than the entomology. But the wind had veered, and he was forced, reluctantly, to humour the captain's impatience to return to the ship. A little white butterfly danced away to sea with them, fluttered a moment up the side of the vessel, and then flew gaily back to her home in Cayo Boca.

When they were fairly in the Gulf of Mexico, creeping past the Tortugas, numbers of sharks were swimming round and under the vessel, accompanied by a multitude of what they at first supposed to be young ones of the same species. As one or two rose to the surface, however, they turned out to be remoras, or sucking-fish. The men struck first one and then another of these curious creatures with a barbed spear, and secured them alive. These specimens my father thus describes :—

"They are about two feet in length, very slender, "slippery, not covered with scales, but a sort of long flat "prickles, concealed under the skin, but causing a rough- "ness when rubbed against the grain. The colour is blue- "grey above, and whitish beneath ; the tips or edges of "all the fins, and of the tail, light blue. The tail is not "wedge-shaped, but slightly forked. The under lip "projects beyond the upper, so that the mouth opens on "the upper surface, as that of the shark does on the "lower. The sucker is a long oval, slightly narrower in "front, having a central, longitudinal ridge and twenty- "four transverse ones, which can either be made to "lie down flat, or be erected, not however perpendicu- "larly, but inclined backward ; the pectoral and ventral "fins are of the same shape and size, as are the dorsal "and anal. . . . While at liberty they were in close "attendance on the shark, one or two on each side, "generally just over his pectoral fins, and keeping their "relative position, turning as he turned ; sometimes they "appeared belly upward, adhering to the fin of the "shark, at others they seemed loose. Numbers, how- "ever, were in their company without so closely follow- 'ing them. Now, in captivity the sucker adheres to

"everything it touches, provided the surface will cover
"the organ, apparently without the volition of the
"animal, and so strongly as to resist one's endeavours
"to drag the fish up, without inserting something under
"the sucker.   I have cut off the sucker of one for
"preservation."

Next morning the captain speared a dolphin (*Coryphæna
psittacus*), and Gosse eagerly watched for those changes of
colour which are popularly supposed to attend the death
of these creatures. He was not disappointed. When the
expiring animal was first brought on board, it was silvery
white, with pearly reflections ; the back suddenly became
of a brilliant green, while the belly turned to gold, with
blue spots.   This was the only change, except that all
these hues became dusky after death. They cooked the
fish, and found it firm and palatable. Little occurred in
the last tedious days of the voyage, beyond a terrific
tropical storm. Once a sailor hooked a king-fish, three
feet long, silvery blue, with opaline changes, and had just
dragged it in, when a shark leaped at it, like a dog, and
drew his fangs through the body. They were happy at
last when, on the morning of May 14, after a voyage
of four weeks, a long, low tongue of land, with a lighthouse at the end of it, announced their arrival at Mobile
Point. The bay is a difficult one to enter ; at last, about
thirty miles up from the gulf, on turning a sandy cape,
covered with pine trees, the city of Mobile came into sight.
Philip Gosse's last entry in the diary of his voyage is thus
worded :—

"Drawing so near to the time on which hangs my
"fate, my means nearly exhausted, and uncertain what
"success I may meet with, I have been all to-day
"oppressed with that strange faintness, a sickness of
"heart, which always comes over me on the eve of any

"expected conjunction. The pilot left us when we got
"within the bay, up which we are rapidly sailing with a
"fair breeze, in delightful weather."

He was conscious of great depression of spirits as he
walked that evening through the streets of the city of
Mobile. The experiment, indeed, which had brought him
so far from all his associations was a bold one. He had no
certainty of any welcome in the strange, crude country
into which he was about to penetrate, and it came upon
him with a shock that he had but one letter of introduction
in his wallet, and that given to him by a stranger. Next
morning this distressing feeling had worn off. He was
glad to be on shore again, and he spent the greater part of
the day in roaming about the woods in the vicinity of
Mobile, where he found great numbers of interesting insects. Near the shore he met with impenetrable hedges
of prickly pear, studded with its handsome flowers and
purple fruit. The latter he rashly tasted, to find his
mouth filled with an agony of fine spines, which gave him
infinite toil and pain to tear out.

There was nothing to detain him in Mobile, and that
same evening he took passage in the *Farmer*, one of the fine
high-pressure steamers which thronged the Mobile wharves,
fifty years ago, far more abundantly than they do now, since
at that time the commerce of the city almost promised to
rival that of New Orleans. After a voyage of two nights
and a day spent in following the interminable windings of
the Alabama river, a voyage through a country which had
no towns or villages, and scarcely a sign of life, except at
the occasional wood-yards in the forest, the vessel arrived
at King's Landing. It so happened that a fellow-passenger
on board the *Farmer* was the Hon. Chief Justice Reuben
Saffold, a jurist then of great eminence in the South, who
had done good service in the Indian troubles, and had for

many years been a member of the legislature of the terri-
tory of Mississippi. Now, in advancing life, he was settling
in that estate at Dallas, Alabama, which was henceforward
to be his residence, and the place of his death in 1847. To
this dignified and agreeable personage, whose polished
manners formed a charming contrast to the rough tones he
had lately been accustomed to, Philip Gosse showed his
open letter of introduction to the planter at Claiborne,
which Mr. Conrad had given him. It fortunately happened
that Judge Saffold was seeking a master for a school composed of the sons of his neighbour proprietors and himself. He instantly engaged Philip Gosse, and when the
steamer reached King's Landing, which was the nearest
point on the river to Dallas, the latter stopped there ; Mr.
Saffold proceeding a little further on business, and pro-
mising to meet him at his own house next day.

An hour before dawn he was landed at the foot of a
long flight of steps which descended from a large cotton
warehouse. His trunks were thrown to him, and the
steamer wheeled away in the darkness. Mr. Saffold's house
was ten miles distant, and how to find it he knew not. He
groped along a path up into the forest, and presently came
to a clearing with several houses in it. He made his way to
the door of one, where a rascally cur kept up a pertinacious
barking, and he knocked and shouted to no purpose. At
length, at another house, the cracked voice of a negro
woman replied. He told her he was on his way to Pleasant
Hill, and asked her to get him some breakfast. All sound
within the house died away, till he knocked and shouted
again, always to receive the same answer, "Sah ? Iss,
sah !" At last, when patience was wearing away, the old
woman appeared, went to another house, and began to
shout, "Mas' James ! Mas' James !" But Master James was
even more impassive than she had been herself, and made

no answer at all. At length, after a prodigious waste of time, and as the soft daylight began to flood the air, a little white boy of twelve years of age appeared at the door. This was Master James, the son of the manager, who rubbed his eyes, stated that the negro woman and himself were the only persons on the premises, and tumbled back into bed. The woman then raked in the ashes and prepared Gosse some breakfast, his luggage all this while remaining on the lowest step at the margin of the river. But before the meal was over, Master James strolled to the threshold, blew a long blast upon a conch, and, on the simultaneous appearance of a dozen negroes out of the woods, sent some of them down for the visitor's trunks. While Philip Gosse waited for them to reappear, in the balmy air of the wood-yard, several fox-squirrels descended and chased one another from bough to bough of the nearest oaks, a pair of summer redbirds (*Tanagra æstiva*) were flirting almost within reach of his hand, and a flock of those delicate butterflies, the hairstreaks (*Thecla*), came dancing to him down a glade in the forest. Under these picturesque conditions he gained his first impressions of Southern life.

At the pace of one mile an hour he spent the remainder of the day in reaching Dallas. The road lay through the romantic forest, descended into cool glens, where hidden rivulets ran brawling under bowers of the profuse scarlet woodbine, emerged in high clearings where brilliant flowers, in veritable bouquets, thronged the angles of the fences. He passed fields where negro slaves, the first he had seen at work, were ploughing between rows of cotton ; he hurried through neglected pastures where turkey buzzards were performing, none too soon, their scavenger's duty on a too-odorous carcase ; he feasted upon wild raspberries and luscious Virginian strawberries ; and, at last, late in the afternoon, arrived at Dallas, where he was hospitably welcomed by the family of Judge Saffold, and in particular by his son, Reuben Saffold, junior, who was to be his pupil. This youth, who was of a charming modesty and courtesy, had been at college, and had learned the rudiments of Greek.

At Dallas Philip Gosse spent several agreeable days while arrangements were being made for his school to be opened. This house was large, but rudely built, and furnished with an elegance which contrasted with its rough architecture. In this respect, no doubt, it was not distinguished from other residences of wealthy planters at the time. What more particularly struck Philip Gosse was the gorgeous furniture which Nature itself, in the rich June weather, had provided for the front of it. The wide passage, with rooms on either side, which ran through the house, was completely embowered with the lovely Southern creepers; the twisted cables of *Glycine frutescens* flung their heavy branches of lilac blossom about the walls, and wherever space was left it was filled with more delicate forms of profuse bloom, with the long pendulous trumpets of the scarlet cypress-vine and of the intensely crimson quamoclit, sweet-briar that made the hot air ache with perfume, and deep vermillion tubes of the Southern honeysuckle, in which great hawkmoths hung all through the twilight, waving their loud-humming fans, and gorging themselves on sweetness. "Here," he says, in a letter from Dallas, "particularly at the close of evening, when the sunbeams twinkle obliquely through the transparent foliage, and the cool breeze comes loaded with fragrance, the family may usually be seen, each (ladies as well as gentlemen) in that very elegant position in which an American delights to sit, the chair poised upon the two hind feet, or leaning back against the wall, at an angle of forty-five degrees, the feet upon the highest bar, the knees near the chin, the head pressing against the wall so as now and then to push the chair a few inches from it, the hands (but not of the ladies) engaged in fashioning with a pocket-knife a piece of pine-wood into some uncouth and fantastic form."

He was not, however, to spend his time lolling and whittling on the verandah of Dallas. The neighbouring village of Mount Pleasant was chosen as the site of his school, and lodgings were found for him in the house of a planter, a Mr. Bohanan, in the hamlet itself. It was a rough frame-house, standing in the middle of a large yard, which, with the combined screaming of stark-naked little black children at play, the squealing of pigs, the gobbling of turkeys, the quacking of Muscovy ducks, and the cackling of guinea-fowls, was scarcely an abode of peace. It possessed a splendid example of that flowering tree of the South, the Pride of China, and a wild cherry, the fruit of which was so tempting that all the noises were not able to scare away from it the persistent attentions of the red-headed woodpeckers. The school-house was a little further off, a couple of miles outside the limits of the village. It was a queer little shanty, built of round, unhewn logs, notched at the ends to receive each other, and the interstices filled with clay. There was no window, but as the clay had become dry it had been punched out of several of these spaces, and the light and air admitted. The wooden door stood open night and day. The desks were merely split and unsawn pine boards, unfashioned and unplaned, sloping from the walls and fastened with brackets. The forms were split logs, and the only exceptions to the extreme rudeness of all the fittings were a neat desk and decent chair for the schoolmaster. The pupils were as rude as the building. Most of them, he writes, "handle the long rifle with much more ease and dexterity than the goose-quill, and are incomparably more at home in 'twisting' a rabbit or treeing a 'possum, than in conjugating a verb." But they proved to be decent lads, and a great affection sprang up in time between them and their strange, insect-collecting, animal-loving master. They grew in time to form a volunteer corps of collectors, and their sharp eyes to be most useful to the naturalist.

The school-house was situated in a very romantic spot. A space of about a hundred yards square had been cleared, with the exception of one or two noble oaks, which had been preserved for shade. "On every side we are shut in by a dense wall of towering forest trees, rising to the height of a hundred feet or more. Oaks, hickories, and pines of different species extend for miles on every hand, for this little clearing is made two or three miles from any human habitation, with the exception of one house about three-quarters of a mile distant. Its loneliness, however," Philip Gosse writes, "is no objection with me, as it necessarily throws me more into the presence of free and wild nature. At one corner a narrow bridle-path leads out of this 'yard,' and winds through the sombre forest to the distant high-road. A nice spring, cool in the hottest of these summer days, rises in another corner, and is protected and accumulated by being en-closed in four sides of a box, over the edges of which the superfluous water escapes, and, running off in a gurgling brook, is lost in the shade of the woods. To this 'lodge in the vast wilderness,' this 'boundless contiguity of shade,' I wend my lonely way every morning, rising to an early breakfast, and arriving in time to open school by eight o'clock."

It is possible to recover something of a record of his typical day in Alabama. It opens with breakfast at six o'clock; the "nigger wenches" bringing in the grilled chicken and the fried pork, the boiled rice and the hominy, the buttered waffles and the Indian bread. A little negro-boy is continually waving a large fan of peacock's feathers over the food and over every part of the table. Breakfast once over, Philip Gosse seizes the butterfly-net which stands in the corner of the room, and which he always carries, as other sportsmen do their gun, and he sallies forth, startling the mocking-bird that is hopping and bobbing on the rails of the fence. He gives himself plenty of time to chase the zebra swallow-tails across the broad discs of the passion-flowers, to lie in wait for hairstreaks on the odorous beds of blossoming horehound, or to watch the scarlet cardinal grosbeak, with his negro face and his mountain crest, leap whistling up and up in the branches of the pines like an ascending flame of fire. He reaches school, however, in time to open that "*alma mater*," as he laughingly styles it, by eight o'clock ; and for no less than nine hours of desultory education, mingled with play and idleness, he is responsible for the troop of urchins.

But five o'clock comes at last, even in the soundless depths of an Alabama forest, and he dismisses his wild covey of shouting boys, following more sedately in their wake. Twilight falls apace, and in a little hollow where the oaks and hickories meet overhead, a barred owl flits like a ghost across the path, and the air begins to ring with the long mellow resounding whoops of the negroes on the plantations, calling home the hogs at sunset. It may be that two or three of these pachydermatous grey-hounds, with their thin backs and tall legs, are rooting and grazing close to the path. From a mile off will be faintly heard the continual unbroken shout of the distant negro. Each hog will instantly pause, snout in air, and then all is bustle ; and, each anxious to be first at home, they scamper off on a bee-line for the village. And so Philip Gosse, too, goes home to supper, and to bed in a room with every window open, but latticed to keep out the bats and birds. Before going to sleep, perhaps, he will sit a few minutes at the window, while the chuck-will's-widows call and answer from all directions in the woods, with their mysterious and extraordinary notes clearly enunciated in the deep silence of the night. Gosse tried on many occasions to see these strange birds, but they are extremely shy, although so neighbourly and familiar ; nor was he ever successful, although he wearied himself in the search.

Mount Pleasant proved to be an excellent centre for entomologizing, and in particular there was a little prairie-knoll, about a mile from Bohanan's house, which was one mass of blue larkspurs and orange milkweed, and a marvellous haunt of butterflies. From this small hill the summit of an apparently endless forest could be seen in all directions, broken only by curls of white smoke arising here and there from unseen dwellings. Here he would find the blue swallowtail (*Papilio phanor*), with its shot wings of black and azure, vibrating on the flowers of the milkweed ; the black swallowtail (*Papilio asterius*), an old friend from Newfoundland ; the orange tawny Archippus ; the American Painted Beauty (*Cynthia Huntera*), with its embroidery of silver lines and pearly eyes ; and, most gorgeous of all, the green-clouded swallowtail (*Papilio Troilus*), over whose long black wings is dispersed a milky way of grass-green dots and orange crescents. The abundance of these large species struck him with ever-recurring wonder. In a letter of July he says : "An eye accustomed only to the small and generally inconspicuous butterflies of our own country, the *Pontiæ, Vanessæ,* and *Hipparchiæ,* can hardly picture to itself the gaiety of the air here, where it swarms with large and brilliant-hued swallow-tails and other patrician tribes, some of which, in the extent and volume of their wings, may be compared to large bats. These occur, too, not by straggling solitary individuals; in glancing over a blossomed field or my prairie-knoll, you may see hundreds, including, I think, more than a dozen species, besides other butterflies, moths, and flies." There remains, as the principal memento of these months in the south, still unpublished, a quarto volume entitled *Entomologia Alabamensis*, containing two hundred and thirty-three figures of insects, exquisitely drawn and coloured, the delightful amusement of his leisure hours in the school-house and at home. His powers as a zoological artist were now at their height. He had been trained in the school of the miniature painters, and he developed and adapted to the portraiture of insects the procedure of these artists. His figures are accurate reproductions, in size, colour, and form, to the minutest band and speck, of what he saw before him, the effect being gained by a laborious process of stippling with pure and brilliant pigments. It has always been acknowledged, by naturalists who have seen the originals of his coloured figures, that he has had no rival in the exactitude of his illustrations. They lost a great deal whenever they came to be published, from the imperfection of such reproducing processes as were known in Philip Gosse's day. The *Entomologia Alabamensis*, however, is one of those collections of his paintings which remain unissued, and it is possible that it may yet be presented to the scientific world by one of the brilliant methods of reproduction recently invented.

When he first proceeded to Canada, he had described himself as a very bad shot; but practice had improved him, and he was now by no means unskilful. He exercised his rifle considerably in Alabama, in forming a collection of birds, and particularly of woodpeckers. He lost himself in the forest one day in June, and in a dense part of the woodland, from the midst of a tall clump of dead pines, he heard a note proceeding like the clang of a trumpet, resounding in the deep silence and waking all the forest echoes. These extraordinary sounds came from a pair of ivory-billed woodpeckers, the largest and most splendid of all the *Picus* tribe. *Picus principalis* is a huge fellow, nearly two feet long, glossy black and white, with a towering conical crest of bright crimson, and, what is the main distinction of the species, a polished and fluted beak, four inches long, which looks as though it were carved out of the purest ivory. With this pickaxe of shell-white bone, the bird hews away the dead wood as it hangs openly on the perpendicular trunk of a tree, its head thrown back and its golden-yellow eyes alert for insects. It is far from being common, and my father was glad to secure these specimens, which were in fine plumage. Other woodpeckers were nearer to his daily haunts. One evening a boy came to him and told him of a gold-winged woodpecker (*Picus auratus*) at his very door. The schoolboy had found a deep and commodious chamber dug out in the decaying trunk of a pine-tree in Mr. Bohanan's peach-orchard. In the twilight the pair of marauders set forth, carrying a ladder with them. After throwing up a few stones to frighten out the old bird, she suddenly rushed out, and left the coast clear. "The boy," Philip Gosse writes, "pulled out one of the callow young, which I gently examined. It was nearly fledged; the young feathers of the wings being very conspicuous from their bright golden colour. It was not pretty—young birds seldom are. I soon put it back again, and then, whether the rest were congratulating it on its return, or what, I don't know, but if you had heard the odd snoring or hissing that the family kept up for some time, you would have thought the whole nation of snakes had been there in parliament assembled. The anxious mother soon flew in again when we had removed our ladder, gratified, no doubt, to find no murder done."

He had no opportunity for making many excursions while he was at Mount Pleasant, and, indeed, the general monotony of the thinly peopled country did not greatly invite a traveller. On one occasion (June 2) he rode to Cahawba and back, and saw something of the central district of Alabama. Cahawba had then until lately been the capital of the state and the seat of government ; it had, however, decayed so rapidly, that the legislature had removed to Tuscaloosa, Montgomery being as yet a little place of no importance. The town of Cahawba stands on a point of land between the Alabama river and the Cahawba river ; it was, even then, a very desolate looking collection of a few stores, a lawyer's office or so, and two or three houses of business. Even the "groceries," as the rum-shops were called, seemed, as the visitor went by, to spread the hospitality of their verandahs almost in vain. To reach Cahawba from Mount Pleasant had involved a long ride through the dense pine forest, with hardly a break save where the path dipped down, through a glade of thickly blossomed hydrangea, to some deep and treacherous "creek" or rivulet. The road led at last to the shore of the broad Alabama, and there seemed no way to cross. A shout, however, soon brought two old " nigger fellows " into sight, slowly pushing a flat ferry-boat across. There was no inn or house near by to put up his horse, so the traveller took him into a little wood, according to the practice of the country, and tied him to a tree.

The squirrels form a prominent feature of forest-life in the Southern States. Deep in the woodlands they are not to be observed, but they abound close to the houses of the planters, seeming to prefer the neighbourhood of man. At Mount Pleasant, the large fox-squirrel was most abundant, chattering, barking, and grunting impatiently all day long, until a shot from the rifle brings him "protracted repose," and prepares him to appear on the planter's dinner-table. A little further away, in the swamps, and hidden under the pale and ragged tufts of Spanish moss that stream from the branches, is the sleepier and less attractive Caroline squirrel, also excellent in the form of pie. While my father was in Alabama the squirrel question was one of great importance in local politics. These delightfully amusing animals are, unfortunately, wasters of the first order; they are in the cornfield morning, noon, and eve, from the time that the grain is forming in the sheath to the moment when what remains of it is housed in the barn. While Philip Gosse was at Mount Pleasant, a fellow from the North sent round an announcement that he would lecture in a neighbouring village, and that the subject of his discourse would be to reveal an infallible preventive for the thefts of the squirrels. The announcement attracted great curiosity, and planters assembled from all sides. A deputation started from Mount Pleasant itself, and Philip Gosse, thinking to hear what would be of interest to a naturalist, was of the party. A considerable entrance-fee was charged, but very willingly paid. At last the room was full, the doors were closed, and the orator appeared on the platform. He began by describing the depredations of the squirrels, the difficulty of coping with them, and various other circumstances with which his audience was familiar. He was a plausible fellow and seemed to have mastered his subject. At last he approached the real kernel of his oration. "You wish," he said, "to hear my infallible preventive, the absolute success of which I am able to guarantee. Gentlemen, I have observed that the squirrels invariably begin their attacks *on the outside row* of corn in the field. *Omit the outside row*, and they won't know where to begin!" The money was in his pocket; he bowed and vanished by the platform door; his horse was tied to the post, he leaped into the saddle and was seen no more in that credulous settlement. The act was one of extreme courage as well as impudence in that land of ready lynching; but my father was wont to say that, after the first murmur of stupefaction and roar of anger, the disappointed audience dissolved into the most good-humoured laughter at themselves.

Another serious depredator, and one of a more sporting size, was the bear. One night in August, a negro boy rushed breathless into Mr. Bohanan's house, inarticulate with importance, and managed to splutter out, " Oh, mas'r, mas'r! big bear in corn-patch; I see 'im get over." All at once was bustle; bullets were cast—"a job," says my father in the letter describing this event, " that always has to be done at the moment they are wanted "—and the planter and his overseer crept out with their rifles to the field. But it was too late. The prints of Bruin's paws were all over the place, but he had prudently retired. Bears are very seldom seen in the woods, being shy and nocturnal in their movements. A curious case happened, however, while Philip Gosse was in Mount Pleasant, of a planter who was riding into the forest to search for strayed cattle, and who, suddenly seeing a huge bear start up before him, could not refrain from giving it a lash with his cow-whip of raw hide. To his dismay, the beast showed a disposition to fight, but turned tail at last, when the thought struck the planter that he might possibly drive it home, like a refractory bullock. He actually succeeded in doing this, whipping the bewildered bear for six miles along one of the cattle-paths, till he came close to his own house, when his son came out and put the weary bruin out of its misery with a rifle. My father was not an eye-witness of this adventure, which I record with all reserve.

On August 14 he was, however, personally engaged in a sporting affair, which it may be amusing to read, described in his own words, in a letter dated the next morning. There had been great complaints of the robberies committed on the estate of a neighbouring planter, Major Kendrick, by the opossums, and Philip Gosse was courteously invited to stay at the house and take part in the nocturnal expedition :—

"About half-past nine we set out, a goodly and "picturesque cavalcade. There was, first, my worthy "host, Major Kendrick, a stout sun-burnt fellow of six "feet two, as erect as a sundial, grizzled a little with "the labours of some sixty years in the backwoods of "Georgia, but still hale and strong, with as keen an eye "for a wild cat or a 'coon as the stalwart nephews by his "side. His attire would be deemed peculiar with you, "though here it is the approved thing. A Panama hat, "made of the leaves of the palmetto, split fine, low in the "crown, and very broad in the flap ; a ' hunting shirt,' or "frock, of pink-striped gingham, open all down the "front, but girded with a belt of the same ; the neck, "which is wide and open, is bordered with a frill, which "lies upon the shoulders ; loose trousers, of no describ- "able colour, pattern, or material ; short cotton socks, "and stout half-boots, of domestic manufacture. Such "is the costume of our ' king of men,' and all the rest of "us approach as near to it as we may.

"But who are ' the rest of us ' ? Why, the two strap- "ping youths who call the planter uncle, Zachariah and "Bill, each emulous of his patron's stature and accom-

"plishments ; Jones, the overseer, a wiry fellow, origin-
"ally from the far east (Connecticut, I believe), but
"grown a Southerner by a dozen years' experience in
"negro-driving ; and the humble individual who pens
"these lines, who begins at length to be known by his
"proper name, instead of 'the stranger.' We five were
"mounted on very capital steeds, and behind and around
"us marched on foot our sable ministers.

"It was a lovely night. The sky, almost cloudless, had
"a depth of tint that was rather purple than blue, and
"the moon, near the full, was already approaching the
"zenith. A gentle breeze, warm and balmy, breathed in
"the summits of the trees, and wafted us the delicate
"perfumes from leaf, flower, and fruit, from gum and
"balsam, with which the night air is commonly loaded.
"Bright as was the night, however, it was thought requi-
"site to have artificial light, especially as we should have
"to explore some tall woods, whose gloomy recesses the
"moon's beams were quite insufficient to illuminate. The
"knots of the pitch-pine answer admirably for torches,
"being full of resin, and maintaining a brilliant flame for
"an hour or more. The glare of broad red light which
"these flambeaux cast on the leafy walls along which we
"rode, and the beautiful effect produced on the sur-
"rounding shrubs and intervening trees when the torch-
"bearers passed through some narrow belt of wood, or
"explored some little grove, was highly novel and
"picturesque ; the flames, seen through the chequering
"leaves, played and twinkled, and ever and anon
"frightened a troop of little birds from their roost, and
"illuminated their plumage as they fluttered by.

"At length we reached the melon-patch, and having
"dismounted and tied our horses to the hanging twigs
"of the roadside trees, we crossed the rail-fence to beat

"the ground on foot. It was a large field, entirely
"covered with melons, the long stems of which trailed
"over the soft earth, concealing it with the coarse foliage
"and the great yellow flowers of the plant ; while the
"fruit, of all sizes, lay about in boundless profusion, from
"the berry just formed, to the fully matured and already
"rotten-ripe melon, as large as a butter firkin. Abundant
"evidences were visible of the depredations of our game,
"for numbers of fine ripe melons lay about with large
"cavities scooped out of them, some showing by their
"freshness and cleanness that they had been only just
"attacked, while others were partially dried and dis-
"coloured by the burning sun. Moths of various species
"were collected around the wounded fruit, some of them
"(which I should have prized for my cabinet, if I had
"had time and means to capture and bring them home)
"inert and bloated with the juices which they had been
"sucking ; others fluttering by scores around, or attracted
"by the light to dance round the torches.

"The party had dispersed. I accompanied the planter
"to the edge of a wood at one side of the patch, while
"the young men took up similar stations at some
"distance. The object was to intercept the vermin in
"their retreat, as, on being alarmed from their repast,
"they at once make for their fastnesses in the lofty trees.
"A negro, with his pine-knot, stood at each station,
"illuminating the hoary trunks of the great trees.

"Meanwhile the other servants were scouring the field
"with the dogs, shouting and making as much noise as
"possible. Again the twinkling lights looked beautiful,
"and the sound of the negroes' sonorous voices, raised
"in prolonged shouts with musical cadences, and now
"and then a snatch of a rattling song, the favourite
"burden being how a ' big racoon ' was seen—

" ' a-sittin' on a rail,'

" fell very pleasantly on the ear. Occasionally the bark-
" ing of the curs gave token that game was started ; and,
" presently, the approach of the sound towards us was
" followed by what looked to be a white cat scampering
" towards the very chestnut-tree before us, closely pur-
" sued by one of the mongrel curs. My friend's fatal
" rifle turned the creature over as soon as seen ; but the
" very next instant another appeared, and scrambling up
" the fissured trunk, made good its retreat among the
" branches.

" In the course of an hour another was shot, one was
" caught and worried by the dogs, and some half a dozen
" others were just glimpsed as they scuttled past us, the
" light for an instant revealing their grey bodies, but too
" briefly to allow an aim. We heard, by the reports of
" our distant friends' rifles, that they had their share of
" success ; and when we assembled at the edge of the
" field, half a dozen opossums and a racoon were thrown
" across the crupper of one of the beasts. The appear-
" ance of the latter had been curiously in accordance
" with the negroes' song ; for one of the young men,
" creeping quietly along the fence, had seen the furry
" gentleman 'sittin' on a rail,' and looking with out-
" stretched neck and absorbed attention into the field,
" wondering, doubtless, what all the uproar was about.
" His senses were not so locked, however, as not to be
" aroused by the gentle footfall of our young friend ;
" before he could raise his rifle, the racoon had leaped
" from the fence, and scoured up an immense sycamore.
" It seemed a hopeless case ; but young Zachariah,
" vexed at being done by a 'coon, continued to peer up
" into the tree, hoping that he might get another glance
" of the animal. Familiar with the habits of the wild

" denizens of the woods, the youth directed his patient
" searching gaze to the bases of the great boughs, well
" knowing that in the fork of one of these the wily crea-
" ture would seek shelter. At last, he saw against the
" light of the moon, what seemed the head of the racoon
" projecting from one of the greater forks, and steadily
" watching it, distinctly saw it move. The fatal ball
" instantly sped, and down came the creature, heavily
" plumping on the ground.

" I had seen racoons before, yet I looked at the car-
" case with interest. You probably are aware that it is
" an animal about as large as a fox, to which it bears
" some resemblance. It seems, however, larger, from the
" fulness of its thick and soft fur, and is more heavy-
" bodied. Its grey coat, black and white face, and bushy
" tail, alternately banded with black and light grey,
" entitle it to admiration ; while the opossum, clothed in
" rough wiry hair, of a dirty greyish-white hue, with a
" long rat-like tail, is anything but prepossessing.

" The torches were extinguished, and we sauntered
" slowly home. The opossum which had been worried
" by the curs was not by any means dead when we
" reached the house, and I had an opportunity of wit-
" nessing the curious dissimulation which has made the
" name of this animal proverbial. Though, if left alone
" for a few moments, the attention of the bystanders
" apparently diverted from it, it would get on its legs
" and begin to creep slily away ; yet no sooner was an
" eye turned towards it, than it would crouch up, lie
" along motionless, with all its limbs supple, as if just
" dead ; nor would any kicks, cuffs, or handlings avail
" to produce the least token of life—not the opening of
" an eyelid, or the moving of a foot. There it was, dead
" evidently, you would say, if you had not detected it

"the moment before in the act of stealing off. The
" initiated, however, can tell a real dead 'possum from
" one that is shamming, and the overseer directed my
" attention to the last joints of the tail. This, during
" life, is prehensile, used to catch and hold the twigs like
" a fifth hand ; and even in the hypocritical state in
" which I saw it, the coil of the tail-tip was maintained,
" whereas in absolute death this would be relaxed per-
" manently. The propriety of correct classification was
" impressed on me during my examination. I inadver-
" tently spoke of it as 'a singular creature ;' but *creature*,
" or rather 'critter,' is much too honourable a term for
" such an animal, being appropriated to cattle. The
" overseer promptly corrected my mistake. 'A 'possum,
" sir, is not a critter, but a varmint.'"

This letter is written, as will be observed, in capital
spirits. It is evident that his first months in Alabama
were very happy ones, and yet there were elements of discomfort which did not fail to become accentuated. He
had not been received ungenerously ; on the contrary, a
rough and tolerant hospitality had desired to make "the
stranger" feel at home. But Philip Gosse was not eminently pliable to social peculiarities. He was proud of his
pure enunciation, and was careful not to adopt an American
accent—his "British brogue" was in consequence brought
up as a charge against him ; nor could he throw aside a
latent jingoism, as we should call it to-day, a patriotism
that was apt to become truculent because it was in exile.
In Alabama the jealousy of the "British" was almost
humorously prominent ; the expression of contempt for
English opinion was so constant as to suggest an extreme
sensitiveness to that opinion. But Philip Gosse was almost
as thin-skinned on this point as the planters themselves,
and he found the continual dropping of ignorant prejudice

very trying. On one occasion, when the papers announced some trifling factory row in Paisley or Glasgow, a wealthy neighbour hastened to condole with him on the fact that "the Scotch were throwing off the British yoke," for the ignorance of European life was such as to make the picture in *Martin Chuzzlewit*, twelve years later, seem in no degree whatever a caricature. "The universal notion here," says my father in July, 1838, "of Scotland, Ireland, and Wales, is that they are conquered provinces, on a par with Poland, kept in a state of galling servitude by the presence of a powerful 'British' army." Nor was it ever supposed that the confident prophecy that America would shortly "whip the British" could be other than pleasant to the young English schoolmaster.. Let those who are ready to condemn such crudity reflect how often, even to the present day, well-bred Americans in this country have to endure with silent politeness sentiments from ourselves which are scarcely less crude in their ignorant misconception.

There was, however, a much more serious reason for discomfort. The population was gallant, cordial, easy-going, and hospitable ; but underneath the agreeable surface of life there was an element of lawlessness which created in a stranger a painful sense of insecurity. Every man was a law to himself, and to curb the passions was not understood to be a part of the science of life. What first opened my father's eyes to the conditions of Alabaman society was a little circumstance which occurred after he had been a month or two at Mount Pleasant, in the next village. A travelling menagerie had arrived there ; but, in some way or other, its proprietor contrived to offend an overseer, who, without scruple, called some of his companions together, and rolled the caravans over the edge of a steep ravine into the creek below. They were broken before they reached the water, and the iron cages, full of beasts, were scattered on every hand. Fortunately they were too strong to burst, but the howlings and roarings of the lions and tigers were something horrible to listen to. The loss of property was very serious ; the aimless cruelty thus passionately inflicted on a quantity of innocent animals was more serious still. But the proprietor of the menagerie knew that he had no redress, and he sought none. Scarcely less daunting than this occurrence, was a duel in the neighbourhood, in which the combatants almost literally hacked each other to pieces with bowie-knives ; and in many cases of vendetta, what the bowie-knife spared, the rifle devoured.

Closely connected with these disquieting elements in society was that central fact in Southern life, the institution of slavery. Philip Gosse was not a humanitarian. The subject of slavery was one which had not troubled his thoughts in coming to the South ; he had been aware of its existence, of course, and he supposed that he had discounted it. But he found it more horrible, and the discussion of it more dangerous, than he had in the least degree imagined. He was looked upon, as an Englishman, with a peculiar jealousy, as a person predisposed to question "our domestic institution," as it was called. He soon had unquestionable proofs that his trunks were surreptitiously opened and his letters examined, obviously to ascertain whether his correspondence touched upon this tenderest of themes. He had, however, warned his friends, and he was careful himself to be most guarded upon this subject. It was not until he was in act of leaving the country that he dared to put pen to paper on this theme. "What will be the end of American slavery?" he asks, and the query was one to which in 1838 there seemed no answer. "There are men here," he proceeds, "who dare not entertain this question. They tremble when they look at the future. It is like a huge deadly serpent, which is kept down by incessant vigilance, and by the strain of every nerve and muscle ; while the dreadful feeling is ever present that, some day or other, it will burst the weight that binds it, and take a fearful retribution."

It was in September, however, when the bustle of cotton-picking made an unusual strain upon the native laziness of the negro, that Gosse was made physically ill by the ruth-less punishments which were openly inflicted on all sides of him. The shrieks of women under the cow-hide whip, cynically plied in the very courtyard beneath his windows at night, would make him almost sick with distress and impotent anger, and I have heard him describe how he had tried to stuff up his ears to deaden the sound of the agonizing cries which marked the conventional progress of this very peculiar "domestic institution." With the Methodist preachers and other pious people with whom he specially fraternized, he would occasionally attempt, very timidly, to discuss the ethics of slavery, but always to find in these ministers and professors of the gospel exactly the same jealousy of criticism and determination to applaud existing conditions, that could characterize the most dis-solute and savage overseer, as he sat and flicked his boots with his cow-hide on the verandah of a rum-shop. My father saw no escape from this condition of things. He was obliged to admit that slaves seemed indispensable in Alabama, and that "free labour is out of the question." But it sickened him, and it had much to do with his abrupt departure.

From the day of his arrival he had kept a copious scientific journal, but in September this begins to fall off, and early in October it ceases altogether. For the last three months of his stay in Alabama there scarcely exists any record, except a private diary which is painful reading.

At no time was Philip Gosse ready to admit that connection between the physical and the spiritual well-being of a man, the relation between bodily health and mental health, which to many of us may seem one of the finest lessons which life has to give. It was very strange that one of such infinitely delicate and accurate perceptions in observation of animals and plants, one to whom the movements of a butterfly and the conscience of an orchid were almost preternaturally obvious, should be unable to adapt the same habit of observation to humanity and to himself. But it must be said that he was never a very subtle judge of man, and always a very bad critic of himself. There were many conditions of his life in Alabama which predisposed him to melancholy and physical depression, and against which he should have been upon his guard. This social isolation, the repressed indignations of his patriotism and of his humanity, his narrow resources and hopelessness of improvement, were enough to cast him down in spirits. But in addition, the autumn in those hot, damp countries is exceedingly distressing to a stranger ; the neighbourhood of the swamp is deadly, and the decay of the monstrous body of vegetation almost fatal to organic elasticity. Unhappily, however, in a manner I need not dwell upon at distressing length, my father, who would have hit with luminous directness on the cause of such symptoms in an insect or a bird, saw in his own condition nothing less serious than the chastisement of God on one who was sinning against light. The more wretched he felt, the more certain was he of the Divine displeasure, and the more did he lash his fainting spirit to the task of religious exercises. His diary is full of self-upbraidings, penitential cries, vows of greater watchfulness in the future ; and it is downright pathetic to read these effusions, and to know that it was quinine that the poor soul wanted in its innocent darkness. He began to wish to return to England, but put the thought behind him, as evidently a temptation of the devil, because it would please him to return. For the first time in his life, he was in a thoroughly morbid condition of mind.

Towards the middle of November his apathy and gloom deepened into positive illness. He began to suffer from a very violent and almost unceasing headache. On December 1 he writes—

"By medicine and care my headache is at length "relieved, though not yet removed. It has been ac- "companied by great prostration of mind and body, "but though I have not been capable of much "devotional exercise, I have been enabled to fix my "mind with filial confidence on God. . . . I have seen "the absurdity of deferring the work of repentance and "conversion to a sick bed, which is very ill adapted "for such work. My school has closed, another gentle- "man having been engaged to succeed me ; in this, too, "I see the hand of God."

From this last statement it would almost seem as though, in consequence of Philip Gosse's failing health, he had been arbitrarily superseded, but of this I find no other record. For the next fortnight the entries in his journal are tinged with the deepest melancholia. On December 16 he says—

"From the representations of Brother Hearne (the "presiding Elder of this district) and Brother Nose- "worthy, and their persuasions, I have given up the "thought of going to England, believing it to be my "duty to labour here. I am not convinced by their "reasons, but I fear that my will stands opposed to the "will of God."

But a few days later he was persuaded to go off for a

visit to Brother Noseworthy at the town of Selma. The ride did him good, and the change of air also. He was bustled up by the activity of Quarterly Meeting. On the 25th he writes, "The Methodist Society at Selma is in a much livelier state than ours, and I have had some profitable seasons, though I find too much of a narrow bigotry with all." He came back to Mount Pleasant persuaded that he had a call to be a Wesleyan minister in Alabama, and convinced that he was to spend his life there preaching and visiting.

What happened next I know not, but I suppose that the visit to Selma had quickened his senses, and showed him that life in Mount Pleasant was impossible, since exactly four days after this conclusion to stay in Alabama for ever, he is found to have packed up all his boxes and cabinets, to have been up to Dallas to say farewell to the Saffolds, and to be positively on board a steamer on the Alabama river, in the highest possible spirits, and bound merrily for Mobile. He ate part of a splendid turkey for his Christmas dinner on board the steamer, his curious objection to everything which in any way suggested the keeping of Christmas as a festival not having as yet occurred to him. The voyage down the river from the upper country occupied two days and a night, considerable delay being caused by frequent stoppages to take in cargo, until the vessel was laden almost to the water's edge with bales of cotton. "I looked with pleasure on the magnificent scenery of the heights. There is something," he writes, "very romantic in sailing, or rather shooting, along between lofty precipices of rock, crowned with woods at the summit. One such strait we passed through to-day (December 30) just at sunrise ; the glassy water, our vessel, and everything near still involved in deepest shadow ; the grey, discoloured limestone towering up on each side ; while the trees, and just a streak on the top-most edge of one cliff, were bathed in golden light from the newly risen sun."

He was greatly amused by the way in which the crew stowed the cargo. The cotton had been already screwed into bales so tightly that further compression might seem impossible. But when the stowed bales in the hold were in contact with the upper deck, another layer had to be forced in by powerful jack-screws, worked by four men. When the end of the bale was seen set against a crevice into which a thin board could scarcely be pushed, it might appear impossible that it should ever get in ; but the screw was continually turned, and though the process was a slow one, the bale would gradually insinuate itself. The men kept the most perfect time by means of their songs. " These ditties,"—says the curious " chiel" who hung above the cotton-bales "making notes,"—"though nearly meaning-less, have much music in them ; and as all join in the perpetually recurring chorus, a rough harmony is pro-duced, by no means unpleasing. I think the leader im-provises the words, of which I have taken down the following specimen ; he singing one line alone, and the whole then giving the chorus, which is repeated without change at every line, till the general chorus includes the stanza :—

> " ' I think I hear the black-cock say,
>   *Fire the ringo ! fire away !*
> They shot so hard, I could not stay ;
>   *Fire the ringo ! fire away !*
> So I spread my wings, and flew away ;
>   *Fire the ringo,* etc.
> I took my flight, and ran away ;
>   *Fire,* etc.
> All the way to Canaday,
>   *Fire,* etc.

> To Canaday, to Canaday,
> All the way to Canaday.
> Gin'ral Jackson gain'd the day;
> At New Orleans he gain'd the day;
> *Ringo! ringo! blaze away!*
> *Fire the ringo! fire away!'"*

Later on the last evening of the year 1838, he entered Mobile, where he had to stay a week before proceeding to England. At Mobile he found his poor shattered insect cabinet from Canada, lying in a warehouse in a shocking condition, but with the contents not so hopelessly destroyed as he had every reason to fear that he should find them. It was pleasant to gaze on his captures, after having been parted from them for nearly a year. From Alabama he carried home about twenty specimens of the skins of rare birds, and a few fur-pelts. In cash he found that he was, when he had paid his passage to England, even poorer than when he left Canada. So poor was he that he was obliged, immediately on his arrival in Liverpool, to part with his furs and skins hastily, and therefore at a wretched price. His entomological collection he sold, for a fair sum, to the well-known insect-buyer, Mr. Melly. As a matter of fact, however, the rolling stone returned to England, after an exile of eleven years, with practically no moss whatever on its surface. He was completing his twenty-ninth year, and life still seemed wholly inhospitable to him. He had not chanced yet on the employment for which alone he was fitted, but he had unconsciously gone through an excellent apprenticeship for it. It was on his return voyage to England in January, 1839, that Philip Gosse began to be a professional author.

CHAPTER VI.

LITERARY STRUGGLES.

1839–1844.

IN his diary of January 4, 1839, Philip Gosse has recorded: "I spent an hour or two in walking through the public burial-ground of Mobile. Many of the epitaphs were ridiculous, but some very touching. I felt my spirit softened and melted by some of the testimonials of affection, and I could not refrain from tears. Then I went on board the ship *Isaac Newton*, lying in the bay, and so bade adieu to American land, probably for ever." This melancholy note is not inappropriate to mark what was in fact a great crisis in his career, while the prophecy in the last words was actually fulfilled, since though his activity in the New World was by no means at an end, he was never to set foot on the American continent again.

As a part of the fresh religious zeal which he had roused in himself during his latest weeks in Alabama, he began on board the *Isaac Newton* the practice of speaking on the condition of their souls to those into whose company he was thrown. This habit he preserved, with varying intensity, till the end of his life, and in process of time it became easy and natural to him to exhort and to examine. But it was difficult enough at first, and nothing but an overwhelming conviction that it was his duty would have enabled him to overcome his reluctance. He was shy, and disliked addressing strangers; he was sensitive, and hated to take a liberty. But he had convinced himself that it was his duty to God to speak of sacred matters "in season and out of season," and he persevered in the same indomitable spirit which forced Charles Darwin, in spite of sea-sickness, to continue his experiments on board the *Beagle.*' In later years, I remember once quoting to my father, in self-defence under his spiritual cross-examination, Clough's—

> " O let me love my love unto myself alone
>   And know my knowledge to the world unknown !
>   No witness to the vision call,
>   Beholding, unbeheld of all ;
>   And worship thee, with thee withdrawn, apart,
>   Whoe'er, whate'er thou art,
>   Within the closest veil of mine own inmost heart."

"Mellifluous lines, enough !" he replied, "but that is not what God asks from a converted man. It is not the luxury of meditation and the cloister, but the unwelcome effort to spread a knowledge of the truth."

The entries in his journal of the voyage of January, 1839, are naïve and pathetic :—

" We have had much rough, cold, wet, and uncomfort-
"able weather, but I have called the crew together, on
"Sabbath days (but not so often as I ought, having
"suffered from extreme reluctance to disturb them), to
"hear the way of salvation. They listen with decorum
"and attention, and perhaps fruit may spring up after
"many days; and if not, I have not failed to be well
"paid even in a present blessing. . . . I made an
"opportunity of·speaking to the captain on the subject
"of religion. He is an amiable and well-informed man,
"a profane swearer, and one who seems to entertain
"considerable contempt for godliness. . . . The captain

"continues to profess infidel sentiments, but kindly per-
"mits his people to be assembled, and himself listens
"respectfully."

The voyage to England occupied five weeks, and during
that time Gosse worked hard at the manuscript of his *Canadian Naturalist*, contriving to finish it, so far as it could
be finished, before the ship entered the Mersey. In some
respects the voyage was pleasant, but the whole vessel was
stuffed with cargo, cotton-bales being piled even in the
cabin, leaving scarcely room to creep in and out. He used
to recline on the top of these soft bales, reading natural
history, and in particular Walsh's *Brazil*, which he had
found on board, and which fascinated him. At last England was again his home, after twelve years' exile. He was
furnished with ample and fervid introductions from his
dear friends the Jaqueses in Canada to their relatives in
Liverpool, and by them he was hospitably entertained for
a fortnight. These kind people became sufficiently interested in him to perceive his talents and to deplore his
poverty. They set themselves, with such slight means as
lay at their hands, to find suitable occupation for him. A
letter addressed to Mr. William Clarke, of Liverpool, who
had obtained for Philip Gosse the refusal of the office of
curator at some museum,—I know not what or where—
may here be quoted in full. It is a very characteristic
document.

To Mr. William Clarke, Liverpool.

"Wimborne, April 25, 1839.

"My dear Sir,

"I know not in what terms to express, in an
"adequate manner, my sense of your most undeserved
"kindness; it really oppresses me. As if it were not
"enough that you loaded me with the kindest atten-

"tions during my pleasant sojourn in your friendly
"family, you are still caring for my welfare, and devising
"schemes for my benefit, now I am far away. It is
"pleasing to know that though out of sight, I am not
"out of mind. Do not think me ungrateful if I cannot
"avail myself of your very obliging proposal. I am
"pained that your goodness should be thrown away ;
"but I am really not qualified for the situation of
"curator. I do not know the art of stuffing birds and
"beasts ; and, though I have some acquaintance with
"natural history, I am totally ignorant of mineralogy,
"which, I observe by the advertisement, is required.
"Attendance, too, is required from 8 a.m. till 9 p.m.—
"thirteen hours a day ; and the whole time to be devoted
"to the duties.

"There are other reasons why I should hesitate to
"fill such an office as that. I should fear that I should
"be thrown into situations in which I might find it diffi-
"cult to keep that purity of intention which I value
"more than life ; and likewise, that my opportunities of
"being useful to my fellow-men, especially to their
"souls, would be much curtailed. I view this transient
"state as a dressing-room to a theatre ; a brief, almost
"momentary visit, during which preparation is to be
"made for the real business and end of existence.
"Eternity is our theatre : time our dressing-room. So
"that I *must* make every arrangement with a view to
"its bearing on this one point.

"Again I repeat my gratitude for your kindness ; and
"pray God to reward you a thousand-fold, for I am
"utterly unable. Should it ever be my lot to revisit
"Liverpool, I shall gratefully renew my acquaintance
"with you and your dear family. I have heard nothing
"from Mr. Jaques since I have been here—have you ?

"My kindest wishes and most respectful regards wait on
"Mrs. Clarke, and my love to the dear young folks—espe-
"cially dear Henrietta, and William, and Charley; and
"indeed Emily, too. There, I have named all; for I
"can make no exception. May every happiness be
"yours and theirs!

"Believe me to be, dear Sir,

"Kindly and sincerely yours,

"P. H. GOSSE."

The excuse for not accepting seems, even from his own
point of view, curiously inadequate. The position of curator
at a provincial museum is not commonly looked upon as
one of peculiar temptation to worldliness, and the writer
was, besides, reduced to a poverty so extreme, that one might
suppose an independent spirit, such as his, would leap at
any honest way of getting a livelihood. But the fact
appears to be that he believed himself called to the
ministry, and that his full intention was to become, if
possible, a Wesleyan preacher. His efforts in this direction also, however, were met with disappointment. The
rough discourses which had served in Alabama were not to
the taste of the Methodists of Liverpool. He wrote: "The
large and fine Wesleyan chapels of Liverpool, the fashionable attire of the audiences, and the studied refinement of
the discourses, so thoroughly out of keeping with my own
fresh and ardent feelings, distress me. I mourn over the
degeneracy of Methodism." And Methodism, in her turn,
looked very coldly at this vehement colonial critic of her
manners.

Early in March, 1839, he went by railway and coach to
Wimborne, in Dorset, where his mother was now residing
with a younger son. Here Philip remained for three
months, taking at first a prominent place as a local

preacher in Wimborne itself and in the neighbouring villages, and frequently supplying the pulpit of the minister
at the Congregational chapel of the town.   The fervour of
religious zeal with which he had left Alabama now, however, began to abate.   Many little things had occurred
which tended to diminish his ardour.   His purpose was
still to seek acceptance from the Methodist Conference as
a travelling preacher.   But much of the enthusiasm which
had prompted him to undertake this form of employment
had evaporated by the summer, and, to his surprise, he
was conscious of not being disappointed when, on application, he found that he was past the limit of age at which
candidates for the regular ministry are received.   He was
not destined to be a Wesleyan preacher after all.

Why he lingered so long at Wimborne it is not easy to
say.   Perhaps it was connected with an episode which must
be recounted in the exact form in which he has chosen to
preserve it among his notes :—

"The widow of a deceased Wesleyan minister, residing
"in Wimborne, Mrs. Button, had two unmarried
"daughters, to the elder of whom, Amelia, an accom-
"plished, pious, and winning lady, older than I, and
"much pitted with the small-pox, I at once formed a
"very tender attachment.   It was as tenderly returned ;
"but the prudent mother made her sanction contingent
"on my obtaining some permanent source of income,
"which at present was wholly *in nubibus*.   This was not
"readily obtained.   Amelia's years could not well brook
"delay : another suitor interposed, a Wesleyan minister
"in full employ ; she accepted him, and I was left to
"mourn.   And mourn I did, sadly and deeply ; for my
"love for her was very earnest.   I could not, however,
"blame her decision."

The conduct of Amelia Button was as proper as that of

Edmund Gibbon under similar circumstances. She sighed as a lover, but she obeyed as a daughter.

It was no time, however, for Philip Gosse to be dallying with the tender passion. His fortunes were at their lowest ebb, and the summer of 1839 marks the darkest point of his whole career. It was a happy thought that made him turn, at last, to what should long ago have engrossed his attention, the field of literature. In the fervid and unwholesome condition of his mind, he had set on one side the manuscript of his *Canadian Naturalist*. It was only by a fortunate accident that, in his full tide of Puritanism, he had not destroyed it. It was now his one and only chance for the future, and London was the sole field into which he could, with hope of a harvest, drop the solitary seed. A constitutional timidity and that fear of London which is sometimes so strong in a sensitive countryman, held him shivering on the brink. At last, on June 7, 1839, he set out on a coach for the metropolis. While he had been in Dorsetshire he had earned just enough to prevent his being a positive burden upon his people, partly by preaching for absent ministers, partly by teaching the elements of flower-painting. He thought to continue the second branch as a lucrative profession in London, his own drawings being, as his Canadian and Alabaman specimens showed, of an exquisite merit. But his ignorance of London and of life were quite extraordinary. His first lodging in the town was quaintly chosen, since, in consequence of some literary reminiscence or another, he selected Drury Lane as the scene of his operations, and took a cheap but infinitely sordid lodging on the east side of that noisy and malodorous street. His room was an attic, a few doors north of Great Queen Street, and the present writer vividly remembers how, in his own boyhood, his father, walking briskly towards the British Museum with Charles

Kingsley, stopped to point out to his friend and to the boy the grimy window from which, in the dreariest hour of his life, he had looked down upon the roaring midnight debauchery of the Drury Lane of fifty years ago.

Philip Gosse's resources were now reduced to a few shillings. Driven by dirt and noise out of the Drury Lane attic, he took refuge in another, a little quieter and cleaner, in Farringdon Street, at the summit of the house then devoted, in its lower part, to the sale of Morrison's pills. The young man's only friend in London was the cousin mentioned in an earlier chapter, Mr. Thomas Bell, a dentist already eminent in the profession, a naturalist, the publication of whose *British Quadrupeds* in 1837 had given him considerable reputation, and a prominent member of the Royal Society. On June 15, 1839, Philip Gosse writes to his sister, Elizabeth Green :—

" Mr. Bell has very kindly offered to read my manuscript
"and give his opinion ; he is going to show it to his own
"publisher, but thinks that it will need some alteration
" before being published. I want to get some permanent
"means of subsistence, and one object of my writing
" now is to ask what you think my prospects would be of
"teaching drawing (the finer branches, such as flower-
"painting, etc. — you know my manner) among the
" aristocracy and gentry of Sherborne, and whether you
"think there would be sufficient chance of success to
" make it worth my while to come down and canvass the
" neighbourhood ? . . . If you write home, give my
" love. I do not like to write there until I know what
" my chance is here. Things look dark at present and
" hopeless enough, but they may brighten. Do not fail
" to write immediately; but rather put it off a day, than
"go about it in such haste as not to make half a letter.
" Adieu ! "

The manuscript here mentioned was *The Canadian Naturalist*, which pleased Mr. Bell so much that he recommended it strongly to Mr. Van Voorst, the distinguished publisher of scientific works. Philip Gosse's pride made him conceal his real state from Thomas Bell, and though the latter knew his cousin to be in need of employment, he did not suspect that he was in such bitter straits. Mr. Van Voorst appointed a day for the young author to call on him. Meanwhile the shillings, nursed as they might be, were slipping, slipping away. The practice of going once a day to a small eating-house had to be abandoned, and instead of it a herring was eaten as slowly as possible in the dingy attic in Farringdon Street. Meanwhile, the response about the "aristocracy and gentry of Sherborne" had been discouraging in the extreme. "Nothing to be done in' Sherborne," was the answer; "better stay where you are." At last the day broke on which Mr. Van Voorst's answer was to be given, and with as much of the gentleman about him as he could recover, the proud and starving author presented himself in Paternoster Row. He was ushered in to the cordial and courteous Mr. Van Voorst. He was no longer feeling any hope, but merely the extremity of dejection and disgust. The wish to be out again in the street, with his miserable roll of manuscript in his hands, was the emotion uppermost in his mind. The publisher began slowly: "I like your book; I shall be pleased to publish it; I will give you one hundred guineas for it." One hundred guineas! It was Peru and half the Indies! The reaction was so violent that the demure and ministerial-looking youth, closely buttoned up in his worn broadcloth, broke down utterly into hysterical sob upon sob, while Mr. Van Voorst, murmuring, "My dear young man! my dear young man!" hastened out to fetch wine and minister to wants which it was beyond the power of pride to conceal any longer.

Mr. Van Voorst, in venerable age, is still living as I write these words. I trust that I may be permitted the pleasure of assuring him of the gratitude which the family of his old friend feel and must ever continue to feel towards him. Since Otway dedicated his *Soldier's Fortune* to Richard Bentley in 1681, many things have been said by authors about publishers, and sometimes not in so amicable a spirit as that of Otway. The relations of the two professions have even, at times, so it is whispered, become positively strained. But between John Van Voorst and Philip Henry Gosse there was sealed, under the circumstances I have just described, a bond of business friendship which held them together for nearly fifty years, without a single misunderstanding or even momentary disagreement.

From this time forward, Philip Gosse had an aim in life. The form of literary work which he had adopted, or, rather, which had at last forced him to recognize its claims, was not a very lucrative one, and he was still, as will be seen, curiously unready in taking to literary work. Nevertheless, he had now made a successful start, and there was Mr. Van Voorst in Paternoster Row always ready to listen to a reasonable suggestion. Mr. George Loddiges, the once famous florist, was also a useful acquaintance gained through Thomas Bell. He was charmed with Philip Gosse's drawings of American flowers, made him free of his own admired series of orchid-houses and nurseries, and recommended him to seek employment in ladies' schools, as a teacher of flower-painting. In the winter of 1839 I find that Gosse has removed into the suburbs, to a lodging at Hackney. He writes, with his customary cheerfulness—for these letters never show the slightest petulance or ill-humour under failure—" Day by day, I trudge wearily through the streets, with my portfolio under my arm, seeking to show my drawings of flowers and insects. I get many praises, but little employment. I have, however, obtained several engagements, in private schools and families. I make frequent visits to the British Museum, and am especially studying the large mammals. I have made careful drawings of the giraffe on the old staircase, and the hippopotamus and rhinoceros at its foot. The other day I met a Chinaman offering a glazed box of Chinese insects, stuffed as full as it could hold. I could not resist the extravagance of buying it, as he wanted but a small sum for it. I have thrown away all but a few of the choice lepidoptera, and have made it quite air-tight." This treasure accompanied him in all subsequent wanderings to the very end.

On February 29, 1840, *The Canadian Naturalist* was published, the first of the long series of my father's works. It was very favourably received, and sold firmly, though rather slowly. The form in which it was written was somewhat unfortunate, for it consisted of a series of conversations between an imaginary father and son, "during successive walks, taken at the various seasons of the year, so that it may be considered as in some degree a kind of Canadian *Naturalist's Calendar.*" The presentment of facts was by no means helped by the snip-snap of the dialogue, and the supposed father was found most entertaining when he talked with least interruption from the young inquirer. The book was adorned by a large number of illustrations, engraved in a very refined and finished manner on blocks drawn in most cases by the author himself, and in all designed by him. In *The Canadian Naturalist*, imperfect as it was as a final expression of his peculiar genius, Philip Gosse opened out a new field of literature. In the eighteenth century, amid the careless pedantry of such zoologists as Pennant, had been heard the clear note of Gilbert White. Twenty years later, Alexander Wilson had begun to issue the eight volumes of his magnificent *American Ornithology.* In 1825 Charles Waterton had published his sensational *Wanderings.* These three works are the only ones which can fairly be said to have preceded *The Canadian Naturalist* in its own peculiar province, and of these Waterton's, at least, had little but a superficial resemblance to the new departure in natural history. It was from Wilson that Philip Gosse had learned most of the zoological art of his book, but it was his chief advantage to have been held long away from masters and teachers of all kinds, and to have been forced to study nature for himself. In his preface he said, modestly enough, that "the author is fully aware how very limited is his acquaintance with this boundless science [of zoology]; having lived in the far-off wilds of the West, where systems, books, and museums are almost unknown, he has been compelled to draw water from Nature's own well, and his knowledge of her is almost confined to her appearance in the forest and the field."

He very soon made himself fully familiar with all that systematic zoologists had arranged and decided. He became a learned as well as a practised naturalist. But the unacademic freshness of his early habit of mind remained, and gave its pleasant tincture to all his subsequent work. His function continued to be, as it had begun by being, that of one who calls his contemporaries out of their cabinets and their dissecting-rooms into the woods and seashore, and bids them observe the living heart of Nature. Since his time, such appeals have grown more and more frequent, until they have begun to seem commonplace. All can raise this particular flower now, but it was Philip Gosse, in a very marked degree, who first found, or at least first popularized, the seed. The moment was one in which, throughout the world, a fresher air was being blown across the fields of biology and natural history. Captain Fitzroy had just published that account of the cruise of the *Beagle* in which the greatest of all biologists, Charles Darwin (my father's senior by one year), made his first public appearance; while in New England one whom, from a purely literary point of view, it is more natural to compare with Philip Gosse, Henry Thoreau, had just made that week's voyage on the Concord and Merrimac rivers which he was to describe some ten years later. The germs of all that made Gosse for a generation one of the most popular and useful writers of his time are to be found in *The Canadian Naturalist*,—the picturesque enthusiasm, the scrupulous attention to truth in detail, the quick eye and the responsive brain, the happy gift in direct description. The pages devoted to the red squirrel, "that fantastic little gentleman, with as many tricks as a monkey;" the disquisition on the hard-woods of Lower Canada; the episode of the skunk,—these may be taken as typical examples of the felicitous character of the best passages, mingled, it is only fair to say, with much that, from want of literary experience, was put together without skill. One passage may be quoted here—a brief description of the phenomena of a Canadian winter tempest :—

"Hark to the wind! how it howls and whistles through "the tops of the trees, like a close-reef gale through "the shrouds and ropes of a ship at sea. Now it sinks "to a hollow moan, then sings again, uttering sounds "which one might fancy those of an Æolian harp. The "leaves fly from those few trees which still retain any, "and the long grey moss streams from the tops of the "scathed hemlocks, stretching far out upon the blast, "like signals of distress. Do you hear that crashing "roar? Some mighty tree has bowed to its destiny.

M

" We are in danger until we can get out of the proximity
" of the forest. Yonder is one prostrate across the road,
" which has fallen since we passed an hour ago : see how
" it has crushed the fence, and torn up the ground of
" the field on the opposite side ! There thunders
" another ! They are falling now on every side ; and
" the air is thronged with pieces of bark, shreds of
" tree-moss, and broken branches, descending. It is
" appalling to hear the shrieking of the gusts, and the
" groaning of the trees as they rock and chafe against
" each other, while they toss their naked arms about, as
" if in agony."

The record of the next two years is a very slight one.
It was a period of obscurity and poverty, borne with an
almost stoic patience. Philip Gosse was still, what indeed
he never wholly ceased to be, timid, reserved, little disposed
to form new acquaintances or to cultivate old ones. The
success of his *Canadian Naturalist* made a ripple in
scientific society, and a more ambitious man would have
felt that his foot was on the ladder and have made his
own ascent secure. But that was not Philip Gosse's way.
He was not easily to be persuaded of his powers, and,
without making the smallest effort to secure work of a
serial or journalistic kind, such work as would have been
easily within reach of his elegant and active pen, he fell
back on his flower-drawing and his elementary teaching.
He was not, at this time, in good health. The miasma
of Alabama was probably still hanging about his system.
His rare letters of this epoch, though always resolute and
patient, have a melancholy tone. He says to his sister
Elizabeth, early in 1840, after a brief visit to Dorsetshire :
" Now I am in London again, lonely and depressed, and
almost without a friend—at least, without *dear* friends.
What a sad word is 'farewell'! But, by-and-by, there

will be a state where the sound of farewell, now familiar as a household word, shall be altogether unheard of and altogether unknown.   May we meet there!"

In his dreary lodgings, his thoughts went back to the haunts of his boyhood in Newfoundland, "the beautiful little silver lakes that sleep among the spruce-covered mountains,—I mean a mile or two in from shore. I should like exceedingly," he writes (April 25, 1840) to his brother William at St. John's, "that you should transfer some views to paper for me, if they were but sketches; the very lovely one from Pack's farm in Carbonear, and the same from Elson's flagstaff down Little Beaver Pond, Black Duck Pond, etc., with the hills of Freshwater in the distance, and the sea peeping out between the peaks. Another from that high round hill on the left hand of the Harbour Grace Road, looking in towards Lady Pond, and over many other ponds. From Mosquito Point there is a noble coast view—Carbonear Island in the foreground, green and woody; behind, the gradually receding headlands of the north shore, becoming more dimly blue until Boccalão is almost invisible. Give my love to all my Bay friends, if you have the opportunity, and don't forget my request to gather flowers, sprigs of bushes, etc.; it is very little trouble, when you are walking, to gather what you see, and when you come home, just shut them into a book. I flatter myself you will do it."

In the summer he was himself applied to to take some views of the neighbourhood of Sherborne, to be lithographed for a history of that town, but was not a little incensed, on the publication of the book, to find the name of a better-known artist appended to them, instead of his own. He complained to the publisher, but obtained neither reply nor redress. He was still staying close to Sherborne, when his only sister, Elizabeth Green, after a brief illness, died on July 26, 1840. The loss of Mrs. Green left him more lonely than ever, for she was one of the few persons to whom he was attached. In the course of this summer he was once more reduced to such straits that he had almost determined to "again cross the Atlantic, either back to the Southern States, or to the West Indies; for," he says, "I cannot live thus. I get no new pupils, and am losing money. In the States I can be sure of £200 or £250 a year, but it is such an exile. I should seek a school as before, and at my leisure get up the material of another book." This idea of a school, either in England or America, had long been haunting him, and early in 1840, as his own acquaintance with Greek was but elementary, he set himself to a close and earnest study, with grammar, lexicon, and Delectus, reading thirty pages a day, until he became, what he remained, a fair Greek scholar. In June he ran down to Colchester, to inquire about a school advertised for sale, but with no result. In September he arranged with a retiring schoolmaster in London Lane, Hackney, to take over his fixtures and three pupils. His printed announcement to the gentry of the neighbourhood now lies before me, a faded scrap of elegant satin paper. It is worded so quaintly, and carries about it such an old-world air, that I cannot refrain from reprinting it :—

ACADEMY.

"MR. P. H. GOSSE respectfully announces to the "inhabitants of Hackney and its vicinity, that he intends "to open a Classical and Commercial School for Young "Gentlemen, at the large and commodious School-room "in London Lane, in the rear of the Temperance "Hotel; where, by assiduous attention to the morals, "comfort, and intellectual progress of the Pupils intrusted

"to his care, he hopes to merit a share of public
"patronage. The School will commence on Wednesday,
"the 30th September, 1840.
"*N.B.—Mr. G.'s residence is at No.* 1, *Retreat Cottages,*
"*Hackney.*"

The school was not quite a complete failure ; indeed, it
enjoyed a mitigated degree of success. Philip Gosse's
ideas of education were as free as his science from
traditional rule. But in his way of teaching there seems
to have been something of the freshness of his natural
observation. From a letter written·at this time I extract
a passage which is not unworthy of preservation as the
contribution of an unbiassed mind to the problem of
education :—

"I am a friend to boys' getting their lessons (the
" mere words of them) well fixed in the memory ; I
" once thought it enough if the *sense* were secured, but
" on considering how little boys in general reflect on the
"meaning of what they learn, and how often the
" verbatim words stick indelibly to the memory in after
" years, I attach a great value to the mere learning of
"words—that is, learning them thoroughly (not hammer-
" ing and stammering, and fingering the buttonhole, with
"'Stop a minute, sir!' 'I could say it, just now, sir!'
" and so forth)—to say nothing of the vast increase of
"the powers of memory, as of every other intellectual
"faculty, by its habitual exercise. Consider, too, how
"very much of school learning is a matter of *mere*
" abstract memory—conjugations, declensions, lists of
" heteroclites and exceptions, conjunctions, prepositions,
" adverbs, in grammar ; names of places, distances, and
" bearings, in geography ; dates in history ; tables in
"arithmetic ; in all which, and many others, no assist-

"ance whatever is derived from the understanding ;
"they are matters of mere memory, and if got at all,
"must be got by heart, and that thoroughly. With
"respect to spelling, you argue against yourself. You
"'have known lads of tolerable capacity spell wretchedly;'
"so have I, and men and women too, hundreds of them ;
"and what does that prove, but the total inefficiency of
"the mode by which they were *pretended* to be taught—
"the common mode of columns? Did you ever know
"one who had been *trained* (not for half a year, but
"through his education) by writing from dictation, to
"spell wretchedly? I have found in spelling that the
"great and most common difficulty consists in not
"knowing how to elect in words of every moment's use,
"which superficially sound alike but differ in import : 'as
"'—has ;' 'which—witch ;' 'were—where ;' 'weal—
"'wheel ;' 'air—are—hair—hare—hear—here—ear—e'er
"'—ere,' etc., etc. Now dictation, by showing the rela-
"tion and connection of words, shows when one form
"should be adopted, and when another. I allow this
"knowledge is very commonly gained without dictation,
"but how is it gained ? Not by learning from a spelling
"book, *in no single instance*, but by what is equivalent
"to dictation, by observation in private reading, till the
"individual acquires a practised, an educated eye. That
"there may be an advantage in learning the definitions
"of words, I am not prepared to deny, but that is an
"exercise quite distinct from spelling."

He had the habit of teaching the elements of geography
by making his boys draw the pattern of a piece of the
carpet, then a ground-plan of the school-room, with all its
furniture, then the garden, with the relative portions of
house and road, until the notion of the principle on which
a map is made was insensibly gained, and then, and not

till then, he would proceed to the geography of large areas. Whether this idea, which proved exceedingly efficacious in the case of his own pupils, has been often carried out in schemes of education, I am not aware. So far as my father knew, it was original to him. In the summer of 1841, as he was growing very weary of solitary lodgings, he took a small house, called Woodbine Cottage, close to the school, and brought his mother up from Dorsetshire to keep it for him. It stood surrounded by a pretty little garden, full of perennials in geometric beds, with thick box edges. From this house he would frequently, in the warmer months, start with all his boys on entomologizing excursions, commonly to the borders of Epping Forest, and he began a collection of English butterflies which soon comprised most of the local species. All this while he was busy enough, since he still had a few pupils in flower-painting, and exercised his leisure to the full in scientific and literary study. These years make little show in the record of his life, but they were full of intellectual energy. He was making up for time lost in Canada and Alabama; he was fitting himself to compete on equal terms with men who had been better equipped than he in starting.

More than anything else, however, he was training and cultivating by ceaseless miscellaneous notes his powers of observing and recording natural facts. To print the multitudinous records of small scientific observations which he accumulated for his own use would be tedious and useless to the general reader. Yet some example ought, perhaps, to be given here as a specimen of his process of self-education. I select at random, and transcribe from the almost microscopic writing in faded ink, one little series of consecutive notes, one brick out of the immense edifice of his records :—

"*February* 18.—Having caught some water insects, and
"put them into water with a little duckweed, I found a
"few Cyclopidæ among them. One was a largish plump
"fellow, which under the lens presented a very pretty
"appearance, being of a pellucid white, brightly shining
"in the light, like a polished egg. On the 16th I put
"this, with two little ones, into a clear phial, with water
"and a little duckweed ; neither had eggs. The next
"day I could see no more of one of the little ones ; but
"to-day the remaining little one has a capsule of eggs
"on each side the tail, projecting.

"*February* 19.—This morning, while I was looking at
"the Cyclopidæ, the large one suddenly darted at the
"little one, and they had a tussle ; immediately I per-
"ceived that nearly the whole of one capsule of eggs was
"gone from the little one, about five eggs only remaining
"on the right side, attached to a portion of the ovary.
"I dare say the former one was devoured. In the after-
"noon, on looking again, I see the large one has got
"two projecting ovaries attached.

"*February* 20.—To-day the small Cyclops was desti-
"tute of eggs, and with a lens I found many little
"creatures, exceedingly minute, darting hither and
"thither, nothing in form like the parent, but much like
"mites, with four projecting feet and two antennæ.

"*February* 22.—The larger Cyclops still carries her
"eggs, but the smaller has acquired another double
"series. I fancy them to be of a paler grey, when first
"extruded.

"*February* 24.—This afternoon I see the large Cyclops
"is divested of her ovaries, and the water now swarms
"with the little quadrupedal young."

It is noticeable, in dealing with these scientific diaries,
that although they were not intended for publication,

literary form is never neglected in them. The extreme clearness of observation found its natural expression in perfect lucidity of language. The consequence was that if, in future years, the naturalist had need to transfer to a manuscript his old notes on any particular species, he could do it almost without revision, and thus save a great deal of labour.

All this time he had continued to act as a class-leader and local preacher among the Wesleyan Methodists. There still exists a manuscript book of skeleton sermons preached by him in the chapels around London, from 1839 to 1842. He has attached to it a note, written forty years later:—"This volume possesses some interest, as showing how very poor and crude my theology was at that time." He was, in fact, approaching a great crisis in his religious life, to be marked, in the first place, by his formally severing his connection, early in 1843, with the Wesleyan Society. The present writer is entirely without competence to deal with this particular phase of religious conviction, which, however, he does not feel at liberty to ignore. To misrepresent it would be even worse than to neglect it, and a succinct account of it will be found printed, in Philip Gosse's own words, in an appendix.* We may return to the more external features of his career. The school, which had for a while promised well, began to fall off; several of the elder and more interesting pupils ceased to attend, and were not replaced by others; so that, by the end of 1843, the number of scholars was reduced to eight. A far more lucrative and interesting source of income was, however, opening up to Philip Gosse at last. In the spring of 1843 the Society for Promoting Christian Knowledge wanted an *Introduction to Zoology.* Professor

---

* Appendix II.

Thomas Bell, who was on the committee, was deputed to ask Mr. Van Voorst who would be a suitable person to write such a book. " Why not your cousin, Mr. Gosse ? " was the reply, and Bell at once assented. With his ordinary diffidence, however, Philip Gosse was far from ready to believe that he was competent to fulfil the task, and it was with difficulty that he could be persuaded to undertake it.

At this point Philip Gosse's career as a man of letters may properly be said to open. He had reached his thirty-fourth year not only without distinction, but without gaining any confidence in his own powers. His practical training had been excellent, but he needed to be pushed into active literary work. At last the impetus had been given, and henceforward to write for the public became the natural and obvious thing for him to do. He had no sooner accepted the commission which the Society offered him, than the plan of his work assumed form in his mind. He entered upon it with a timidity which soon gave way to enthusiasm, and he pursued it expeditiously with ever-increasing zeal and interest. In this and future relations with the Society my father invariably met with great consideration and courtesy. He had scrupulously felt obliged to let the committee know that he was a noncon-formist, but they desired that that matter might never again be alluded to. For the two volumes of the *Intro-duction to Zoology*, the Society paid him £170. It was composed in less than a year, without interfering in any way with the author's other pursuits. It was therefore the cause of valuable augmentation to his small means of subsistence.

The preparation of these volumes took Gosse a great deal to the Natural History Department of the British Museum, and he began to form acquaintanceships which ripened into valuable friendships. Edward Newman had been one of the first to welcome with enthusiastic appreciation the peculiar qualities of the new writer, and he had not only reviewed *The Canadian Naturalist*, but had sought out its author as a contributor to his own periodical, *The Entomologist*. He was introduced by Newman in 1843 to Edward Doubleday, a naturalist of great promise, a little younger than Philip Gosse, and these two formed a friendship eminently profitable to each of them, which only terminated with the premature death of the entomologist in 1849. Edward Doubleday, like his new friend, had travelled in America as a collecting naturalist, having returned laden with treasures in 1837. In 1839 he had obtained the position of assistant at the British Museum, and was put in charge of the lepidoptera. When Philip Gosse first became intimate with him, he had just arranged the national collections of moths and butterflies in an admirable manner. In company with Edward, Gosse made frequent pilgrimages to the home of the Doubledays at Epping, where the widowed mother and the more eminent and the elder of the two brothers, Henry Doubleday— probably the greatest entomologist whom England has produced—involved a demure and noiseless Quaker home in an atmosphere of camphor. But Gosse never came to know Henry Doubleday, whom he found reserved and dispiriting, so well as the mercurial Edward, with whom he formed one of the warmest and most easy friendships of his life. It was through the Doubledays, if I mistake not, that Philip Gosse was encouraged to become a contributor to the Proceedings of the Royal Society. The first of his lengthy series of papers read before that body was a *Note on an Electric Centipede*, published in this year, 1843.

Other associates of this period were Baird, Whymper, Westwood, Adam White, and the Grays. Dr. William

Baird, a biologist of some distinction in his time, had been an assistant in the British Museum since 1841 ; Whymper, the principal water-colour painter and engraver of scientific illustrations in that generation, was an *habitué* of the scientific departments of the Museum, in which John Edward Gray and George Richard Gray already held positions of considerable influence. Of the brilliant, affectionate, and eccentric Adam White, little now remains in memory, but if he was the least distinguished, he was far from being the least beloved. Of the whole group of young naturalists, then all full of ardour, and already either famous or on the road to fame, the only one who survives is the venerable John Obadiah Westwood, now in his eighty-sixth year, but still Hope Professor of Zoology at Oxford, who in 1843 was already eminent for his *Entomologist's Text-Book* of 1838 and his *British Butterflies* of 1841.

Association with those and other scientific friends effected a rather sudden expansion in Gosse's social nature. The reserved and saturnine young man, absorbed in his own thoughts, developed into the enthusiastic companion in and sympathizer with the studies of others. The journey from Hackney to the British Museum began to prove a tedious waste of time, and towards the close of 1843 he moved further into London, renting a small house in Kentish Town, No. 73, Gloucester Place, the last, at that time, on the northern side of the street, recently built, having behind it a long "garden" of heavy clay soil, mere broken meadow not yet subdued. Hither he and his mother removed, and soon he invited his aged father—who was now quite an invalid, and in his seventy-eighth year—to come up from the West of England and join them. Behind the garden of this house, there stretched away waste fields to the north, and here, one night in the early summer of 1844, Philip Gosse, for the first and last time in his life, was "run in" by the police. He had fastened a bull's-eye lantern to a tree, and was anxiously watching for the advent of insects, when the would-be capturer was himself suddenly captured, on suspicion, by a couple of active constables. He had no great difficulty in explaining that his conduct, if eccentric, proffered no real danger to society.

A little before Christmas, 1843, Whymper suggested to him that he should write a book about the ocean. There was a sudden access of public interest in the new and mysterious theories of deep-sea fauna. Sir James Ross had just returned from his epoch-making voyage in the Pacific Ocean, and had brought up living shell-fish from what then seemed the astounding depth of a thousand fathoms. It appeared that a general treatise on the popular zoology of the deep sea might be acceptable, and Philip Gosse proposed to write one for the Society for Promoting Christian Knowledge. The committee were delighted with the idea, and asked him to prepare a sample of his method. He did so, and wrote a little essay of which only half a dozen copies were printed for the use of the committee. The work, as it finally appeared, did not contain this fragment, which has never been published. I print it here as a characteristic specimen of the style of the author at this period :—

"Waiving our privilege of breathing the thin and
" elastic air, let us descend in imagination to the depths
" of ocean, and explore the gorgeous treasures that
" adorn the world of the mermaids. We will choose for
" our descent one of those lovely little groups which
" speckle the Pacific, the wondrous labour of an insig-
" nificant polyp. The sun is no longer visible through
" the depth of the incumbent sea; but a subdued

" greenish light, soft and uniform, sufficiently reveals the
" wonders of the scene.   We find ourselves at the foot of
" a vast perpendicular cliff, the base of a coral island,
" entirely composed, to all appearance, of glistening
" madrepore, of snowy whiteness, but, in reality, perhaps
" only encased by it. Every part of its surface is seen,
" on close examination, to be studded with minute
" orifices, from each of which projects a little fleshy
" polyp, which spreads its six green arms, like the rays of
" a star, waiting for prey.   On touching one, though ever
" so slightly, it contracts its arms and withdraws.   Many
" other corals rise around us, most of them assuming the
" form of stony trees or shrubs, of singular variety and
" beauty, some crimson, some grey, some white, some
" black, while the rocks at our feet are almost covered
" with brainstones of vast size, mushroom-corals, and
" other madrepores, of the most grotesque forms.
" Enormous sea - fans wave their netted expansions
" slowly to and fro in the long heavy swell of the sea,
" embraced here and there by the slender branches of
" the jointed corallines.   The beauty of form and colour
" displayed by these productions is contrasted with the
" sober hue of the sponges, which, in endless diversity,
" overspread the bottom of the sea.   Their forms are no
" less fantastic than those of the corals, and resemble
" vases, or tables, or horns, or tubes, or globes, or many-
" fingered hands ; while from the larger orifices on their
" surface, as from so many mouths, they pour forth
" incessant streams of water with untiring activity.   The
" vegetable productions, however, display little of the
" variety which marks their sisters of the upper world ;
" but the dull yellow bladder-weed and other fuci creep
" among the rocks, and the brown sea-thong and fea-
" thery conferva wave amidst the coral branches.

"All this forms the *scenery*, as it were, of our novel
"position. But these dim recesses are not solitudes;
"the water teems with life to an extent utterly unknown
"to the sunny earth above. Minute crustaceous animals
"swarm in every part, and gelatinous animalcules so
"abound as almost to touch each other. Beautiful
"shells, whose loveliness, however, is partly concealed
"by their leathery skin, glide slowly over the rocks;
"the paper nautilus darts by in its graceful but fragile
"habitation; and the giant clam opens its immense
"valves to feed in security in the shelter of yonder
"cavern. The loggerhead turtle, however, explores the
"caverns for his prey, within whose formidable jaws
"even the stony shells of the great conchs are crushed
"like a walnut; nor is the depth of ocean inaccessible to
"him who urges his arrowy course through the waters
"with the swiftness of a bird upon the wing. We are
"tempted at first sight to believe that these slimy rocks
"give birth to the most brilliant flowers; so close is the
"resemblance borne by the expanded actiniæ to these
"lovely productions of the garden. We can almost
"identify the aster, the anemone, the sunflower, the
"daisy, the cactus, the carnation, and other favourites of
"the *parterre*, in these fleshy animal-flowers that

"'The dark unfathom'd caves of ocean bear.'

"The water is now become our atmosphere; in which
"the place of the feathered tribes is supplied by the no
"less varied tribes of fishes, which cleave the waters
"with a fleetness emulating that of the most favoured
"inhabitants of the upper air. The gemmed and glitter-
"ing mail in which many of these tenants of the deep
"are arrayed, rivals the hues of the parrots or the
"humming-birds. The labrus, which has just shot past

"us, is a notable example ; possessing in its silvery
"body, yellow head, and crimson tail, an undoubted
"claim to beauty of decoration ; nor are the gleaming
"hues that flash from the pearly sides of that troop of
"coryphenes, as they play in the changing light, less
"charming. Now they have caught sight of yonder
"shoal of timid little flying-fishes which are making
"their way to surface, to seek a momentary refuge in
"another element,—and away they dart, pursuing and
"pursued. And here comes, stealing by, the fellest
"tyrant of the deep, the grim shark, attended by his
"*fidus Achates*, the little pilot-fish, in a livery of brown
"and purple. The very countenance of this grisly
"monster, the expression of settled malice in his eye,
"inspires an involuntary horror, scarcely increased by
"a glimpse of the serried lancet-like teeth which arm
"those fatal jaws.

———

"It is night. Yet darkness has not fallen upon the
"scene, for the whole mass of the sea is become imbued
"with light. A milky whiteness pervades every part,
"slightly varying in intensity, arising from inconceivably
"numerous animalcules, so small as to be separately
"undistinguishable, but in their aggregation illuminating
"the boundless deep. Among them are numerous
"swimming creatures, of perceptible size and greater
"luminousness, which glitter like little brilliant sparks ;
"and when a fish swims along, its path becomes a bed
"of living light, and we may trace it many fathoms by
"its luminous wake. Some of the larger creatures also
"are vividly illuminated ; the medusæ, which by day
"appear like circular masses of transparent jelly, now
"assume the appearance of cannon-balls heated to

"whiteness; and yonder sun-fish seems like a great
" globe of living fire."

The composition of the book of which this little essay
was intended to be a specimen was the principal occupation
of 1844. He was paid £120 for the copyright of *The
Ocean*, which was published early in 1845, while the author
was away in Jamaica. The success of this volume was
surprising, and first opened the eyes of Philip Gosse to the
fact that he had in him the making of a popular author·
Edition after edition was sold out, and of all his subsequent
works few showed a more steady vitality than *The Ocean*.
It was the popularity of this book, and regret that he had
parted with the copyright, which set him meditating on
schemes of publication which should be more lastingly, if
less immediately, lucrative ; but some years passed before
Philip Gosse took the management of his books into his
own hands.

The Ocean is a volume which has probably reached a
more varied circle of readers than any of my father's
books. It is not the most read or best liked of them, but
is the one which has perhaps enjoyed the widest circulation. It is eloquently written, and in freedom of
style marks an immense advance on *The Canadian
Naturalist*. The opening chapter deals with the general
features of ocean, treated poetically and sentimentally ; the
writer then turns to the subject of which he as yet knew
little at first hand, but which was presently to absorb
him entirely, the fauna and flora of the shores of Great
Britain. The succeeding chapters deal successively with
the Arctic seas, the Atlantic, the Pacific, and the Indian
Oceans. The book is copiously illustrated by Whymper
and by the naturalist himself ; the natural history subjects
being drawn on the block by Gosse and cut by Whymper
in a way which often does great credit to each artist. The

drawing of the white shark, on p. 284, is a capital instance of this double skill. With the warm reception of *The Ocean*, in 1845, Gosse may be said to have begun to be distinguished ; but when fame found him, he was far away in the tropics. A new chapter of his career had opened.

Early in 1844, while he was chatting one day with his friends in the insect-room of the British Museum, Edward Doubleday suggested that Philip Gosse would do well as an insect-collector in the tropics. Demerara was originally proposed ; then Jamaica, as being less known to naturalists, and, entomologically, absolute virgin ground. The British Museum had almost nothing from Jamaica, nor was anything known of the natural history of the island since the days of Sloane and Browne. Gosse jumped eagerly at the suggested proposal. He had already had some experience in Newfoundland, in Canada, and in Alabama, and the prospect appeared to him delightful in the extreme. He immediately began to prepare. He read up all works which touched upon the zoology of the West Indies, made drawings of desiderata, especially of orchids, butterflies, and humming-birds, constructed collecting-boxes, and gradually bought the necessary materials.

Doubleday introduced him to Hugh Cuming, of Gower Street, as an agent for selling the collections to be made, and this gentleman, himself a successful collector, gave Gosse some useful instructions. He also took him down to Kew Gardens, where he began that life-long acquaintance with Sir William Hooker, which was to be of such lasting profit and pleasure to him. His latest occupation of a purely literary nature, before starting, was to write for Messrs. Harvey and Darton a Christmas annual, which appeared the ensuing winter under the title of *Glimpses of the Wonderful.* This little volume, gaily illustrated in the taste of the time, was a " pot-boiler," if ever there was one, and the author, though he had not scamped his perfunctory task, declined to allow his name to appear on the title-page. In the autumn the elder Mr. and Mrs. Gosse were removed from Kentish Town to a little house at the Oval, Hackney. On October 20, 1844, their son sailed from the Thames on board a vessel bound for Jamaica. Just about the same time two other young naturalists set out on collecting expeditions, Hugh Low for Borneo, and David Dyson for Honduras, both having made like agreements with Cuming to be their sole agent.

CHAPTER VII.

JAMAICA.

1844–1846.

IN 1770 Gilbert White of Selborne wrote to Daines
Barrington : " A sight of the *hirundines* of that hot
and distant island of Jamaica would be a great entertainment to me." Seventy-four years later the ornithology of
that ancient colony remained, as Bell has said, scarcely
better known than it was in White's time. It was now
to be carefully and indeed exhaustively investigated, with
the result that since Gosse's visit but few new facts of any
importance have been added to knowledge. He spent
eighteen months in Jamaica, during which time his attention was mainly, though not exclusively, directed to the
birds of the island. When he arrived, the ornithology of
Jamaica was in a chaotic state ; when he left, nearly two
hundred species of birds were clearly ascertained to belong
to the island fauna. Of mammalia, reptiles, and fishes
he was able to add twenty-four new species to science.

The voyage out was not a remarkable one. From the
zoological point of view its interest culminated in the
observation, in mid Atlantic, of a very rare, if not absolutely
undescribed, cetacean. There seems to be very little
doubt that the troop of large dolphin-like whales which
sported about the vessel for nearly seventeen hours, on
November 22 and 23, was identical with the toothless

whale of Havre (*Delphinorhynchus micropterus*), of which at that time a solitary specimen, washed up at the mouth of the Seine, was the only one described by any naturalist. A little further on, off the west extremity of Puerto Rico, a shoal of the other species of this rare genus, *Delphino-rhynchus rostratus*, or the rosy-bellied dolphin, fell under Philip Gosse's observation, and he thus had the opportunity, in the course of the same voyage, of seeing two cetaceans, closely allied, neither of which had, probably, been observed alive by any existing zoologist. After entering the West Indian seas, the flying-fishes became abundant, and he had the opportunity of closely examining their habits. He writes at last, under date of December 4, as follows :—

"My first sight of Jamaica was one that I can never "forget. . . . During the forenoon the mountains of "Jamaica were seen, and gradually grew more distinct "as we neared the island. Yet the cloudiness of the day "prevented my having any satisfactory view of it until "evening. About sunset, I was standing forward, when "one by my side said, 'Look at the Peak!' I looked "intently, directing my gaze to the neighbourhood of the "horizon, where I supposed it was to be seen ; but nothing "but the dull white clouds met my eye. 'Up there!' "said my informant ; and his finger pointed up into the "sky ; and there indeed was its noble head (perhaps "elevated by refraction), a conical mass, darkly blue, "above the dense bed of clouds that hung around its "sides, and enveloped all beneath its towering elevation. "Yet it is situated far inland, and was then full forty "miles distant from our ship. But night soon fell, and, "as we were somewhat anxiously watching for the light "on Point Morant, I had the pleasure of first seeing it "from the main rigging. We were soon abreast of it, and

"as we passed on before an increasing breeze, that
"tempered the tropical heat with its refreshing breath,
"we saw the coast dark and high only a few miles off.
"Many lights were seen in the scattered cottages, and
"here and there a fire blazed up from the beach, or a
"torch in the hand of some fishermen was carried from
"place to place. My mind was full of Columbus, and of
"his feelings on that eventful night when the coast of
"Guanahani lay spread out before him, with its moving
"lights and proud anticipations. With curiosity and
"hope, somewhat analogous (*parva componere magnis*), did
"I contemplate the tropical island before me, its romance
"heightened by the indefiniteness and obscurity in which
"it lay. I was on deck several times during the night,
"and in the intervals was still engaged, in dreams, in
"endeavouring to penetrate the darkness of the shore."

At daybreak next morning they were off Port Royal,
but becalmed ; they had leisure to enjoy one of the most
brilliant views in the world, the blue crystal sea, the white
city of Kingston, the majestic Peak, towering eight
thousand feet into the azure sky, and contrasting, in its
uniform tone of blue, with the purple ridges of the lower
mountain ranges. Three black pilots boarded the vessel
about nine, but it was noon before a gradual breeze sprang
up and carried them in to Port Royal. Gosse was put
ashore at the wharf, and walked off to the Palisades, the
long sandy spit which makes a sea-lake of the ample
harbour of Kingston.

"I found it barren enough ; but it all was strange, and
"to feet which for nearly two months had not felt the
"firm earth, even a run along the beach was exhilarating.
"The graceful cocoa-nut palm sprang up in groups from
"the water's edge, waving its feathery fronds over the
"rippling waves that dashed about its fibrous foot.

"Great bushes of prickly pear and other cacti were
"growing on the low summit of the bank, covering large
"spaces of ground with their impenetrable masses,
"presenting a formidable array of spines ; as did also a
"species of acacia that grew in thickets and single trees.
"All along the line of high water lay heaps of seaweeds,
"drying in the sun, among which was particularly
"abundant a species of *Padina*, closely resembling the
"pretty 'peacock's-tail' of our own shore, though less
"regularly beautiful. Sponges of various forms, and
"large fan corals, with the gelatinous flesh dried on the
"horny skeleton, were also thrown up on the higher
"beach ; and I found in some abundance a coralline of
"a soft consistence, and of a bright grass-green hue. . . .
"Shells were very scarce on the sea-beach. Several
"specimens of a brilliant little fish, the *chætoden*, were
"swimming and darting about the narrow but deep
"pools ; they were not more than an inch in length,
"marked with alternate bands of black and golden-yellow.
"In the vertical position in which they swim, with the
"eye of the observer looking down upon them, they
"appear to bear the slender proportions of ordinary fishes ;
"and it is only by accident, as in turning, or on capturing
"one, that we detect the peculiar form, high and vertically
"flattened, of this curious genus."

Next day (December 7), they got under way at daybreak,
and, avoiding Kingston altogether, sailed for Alligator
Pond, a dreary little settlement surrounded by heavy
drifts of sand, where Gosse became first personally introduced to the exquisite *Heliconia* butterflies, and to a mango
humming-bird (*Lampornis porphyrurus*), flashing his ruby
gorget in the sun while probing the sulphur-coloured
blossoms of the prickly pear. The vessel stayed several
days in the neighbourhood of Alligator Pond, and the

young naturalist took advantage of this fact to make every day a fresh excursion inland with his net. A planter, Mr. Haffenden, of New Forest, hearing of the arrival of an English *savant*, hospitably invited him to dine and sleep at his house, and sent a horse for him. The estate was some miles up the valley, and the house one in the most splendid colonial style. The balcony offered a view of great breadth and magnificence ; the eye roamed over many miles of open savannah. "But the most striking feature was an enormous mountain rising immediately in front of the house, covered to the summit with dark woods ; so steep and towering that, as I lay in bed in a lofty room, I could but just see a little portion of the sky in the upper corner of the window." The top of this mountain was Mr. Haffenden's coffee-plantation. While Gosse was staying at New Forest, he occupied himself in collecting specimen blossoms of the various exquisite orchids, especially *Broughtonia* and *Brasavola*, which grew about the rocks in the forest. The negro groom who had been sent to accompany him was bewildered at this behaviour, and afterwards confided to Mr. Haffenden that the "strange buckra had taken the trouble to get *parcels of bush !* "

The *Caroline* had landed her mails and principal passengers for Kingston at Port Royal, and was now very leisurely, chiefly at night, creeping from port to port round the south-western coast of Jamaica. It was not until December 19 that she reached the point at which Philip Gosse had determined to leave her, that port of Savannah-le-Mar which lives in literature in a most brilliant and paradoxical fragment of De Quincey. In entering the harbour, the ship suddenly struck upon the reef that divides the former from the expanse of Bluefields Bay. This might have proved a fatal accident, but she did not strike heavily, and, after two hours' arduous exertion, the ship was off again. When morning broke, they were running into Savannah-le-Mar through a very narrow channel, the coral reef almost touching them on either side. Gosse mounted a little way up the shrouds, and saw the beautiful bay beneath him, so calm, pure, and transparent that it seemed simply like gazing down through a broad sheet of plate glass. After some days in the deplorably dead-and-alive town of Savannah-le-Mar, the captain of the *Caroline* lent Gosse the cutter to Bluefields, the house of a Mr. and Mrs. Coleman, Moravian missionaries, with whom he had made arrangements to lodge. Several kindly faces were waiting to welcome him on the beach, and the good-natured negroes competed for the honour of taking his boxes and cases up to the mansion.

Bluefields, which was now to be his home for eighteen months, is marked on the maps as if it were a town of some importance on the coast-road from Savannah-le-Mar to Black river, on the south-west shore of Jamaica. In point of fact it is, or was, but a solitary house; one of the oldest and largest of the planters' mansions in the prosperous times, but already, in 1844, fallen into partial decay in the midst of what was called a "ruinate" plantation. It figures in literature in the pages of that very spirited and entertaining novel, *Tom Cringle's Log*, which gives an unsurpassed picture of what Jamaica was in the opening years of the century. The gaiety and opulence of Michael Scott's Jamaica had, however, given place to commercial dejection within the forty years that preceded Philip Gosse's visit. In 1844 the beautiful sugar estates throughout the island were half desolate, and the planters had either ceased to reside in their mansions, or had pitifully retrenched their expenses. With all this had come a spirit of pietism, and Bluefields, in particular, seems to have been the centre of a missionary activity, in the hands of the

Moravians, which radiated into all parts of the county of Westmoreland.

On board the *Caroline* Philip Gosse had made the acquaintance of a Mr. and Mrs. Plessing, German Moravians, who were coming out to Jamaica to be employed as missionaries. Their account of Bluefields had struck him as singularly attractive to the naturalist, while the religious views of the Moravians, which were quite novel to him, exercised a fascination over his religious curiosity. On arriving at Alligator Pond, therefore, the Plessings had written to know whether he could be received at Bluefields as a tenant, and without waiting for a reply— since Bluefields was large enough to admit a regiment of tenants—they proceeded on their leisurely voyage thither. Had they waited for an answer, the reply would have been in the negative ; for Mr. Coleman and his wife were both dangerously ill, and in no position to receive a guest. In that climate, however, in a very large house, and surrounded by willing negroes, the responsibility of a hostess may be minimized, and Philip Gosse took up his abode in a suite of lightly furnished rooms without disturbing the Colemans.

The position of Bluefields was one not only of exceptional beauty, but of singular convenience to a collecting zoologist. It lies a little above the sea, on a gentle slope, with steep woods rising to the back of it, and a noisy rivulet, always exquisitely fresh, brawling under its bamboos and guava trees down to the sea through the heart of the estate. Behind the house, a ride of four or five miles leads to the summit of the lofty Bluefields Mountain, from which the south-western coast of Jamaica is seen as in a map from South Negril to Grand Pedro Bluff, with " the sparkling Caribbean Sea stretching away to the far, far distant horizon " in the direction of Cuba. On his first ascent, the naturalist was charmed with an unexpected scene on the very brow of the mountain, for this is cultivated as a garden of allspice, and around each tree a group of negro children were plucking the aromatic twigs in clusters, while flocks of green parrots and parroquets were shooting from bough to bough, and screaming discordantly as they went. The very Peak itself is densely covered with primal forest, "all," as he says, "in the rude luxuriant wildness that it bore in the days when the glories of these Hesperides first broke upon the astonished eyes of Europeans."

In every direction the neighbourhood of Bluefields proved to be a rich field for zoological investigation. The mountain-forest rose on one hand ; the seashore, with its wall of mangroves, was stretched upon the other ; while close around the house the grove of avocado-pear trees, a dozen acres of open pasture, the low walls festooned with creepers, the valley of the rivulet, the orchid-nurseries on the trunks of the straggling calabash trees, all formed so many happy hunting grounds at the very threshold of home. Gosse's first anxiety was to send something of value back by the *Caroline*, on her return voyage. Without, therefore, settling down to any very systematic labour, he hastily set about forming a small collection of the *Oncidiums*, *Angræcums*, and other orchids which he found growing in the angles of the calabashes, and in gathering land-shells, of which he sent back a cabinet of seven hundred and fifty specimens. These, with the addition of a few birds, sponges, and ferns, being despatched, he had time to turn round and consider himself at home.

He found himself unable to take the whole trouble of collecting without much loss of time, and therefore, on January 1, 1845, he engaged a negro lad of eighteen, Samuel Campbell by baptism and Sam by name, to give him his entire services for a salary of four dollars a month. This arrangement continued until the naturalist returned to England, and proved eminently successful. He says :—

" Sam soon approved himself a most useful assistant
" by his faithfulness, his tact in learning, and then his
" skill in practising the art of preparing natural subjects,
" his patience in pursuing animals, his powers of obser-
" vation of facts, and the truthfulness with which he
" reported them, as well as by the accuracy of his
" memory with respect to species. Often and often,
" when a thing has appeared to me new, I have appealed
" to Sam, who on a moment's examination would reply,
" ' No, we took this in such a place, or on such a day,'
" and I invariably found on my return home that his
" memory was correct. I never knew him in the slightest
" degree attempt to embellish a fact, or report more than
" he had actually seen."

Sam became so intelligent and serviceable, that, at length, he could be trusted upon expeditions of his own, and he added not a few specimens, and some of them unique, to the general collection.

For a long time, almost the only breaks in the tranquil life at Bluefields were occasional visits to Savannah-le-Mar. After the silence of the week, Saturday would present a scene of unusual bustle, and not less than one hundred persons would assemble at sunrise on the beach at Bluefields, a population drained from many square miles of the interior. Three or four canoes, laden with fruit and vegetables, are slowly packed for the market of Savannah-le-Mar, and but little room is left for the legs of any would-be passengers :

" The jabber is immense ; a hundred negroes, many of
" them women, all talking at once, make no small noise ;

"and the white teeth are perpetually shining out in the
"sable faces, as the merry laugh—the negro's own
"laugh—rises continually. The figures of the women,
"many of them not ungraceful, though plump and
"muscular, are picturesque, clad in short gowns of
"showy colours, and wearing the peculiarly set handker-
"chief for a head-dress, in form of a turban, often also
"of bright hues, though in most cases white as snow.
"They move about amongst the bustle, crowding up to
"the canoes to stow their ware ; tucking up their frocks
"still higher as the depth of water increases, regardless
"of displaying their bronzed legs. At the edge of the
"water, on whose mirror-like surface the mounting sun
"begins to pour torridly, the little children sit, sucking
"cane or oranges, while the elder ones play about them,
"helping to augment the noise."

It was during one of these occasional visits to Savannah-
le-Mar that he received the news of his father's death.
Almost immediately after Philip's departure for Jamaica,
the old gentleman had been seized with an ailment which
defied medical skill ; it proved fatal on November 26, 1844,
while his son was crossing the Atlantic. Mr. Thomas Gosse
was serene in mind to the last, and died apparently without
pain, and almost without a sigh, conscious, but entirely
tranquil. He would, in eight months more, have completed his eightieth year. The only thing which fluttered
in the calm of his resigned cheerfulness was the memory
of one of those hopeless works in prose and verse which
he had so vainly urged upon the publishers for more than
half a century. His latest words referred to an epic poem,
The Impious Rebellion, that he thought he had, on one of the
last occasions upon which he walked out, left for inspection
with Messrs. Blackwood, at their London agents'. He was
doomed, however, to live and die inedited, and when his

heirs inquired for *The Impious Rebellion*, behold ! as rare things will, it had vanished.

Philip Gosse's life at Bluefields now took an almost mechanical uniformity. The house was, as has been said, a well-built mansion ; it was raised, in the colonial fashion, high above the ground, so that its dwelling-rooms were reached by climbing an exterior staircase. The naturalist had no return of those malarial symptoms which had troubled him in Alabama. His health in Jamaica was very good, at all events during the first year, and his spirits excellent. He attributed his good health in great measure to the tonic waters of the Paradise River, the foaming and brawling rivulet which danced through the estate on its way to the ocean. In a hollow of the lime-stone rock, under a little cascade, he was in the habit of taking a long cool bath every day at noon, under the shadow of the bamboos, lounging here for half an hour at a time. On one occasion, he was lying motionless, just beneath the surface, when he observed that a vulture was beginning " to descend in circles, swooping over me, nearer and nearer at every turn, until at length the shadow of his gaunt form swept close between my face and the light, and the rushing of his wide-spread wings fanned my body as he passed. It was evident that he had mistaken me for a drowned corpse ; and probably it was the motion of my open eyes, as I followed his course, that told him all was not quite right, and kept him sailing round in low circles, instead of alighting." Here, too, in languid passages of the day, Philip Gosse would sit and fish for mullet with pieces of avocado pear, or grope for crayfish with a fish-pot.

These, however, were his idler moments, and in such he did not very often indulge. He would commonly set forth, about daybreak, in company with Sam, riding into the forest, alighting to gather shells, orchids, or insects, and pausing to shoot birds. At first, he was fain to borrow a gun when he could, but after a month or two, as he saw the paramount importance of making a special study of the birds of the island, he bought himself a gun, and was never without it. He was disappointed in the insects, and especially in the butterflies, which he found, at all seasons of the year, to be far less numerous than he had anticipated. Butterflies could be obtained but casually, and moths were still more rare. He had brought with him, on purpose, a bull's-eye lantern, so useful an instrument in the hands of northern entomologists, but although he repeatedly took it out after nightfall, searching in every direction, he never made a single capture in Jamaica by this means. There were one or two local exceptions to this general scarcity; a certain mile on the road above Content was alive with insects, and most of the specimens Gosse secured were captured in this one locality, which did not appear to differ in any other way from all neighbouring places where no beetles or butterflies could be found. When he was at home, or during the periods of tropical rain, he was actively engaged in drying and packing his plants, preparing his birds, wrapping up his orchids, cleansing his shells, and putting all these captures into a proper condition to be sent off to his sale agent in London. He made seven successive shipments to England during his stay in the island, and all of these arrived in favourable condition. He had become very adroit in the preparation of specimens for transit by sea, and, except in orchids, suffered few and inconsiderable losses.

It might be supposed that a missionary station was not a favourable centre for the pursuit of scientific enterprise. But this was not the case. Gosse's sympathies were with the Moravians, and their gentle manners won his affections. To collect " bush " and " vermin " was, no doubt, eccentric;

but, then, the whole habit of life at the Moravian settlement was averse to rule and tradition of every kind. In this collection of odd, pietistic, and irregular white men, surrounded by an emotional crowd of affectionate and half-converted blacks, nothing was considered irregular, except regularity. They were exceedingly averse to anything which savoured of formality, even in their religion, and one or two of the leaders, after the lengthy Sunday services, would go out with their guns on horseback for the purpose of "testifying" against any supposed sanctity in the Lord's Day as a day. If on their side they never criticized or disturbed the naturalist, he on his was much interested in their form of Christianity. It is true that some of their oddities puzzled him. He notes in his journal, after the first meeting at which he was present, which lasted six mortal hours, "the great weariness of body which so long a sitting induced prevented me from enjoying the occasion nearly so much as I had anticipated." But he soon fell into their ways, and consented to help them in their services. It was presently proposed that he should preach each alternate Sunday at a coffee plantation called Content, fifteen miles east of Bluefields, high up in the mountains.

This proposal fell in well with his scientific projects, for the fauna and flora of Content differed very considerably from those of Bluefields, and represented a less marine atmosphere and a higher altitude. There was a little cottage at Content, romantically perched on a mass of bare rock under the shadow of the mountain, and here he made it a practice to lodge for three or four days every fortnight, shooting and collecting in the vicinity. In this way he would ride far into the interior, sometimes staying all night at a hospitable planter's house, and becoming thoroughly acquainted with the aspect and the products of this part of the colony—never before or since, perhaps, visited by any

one accustomed to express his observations in words. His
Naturalist's Sojourn in Jamaica is full of exquisite descriptions of the varied and picturesque scenery of the interior
of the island.

His most delightful memories in later years were associated with one particular series of scenes, which he visited,
perhaps, more often than any other. A lonely road led
over the shoulder of Bluefields Mountain to a half-de-
serted coffee plantation called Rotherhithe. Philip Gosse
was frequently accustomed to rise two hours before dawn,
and, sitting loosely in the saddle, to ride slowly up this
romantic ascent by the light of the stars, "listening," as
he says, "to the rich melodies poured forth by dozens
of mocking-birds from the fruit trees and groves of the
lower hills," managing to arrive at the brow of the mountain at sunrise. Then he would leave his horse, and,
"throwing the bridle over his neck, allow him to graze on
a little open pasture until my return," while he would
pursue on foot the road towards Rotherhithe which has
been mentioned. This was the haunt of several rare birds
of peculiar interest—of the eccentric jabbering crow, of the
solitaire, and of the long-tailed humming-bird. It was
fascinating, in intervals of labour, "to sit on a fallen log
in the cool shadow, surrounded by beauty and fragrance,
listening to the broken hymns of the solitaires, and watching the humming-birds that sip fearlessly around your
head, and ever and anon come and peep close under the
brim of your broad Panama hat,—as if to say, 'Who are
you that come intruding into our peculiar domain?'"

One great difficulty which Philip Gosse met with was
the absence of all scientific sympathy in Jamaica. He
could not hear of any other naturalist, native or imported,
who was working in earnest at the fauna of the island.
At length, however, his inquiries were rewarded by news of

a gentleman at Spanish Town, a magistrate and leading planter of the name of Richard Hill, who was understood to shoot birds and to preserve their skins. To him, then, wholly without introduction, Philip Gosse had the happy inspiration to write in the autumn of 1845, and the result was such as to make him wish that he had written a year earlier. The following was the very agreeable reply which he received :—

" Spanish Town, November 6, 1845.

"DEAR SIR,

"On the receipt of your letter, I took down from "my bookshelves *The Canadian Naturalist*, and finding "the same 'P. H.' preceding your name there, as in "your letter, I perceived that you were already known "to me. I acknowledge with pleasure the receipt of "your communication, and, as an earnest of my desire "to assist in turning your time to profit during your "sojourn among us, I send you a list of the birds of this "country, both migratory and stationary, which are "common to us with Central and Northern America. "As I have set them down from the list of the prints of "Musignano, you will be in no uncertainty as to the "objects to which I direct your attention. The advan-"tage of this list to you will consist in the number of "birds with which your North American experience "will make you intimately acquainted. I have added "another list containing what may be considered our "peculiar ornithology. I have given with this such of "the scientific names as I can determine with cer-"tainty.

"My peculiar walk in natural history has been con-"fined to birds, with the view of illustrating that branch "of our local history ; in other departments my ac-

"quaintance is only general. Our vertebrate animals
"consist but of the agouti, *Dasyprocta;* and the aleo,
"a dog now extinct, but common as a domestic com-
"panion of the Indians at the time of the discovery.
"You will find that it was a curly-haired, brown variety
"of the Mexican terrier, now so generally known as
"the favourite lap-dog called the Mexican mopsy, the
"Mexican being the white woolly variety. Our reptiles
"are not numerous, but they are new to the naturalist ;
"the alligator and the pretty changeable anolis, with the
"dilatable gorge, being almost the only ones yet de-
"scribed to European readers. Our fishes have scarcely
"been made the subject of investigation. Dr. Parnell,
"of the British Museum, who was in this island some
"four years ago, attended, however, exclusively to this
"field of inquiry, in conjunction with the reptiles. On
"your return to Europe, you will be able to determine
"from your own observations in these two departments
"of vertebrata by the ascertained species in the British
"Museum.

"I have nearly completed a series of papers on the
"migratory instincts of birds, with a view of illus-
"trating our ornithology, intending, after the manner of
"Alfred de Malherbe in his *Faune Ornithologique de la
"Sicile,* to describe what was particularly our own, and
"to direct attention to the published descriptions already
"known of those that were common to us and the
"neighbouring continent.

"In our *Jamaica Almanac,* from 1840 to 1843 inclusive,
"you will see all that I have published on our local
"natural history, if I except some few papers on
"insects in the Royal Agricultural Society's *Reporter.*
"I write you hurriedly, having our quarter sessions
"sitting, and with little time at my disposal; but I

"shall not fail to renew my intercourse with you, if
"you should in any further communication desire it.
"With much respect, pray believe me to be, dear sir,
"Very faithfully yours,
"RICHARD HILL."

This was the opening passage in one of the warmest
and most intimate friendships of my father's life, assiduously cultivated long after his departure from Jamaica,
and not wholly interrupted until the death of Mr. Hill. In
1851, when sending the preface of his *Naturalist's Sojourn
in Jamaica* to the press, Philip Gosse wrote that he considered it "one of the happiest reminiscences of a visit
unusually pleasant, that it gave him the acquaintance of a
gentleman whose talents and acquirements would have
done honour to any country, but whose excellences as a
man of science, as a gentleman, and as a Christian, shine
with peculiar lustre in the comparative seclusion of his
native island;" and he insisted, in the face of his friend's
modest entreaties, in appending the words "assisted by
Richard Hill" to the title-page of each of his own Jamaica
volumes. They did not meet till 1846, on an occasion
which shall presently be described.

In October, 1845, Gosse had occasion to visit the north
coast of the island of Jamaica, his friend Mr. Deleon
offering him a seat in his gig. He had thus the opportunity of crossing the country twice, and of seeing the
interior to advantage; but he found it, from the scientific
point of view, disappointing. They passed, among other
things, the remote plantation of Shuttlewood, remarkable
from the circumstance that it was here that a bag of grass
seed, brought from Africa to be the food for a cage of
finches, was emptied out upon the fertile soil, and in due
time became the nucleus from which guinea-grass, one of

the best pastures in the West Indies, spread to all parts of Jamaica. The approach to the town of Montego Bay was very fine, and so clear was the atmosphere that the highlands of Cuba, ninety miles away, were seen faintly on the north-western horizon. Philip Gosse was the guest while at Montego Bay of Mr. and Mrs. J. L. Lewin. With this gentleman he had already corresponded on zoological questions, and had obtained useful notes from him. The naturalist's experience in the north of Jamaica was sufficient to persuade him that he had done perfectly right to settle in the southern district of the island. He found the fauna and flora in the country of St. James distinctly more scanty and less valuable than in his own Westmoreland and St. Elizabeth. This was the most extensive of many excursions which he took from the central stations of Bluefields and Content, sometimes riding out until nightfall, and trusting to the never-failing Jamaica hospitality to supply him with a bed.

For a whole year his health was excellent, and even when Sam got the fever in consequence of their explorations in damp hot hollows of the forest, his master escaped scot-free. Towards the end of December, 1845, however, after stalking yellow bitterns for a day or two in the morass, and ending up with several hours spent knee-deep in the deep mud of the fœtid creek, getting pot-shots at pelicans and kingfishers, both the white naturalist and the black one were laid up with a very sharp attack of fever. Four days later, they were both down in the creek morass again, shooting snipe and ground-doves, but from this time forth Philip Gosse was liable to violent headaches and sickness at quickly recurring intervals. He consequently began to put his house in order, cataloguing his captures and preparing to leave the country.

On March 3, 1846, he rode with Sam to Savannah-le-

Mar, and took berth on board the steamer *Earl of Elgin*, which was coasting eastwards. After a day's pleasant steaming along the south shore of Jamaica, they got into Kingston Harbour at nightfall. The tossing of the Caribbean Sea was exchanged for the smooth surface of the land-locked harbour, over which a flock of gulls were flying and hovering. He proceeded to a noisy hot hotel, where the contrast with the still cool nights of Bluefields, scarcely broken by the note of a bird or a bat, kept him awake till near morning, or at least till long after a riotous party of billiard-players had finally decided to break up. He rose early and walked about the dirty and unattractive capital of Jamaica. Having despatched a note to Mr. Richard Hill, in Spanish Town, to announce his arrival, he paid some calls, and drove out a little way into the country, to find, on his return to the hotel, that Mr. Hill had instantly responded to his summons, and was in the parlour waiting to welcome him. This was the first meeting of the brother ornithologists. The next day Mr. Hill did the honours of Kingston, and in particular took Gosse to the rooms of the Jamaica Society, where they examined together Dr. Anthony Robinson's drawings of birds and plants. The specimens in the town museum were few and in wretched preservation, yet the objects in themselves mostly good. By the afternoon train the friends left Kingston for Spanish Town, and spent the evening in examining a large collection of drawings of birds, made by Richard Hill himself.

Philip Gosse's brief stay at Spanish Town was made extremely pleasant to him by the assiduous hospitalities of Richard Hill. On the 10th, in company with Mr. Hill and a young collector, Mr. Osborne, who had been invited to meet the English naturalist, Sam and the latter ascended Highgate, a peak of the Liguanea Mountains, about three thousand feet above the sea. From this point there is a famous view, which has several times been described ; not only does the sinuous southern coast of Jamaica lie spread out before the spectator, but the northern sea, near Annotto Bay, can also be seen shining between the peaks. The ascent occupied six hours, and when another hour had been spent in searching for shells and insects, it was time to take shelter for the night in a house under the brow of the mountains. Here the temperature was delightfully cold, and the travellers were even glad to roll blankets around them in their beds. Next morning they gazed again on the magnificence of the unrivalled prospect at their feet, but soon after sunrise it was necessary to start for Spanish Town. He thus describes the drive back in his journal (March 11, 1846) :—

"We returned by a different route, skirting the sum-
"mits of the Liguanea Mountains, and passing through
"smiling plantations, in order to descend into the
"romantic parish of St. Thomas in the Vale. After a
"while, we crossed and recrossed, many times, the
"winding Rio d'Oro, and at length entered the magnifi-
"cent gorge called the Bog Walk (i.e. *bocacaz*, a sluice),
"through which runs the Cobre, formed by the union of
"the Negro and the D'Oro. The road lay for four
"miles through this deep gorge, by the side of the river,
"and afforded at every turn fresh scenes of surpassing
"wildness, grandeur, and beauty. The rock often rose
"to a great height on each side, leaving only room for
"the rushing stream which seemed to have cleft its
"course, and the narrow pathway at its side. Some-
"times, across the river, the side of the ravine receded
"in the form of a very steep but sloping mountain,
"covered with a forest of large timber, and so clear of
"underwood, that the eye could peer far up into its

"gloomy recesses. Here and there the course of the
" river was dammed up by islets; some of them mere
" masses of dark rock, others adorned with the elegant
" waving plumes of the graceful bamboo. But the most
" remarkable object was the immense rock called
" Gibraltar, which rises on the opposite bank of the
" river, from the water's edge, absolutely perpendicular,
" to the height of five or six hundred feet; a broad mass
"of limestone, twice as high as St. Paul's."

At nightfall the same day, their carriage drove into the
streets of Spanish Town. Two or three days later, the
friends began a revised list of the birds of Jamaica, the
discoveries of each being able to fill up gaps in the experience of the other; and this was the occupation of each
successive evening. On the 17th they finished their list,
making out 184 species of birds more or less clearly. Sam
was all this time actively engaged on daily excursions,
usually alone, and he rarely failed to bring home at night
at least one interesting rarity. The next day the friends
betook themselves to Kingston, and in the rooms of the
Jamaica Society carefully compared their list of birds with
that in Robinson's manuscripts. It should here be explained that Dr. Anthony Robinson, a surgeon practising
in Jamaica in the middle of the eighteenth century, had
left behind him a very valuable mass of information on
the zoology and botany of the island, which had been
preserved, in five folio volumes, in the archives of the
Jamaica Society in Kingston. " The specific descriptions,
admeasurements, and details of colouring," Philip Gosse
wrote in reference to these collections, " are executed with
an elaborate accuracy worthy of a period of science far
in advance of that in which Robinson lived, and accompanying the manuscripts are several volumes of carefully
executed drawings, mostly coloured." On March 23,

Philip Gosse, accompanied by the ever-faithful Sam, took leave of his hospitable friend, and started from Kingston in the coasting steamer *The Wave.* An easterly breeze from Port Royal carried them roughly but swiftly back to Bluefields, the captain making a special exception in the naturalist's favour by dropping the two passengers at Bluefields, instead of carrying them on to Savannah-le-Mar. No one had ever enjoyed this privilege before, and the wanderers were welcomed with as much bewilderment as delight. They had been exactly three weeks away from home, three weeks which formed a delightful oasis of intellectual excitement in Philip Gosse's monotonous existence. He had left Bluefields dispirited and poorly; he returned in buoyant health and spirits.

He once more fell into the regular and monotonous life of the collector, riding out to shoot every day, sending Sam, and other lads whom he had trained, into the forest for plants and insects, and spending his evenings in preparing his captives for the transit to England. On June 18, 1846, he rather suddenly determined to bring his stay at Bluefields to a close, and sent to the bay to engage a passage for himself and Sam on board a sloop, or *drogger*, which was just starting for Kingston. His parting with the kind and faithful Colemans was a pathetic one, and when he set foot on the vessel, he turned "to gaze for the last time at a place where I have spent so many pleasant months." The voyage occupied seven dreary days, mitigated by a day agreeably spent on shore, at Black River, with some friends. He had the pleasant consciousness, while knocking about under Pedro Bluff, that the English packet, which he had hoped to catch, must be then just leaving Kingston. On the morning of the last day (June 26) he had a curious and very embarrassing experience. While lying in the berth of the little close cabin, he was awakened by a severe twinge in the side of his neck; on putting his hand to the place, he took hold of some object which was so firmly fastened to the flesh that it required a sharp tug to make it let go. By the dim light of the cabin-lamp he discovered that he had caught, fortunately by the tail, a large scorpion. The pain was sharp, but perhaps not greater than that of a wasp-sting; the wound swelled rapidly, but, being rubbed with rum by the old skipper, speedily healed. "One of the most curious of the results was a numbness of some of the nerves of the tongue, perceptible in the *papillæ* of the surface, which felt as if dead."

They entered Kingston Harbour that night, and finding that, as he anticipated, he had missed the packet, Philip Gosse took lodgings in the town, not altogether displeased to be forced to see something more of the capital of Jamaica. Next day he engaged a berth on board the steamer *Avon*, which was to sail on July 9. He met Richard Hill, by a fortunate accident, that same afternoon, and received from him the welcome news that the Jamaica Society had resolved to entrust him with the Anthony Robinson manuscripts to take with him to Europe. He went up then and there to the society's rooms, and secured these valuable papers. After a fortnight, divided between Spanish Town and Kingston, and much spoiled by the distress of an ulcerated leg, he at length said farewell to his friends and to Jamaica, Richard Hill waving adieu to him from the quay at Kingston, and another friend, Dr. Fairbank, kindly accompanying him, for company's sake, so far as Port Royal. His last glimpse of Jamaica was the twinkling of the lighthouse on Point Morant. Next day, at daybreak, the mountains of Hayti were visible, and "during the whole day we ran along the great promontory of Tiburon, the ancient province of Xavagna, once the happy domain of the beautiful and unfortunate Princess Anacaona." On the following morning, when he came on deck, the *Avon* was putting off mails in the land-locked harbour of Jacmel, in Hayti. " There had been rain in the night, and the shaggy hill-tops were partially robed in fragments of cloud, undefined and changing, which contrasted finely with the dark surface of the forest. Inland the mountains in the morning sun looked inviting ; and I noticed that they displayed the same singular resemblance to crumpled paper, as those in the eastern part of Jamaica."

The *Avon* steamed across to Puerto Rico, and ran, all through the 13th, along the northern shore of that island, " the land thickly strewn with cultivated estates, spotted with clumps of trees, and presenting a very beautiful appearance, contrasting in this respect with both Jamaica and Hayti, whose forest coasts display little trace of cultivation, and look rude and uninviting." Soon after noon, the Moro, or fortification which protects the town of San Juan, was in sight, like a white wall projecting into the sea, and four hours later the steamer moored under it.

" The town, walled and strongly fortified, reminded " me, with its turret-like houses, and little balconies to " each window, of engravings of Spanish cities ; and " when I went ashore and wandered through the streets, " ladies in black mantillas, opening and shutting their " fans as they walked, solemn priests in black robes and " shovel hats, the children, the men, the *posadas* (taverns), " everything had such a novel character as I had never " before seen. For, in all my travels, I have never before " set foot in any other country than such as are inha- " bited by the Anglo-Saxon race. After partaking of a " little nicety in a *posada*, and seeing the paved parts of

" the town, I and a single companion who had separated
" from the main party found that we could not get a
" boat for less than four dollars, for about fifteen minutes'
" rowing.   The steamer, however, was under way, and
" we had no alternative but to pay it, and I found that
" my afternoon's stroll had cost me half a guinea."

The reason of his separation from the others was that
they had all trooped into the cathedral, where Philip
Gosse's strong conscientious objection to the Roman
Catholic forms of worship made it impossible for him to
follow them.   To the end of his days he never, on one
single occasion, entered what it was his uncompromising
habit to call a "popish mass-house."

A little before daybreak next morning, the steamer got
into the Danish harbour of St. Thomas.   Though it
rained hard until after sunrise, and the mist enveloped the
hills, yet the beauty of the town, rising from the sea on
the sides of three conical mountains, could not be concealed.   Gosse walked a little way into the bush, and
captured fifty-two insects, almost all of them new to him,
among which were some fine and curious *Curculionidæ*
and *Longicorns.*   In the evening he took another pleasant,
though rather fatiguing walk, and saw the Slip, "a noble
work on which the largest ships can be hauled up and
repaired."   Next morning he again entomologized in the
bush, and captured fifty-four insects.   He saw all the
sights of St. Thomas, visited the Moravian mission, "called
on Mr. Nathan, the Chief Rabbi, a very friendly and gentleman-like man," and went back to the steamer to sleep.
At sunrise on the 16th, they quitted the beautiful harbour
of St. Thomas, having received many new passengers, and
steamed north for Bermuda.   These two slight excursions,
at San Juan and St. Thomas, were the only occasions,
during the whole of my father's life, when he stepped on
land that was not Anglo-Saxon.

On the 20th the *Avon* arrived at Bermuda, where the traveller "admired the English-looking beauty of the islands, divided into fields and strewn with pretty white houses." Off the small island of Ireland, the goods and passengers were transferred to the steamer *Clyde*, and the *Avon* made her way back to Havannah. Scarcely had the former vessel started eastward on the following day, than Philip Gosse was attacked with violent headache. The symptoms of brain fever rapidly displayed themselves, and for a fortnight he was very dangerously ill. On August 4 he was permitted by the ship's doctor to creep up on deck for the first time, and to enjoy the pleasing sight of the Land's End, dimly visible at a distance of twenty-five miles. Next day, still very weak and wretched, yet steadily gaining strength, he was put on shore at Southampton, and enjoyed a long sleep in an hotel bed. Next morning (August 6, 1846) he took an early train for London, reached his mother to find her well, and had the satisfaction, in unpacking his specimens, to discover all uninjured. Moreover his living birds, which some kind person on board the steamer had attended to during his brain fever, were in good health, only two, the blue pigeon and the mountain witch, having died.

My father's single episode of tropical life had now closed. It had been in every respect a signally successful one. Those theoretical zoologists who had encouraged him to go out to Jamaica were satisfied, and far more than satisfied, with the practical result of his labours. The chronicle of his life in Jamaica is monotonous, because it was so crowded with scientific incident. He stuck to his work, and not a single week-day passed in which he did not add something to his experience.

CHAPTER VIII.

LITERARY WORK IN LONDON.

1846—1851.

THE record of the next two years is scanty. They were spent in close retirement and in almost incessant literary labour. Philip Gosse came back from Jamaica considerably altered and matured; from a belated youth he had slipped rather suddenly into premature middle age. The climate of the West Indies, his solitary conditions there, coinciding with a period of life which is often critical, had their effect upon his person and his temperament. It may be well, at this point, to give some description of the former, which underwent no further perceptible change for many years. He was under middle size; slight, and almost slim, when he had left England, he returned from Jamaica thick-set and heavy-limbed, troubled with a corpulence that was not quite healthy. His face was large and massive, extremely pallid, with great strength in the chin, and long, tightly compressed lips; decidedly grim in expression, but lighted up by hazel eyes of extraordinary size and fulness. These eyes, which have been compared (I suppose more with regard to their luminous character than their shape) with the eyes of Lord Beaconsfield, were the most obvious peculiarity of the face, which was, nevertheless, chiefly remarkable, to a careful observer, for the tense and exalted nature of the expression it habitually wore. Nothing was

more common, even among my father's own family, than
for a person who approached him with the design of asking
a question or making a remark, to hesitate, scared by his
apparent austerity. No one can doubt that, without intending to be so, he was often not a little awe-inspiring.
This was partly caused by his introspective habit of mind,
self-contained in meditation; partly also by his extreme
timidity, which found a shelter under this severe and
awful mien. Very often, when the person who approached
him wondered whether those oracular lips would fulminate,
the oracle himself was only speculating how soon he could
flee away into his study and be at rest. The air of
severity was increased by the habit of brushing his straight
black hair tightly away from the forehead; it was occasionally removed by a cloud of immeasurable tenderness
passing across the great brown lustrous orbs of his eyes.
His smile was rare, but when it came it was exquisite.*

That his standard, both for himself and others, was high,
and that his manner towards an offender could be formidable, it would be easy to prove. At this juncture one
striking example may suffice. One of the difficulties of
the Moravian mission at Bluefields had been the unalter-
able prejudice against treating the negroes as exact
equals with white men and women. It was especially
hard to overcome the feeling of shame and repulsion with
which West Indian society regarded the idea of mixed
marriages between whites and blacks. To the Moravians,
however, it appeared that no difference should be made
when the Church had received members of the two races

---

* A very remarkable accidental portrait of my father, as he looked when he
was about sixty years of age, exists in the museum at Brussels. Philip Gosse
might have sat for the man, holding a crimson missal, who kneels in the left-
hand wing of the triptych, by Bernard van Orley (No. 40 in the Catalogue),
except that the nose is too large and flat. The eyes and mouth, the general
form of the face, and the colour of the skin are marvellously identical.

to a like communion, and a certain person, apparently to gain prestige with the body, had expressed himself willing to marry a converted negro girl, and had gone through the ceremony of betrothal at Bluefields.   But on his returning to England no more had been heard of him, and Philip Gosse was commissioned to remind him of his promise. He did so immediately on his own arrival in London, and received a flippant reply.   To this he returned the following answer :—

"I have received your note of yesterday. I cannot
"say that it would give me any pleasure to see you,
"knowing as I do your behaviour to Sister Stevens. I
"desire to write in a humiliating sense of my own failure,
"yet in faithfulness I must say that the whole affair,
"the breaking of a solemn engagement, the coolness
"with which you could crush a sister's happiness, and
"above all the insincerity, I had almost said the duplicity,
"which has marked your whole course in it, renders any
"communion with you out of the question. I cannot
"help believing, with almost a moral certainty, that even
"when you recorded your betrothal before the Church at
"Bluefields, you had not even the slightest intention of
"returning to fulfil it. And when the tenor of your
"letters began to intrude painful suspicions on our
"minds, and Coleman and myself felt constrained to-
"wards you, your replies (at least that to me) insinu-
"ated that you were still unchanged in intention, and
"that *your health* was the only obstacle.   But when
"I read (I cannot help adding *with indignation*) in your
"late letters to Sister S. your heartless breach of
"promise, a breach which would evoke the scorn of
"every worldly man of honourable feeling, and which
"in a court of law would be visited with heavy damages,

"I saw at once how egregiously our love and confidence
"had been misplaced. I know not the nature of the
"purification of which you speak, but if this is the fruit
"of it, I desire not to know it.

　"Perhaps you may think I am severe ; I write not in
"bitterness, but in grief. To me the transaction seems
"a very shocking one ; and it is not the least painful
"trait in it, that you can write of it so lightly, as if it were
"an everyday matter. I trust the Lord may trouble
"your conscience about it, which I had much rather see
"than your present complacency ; to Him I leave you.

"Remaining

"Yours in much sorrow,

"P. H. GOSSE."

The conditions under which Philip Gosse had gone out
to Jamaica, and those under which he now returned, may
be gathered from the following letter addressed to the
well-known collector of natural objects, Mr. W. W.
Saunders :—

"Dalston, August 8, 1846.

"MY DEAR SIR,

　　"Your favour of the 16th of April, acknow-
"ledging the receipt of the first consignment of woods,
"was received in due course. In May I shipped another
"lot of specimens, and that vessel, I understand, has
"been here some little time. That I did not write by
"her, giving you an account of the consignment, was
"owing to the fact that I believed myself on the point
"of sailing for England by the steamer ; and, fully ex-
"pecting to be in England long before the specimens,
"I intended to write to you from London. I was, how-
"ever, strangely disappointed of two successive packets,

P

"and am now only just arrived by the *Clyde*. I have
"taken some pains to ascertain the botanical names of
" the woods, but have not succeeded in all cases. What-
"ever little personal trouble I have been at in procuring
" these woods, I beg you to consider has been undertaken
"*con amore*. It is but a very small return for the kind-
"ness you exhibited towards me in so very promptly
"advancing me aid when I was rather short of cash.
" Any allusion to pecuniary remuneration, direct or
" *indirect*, for this, will only grieve my feelings, so that
" you will permit me gratefully to decline it. The
" expenses actually incurred I have no objection to your
"refunding, though it will be pleasing to me if you will
" accept this also. But as you might find this disagree-
" able, I enclose a little note of the expenses incurred in
"procuring and shipping the specimens. Should you
"have an opportunity of seeing Mr. John A. Hankey,
" I beg that you will present my compliments to him,
"with cordial thanks for his politeness in allowing my
" specimens of natural history to pass freight free."

It appears from this letter, and from other documents,
that, eminently successful as the Jamaica trip had been, it
had not led to any definite addition to Gosse's means of
income. He had supported himself with independence in
the West Indies, and he had brought back, in addition to
his sales, a collection of miscellaneous objects for which he
slowly found purchasers ; but he had no security for the
future. The British Museum proposed another excursion,
this time to the Azores, and he made some preliminaries
towards starting in the winter of 1846, bought a Portuguese grammar, learned the mode of arriving at Fayal
from Madeira, and began a list of Azorean desiderata.
But the scheme fell through, mainly because an abundance

of literary work immediately came in his way, and promised to be quite as lucrative as a tropical excursion and much less laborious. He was very properly anxious, moreover, to give due literary form to the ornithological discoveries which he had made in the West Indies, and before he had been a month in London, he began to write for Mr. Van Voorst his volume on *The Birds of Jamaica,* which he completed in the following March. This was one of the most important and compendious of his works, and he tempered the strain of its composition by compiling, at the same time, for his old friends the Society for Promoting Christian Knowledge, a volume on *The Monuments of Ancient Egypt,* which, however, was not published until November, 1847. This book professes to be no more than "a plain treatise for plain people," and Philip Gosse had no first-hand knowledge of archæology. He was, however, helped in writing it by two distinguished Egyptologists—Dr. Samuel Birch, of the British Museum, and the Rev. G. C. Renouard, Rector of Swanscombe, in Kent. It is, of course, long since obsolete, but it ran with esteem through several editions.

The Birds of Jamaica was published on May 1, 1847, and was received with great respect by the world of science. He says, in one of his letters, speaking of this book, "It sells rather slowly, but every one praises it, and it has been well reviewed in Germany." The publication of *The Birds of Jamaica* raised Philip Gosse's reputation with a bound, and among those ornithologists who took this opportunity of making his personal acquaintance, and gave expression to their admiration, were prominent Sir William Jardine, the Vicomte du Bus, John Gould, and D. W. Mitchell. The book filled a gap in the existing records of science, and it contrived to please two classes of readers, since, while its scientific definitions were accurate and detailed, no observation of habits and no characteristic anecdote was omitted to fill up the portrait of each successive bird. The only complaint which was made by the reviewers was the entire lack of illustrations, the absence of which was presently explained and removed, as we shall see in due course. On the title-page of *The Birds of Jamaica* the words "assisted by Richard Hill, Esq., of Spanish Town," succeeded the name of the author, although greatly against that modest gentleman's wish, and the publication was delayed by the fact that every sheet was sent out to Spanish Town to be read in proof by Mr. Hill. *The Birds of Jamaica* once launched, Philip Gosse immediately began, in a quiet way, that labour in the popularization of science which was ultimately to form so large a proportion of his life's work. Once more the S.P.C.K. suggested to him that a series of small volumes, strictly accurate from a scientific point of view, but giving zoological facts in a form easily to be comprehended by the public, would be of great service to the general reader. Nothing of the kind existed, and he gladly undertook to open such a series. He began the *Mammalia* in June, 1847, and it was published a year later, having occupied but a small part of those months. It was copiously illustrated with woodcuts designed by the author and by J. W. Whymper.

In the spring of 1847, while stooping to dig up gladiolus bulbs from the grass-plot of his friend, Mr. William Berger, my father was suddenly conscious of pain, apparently caused by a strain to the liver, and from this time forth, for fifteen years at least, he was more or less continuously subject to what was supposed to be dyspepsia, often very acute in character, and causing great depression of spirits. The fact that he was constantly reading and writing, and that he took no exercise of any kind, except a little work in his garden, did not improve matters. In the record of his career at this time, his religious life must not be omitted. After his return from Jamaica in 1846, he was for some time connected with no body of Christians, but in April of the following year he joined a few other persons, almost all of them educated men, in forming at Hackney a meeting of the communion then recently united, throughout England, under the title of " Brethren," or " Plymouth Brethren," as they were usually called, apparently from the circumstance that their central meeting was at Bristol, which, like Plymouth (where for some time they did not exist), is in the west of England. The tenets of this body are perhaps well known. They may be best described by a series of negations. The Brethren have no ritual, no appointed minister, no government, no hierarchy of any kind ; they eschew all that is systematic or vertebrate ; their manner of worship is the most socialistic hitherto invented. Their positive tenets are an implicit following of the text of Holy Scripture, the enforcement of adult baptism, subsequent upon conversion and preliminary to the partaking of the Lord's Supper in both kinds, the loaf of bread and the cup of wine being passed from hand to hand in silence, every Sunday morning.

Whether this interesting sect still exists in anything like its early simplicity I cannot say, but I think not. It is at all events certain that it very soon suffered from a violent split in its own corporation, if such a word may be used of a conglomeration of atoms, and that its obscure meetings became a byword for bigotry and unlovely prejudice. But in its beginning, and when Philip Gosse and his friends first gathered round a deal table in a bare room in Hackney, this Utopian dream of a Christian socialism, with all its simplicity, *naïveté*, and earnest faith, was one at which those who knew human nature better might smile, but which was neither ignoble nor unattractive. These early Brethren had at least one strong point. The absence from their ritual of any other book threw them upon the study of the Bible, and the fact that most of the founders of the sect were educated and, perhaps it may be added, somewhat eccentrically educated men, made their exposition of the Scripture deep, ingenious, and unconventional.

One result of these new religious ties was the formation of fresh scruples with regard to any action of a worldly kind. The Brethren held that it was the duty of the Christian to leave all revenge to God, to bow to injury and insult, and, above all, on no occasion to use any form of words stronger than affirmation. In the autumn of 1847, while Philip Gosse was looking into the window of a print shop, at the corner of Wellington Street, Strand, a boy picked his pocket of a silk handkerchief. A policeman saw the thief, caught him, and dragged him to Bow Street, where the victim of the theft was asked to prosecute; "but I," says my father in a letter recording the incident, "from Brethren's notions of grace, refused, and they would not restore me the handkerchief." Soon afterwards, while his mother, he, and the servant-maid were all out at meeting one Sunday morning, the house was broken open and robbed. A watch, some miniatures, and other valuables were stolen. The police came to make inquiries, but, for conscience' sake, the owner refused to take any steps in pursuit. I should add that the extreme punctilio of which these trifling occurrences are examples was afterwards modified; but my father always retained a great repugnance to the prosecution of individual criminals, though very severe on crime in the abstract.

Among those who met, with this austere simplicity, at

the meeting-room at Hackney, was a lady of American parentage, equally remarkable for her outward charms and her inward accomplishments. Of this lady, destined to take so large a part in the life of Philip Gosse, her only son may be permitted to give at this point a more particular account. Although Miss Emily Bowes was born in England, on November 10, 1806, both her father, William Bowes, and her mother, Hannah Troutbeck, were Bostonians of pure Massachusetts descent. Her people had taken the English side in 1775. When "the Boston teapot bubbled," her father—who had been duly baptized, as befitted a good Bostonian, by Dr. Samuel Cooper, at Brattle Street meeting-house—was hurried away by his parents, whose nerves the "tea-party" had shaken, to North Wales, where the family settled in the neighbourhood of Snowdon. But William Bowes, with his undiluted Massachusetts blood, had been forced to be a loyalist in vain, for, once grown to man's estate, to Boston he went back for a wife, and secured a New Englander as true as himself in Hannah, daughter of the Rev. John Troutbeck, formerly King's Chaplain in Boston, U.S.A. Mrs. Bowes was born in 1768, close to Governor Winthrop's house in South Street, Boston. She lived to be eighty-three, and the writer of these lines has been seated in her arms. In Dr. O. W. Holmes's words—

"She had heard the muskets' rattle of the April running battle;
   Lord Percy's hunted soldiers, she could see their red coats still,"

and, when he thinks of her, her grandson thrills with a divided patriotism.

Through her father, Miss Bowes was directly descended from one of the most distinguished families of New England. Her great-grandfather, Nicholas Bowes, of Boston, born in 1706, graduate of Harvard, and for twenty years minister of New Bedford, married Lucy Hancock, aunt of the famous Governor John Hancock, whose signature stands so big and bold on the Declaration of American Independence. Succeeding Boweses had intermarried into good Massachusetts families—Whitneys and Stoddards and Remingtons—and had thus preserved to an unusual extent the purity of their local strain.

Miss Emily Bowes had suffered from severe vicissitudes of fortune. Her infancy, and that of her two younger brothers, had been spent in moderate circumstances; but her father, who had a splendid capacity for the dispersion of wealth, had meanwhile inherited a large property and spent it, nearly to the last penny. Almost the only advantages which had accrued to his daughter from the few years of their opulence, were comprised in the very complete and extensive education which Mr. Bowes, proud of her intellectual gifts, had provided her. She was not only taught all that girls at that time were supposed capable of learning, but, at her own desire, excellent tutors had been engaged to ground her in Latin, in Greek, and even in Hebrew. She had great force of character and rapidity of action. When the crash came, her brothers were at that critical age when to pursue education a little further is the only means by which what has been learned can be made of any service in the future. Emily Bowes undertook the training of the boys, and when the time came for the eldest to go to college, she devoted the interest of her own small capital to his maintenance there, and went out as a governess that she might add to that scanty sum. A governess she remained until her brothers —excellent young men, but with none of her force of mind—were started in life, and then, with deep thankfulness, she retired from work to the irksomeness of which she preferred the most straitened independence. At the time that my father became acquainted with her, she was living in a very quiet way, keeping house in Clapton for her aged parents.

Emily Bowes was in her forty-third year when Philip Gosse first met her, but she retained a remarkable appearance of youth. Her figure was slim and tall, her neck of singular length and grace ; her face small, with rather large and regular features, clear blue eyes delicately set in pink lids, under arched and pencilled auburn eyebrows ; the mouth very sensitive, with something of the expression of Sir Joshua's little " Child with the Rat-Trap ; " the whole face surmounted by copious rolls and loops, in the fashion of the period, of orange-auburn hair. In earlier life the complexion had been brilliant, but almost the only sign of the passage of years, in 1848, was the pallor of the skin, which was, moreover, badly freckled. But for her complexion she would still have been a very pretty woman, of the type admired by the painters of to-day. She was painted several times, and in particular there existed of her a very amusing full-length oil portrait, by G. F. Joseph, A.R.A., which represented her in a pink satin dress, at the age of six, bareheaded and barelegged, on the top of Snowdon in a storm, with forked lightning playing behind her. This was hung, in its day, in the Royal Academy, and was stolen, alas ! a few years ago, by a person who certainly could obtain very little satisfaction from a theft which left our family sensibly poorer.

Miss Emily Bowes was one of those who had accepted the views of the Plymouth Brethren, and as there was no meeting of these Christians in Clapton, she was in the habit of walking over to Hackney on Sunday mornings, usually lunching there, and returning home after the evening meeting. In this manner she naturally formed the acquaintance of Philip Gosse, who was immediately attracted by her wide range of knowledge and by her literary tastes. She was the author of two little volumes of published poems of a religious cast ; she was almost as great a lover of verse as he was himself. She was sympathetic, gentle, quick, eminently intelligent. He, on the other hand, little accustomed to the company of any woman but his aged mother, felt himself awkward with girls. He had no small-talk, no common change of conversation. The charm of Emily Bowes lay in the maturity of her mind, the gravity of her tastes. Yet it was quite abruptly, and without premeditation, that he took the step of asking for her hand. It was on Sunday evening, September 17, 1848, that the sudden resolution took him as he was about to say farewell to her at her garden-gate. When he reflected that he had proposed marriage to her, and that she had not rejected him, there was a moment of intense remorse. He was too poor, he reflected, too little likely to make a proper competence, to have the right to link another life to his own. But she was accustomed to poverty, she loved him already, she believed in his future, and she was eminently careless about luxury. They were betrothed, and, after a short delay, they were married at Tottenham, on November 22, 1848, from the house of the late Mr. Robert Howard, whose venerable and beloved widow still survives as I write these lines.

It is necessary, however, to go back a little to resume an account of the literary activity of 1848, which was very considerable. We have seen that the reviewers complained of the want of figures to accompany *The Birds of Jamaica*. In January, 1848, Philip Gosse sent out circulars proposing to publish by subscription a folio volume of lithographic drawings, coloured by hand, if desired, of one hundred and twenty species of Jamaica birds, very largely new to science. This work was to be issued in monthly parts. The response was so immediately favourable, that in March he began to make the drawings on the stone, and he laboured away so assiduously, in spite of other work, that the book, an exquisite portfolio of plates, was given to the public, as *Illustrations of the Birds of Jamaica*, in April, 1849. Unhappily, however, the price at which he had undertaken to bring out the coloured illustrations was so low that there was, through an error in his calculations, a slight loss on every copy subscribed for, and if the demand for the book in this condition had been great, he would have been in dreadful straits. This was a lesson for which he had himself alone to thank, and he never made that particular error again.

In February, 1848, he began his *Birds*, the second volume of the popular series for the S.P.C.K., and being now more prosperous, and secure of plenty of tolerably remunerative work, he moved from the incommodious little house in Richmond Terrace, to a pleasanter dwelling, No. 13, Trafalgar Terrace, De Beauvoir Square. At this time he was greatly excited by the news of the Revolution in France, and the rapid spread of revolutionary sentiment through Europe, with the Chartist demonstration in London on April 10. "All this," he writes, "greatly excites our hopes of the near Advent;" and from this time forward, for nearly forty years, each political crisis in Europe reawakened in his breast this vain hope of the sudden coming of the Lord, and the rapture of believing Christendom into glory without death. This minute and realistic observer of natural objects possessed one facet of his soul on which the rosy light of idealism never ceased to sparkle. He was a visionary on one side of his brain, though a biologist on the other.

In June, 1848, he suggested to the Society for Promoting Christian Knowledge that he should write them a *History of the Jews*. They accepted the proposal, but he

found the task a more difficult one than he had anticipated.   It hung around his neck like a weight, and it
was not until 1850 that he published what is perhaps the
most perfunctory of all his longer writings.   Three, if not
four, editions of this work were, however, exhausted.   In
July the *Mammalia* was issued ; and in September he was
already beginning, for another firm of publishers, his
Popular British Ornithology, a work intended as a sort of
bird-calendar for the instruction of young naturalists, a
guide for use through the English bird-year.   This book,
which is illustrated by a variety of exquisite coloured
plates, drawn and lithographed by the author, was peculiarly the labour of his betrothal, since he wrote his first
page the day before he proposed to Miss Emily Bowes,
and the last on the night preceding his marriage.   In
designing and colouring the illustrations, he mainly drew
from the specimens in the British Museum.   Even in work
so modest as this was, he was unwilling to copy the
observations of others whenever it was in his power to
give an impression of his own, and he was in the habit
of remarking that, however hackneyed an animal may
seem to be, the labour of describing or copying it minutely
at first hand will reveal some characteristic in it which has
escaped previous observers.   This is, no doubt, far less
true to-day, when the illustration of natural objects has
been carried to so great a pitch of perfection, than it was
fifty years ago, when all but the best illustrations were of a
very rough character.

From Tottenham, on November 22, 1848, he brought
home his bride to the little house in Trafalgar Terrace
without so much as a single day's honeymoon.   He
immediately took up again the suspended task of *The
History of the Jews*, which, however, occupied him for many
more months.   The next year was one of extreme seclu-

sion. To Philip Gosse, secure of the sympathetic presence of his wife, there was now no need of entertainment away from home ; but to the new wife the strain of the change was not a small one. Emily Bowes had been of an eminently modern temperament—lively, sociable, talkative, accustomed to see moving around her a cloud of female friends. She soon found that visitors were not welcome to her husband, that fresh faces disturbed his ideas and awakened his shyness. His ideal of life was to exist in an even temperature of domestic solitude, absorbed in intellectual work, buried in silence. For hours and hours Mrs. Philip had no one to speak to but the servant-maid or her formidable mother-in-law, who, possessing no intellectual resources herself, looked with suspicion on those who did. Emily Gosse's only refuge was in her husband's study, which no one but herself might enter, and where she would sit for hours and hours, fretted by the unwonted restraint, in a silence broken only by the regular whisper of the pen on the paper or of the pencil on the stone. She possessed great command over her feelings, and she was very intelligent and sensible. Before long, she had the approach of other cares and busier interests to occupy her ; but for the time being the strain was very real, the sudden cloistered seclusion from the open world very trying and distressing. She fell back upon her studies, and began in an elegant Italian hand, in the bright blue ink of the period, to annotate an interleaved copy of the Hebrew Bible, which still exists to testify to her industry.

On February 1, 1849, the *Birds*, in the S.P.C.K. series, was published ; and on the 9th of that month the author began the volume called *Reptiles*. In this same February the *Popular British Ornithology* was published, and on May 9 Philip Gosse began to write his *Text-Book of Zoology for Schools*. The composition of this volume not published until 1851, led to a very important crisis in his intellectual career. He had hitherto taken but a super-ficial interest in the lower forms of life. In order to write the first chapters of his *Text-Book*, he found himself obliged to study what was known of these forms, and the fascina-tion of invertebrate, and particularly of microscopic natural history, suddenly took hold of him. He determined to study these forms at first hand. Early in June he bought a microscope, and this purchase revolutionized his whole life. He instantly threw himself, with that fiery energy which characterized him, into the literature of the subject, and particularly into Pritchard's still classical *History of the Infusoria*.

On June 11, 1849, he made his first independent exami-nation of a *rotifer* under the microscope, and the date may be worth noting as that of the opening of one of the most important of all the branches of his labours. The extreme ardour with which he took up subjects sometimes wore itself out rather rapidly. He grew tired of birds; after-wards he grew tired of his once-beloved sea-anemones. But in the *rotifers*, the exquisite little wheel-animalcules, whose history he did so much to elucidate—in these he never lost his zest, and they danced under his microscope when he put his faded eye to the tube for the last time in 1888. A week after June 11, he was already deep in observation of *Stephanoceros*, that strange and beautiful creature, whose "small pear-shaped body, with rich green and brown hues glowing beneath a glistening surface, is lightly perched on a tapering stalk, and crowned with a diadem of the daintiest plumes; while the whole is set in a clouded crystal vase of quaint shape and delicate texture." He was seized with a determination to collect on a large scale. From a wholesale glass factory in Shoreditch he bought an army of small clear phials, and rose at three a.m. next morning, walking to the Hampstead Ponds for dirty water which might prove to contain sparks of life, leaping, twinkling, and kicking, under the microscope.

Almost immediately he began to correspond with the leaders of microscopic science at that time, with John Quekett and with Bowerbank, neither of whom, however, had given any special attention to the *Rotifera*. He presently fixed in his garden a set of stagnant open pans or reservoirs for infusoria, which, from the prevalence of cholera at the time, were looked upon with great suspicion by the neighbours. In the midst of all this, and during the very thrilling examination of three separate stagnations of hempseed, poppy seed, and hollyhock seed, his wife presented him with a child, a helpless and unwelcome apparition, whose arrival is marked in the parental diary in the following manner:—" E. delivered of a son. Received green swallow from Jamaica." Two ephemeral vitalities, indeed, and yet, strange to say, both exist ! The one stands for ever behind a pane of glass in the Natural History Museum at South Kensington ; the other, whom the green swallow will doubtless survive, is he who now puts together these deciduous pages.

The absorbing devotion to the microscope, which now began to be the dominant passion of Philip Gosse's life was distinctly unfavourable to the prosecution of paying work. During the second half of 1849 he produced comparatively little of a marketable character, although at no time of his life was he engaged more closely or on labour which demanded more intellectual force. But what he was doing was noted with full appreciation in the scientific world, and he was regarded with greater seriousness than ever before. On November 14, upon Bowerbank's proposition, he was elected a member of the Microscopical Society, at whose meetings he forthwith became a regular attendant. This was a much-needed refreshment and stimulus in his monotonous life. He was, meanwhile, making very rapid progress in his investigation of the *Rotifera*, a class at that time, and for many years afterwards, but little understood or studied. In 1849 the one published authority on these creatures, the book which—as Hudson and Gosse have put it in their great monograph—"swallowed up, as it were, the very memory of its predecessors," was the *Die Infusionsthierchen* published at Leipsic by Ehrenberg, in 1838. Philip Gosse found it impossible to proceed without knowing what Ehrenberg had said, but unfortunately the Prussian *savant* wrote only in German, a language with which the English naturalist was not acquainted. Emily Gosse, however, knew German enough, and during the winter of 1849–50 he borrowed the precious volume from the council of the Microscopical Society, and they turned Ehrenberg into English between them, Gosse's feverish anxiety to know what Ehrenberg was saying acting on his language-sense, for the moment, like a sort of clairvoyance. It was long his intention to publish this translation of Ehrenberg, which his wife and he soon completed, with illustrative notes and additions of his own, but he did not find any opportunity of doing this, and the version remains inedited.

It becomes necessary, however, to write when—

> " A life your arms unfold
> Whose crying is a cry for gold,"

and with the opening of 1850 Philip Gosse so arranged his days that the book-making should occupy the mornings, and the afternoons and evenings only be given to the microscope. The *Handbook of Zoology* was finished on February 4, and the very next day *Sacred Streams*, a volume describing the natural history and the antiquities of the rivers mentioned in the Bible, was begun. This was completed early in August, and was instantly succeeded, without a day's interval, by the volume called *Fishes*, in the S.P.C.K. series. The last three months of the year were occupied in the composition of a work far more important than all these, *A Naturalist's Sojourn in Jamaica*, which was a record of his stay in that island, mainly printed from the copious manuscript journal which he had preserved. Hitherto he had not known what it was, since his first success, to have a book rejected ; but this, which is certainly in the first rank among his original volumes, was returned to him by Mr. John Murray, only to be accepted, to their ultimate advantage, by Messrs. Longmans.

The second year of married life was much more comfortable than the first had been. Mrs. Gosse was occupied by the care of her child, and her husband was neither so self-contained nor so isolated from outer sympathies as he had been. In 1850 he was elected an Associate of the Linnæan Society, and he greatly enjoyed the meetings of this, as of the Microscopical Society. He was taken out of himself by being more and more sought as an authority on zoological matters, and the life of eremitical seclusion which he had chosen to adopt was broken in upon by a variety of human interests. The circumstances of the pair, moreover, were considerably less straitened. His books were not ill paid for, and they had become so numerous that the little sums mounted up. In July, moreover, Mr. and Mrs. Gosse were called down to Leamington to the death-bed of an aunt, who left them a legacy. This was trifling in amount, but the interest of it was enough to form a pleasant increase to an income so small as theirs had been. The pinch of poverty was now relaxed, for the first time in Philip Gosse's life,

Q

although industry and thrift were still necessary to insure anything like comfort.

A labour which belongs to the year 1850, and which must not be left unrecorded in the chronicle of his career, was his investigations into the genus of *Rotifera* called by Ehrenberg *Notommata*. The German *savant* had left *Notommata* in an unwieldy and heterogenous condition; Philip Gosse now directed his particular attention to it, and in a succession of papers, read before his two societies, he reduced it to well-defined proportions. These, and his monograph, in the *Annals and Magazine of Natural History*, on the new genus *Asplanchna*, which he dis-covered in 1850 in the Serpentine, attracted a great deal of attention from specialists, and opened up a long series of similar contributions to exact knowledge. During the latter part of the autumn he was once again in daily attendance at the Natural History Departments of the British Museum. On October 10 he was fortunate enough to be leaving the central hall at the very moment when the winged bull from Nineveh was being brought in. Thirty years later my father met, for the first time, with Dante Gabriel Rossetti's striking poem, *The Burden of Nineveh*, recording the same experience :—

> " Sighing, I turned at last to win
> Once more the London dirt and din ;
> And as I made the swing-door spin
> And issued, they were hoisting in
> A wingèd beast from Nineveh."

It was interesting, and it greatly interested Philip Gosse to think, that in the little crowd that watched the bull-god enter his last temple, he had unconsciously stood shoulder to shoulder with the brilliant young poet, those two, perhaps alone among the spectators, sharing the acute sense of mystery and wonder at the apparition.

In November much reading of Jamaica notes caused a revival of intense desire to revisit the West Indies, resulting rather suddenly in a positive design to visit the Virgin Islands and Tortugas. But once more the scheme came to nothing, Mrs. Gosse's health precluding the possibility of her sharing so painful a romantic enterprise. Philip Gosse was one of those people who find it exceedingly difficult to speak of what lies closest to their hearts, and he sometimes preferred to convey his intentions in writing, even to those who were around him. I find a letter addressed on this occasion by my father to my mother, announcing to her his final determination not to start for the West Indies; this letter being, apparently, handed to her in the house. In it he begs her not to refer to the subject in conversation, nor to make the slightest effort to change his plans. The letter is worded in terms of the most devoted affection, and that he wrote it at all is a proof of the almost impassioned longing which had seized him to revisit those luminous archipelagos. If Mrs. Gosse had been strong enough to bear the journey, she could not have left her mother, who was dying, and who passed away on January 14, 1851. Mr. Bowes had preceded his wife by six months; he died, in his eightieth year, on June 10, 1850.

The year 1851 was notable for the publication of no fewer than four of Philip Gosse's works. In the month of March his *Text-Book of Zoology for Schools* and his *Sacred Streams, the Ancient and Modern History of the Rivers of the Bible*, were issued. In February he began *Fishes*, the fourth volume of his series of manuals of zoology for the S.P.C.K., and this was published in October of the same year. Moreover, on October 17, appeared *A Naturalist's Sojourn in Jamaica*, a production of far greater importance than any of these, a handsome volume adorned with lithographic plates designed and coloured by the author.   In the preface to this work, Philip Gosse took up a position which was new to the world of zoologists. "Natural history," he boldly declared, "is far too much a science of dead things; a *necrology*. It is mainly conversant with dry skins, furred or feathered, blackened, shrivelled, and hay-stuffed; with objects, some admirably beautiful, some hideously ugly, impaled on pins, and arranged in rows in cork drawers; with uncouth forms, disgusting to sight and smell, bleached and shrunken, suspended by threads and immersed in spirit (in defiance of the aphorism, that 'he who is born to be hanged will never be drowned') in glass bottles. These distorted things are described; their scales, plates, feathers counted; their forms copied, all shrivelled and stiffened as they are; . . . . their limbs, members, and organs measured, and the results recorded in thousandths of an inch; two names are given to every one; the whole is enveloped in a mystic cloud of Græco-Latino-English phraseology (often barbaric enough); and this is natural history!"

The tradition thus scornfully condemned was that which it was the writer's peculiar function to break through. And he was not, like so many reformers, ready to tear down without having any fresh materials or the design for a new edifice. This is how, in the elegant preface to the *Naturalist's Sojourn*, he describes the science of zoology as he fain would see it conducted :—

"That alone is worthy to be called natural history
"which investigates and records the condition of living
"things, of things in a state of nature; if animals, of
"*living* animals :—which tells of their 'sayings and
"doings,' their varied notes and utterances, songs and
"cries; their actions in ease, and under the pressure of
"circumstances; their affections and passions towards
"their young, towards each other, towards other animals,

"towards man ; their various arts and devices to protect
"their progeny, to procure food, to escape from their
"enemies, to defend themselves from attacks ; their
"ingenious resources for concealment ; their stratagems
"to overcome their victims ; their modes of bringing
"forth, of feeding, and of training their offspring ; the
"relations of their structure to their wants and habits ;
"the countries in which they dwell ; their connection
"with the inanimate world around them, mountain or
"plain, forest or field, barren heath or bushy dell, open
"savannah or wild hidden glen, river, lake or sea :—this
"would be indeed *zoology*, viz. the science of *living*
"creatures."

At the time when these words were written many of
the animals of Europe, and, in the persons of Wilson and
Philip Gosse himself, the birds of America, had found
biographers, but little indeed was known of the mass of
species distributed throughout the rest of the world, and
of the lower orders of life, in their living state, practically
nothing. It was Gosse's privilege to inaugurate this
species of observation, and to live to see the actual study
of living forms take its place as one of the most important
branches of scientific investigation. The public was
instantly attracted by the freshness of this new manner
of writing. The books Philip Gosse had been composing
for the Society for Promoting Christian Knowledge had,
in accordance with a strange whimsey that long prevailed
with the council of that Society, been sent to none of the
reviews. Their sale, accordingly, though it had been considerable, had not been aided or gauged by the publicity
of the journals. *A Naturalist's Sojourn in Jamaica*, of
course, was sent to the newspapers by Messrs. Longmans,
and it received a welcome from the press which was something quite new in Philip Gosse's experience. One of the

best notices was written, as the author had reason to believe, by the distinguished ornithologist, Dr. Stanley, Bishop of Norwich, who sang the praises of the book wherever he went.

In all quarters the freshness of the new mode of observation met with instant appreciation, nor were zoologists less forward than the general reader in commending the novelty of attitude. Charles Darwin and Richard Owen were among those who expressed their approval of this bright, fresh, and electrical mode of throwing the window of the dissecting-closet wide open to the light and air of heaven. The latter wrote (November 29, 1851): "Mr. Gosse is a very true observer and a very beautiful describer of what he sees. His book, all about things I am so very fond of—birds and fishes, crocodiles and lizards, butterflies and crabs, both in and out of shells, to say nothing of sea and sunshine—has made me quite long for a holiday in Jamaica." About the same time Philip Gosse formed the acquaintance of the amiable and charming James Scott Bowerbank, who was then already at work upon his great monograph on the sponges. He occasionally attended those delightful gatherings which the hospitality of Bowerbank collected around him, and the two naturalists corresponded closely for several years. Philip Gosse was not perturbed by the fame thus suddenly thrust upon him, and he resisted the kind attempts which were made to "lionize" him. He was pleased at his success, and grateful to those who assured it to him ; but he remained at home. Save that he was elected to the council of the Microscopical Society, and served in this capacity, he scarcely made the smallest change in the even tenor of his existence.

In the summer his views regarding the *Rotifera* received momentary modification, and his interest in these animalcules was increased, by his meeting with Dujardin's ingenious work on the *Systolides*, as the French *savant* called the rotifers. Gosse studied Dujardin with great care, and was at first inclined to lay much stress on his criticisms of Ehrenberg, but this view ultimately gave way to a confirmation of his faith in the solidity and value of the observations of the Prussian naturalist. In this year, 1851, Philip Gosse published in the "Annals of Natural History" his *Catalogue of Rotifera found in Britain*, a list which extended far beyond any previous catalogue of the kind, but yet looks meagre enough now in comparison with the results of later investigations. By the side of these apparently conflicting labours he was engaged, throughout the year 1851, on another and very distinct work. Since the occasion when he had watched the winged bull of Nineveh being brought into the British Museum, his imagination had constantly been occupied in trying to rebuild that mysterious and sinister Eastern civilization, the character of which it is scarcely too much to say had then recently been discovered by the excavations of Botta and Layard at Nimroud. The splendid folios published, in Paris and London respectively, by these intrepid archæ-ologists, had excited, in conjunction with the discoveries of Rawlinson, interest throughout Europe. To allay his own curiosity, and with no idea of competing with these masters of the field, Philip Gosse prepared at odd moments throughout 1851 what proved at last a bulky volume on *Assyria; her Manners and Customs, Arts and Arms*, which the S.P.C.K. published early in 1852.

With the close of 1851 we reach another critical point in the career of the subject of this memoir, and we may review for a moment the results of these five years of incessant labour. Since Philip Gosse had returned from Jamaica in the autumn of 1846, he had completed thirteen distinct works, a row of volumes enough in themselves to form the whole baggage of many a literary traveller. Of these, four had been compilations of an historical and archæological cast, undertaken solely on account of their semi-religious subject. Six others were handbooks of zoological information—"pot-boilers," as they might be called in the slang to-day—but all of them conscientiously, minutely, and eloquently written, and brought up in every case to the momentary limit of the ever-advancing tide of the scientific knowledge of the age. There remain the three Jamaica volumes, and if these alone had been published during these five years, it may be that their author's fame would have been quite as flourishing as it was. These were genuine contributions, not only to zoological knowledge, but to the new methods of natural history, the methods which their author now so openly defended. Then, of a less public character, there were those technical monographs read at the Proceedings of the Royal, and printed by the Linnæan and Microscopical Societies, in which the new naturalist showed himself just as competent and as accurate in measuring, defining, and copying cabinet specimens as had been any of the old closet *savants* whose exclusiveness he deprecated. On all sides, the author of so many and so incongruous writings, he had widened the field of his experience, and he was now rapidly advancing along the pathway to distinction. A sudden event changed the entire current of his being.

The life he had led for these last five years had been cloistered and uniform in the extreme. Nothing could exceed the monotony of his daily existence. As he became better known, social opportunities had not been lacking; invitations had reached him which, had they been accepted, might have led to others. But he accepted none of them.

He was shy, he was poor, he grudged the time which such visits would consume ; but above all these considerations there was the inherent dislike, constantly on the increase, of being compelled to adopt the artificial manner of general conversation. During these five years his social exercises were strictly limited to occasional visits, mainly in the daytime, to a few scientific friends, such as Edward Double-day and Adam White, and to such a limited circle of religious companions as straitly shared his own peculiar convictions. He stayed at home at his study-table, writing, drawing, or observing, every week-day, and on Sunday he took no rest from his labours, for he usually preached one, if not two, extempore sermons. The monotony of this round of life was perhaps even more deleterious than its severity. He gave himself no holidays of any description. With the exception of a few days in the summer of 1850, spent at Leamington in attendance upon the death-bed and the funeral of a relative of Mrs. Gosse's, he was not out of the neighbourhood of London, even for one day, from August, 1846, until December, 1851. His most· adven-turous excursions had extended no further than Kew Gardens, Hampstead Heath, and the Isle of Dogs.

Such a strain could not be kept up indefinitely ; the wonder was that his constitution sustained it so long. In November he began to be the victim to persistent head-ache, and early in December, after starting to go to the British Museum one morning, he became violently ill, and returned · home in a state of great depression and alarm. His brain seemed to have suddenly collapsed, and he supposed¦ himself to be paralyzed ; but the doctors pro-nounced the symptoms to be those of acute nervous dyspepsia. They attributed the illness mainly to his seden-tary existence, and they insisted that he should leave town at once, and be much in the open air. He himself wrote :

" Sitting by the parlour fire, doing nothing, is dreary work ; and it is not much mended by traversing the gravel walks of the garden in my great-coat. There is nothing particularly refreshing in the sight of frost-bitten creepers and chrysanthemums. To walk about the streets in the suburbs, or even in the City, is dreary too, when there is no object in view, nothing to do, in fact, but spend the time. But, after all, the dreariness is in myself: I am thoroughly unwell, overworked, and everybody says there must be rustication." On December 15 his wife and he started for five days' ramble in the Isle of Wight, hoping that this modest excursion would meet the requirements of the case. But the symptoms of congestion of the brain returned. It was impossible for the patient to read or write, and to put his eye to the microscope was agony. The last day of the year 1851 saw the whole family in bed, each distressingly ill in his or her way. Old Mrs. Gosse had before this gone into separate lodgings of her own. It was determined that the establishment at Hackney should be broken up, and that the invalids should go southward and seaward. On January 27, 1852, they started for South Devon.

CHAPTER IX.

1852–1856.

AT the present time, when the principle of the marine aquarium has become a commonplace, it is difficult to realize that forty years ago it had occurred to no one that it might be possible to preserve marine animals and plants in a living state under artificial conditions. In 1850, when Philip Gosse was first engaged in the study of the *Rotifera*, he had noticed that by allowing aquatic weeds, such as *vallisneria* and *myriophyllum*, to grow in the glass vases of fresh water in which he kept his captures, both *Infusoria* and *Rotifera* would live in captivity, and even breed and multiply. This observation was the first germ of the invention of the marine aquarium, and towards the close of 1851 it occurred to him to apply this principle— the supply of oxygen from living plants under the stimulus of light—to the preservation of animals in sea-water. He reflected that if seaweeds, *algæ*, in the more delicate varieties, could be induced to live in vases of sea-water, they might assimilate carbon and give out oxygen in such proportions as to keep the water pure and fit for the support of animal life. This proved in due time to be the case. To carry out the scheme was a matter of experiment, but the idea was already ripe before the Gosses—" wife, self and little naturalist in petticoats "—proceeded to Devonshire.

His choice of that particular county was made partly because of its warmth in winter, partly because of its geographical position at the gates of the populous Atlantic, but also for a reason which would have occurred only to a practical naturalist. The researches of a littoral zoologist are carried on with most success at spring tides. In many parts of the English coast the lowest water occurs at about six o'clock in the morning or evening, a time inconvenient in many ways, and particularly to an invalid. In Devonshire, on the days of new and full moon, the lowest tide is near the middle of the day. After great hesitation as to a point at which to begin, Torquay was finally chosen, although the doctors considered it too relaxing for a nervous disorder. On January 29, 1852, the family arrived there, and immediately proceeded to the village of St. Marychurch, about a mile and a half to north, an ancient but not picturesque assemblage of whitewashed cottages and small shops, close to the sea-cliff, but out of sight of the sea. This place had the advantage of a considerable altitude above Torquay, which slumbered among its groves of arbutus, by the side of its land-locked azure bay, as in a warm bath, and had alarmed its feeble visitors by the relaxing quality of its atmosphere. St. Marychurch lay open to the east, on a level with the tops of the cliffs, and enjoyed, on clear days, a refreshing view of the purple tors of Dartmoor away in the west. It was little in Philip Gosse's mind, when he first stepped up the reddish-white street of St. Marychurch, that in this village he would eventually spend more than thirty years of his life, and would close it there. For the present his stay was transitory. They took lodgings at Bank Cottage, a little detached villa in the main street.

After the long imprisonment within the gloom of London, Philip Gosse's eyes were acutely sensitive to the pleasure of country sights. The coast of South Devon is peculiarly brilliant in colour; the weather happened to be superb, and the unexpected beauty of every object on which the sun lighted was almost intoxicating. His journal is full of rapturous ejaculations of delight. On the very first afternoon he went down through the embowered hamlet of Babbicombe "to see what promise the beach might afford." That beach is now familiarized and vulgarized; carriage-roads wind down to it, where breakneck paths used to descend; it is all given up, with but small trace of its ancient wildness, to the comfort of nursemaids and trippers. But in those days no bathing-machines had invaded its savage coves and creeks. Descending at Babbicombe, and climbing along the beautiful arc of alternate rock and shingle to the further extremity of the beach at Oddicombe, he discovered on that first afternoon a feature of extraordinary charm, a natural basin in the face of the rock, a veritable little bath where one might conceive the Nereids indolently collecting to gossip at high noon as they plashed the water with their feet :—

"Climbing and crawling around the face of the rough "cliff," he writes, "I found a delightful little reservoir, "nearly circular, a basin about three feet wide and "the same deep, full of pure sea-water, quite still, "and as clear as crystal. From the rocky margin and "sides, the puckered fronds of the sweet oar-weed "(*Laminaria saccharina*) sprang out, and gently droop-"ing, like ferns upon a wall, nearly met in the centre; "while other more delicate seaweeds grew beneath their "shadow. Several sea-anemones of a kind very different "from the common species, more flat and blossom-like, "with slenderer tentacles set round like a fringe, were "scattered about the sides."

This tidal basin became one of the most constant of his haunts, and he nourished a jealous and almost whimsical affection for it, suffering from a constant fear that its crystal beauty might be profaned. Every day the high tide renewed its freshness, and then, retreating, left the basin to settle into glassy calm. "Procul, o procul este!" my father used to murmur, affecting the airs of a lapwing when idle men or lads approached the scenes of his devotion. Strangely enough, this exquisite little freak of nature survived, untouched, for nearly twenty years after its discovery. At last, one day when my father climbed up to look into it, behold! some thrice-wretched vandal had chiselled a channel on the seaward side, not very deep indeed, but enough to destroy its unique regularity of form. He never went to it again.

Early in February he began to feel a marked improvement in health. He bought a hammer and chisel, and spent many hours every day in chipping off fragments of rock bearing fine seaweeds and delicate animal forms. These he preserved in vases and open pans, and thus began to carry out his dream of a marine vivarium. He found the under surfaces of the pebbles on Babbicombe beach singularly rich in those fantastic and gem-like creatures, the nudibranch mollusca, of which he set about forming a considerable collection, in correspondence with Alder and Hancock, the historians of those graceful sea-slugs. With the very first dawn of convalescence, he returned to his literary work. He started in March a fifth volume of the series of handbooks for the S.P.C.K., this time on the *Mollusca ;* and before this he began to put his daily observations into the shape which finally assumed the dimensions of *A Naturalist's Rambles on the Devonshire Coast.*

It was singular that on wholly untrodden ground, and

without previous experience, he immediately fell into the ways of a collector of marine objects, discovering almost by intuition what species were and what were not suited for artificial preservation, and how the sensitive varieties of plants and fixed animals were to be transported without injury. Nevertheless he was not entirely satisfied with St. Marychurch as a centre; it suited him zoologically, but not medically. His headaches returned, and the soft luscious air seemed to leave him constantly weaker. In March he tried Brixham, on the south side of the bay; but this was warmer still, and not so favourable for collecting. At the end of April he determined to try the northern coast of the county. The prevalence of a heavy surf upon the shore below St. Marychurch, in consequence of an undeviating wind from the east, had prevented him from being as successful as he had hoped to be. Still he had gained great experience, and had added many new species to the English fauna. Among the sea-anemones, in particular, which had hitherto been greatly neglected, he had already secured several novelties. Two beautiful species, now widely known to zoologists, *rosea* and *nivea*, Philip Gosse had the good fortune to discover on the same day, April 20, the one on the south, the other on the north side of the limestone headland called Petit Tor. These were his latest trophies there, for in the course of the following week the family transferred themselves to Ilfracombe, on the Bristol Channel, then already a summer resort of some local repute.

The change was instantly beneficial. The air of North Devon proved much more exhilarating, and the rock-pools even richer than those of the Oddicombe district. He found the angular basins in the slaty coast densely fringed with seaweeds, under whose lucent curtains lurked an immense and luxuriant variety of zoophytes of every description.   In the *Devonshire Coast* he has given an eloquent account of his successive discoveries, and of the ardour with which he threw himself into the work of exploration.   The beautiful Devonshire cup-coral (*Caryophyllia Smithii*) had long been known as a skeleton in the drawers of museums ; he was fortunate enough to find it in profusion, throwing upwards its globose white tentacles, and covering with its fawn-coloured flesh the granular plates of its coral structure.   In September he made a discovery of extraordinary interest, and in a manner so characteristic that I give his own account of the incident :—

"It was a spring tide, and the water had receded "lower than I had seen it since I had been at the place. "I was searching among the extremely rugged rocks "that run out from the tunnels, forming walls and "pinnacles of dangerous abruptness, with deep, almost "inaccessible cavities between.   Into one of these, at "the very verge of the water, I managed to scramble "down ; and found, round a corner, a sort of oblong "basin, about ten feet long, in which the water remained, "a tide-pool of three feet depth in the middle.   The "whole concavity of the interior was so smooth that I "could find no resting-place for my foot in order to "examine it ; though the sides, all covered with the "pink lichen-like coralline, and bristling with laminariæ "and zoophytes, looked so tempting that I walked round "and round, reluctant to leave it.   At last I fairly "stripped, though it was blowing very cold, and jumped "in.   I had examined a good many things, of which the "only novelty was the pretty narrow fronds of *Flustra* "*chartacea* in some abundance, and was just about to "come out, when my eye rested on what I at once saw "to be a madrepore, but of an unusual colour, a most "refulgent orange."

It proved to be *Balanophyllia*, a fossil coral, the existence of which, with an actinia-like body of richly coloured living flesh, had never been suspected.

This episode may be taken as an example, not merely of the discoveries in science which Philip Gosse was now constantly making, but of his manner of life. He was accustomed every day at low tide, if the hour was at all convenient, to go down to the shore, and for several hours before and after the lowest moment to examine the weedy rocks, the loose flat stones under which molluscs and crustaceans lurked, the shallow tidal pools, and the dripping walls of the small fissures and caverns. It was extraordinary how wide a range of animal life was included within the tidal limits. After some hours of severe labour, he would tramp home with his treasures, arrange them in dishes and vases with fresh sea-water, and then proceed to a scientific examination of what was unique or novel. The notes taken in this way, with the lens in one hand and the pen in the other, were transferred bodily to the pages of *A Naturalist's Ramble on the Devonshire Coast*, which was rapidly taking form. He was particularly ardent in his study of the sea-anemones, a group which he was presently to take under his special patronage. He had no thought as yet of the generic distinctions which he was to introduce later, and throughout 1852, and for some years to come, what were afterwards distinguished as *Sagartia*, *Bunodes*, and the rest, were classed in one vague genus, *Actinia*. The examination of the sea-anemone was pushed, this summer, to the length of a gastronomical test. A few specimens of the gross strawberry species, *crassicornis*, were boiled and eaten. His account of this courageous experiment runs as follows :—

"I must confess that the first bit I essayed caused a "sort of lumpy feeling in my throat, as if a sentinel there

"guarded the way, and said, 'It shan't come here.' This
"sensation, however, I felt to be unworthy of a philo-
"sopher, for there was nothing really repugnant in the
"taste. As soon as I had got one that seemed well
"cooked, I invited Mrs. Gosse to share the feast; she
"courageously attacked the morsel, but I am compelled
"to confess that it could not pass the vestibule; the
"sentinel was too many for her. My little boy, however,
"voted that "tinny [*actinia*] was good,' and that he 'liked
""'tinny;' and loudly demanded more, like another Oliver
"Twist. As for me, I proved the truth of the adage,
"'Il n'y a que le premier pas qui coûte;' for my sentinel
"was cowed after the first defeat. I left little in the dish.
"In truth, the flavour and taste are agreeable, somewhat
"like those of the soft parts of crab (May 21, 1852)."

In July Philip Gosse made an interesting excursion of
a week's duration to Lundy Island. The description he
presently wrote of this curious and remote fragment of
the British empire appeared in serial form in the periodical called *The Home Friend*, and was long afterwards
reprinted in *Sea and Land* (1865). For the Society for
Promoting Christian Knowledge he wrote this time, in
conjunction with his wife, a little anonymous volume
called *Seaside Pleasures*, consisting, in reality, of four
essays on Ilfracombe, Capstone Hill, Barricane, and the
Valley of Rocks, describing in a graceful manner the
antiquities and scientific attractions of the neighbourhood.
Of these essays the fourth was wholly written by Emily
Gosse. Meanwhile, with her constant help, he was preparing the *Devonshire Coast*, and, in spite of all the exercise in the open air, the ozone from the seaweeds, and
the exquisite freshness of the oceanic winds, both husband
and wife were overtaxing their nervous strength. In
August both of them were ill with headache, and able to

do little or nothing. He was soon well again, writing monographs for the Microscopical Society, corresponding about his captures with Johnston, Alder, Bowerbank, and Edward Forbes, drawing from specimens under the microscope, and recording his discoveries in exact form. At last, in November, the weather grew too cold for collecting on the shore in comfort, and the health of neither husband nor wife was what it should be. They determined to go back to London for the winter, and, after an absence of nearly ten months in Devonshire, they took lodgings at 16, Hampton Terrace, Camden Town.

One reason for coming back to London was the desire to carry on a stage further the invention of marine vivaria, which had been occupying the mind of Philip Gosse all through the year. On May 3, after some slighter experiments, he had put about three pints of sea-water, with some marine plants and animals, into a confectioner's show-glass, which was about ten inches deep by five and a half inches wide. This was the first serious attempt made to create a marine aquarium. Without changing the water otherwise than by adding a little to supply loss from evaporation, this vase was kept fresh, and its contents healthy, for more than two months ; when the experiment came to a close, in consequence of lack of experience. The principle, however, upon which the preservation of marine animals in captivity could be maintained was now discovered, and it was merely a question how to bring it to perfection in practice. Curiously enough, another naturalist, Mr. Robert Warington, of Apothecaries' Hall, had, quite independently, been occupied with a similar series of experiments. In October, 1852, my father heard of this, and immediately corresponded with Mr. Warington. This gentleman, it then appeared, had carried the vivarium to a greater pitch of elaboration, but had as yet only applied himself to the preservation of fresh-water animals by means of the exhalation of oxygen by living water-plants. Philip Gosse at once supplied him with particulars of his own experiments with marine forms, and when he returned to London in November, he brought Mr. Warington a small collection of living seaweeds and animals which were successfully ensconced in one of that gentleman's vivaria. There was no sort of rivalry between these earnest and amiable investigators, but a little later on, when the aquarium had become a fashionable thing, Philip Gosse was accustomed to say that if it was needful to dispute about an invention which was virtually simultaneous, it might be said that Warington had invented the vivarium and he the marine aquarium.

Little time was lost in making a practical use of the experience of the summer. Early in December, with the active co-operation of the secretary, Mr. D. W. Mitchell, a large glass tank was set up in the Zoological Gardens, in Regent's Park, and stocked by Philip Gosse with about two hundred specimens of marine animals and plants brought up from Ilfracombe two months before, and still in a perfectly healthy condition. The Zoological Society soon found that this tank, in the new Fish House then just erected, was exceedingly popular, and they determined to make the newly invented aquarium a feature of the Gardens. They projected a series of seven tanks, and in order to fill them they made a proposition that Gosse should go down again to the seaside for the sole purpose of collecting specimens. This suited him very well. He found that it was absolutely needful for his health that he should not work much indoors, but be out in the fresh air for a great part of each day, and he agreed that so soon as the spring began he should go down to the coast of Dorsetshire.

By the last days of 1852 *A Naturalist's Ramble on the Devonshire Coast* was finished. He was determined that, now that the public had begun to demand his literary work, he would get the profit of it himself. He therefore arranged to be his own publisher, and the book was accordingly set up for him by a firm of printers in Bath. It was eventually sold, on commission, by Mr. Van Voorst, whose name appeared on the titlepage. The volume was expensive to produce, for it contained a large number of coloured plates ; the subject, the marine zoology of an English county, treated in a desultory style, with a mixture of antiquities, gossip, sentiment, and poetry, was one entirely novel, the success of which might well be dubious. My father, however, was willing to try the experiment, and he was amply justified. In these days, when the business details of literature attract so much popular curiosity, it may perhaps be of some interest to mention that the net profits of *The Devonshire Coast* exceeded £750, no poor sum in those days for one small volume to bring to the pocket of its author. The book was published in May, 1853.

In February of that year Philip Gosse was asked to lecture. He had never attempted such a thing, but he said he would willingly make a few remarks about sponges, the siliceous skeletons of which he was studying at that moment in correspondence with Bowerbank. He accompanied the lecture with some large drawings in chalk on the blackboard, and the success of the experiment, which was novel at that time, was such, that he adopted lecturing as a branch of his professional labours, and became a very popular lecturer during the next four or five years. On April 8 the family once more left London, and settled in lodgings at Weymouth, in Dorsetshire. Here they continued to reside until December of the same year, when, as before, bad weather and exhaustion drove them back to London. These were eight months of intense and concentrated activity out of doors, during which comparatively little purely literary work was done. The mode in which these months were spent is fully described in that chatty and delightful record, *The Aquarium.* It was much less desultory and amateurish than the way in which the previous year, in Devonshire, had been occupied. Philip Gosse now clearly understood what objects he wished to secure, and the way to secure them. Almost every evening he sent off to the Zoological Gardens in Regent's Park a package of living creatures, the "bag" of the day, and sometimes this would mean seventy or eighty specimens. His first care was to secure seaweeds, carefully selecting those which were in full health, and, by preference, the finer and cleaner varieties, firmly affixed to rocks. He became an adept in chipping off just as much of the rocky support as the roots required, and no more. To these he would add such specimens of the littoral fauna, annelids, sea-anemones, shells, nudibranchs, and crustaceans, as he found, by experience, had the best chance of surviving the journey, and these he packed, as a rule, not in water, but swathed in wrappings of wet seaweed.

His principal exercise, however, at Weymouth, was dredging in the bay. He declared that Ovid knew more about the arts of dredging than any later naturalist, and used to point, by way of proof, to a passage in the *Halieuticon,* which he took the liberty of paraphrasing thus :—

> "When you the dredge would use, go not away
>   Far out to sea. Mind that your haul be made
>   According to your bottom. Where the ground
>   Is foul and ledgy, be content to fish
>   With hook and line. But when upon the sea

> The morning sun casts shadows deep and long
> From lofty Whitenose,—over with your dredge;
> When 'neath your keel the verdant sea-grass waves,
> The keer-drag try for nudibranchs and wrasse."

The man with whom he habitually sailed was a fisherman of the name of Jonas Fowler, who was glad to be hired day after day, and who took a pride in association with the naturalist. "Me and Mr. Gosse" were a pair of knowing ones, in the eyes of Jonas, whose portrait has been painted thus by his companion :—

"There is nobody else in Weymouth Harbour that "knows anything about dredging (I have it from his "own lips, so you may rely on it); but *he* is familiar "with the feel of almost every yard of bottom from "Whitenose to Church Hope, and from Saint Aldhelm's "Head to the Bill. He follows dredging with all the "zest of a *savant;* and it really does one's heart good "to hear how he pours you out the crack-jaw, the "sesquipedalian nomenclature. 'Now, sir, if you do "'want a *gastrochœna*, I can just put down your dredge "'upon a lot o' 'em; we'll bring up three or four on a "'stone.' 'I'm in hopes we shall have a good *cribella* or "'two off this bank, if we don't get choked up with them "''ere *ophiocomas.*' He tells me in confidence that he has "been sore puzzled to find a name for his boat, but "he has at length determined to appellate her '*The* "*Turritella*,'—'just to astonish the fishermen, you know, "'sir,'—with an accompanying wink and chuckle, and a "patronizing nudge in my ribs."

Every haul of the dredge was an excitement and a delight. Its results were widely different, according to the nature of the bottom. Rough stones, sand, shells, even broken bottles, would form the base of the matter dragged up—no fragment of all this to be lightly thrown away without examination, since it might contain star-fishes, urchins, the tubes of *serpulæ*, delicate nudibranchs and ascidians, and many other attractive captives for the aquarium. The univalve shells might be inhabited by soldier-crabs, with their charming guardian, the crimson *Adamsia*, or cloak-anemone. Skipping among the stones might be tiny fishes and pretty painted shrimps and prawns of various genera ; the long arms of spider-crabs might wave mysteriously above the mass ; sometimes the most gorgeous of the denizens of the British seas, the sea-mouse, with its refulgent silk, would glimmer, like a fragment of a fallen rainbow, through the mud. The keer-drag on the sand would bring ground-fishes, weavers, soles, and rays, rare sea-anemones, and the hump-backed Æsop prawns, with their lovely clouded tones of green and scarlet. The great advantage of dredging, for Philip Gosse's purpose, was, not merely that it supplied him with forms not attainable along the shore, but that it produced the maximum of results, in the way of number of speci-mens, with the minimum of labour.

His keen enjoyment of this healthy and invigorating existence was suddenly interfered with in the month of July by a deplorable misunderstanding with the Zoological Society. He had succeeded in obtaining specimens in much greater numbers than were necessary for Regent's Park, and he was now sending them also to the Crystal Palace and to other proprietors of aquaria in the neigh-bourhood of London. In doing this he broke no pledge, written or spoken. On the contrary, he was acting strictly in accordance with the principles which he had always maintained. When, in the *Annals of Natural History* for October, 1852, he had first mooted the question of marine vivaria, he had suggested that "such collections should be formed in London and other inland cities," and this desire was repeated, with enlarged details, in the *Devonshire Coast.* When he submitted his plan to the Zoological Society, in November of the same year, and offered to supply living specimens at a fixed rate, not the least stipulation that he should limit his supplies to that society was made or hinted at. Indeed, so far was any such thing from his intention, that he mentioned his plan for bringing out a parlour aquarium for sale. He was not the salaried servant of the Zoological Society, and its council had no more right to forbid him to sell specimens elsewhere than to prohibit the tradesman who glazed their tanks from selling glass to any one else. But the fact indubitably was that the notion of the marine aquarium having suddenly seized the public, the tank in the Fish House had proved to be an exceedingly paying attraction. It was, perhaps, not in human nature that the secretary should with equanimity see the same advantages offered to rival and imitative establishments. No doubt it would have been possible to make an arrangement by which Philip Gosse's services would have been exclusively retained for the Zoological Society. But in default of such an arrangement, to turn suddenly from blessing to cursing, and angrily to denounce his want of consideration for the society, was scarcely wise and certainly unjust.

When, in 1852, the state of his health seemed to render precarious the continuance of that kind of work by which Philip Gosse had hitherto maintained himself, he looked with hope to the scheme of the marine aquarium, as to a possible means by which he might obtain a livelihood without much mental labour indoors, and when his proposals were entertained by the Zoological Society, he congratulated himself. But he never considered this engagement as more than temporary, and he principally looked forward to parlour aquaria, supplied by him with animals, in the hope that these might be extensively patronized by wealthy amateurs. Hence it became an object with him to be widely recognized as the man who had been the first to give attention to the subject, and who possessed unique experience in it. On his side, from a business point of view, he was disappointed that the Zoological Society had not permitted some slight allusion to his name to appear in connection with the numerous descriptions of the new vivaria which were communicated to the public prints. Relations had certainly become strained on both sides, and it is impossible, with the correspondence before me, to exculpate the Zoological Society from some lack of justice, as well as generosity, in the matter. By the intervention of Professor Thomas Bell, however, civilities were resumed, but Philip Gosse ceased to supply the Zoological Gardens in Regent's Park with specimens; .nor was the dispute brought to a close until fourteen months later.

Partly owing to the worry involved in this dispute, he began in August to suffer again from violent pains in the head. He went on, however, very assiduously collecting animals, the public having thoroughly awakened to the interest which attached to the vivaria. In particular, the Surrey Zoological Gardens, at the Crystal Palace, were abundantly stocked by Philip Gosse. In September he writes from Weymouth: "We have not at present any thoughts of leaving this place. Perhaps we may remain here all the winter." He was busily occupied in constructing a small tank for himself, and this was set up, filled with living creatures, and started as an article of drawing-room furniture, in the Weymouth lodgings on September 5, 1853. This, the first private marine aquarium ever made, still exists in my possession.

The *Devonshire Coast* had been published, as we have

seen, in May, and had enjoyed a brilliant success. Letters of compliment, questions, and suggestions poured in upon the author, and among the flood of correspondence there floated to his door one missive from a stranger who was destined to become a beloved and intimate friend. In July, 1853, Philip Gosse received his first letter from the Rev. Charles Kingsley, a young poet and novelist already distinguished, and full of energy and intelligent curiosity. In his first letter, Kingsley urged my father to try Clovelly as a hunting-ground, and suggested that they should meet in Devonshire. To this Philip Gosse did not respond in his habitually cautious tone, but warmed up into an infectious enthusiasm. "How pleasant it would be," he wrote, "to have such a companion as yourself in the investigation of those prolific shores!" He adds: "I have sent up to London this summer nearly four thousand living animals and plants. ·Of course many rarities and some novelties have occurred in such an amount of dredging and trawling as this involved. Be assured, my dear sir, I shall esteem it a favour and a privilege to continue the correspondence you have commenced." Charles Kingsley became, almost immediately, one of the most ardent, and certainly the most active, of his allies.

In September Philip Gosse began to write the volume now known as *The Aquarium*, but entitled, until it was actually in the press, *The Mimic Sea*. This was a record of his deep-sea adventures off Weymouth, and a full description of the theory and practice of the marine aquarium. The confirmed ill-health, or rather feeble health, of Mrs. Gosse, and a return of his own brain-trouble, combined with the cold and gusty weather of December to disgust them with Weymouth, and just about the time when it had been proposed that they should join Kingsley in

North Devon, the latter proceeded to Torquay, and the Gosses came up to London. They took a small house in Huntingdon Street, Islington, and this became their home for some years.

There is not very much to record regarding the year 1854. Gosse worked much at the *Rotifera*, and he established several marine tanks, which he supplied with animals and plants from Torquay and Weymouth. Edward Forbes, C. Spence Bate, and Charles Kingsley were his most constant correspondents, and the latter threw himself with his customary splendid energy into the popularization of the marine aquarium. In December, 1853, Kingsley had written from Livermead, on Tor Bay, to know whether he could be useful in sending "beasts" up to town. Gosse replied with eager gratitude, and supplied him immediately with a hamper of suitable wicker-covered jars. These Kingsley promptly returned very successfully packed with desirable specimens, and a brisk correspondence of this nature went on all through the first six months of 1854. On May 30 Gosse writes to Kingsley: "My most charming tank is now thirteen weeks old, and contains nearly a hundred species of animals, and perhaps twice that number of individuals, all in the highest health and beauty. They include four fishes, viz. *Labrus Donovani, Gobius minutus, Gobius unipunctatus*, and *Syngnathus anguineus;* besides many of the treasures you have kindly sent me,—our old friend the 'say-lache' among them,— and the seaweeds which are the subject of my paper in the *Annals of Natural History* for the coming month."

In June the Gosses went down somewhat suddenly to Tenby, in Pembrokeshire. *The Aquarium* had just been published, and was selling like wild-fire. This book, I may mention, was the most successful of all my father's literary adventures; although the coloured plates with which it was lavishly adorned were so costly that no publisher would have faced the risk of their production, the profit on the sale of the volume amounted, in process of time, to more than £900. From Tenby Gosse wrote as follows to Charles Kingsley (June 29, 1854)—

"A most lovely place this is: I know not whether to "admire most the inland scenery, the noble cliffs and "headlands and caverns of the coast line, or the pro-"fusion of marine animals which I meet with. It is by "far the most prolific place for the naturalist that I have "explored, and I expect to get some treasures here. "The pretty *Actinia nivea* that I described from a speci-"men found at Petit Tor is here the characteristic "species, occurring by hundreds; and there is a most "charming variety (if it be not indeed specifically dis-"tinct) which has the whole disc of a miniate or orange "hue, very brilliant, and the tentacles pure white."

The Aquarium was made the peg upon which, in November, 1854, Kingsley hung an article in the *North British Review*, afterwards (May, 1855) enlarged and published as the charming little volume called *Glaucus; or, the Wonders of the Shore*, through the pages of which the lilies of my father's praise are sprinkled from full hands.

Bowerbank had in 1852 assured Philip Gosse that he would find Tenby "the prince of places for a naturalist," and Pembrokeshire, though now first visited, had never been absent from his mind. The very first evening, after securing lodgings, the family strolled out at low tide to the island of St. Catherine, and the naturalist saw enough to assure him that "its honeycombed rocks and dark weedy basins are full of promise for to-morrow." A few days afterwards, he wrote to Bowerbank that "the zoological riches of these perforated caverns amply bear out your laudatory testimony; indeed, I have not met with any part of our coast which can compare with them in affording a treat to the marine naturalist." In his volume called *Tenby* he has given an account, as minute as it is graphic, of the experiences of these summer weeks, and of the results to his aquarium collections. His very delightful and almost uniformly brilliant and successful visit to Pembrokeshire came to a close on August 18. These eight weeks were among the most enjoyable of his life. His bodily condition was unusually good, and Mrs. Gosse was in better health than she had been for two years past; while he was actively and constantly making additions of a more or less important character to the existing knowledge of seaside zoology. His important discoveries, leading to a redistribution of genera, and the naming of many new species, of British sea-anemones, belong to this summer of 1854, although they were not then published.

In the course of the summer, as he was exploring the caverns of St. Catherine's Island, he was accosted by a gentleman who introduced himself as the Bishop of Oxford, and who entered with great gusto into the pleasures of the seashore. The acquaintance thus oddly formed ripened into a daily companionship as long as they were both at Tenby, and after they parted, Dr. Wilberforce and my father kept up a desultory correspondence for a while. Another and more permanent friendship formed at Tenby was that with Mr. Frederick Dyster, the zoologist; from whom he bought, for £30, the microscope which he continued, regardless of modern improvements, to use until near the end of his life. His acquaintance with Professor Huxley, then a young surgeon whose investigations into the oceanic Hydrozoa, on board H.M.S. *Rattlesnake*, had recently given him scientific prominence, and whose contributions to his own collection Gosse records in *Tenby*, began in this year; but his principal scientific or literary correspondent continued to be Charles Kingsley, who in June had taken a house at Northdown, near Bideford, and was writing *Westward Ho!* On Gosse's return from Tenby he had found Edward Forbes in London, shrunken to a phantom of his former self, but still cheerful and brave. He was to die in November, and thus to terminate prematurely one of the most brilliant careers of the time. To Edward Forbes my father was strongly attached by friendship as well as admiration, and his was in later years one of the names which he was wont most affectionately to recall.

The autumn and winter of 1854 were almost exclusively occupied with the study of the *Rotifera* under the microscope, culminating in a treatise of great though strictly technical importance, *On the Structure, Functions, and Homologies of the Manducatory Organs in the Class Rotifera*, published eventually in the *Philosophical Transactions* of the Royal Society for 1856. This work is illustrated with a great many drawings of the mastax and trophi of various species, and " discusses the changes that they undergo, in passing from the typical to the most aberrant forms. It is in this treatise that Mr. Gosse contends that the dental organs of the rotifera are true mandibulæ and maxillæ, and that the mastax is a mouth ; and assigns to the class a position among the *Articulata*," says Dr. Hudson, who gives this work a high rank in the literature concerning the rotifera. Having sent this monograph in to the council of the Royal Society, Philip Gosse immediately returned to the revision of his old translation of Ehrenberg's *Die Infusionsthierchen*. The monograph was accepted, and read at the Royal Society on February 22, 1855, and on successive evenings. It began to seem as though it were impossible for Philip Gosse, however, to live in London, or bear the least social excitement. Quiet as his winter was, it was not quiet enough, and he began again to suffer from such excruciating pains in the head, that he was forced to abandon almost wholly the exercise of writing. He discovered it possible, although very irksome, to dictate, but having found a rapid and sympathetic amanuensis, he reconciled himself to this mode of composition. It even exaggerated his flowing and confidential style, the characteristics of which are seen, almost to excess, in the pages of *Tenby*.

The year 1855 was not marked by any incidents of a very unique character. The manner of life of the Gosses remained almost unchanged, my father merely pushing further and further along the various paths of scientific investigation of which he held the threads. In February was published *Abraham and his Children*, a volume on religious education, the most ambitious work which Emily Gosse had hitherto produced; and Philip Gosse began, at the same time, a book called *The Pond-Raker*, which was to be a popular introduction to the study of the Rotifera. It proved difficult to popularize so abstruse a subject, and *The Pond-Raker*, in spite of enthusiastic encouragement from Charles Kingsley, soon quitted his pond and dropped his rake, to be replaced by the *Manual of Marine Zoology*, a work of reference of real importance. On March 20, 1855, Gosse read before the Linnæan Society an important paper on Peachia, a new genus of unattached, cylindrical sea-anemones, buried in sand, which he had characterized from specimens secured in Torbay, and sent to him by Charles Kingsley. This paper attracted a good deal of attention, and among those present on the occasion of its reading was Charles Darwin, to whom my father was that evening presented for the first time. Gosse was captivated at once, as all who met him were, by the simplicity, frankness, and cordiality of this great and charming man.

Late in March the family proceeded again to Weymouth for a month, and Philip Gosse immediately resumed his work of collecting on the shore and dredging in the bay, encouraged and cheered through rather bad weather by the unexpected companionship of Bowerbank. The text of the first volume of the *Manual* was finished in June and published in July, upon which the Gosses, without delay, started for a second visit to Ilfracombe. For some time previously circulars had been sent out inviting persons who desired to make themselves acquainted with the living objects which the shore produced, and who wished to learn at the same time how to col ect and how to determine the names and the zoological relations of the specimens when found, to join the writer on the shore of North Devon.

But, before these circulars were issued, in the spring of 1855, Kingsley had already committed a discreet indiscretion concerning the project. He had written in *Glaucus :* " That most pious and most learned naturalist, Mr. Gosse, whose works will be so often quoted in these pages, proposes, it is understood, to establish this summer a regular shore class, . . . and I advise any reader whose fancy such a project pleases, to apply to him for details of the scheme." The consequence was that Gosse was received at Ilfracombe by a small party of ladies and gentlemen, who formed themselves into a class for the study of marine natural history. An hour or two was spent on the shore every day on which the tide and the weather were suitable ; and when otherwise, the occupation was varied by an indoor lesson on the identification of the animals obtained, the specimens themselves affording illustrations. But the weather was generally fine, and not a few species of interest, with some rarities, came under the notice of the class, scattered as they were over the rocks, and peeping into the pools, almost every day for a couple of months.

Then the prizes were brought home, where each member or group of the class had a little aquarium for the study of their habits ; their beauties investigated by the pocket-lens, and the minuter kinds examined under the microscope. A little also was effected in the way of dredging the sea-bottom and in surface-fishing ; but the chief attention of the class was given to shore-collecting, and very novel and agreeable the amusement was unanimously voted.

Here for the first time I can trust my own recollection for one or two of those detached impressions which remain imprinted here and there on the smoothed-out wax of a child's memory. I recall a long desultory line of persons on a beach of shells,—doubtless at Barricane. At the head of the procession, like Apollo conducting the Muses, my father strides ahead in an immense wide-awake, loose black coat and trousers, and fisherman's boots, with a collecting-basket in one hand, a staff or prod in the other. Then follow gentlemen of every age, all seeming spectacled and old to me, and many ladies in the balloon costume of 1855, with shawls falling in a point from between their shoulders to the edge of their flounced petticoats, each wearing a mushroom hat with streamers ; I myself am tenderly conducted along the beach by one or more of these enthusiastic nymphs, and "jumped" over the perilous little watercourses that meander to the sea, stooping every moment to collect in the lap of my pink frock the profuse and lovely shells at my feet. This is one memory, and another is of my father standing at the mouth of a sort of funnel in the rocks, through which came at intervals a roaring sound, a copious jet of exploding foam, and a sudden liquid rainbow against the dark wall of rock, surrounding him in its fugitive radiance. Without question, this is a reminiscence of the Capstone Spout-Holes, to which my father would be certain to take the class, " the ragged rock-pools that lie in the deep shadow of the precipice on this area " being, as he says in the *Devonshire Coast*, " tenanted with many fine kinds of algæ, zoophytes, crustacea, and medusæ."

Of the members of the class, one of the most enthusiastic was Sir Charles Lighton, with whom, on frequent occasions, after sending the others home laden to their aquariums, my father would start for a dredging excursion off Lee or Smallmouth. In August the class dispersed, and on September 6 the Gosses returned to town, followed by hampers of living creatures, most of which bore the journey very successfully. Philip Gosse immediately took up the composition of his *Handbook to the Marine Aquarium*, a practical supplement to the work which he had lately been engaged upon ; it was soon finished, and he resumed the notes and observations which he had made in Pembrokeshire in 1854, and began actively to rewrite the volume eventually published under the name of *Tenby*. The *Handbook* was published early in October, and an edition of no less than two thousand copies speedily exhausted, so great was the interest and curiosity now excited among the educated classes by the invention of the marine aquarium. The year closed uneventfully, except that just before Christmas the pains in the head, which had left him unattacked now for many months, set in again with extreme severity, and threatened to check his work.

Besides the first volume of the *Manual of Marine Zoology* and the *Handbook to the Marine Aquarium*, Philip Gosse composed in 1854 a little guide-book to *Kew Gardens*, and wrote a number of technically scientific papers for the Royal Society, the Linnæan Society, the Microscopical Society, and the " Annals of Natural History." This may, then, be taken as one of his fullest years, for he was actively lecturing at the same time on popular invertebrate zoology at a variety of institutes and public rooms.   He recovered his usual condition of health before the close of the year, and 1856 seemed to dawn upon his wife and himself with a more than common promise of happiness and peace.   Emily Gosse had begun to undertake a species of religious work, in which she was to achieve a singular success.   In the autumn of 1855 was published the *Young Guardsman of the Alma*, a Gospel Tract issued in leaflet form by the Weekly Tract Society, and founded on an incident of the Crimean War personally known to the writer.   She had already printed six of these leaflets, and the enormous demand for this particular one led her to concentrate her attention, during the brief remainder of her life, upon this species of composition.   Forty-one of these tracts were published in all, collected after her death in a general volume.   It has been stated that not less than half a million copies of these Gospel Tracts of hers were circulated, and they have been spread to the remotest corners of the globe, effecting, as one cannot question, no small benefit by their pious candour and their direct appeal to the unawakened conscience.

My own memories of her during this winter of 1855-56, the last which we were to spend together in peace, are vivid enough.   I specially recollect sitting on a Sunday morning upon a cushion at her knees, one of her long, veined hands resting upon mine, to learn a chapter of the Gospel of St. Matthew by heart ; and, while her soft voice read out the sacred verses, suddenly seeing something in her large eyes and wasted features, which gave me a premonition that I should lose her.   Most clearly I recall the terror of it, the unexpressed anguish.   It is the more strange, because I am sure that this was in the winter, and before any one had guessed that she was stricken with mortal disease.

In March Philip Gosse read before the Royal Society an important monograph on the *Diœcious Character of the Rotifera*, which attracted a great deal of attention, and led to his election as F.R.S. on the next occasion, the 4th of June of that year, Dr. Lankester being his proposer. In March also was published *Tenby*, the third of his chatty, popular volumes, describing the zoological adventures of a summer on the British shores, and adorned with coloured plates. For some reason or another, in spite of the increased distinction of the author, this was not nearly so successful as either of its immediate predecessors ; although a book which brought in a net profit of over £500 can only be spoken of as relatively, not positively, unsuccessful. *Tenby* had the disadvantage, as I have said, of being in great part dictated, not written, by the author. The gossipy and confidential manner, too—what *The Saturday Review* called " Mr. Gosse's air of taking us upon his knee like a grandpapa "—was carried in certain of its chapters to some excess, and, what was after all probably the main reason, the style itself and the matter were no longer so deliciously fresh and novel to the public as they had been in 1852. None the less, *Tenby* is a charming book, and must be read with *A Naturalist's Ramble on the Devonshire Coast* and *The Aquarium,* as giving the completest expression of one most important branch of my father's literary work, namely, his picturesque introduction of and apology for the pleasures of collecting animals and plants on the seashore.

My father and mother had now been married between seven and eight years. Their wedded life, which had opened under circumstances which might have seemed not wholly favourable to their happiness, had become year by year a closer, a tenderer, and a more sympathetic relation. As each had grown to know the other better, the finer faculties of both had been drawn out. My father, formerly so stiff and self-reliant, had learned to repose more and more easily on my mother's tact and wisdom ; she had, by a magnificent effort, trained herself in mature life to take an interest in subjects and in a course of technical study which had been foreign to her inclination. She was now a part of his intellectual as well as his emotional life. Not a rotifer was held captive under the microscope, not a crustacean of an unknown species shook a formidable clapper at the naturalist, but the cry of " Emily ! Emily ! " brought the keen eye and sympathetic lips on to the scene in a moment. Under her care, all that was warmest and brightest in Philip Gosse's character had been developed ; he had ceased to shun his kind ; he had lost his shyness, and had become one of the most genial, if still one of the most sententious of men. Every year this mellowing influence became more apparent ; every year brought more of sunlight into the circle of their hopes and interests. But now the gloom was to close again over their life, and they were to pass together, through anguish of body and mind, into the valley of the shadow of death.

Late in April, my mother became conscious of a local discomfort in her left breast, the result, she supposed, of some slight bruise. But on May 1, being with her old friends at Tottenham, Miss Mary Stacey persuaded her to consult a physician, who rather crudely and roughly pronounced it to be cancer. She returned very calmly to her home, and in the course of the evening she quietly told her husband. Next day they called on Dr. Hyde Salter, F.R.S., and on Mr. (now Sir) James Paget, both of whom declared that the presence of that disease was indubitable. Each of these eminent practitioners recommended a surgical operation. But from this the sufferer shrank. My mother had an excessive dread of physical pain, and in those days the modern ingenuities of anæsthetics were unknown. Dr. Salter, sympathizing with this weakness of nerve, and recognizing her exhausted condition, mentioned to the couple the name of a certain American who was then in London, professing to cure cancer by a new process, without the requirement of excision. It is needless for me to enter here into any of the harrowing details of his method. Enough to say that he used "a secret medicament," and that he declared his treatment to be painless. In some cases, of a less serious kind, he may have been successful. Hard words and reproaches are out of place now after so great a lapse of years. It is but charity to hope that in deceiving others he was himself in some measure deceived.

On May 12, 1856, my mother began to attend the consulting-room of this person, and to subject herself to his treatment. So far from the secret ointment being painless, it caused "a gnawing or aching in the breast, which at times was scarcely supportable." The doctor lived in Pimlico, and the double journey from Islington was not a little tedious and distressing. Meanwhile both my father and mother, with that happy unconsciousness of the future which alone makes life endurable, were buoyed up with hope, and suffered no depression of spirits. His literary work and his lecturing proceeded. The second volume of the *Manual of Marine Zoology* was completed before the end of May, and Philip Gosse's election and admission to the Royal Society were equally enjoyed by them both. The diaries of these summer months give little or no indications of distress. In July he was away for a little while, dredging off Deal and "anemonizing," as he called it, in St. Margaret's Bay. He had made arrangements to meet a natural history class, as in 1855, on the seashore in August, and this time the rendezvous had been fixed at Tenby, on the coast of South Wales. "It had been a subject of some solicitude with us," he says, " whether that sweet companionship, which had never been interrupted more than a few days at a time since our union, would be vouchsafed to us there.　Dr. ——, however, had from time to time encouraged us to expect it ; and, when the time arrived, he gave his full and hearty consent, furnishing my dear Emily with a supply of medicaments, and giving her instructions for their application.　His confidence had by this time communicated itself to us, so that our minds scarcely contemplated a fatal issue, except as a very improbable, or at least very remote, contingency."

They went down to Tenby on August 29, and the meetings of the class began on September 1.　The order of the day was what it had been at Ilfracombe the year before—excursions on the rocks, lectures indoors, collections in small private aquariums, more limited and occasional dredging parties outside in the bay.　One considerable disappointment, however, awaited the class. In the noble perforate caverns around Tenby my father had found the most exquisite creatures in abundance in 1854.　"Almost every dark overarched basin hollowed in the sides of the caves, or in similar situations, at Lidstep, at St. Margaret's Island, and under Tenby Head, each filled to the brim with crystalline water, has its rugged walls and floor studded with the full-blown blossoms " of these lovely animal flowers.　But when he came in 1856, these caverns and almost every accessible part of the neighbouring coasts had been hacked by the hammers and chisels of amateur naturalists.　He wrote with justified indignation : "If the visitors were gainers to the same extent that the rocks are losers, there would be less cause for regret ; but owing to difficulty and unskilfulness combined, probably half a dozen anemones are destroyed for one that goes into the aquarium."

The romantic caverns of the island of St. Catherine were still the main, and on the whole the happiest, hunting-grounds; but sometimes the entire class was conducted to Monkstone and Sandersfoot, or even so far as to Scotborough. For the first time Mrs. Gosse was unable to take part in these rambles, and her days would be spent, in the long warm September, in sitting on the sands, writing, or chatting to one of those improvised friends whom her sweet and dignified cordiality created wherever she went. She had always possessed an unusual power of attracting the confidence of strangers, and those who were sad, poor, and forlorn could seldom resist the temptation of pouring the burden of their sorrows into her ear. As she herself grew more and more the confidant of pain and weariness, instead of her temper becoming fretful, her sympathy took a deeper colouring, her interest in the griefs of others grew more patient and sincere. All this time she was growing worse, and when they returned to London on October 2, neither could conceal from the other their secret sense of dismay at the change in her power of enduring the fatigue of travel.

More drastic methods were now recommended by the doctor, and to carry them out it was necessary that the patient should be close to him. My mother and her little seven years' old son, therefore, moved into bleak and comfortless lodgings in Cottage Road, Pimlico, the only advantage of which was the fact that they were next door to the doctor's house. My father could only be with us from Saturday night to Monday morning. During the rest of the week we two supported and comforted each other as well as we could; through dreary days and still more dreary nights, which have left their indelible impression on the temperament as well as the memory of the survivor, we were alone together. This prolonged illness, and the heavy fees of the practitioner, made severe drains upon the family finances, and demanded ceaseless labour on my father's part. Yet there was some work of a different and a higher kind performed through this distressing winter. One of the most brilliant of all his monographs —his own special favourite in later years—the paper on *Lar sabellarum*, was read before the Linnæan Society in December, and was received with great respect. There was much close correspondence, too, and interchange of specimens, with Joshua Alder in the North, and with Robert Battersby in Torquay. Philip Gosse, moreover, was engaged at this time in the delightful task of helping Charles Darwin to develop his various important theories, and the three succeeding letters (now first published) may be taken as specimens of this correspondence :—

"Down, Bromley, Kent, September 22, 1856.
"My dear Sir,

"I want much to beg a little information from " you.

"I am working hard at the general question of varia-"tion, and paying for this end special attention to "domestic pigeons. This leads me to search out how "many species are truly *rock* pigeons, *i.e.* do *not* roost "or willingly perch or nest in trees. Tenminck puts *C.* "*leucocephala* (your bald-pate) under this category. Can "this be the case? Is the loud coo to which you refer "in your interesting *Sojourn* like that of the domestic "pigeon? I see in this same work you speak of rabbits "run wild; I am paying much attention to them and "am making a large collection of their skeletons. Do "you think you could get any of your zealous and "excellent correspondents to send me an adult (neck "*not* broken) female specimen? It would be of great

"value to me. It might be sent, I should think, in a
"jar with profusion of salt and split in the abdomen.
"I should also be very glad to have one of the wild
"canary birds for the same object ; I have a specimen
"in spirits from Madeira.

  "Do you think you could aid me in this, and shall you
"be inclined to forgive so very troublesome a request?
"As I have found the good nature of fellow-naturalists
"almost unbounded, I will venture further to state that
"the body of any domestic or fancy pigeon which has
"been for some generations in the West Indies would
"be of extreme interest, as I am collecting specimens
"from all quarters of the world.

"Trusting to your forgiveness,

"I remain, my dear sir,

"Yours sincerely,

"CH. DARWIN."

"Down, Bromley, Kent, September 28, 1856.
  "MY DEAR SIR,

       "I thank you warmly for your extremely kind
"letter, and for your information about the bald-pate,
"which is quite sufficient. When we meet next I shall
"beg to hear the actual coo !

  "I will by this very post write to Mr. Hill, and will
"venture to use your name as an introduction, which I
"am sure will avail me much ; so you need take no
"trouble on the subject, as using your name will be all
"that I should require. With my sincere thanks,

"Yours truly,

"CH. DARWIN.

  "I am very anxious to get all cases of the transport
"of plants or animals to distant islands. I have been
"trying the effects of salt water on the vitality of seeds

"—their powers of floatation—whether earth sticks to
"birds' feet or base of beak, and I am experimenting
"whether small seeds are ever enclosed in such earth,
"etc. Can you remember any facts? But of all cases
"whatever, the means of transport (and such I must
"think exist) of land mollusca utterly puzzle me most.
" I should be very grateful for any light."

    "Moor Park, Farnham, Surrey, April 27, 1857.
  "MY DEAR SIR,

        "I have thought that perhaps in course of the
"summer you would have an opportunity, and would be
"so very kind as to try a *little* experiment for me. I
"think I can tell best what I want by telling what I
"have done. The wide distribution of some species of
"fresh-water molluscs has long been a great perplexity
"to me ; I have just lately hatched a lot, and it occurred
"to me that when first born they might perhaps have
"not acquired phytophagous habits, and might perhaps
"like nibbling at a duck's foot. Whether this is so I do
"not know, and indeed do not believe it is so, but I
"found when there were many *very* young molluscs in
"a *small* vessel with aquatic plants, amongst which I
"placed a dried duck's foot, that the little barely visible
"shells *often* crawled over it, and then they *adhered* so
"firmly that they could not be shaken off, and that the
"foot being kept out of water in a damp atmosphere, the
"little molluscs survived well ten, twelve, or fifteen hours,
"and a *few* even twenty-four hours. And thus, I believe,
"it must be the fresh-water shells get from pond to pond,
"and even to islands out at sea. A heron fishing, for
"instance, and then startled, might well on a rainy day
"carry a young mollusc for a long distance. Now you
"will remember that E. Forbes argues chiefly from the

"difficulty of imagining how *littoral* sea-molluscs could
"cross tracts of open ocean, that islands, such as Madeira,
"must have been joined by continuous land to Europe;
"which seems to me, for many reasons, very rash
"reasoning. Now, what I want to beg of you is, that
"you would try an analogous experiment with some sea-
"mollusc, especially any strictly littoral species—hatching
"them in numbers in a smallish vessel and seeing
"whether, either *in larval* or *young shell state*, they can
"adhere to a bird's foot and survive, say, ten hours in
"*damp* atmosphere out of water. It may seem a trifling
"experiment, but seeing what enormous conclusions
"poor Forbes drew from his belief that he knew all
"means of distribution of sea-animalcules, it seems to
"me worth trying. My health has lately been very in-
"different, and I have come here for a fortnight's water-
"cure.

"I owe to using your name a most kind and most
"valuable correspondent, in Mr. Hill of Spanish Town.

"I hope you will forgive my troubling you on the
"above points, and believe me, my dear sir,

"Yours very sincerely,

"CH. DARWIN.

"P.S.—Can you tell me, you who have so watched all
"sea-nature, whether male crustaceans ever fight for the
"females? is the female sex in the sea, like on the land,
"'*teterrima belli causa?*' I beg you not to answer this
"letter, without you can and will be so kind as to tell
"me about crustacean battles, if such there be."

To this my father replied with ample notes, as, a little
later, he helped Darwin to collect facts with regard to
the agency of bees in the fertilization of papilionaceous
flowers.

My mother's condition, however, was growing more
hopeless week by week, and, under the cruel severity of the
treatment, her anguish had become absolutely constant.
She now slept only under the inducement of opiates ; and,
at last, after torturing her delicate frame so savagely for
eight months, the doctor confessed that the malady was
beyond his skill. On December 24 she was taken home,
a wreck and shadow of herself, to Huntingdon Street, and
for the brief remainder of her life she was under the
soothing care of the eminent homœopathic physician,
Dr. John Epps, whose principle appeared mainly to consist
in the alleviating and deadening of pain. Now, for the
first time, these sanguine lovers realized that the hour
of their parting was at hand ; and they faced the knowledge with fortitude. The extreme kindness of a cousin,
Mrs. Morgan, was an immense relief to both. This lady
came up from Clifton, unsolicited, and undertook the
night-nursing of the patient until near the end. The
harrowing details of these last weeks are given with too
faithful and self-torturing minuteness by my father in his
Memorial. The long-drawn agony, borne to the very last
with an ever-increasing saintly patience, came to a close
at one o'clock on the morning of Monday, February 9,
1857. My mother lies in the remotest corner of Abney
Park Cemetery.

CHAPTER X.

LITERARY WORK IN DEVONSHIRE.

1857–1864.

THE death of Emily Gosse marked a crisis in the career of her husband. None of the customary expressions which are used to denote the grief and despair of a bereaved person are applicable in his case. He showed few outward signs of distress. His faith in God, his implicit confidence that what was called the death of the redeemed was but a passage from the ante-chamber of life to its recesses, to that radiant inner room into which he also would presently be ushered, removed the bitterness of separation. He was not tortured by that *desiderium*, that insatiable and hopeless longing, which saps the vitality of those who have loved, and lost, and do not hope to regain. Yet when faith, with its clearest and fullest vision, has done all it can to comfort, nature will assert itself, and grief takes other forms. My father was now completing his forty-seventh year, and had reached an age when the first eagerness of life is over, and when sympathy and encouragement are necessary, if the strenuous effort is to be maintained. It is probable that he did not realize at once, in his determination to be at peace, in his violent subjection to the will of God, how much had been taken away from his power of sustaining an active intellectual life. He survived to recover his happiness, to be more happy, perhaps, than ever before, but he never entirely regained his energy. From this year forward he was retrenching, suppressing, withdrawing his forces, and preparing for the long-drawn seclusion of his later years.

Although my mother had shared his views on all religious questions, and although on several occasions my father has noted that she stirred the embers of his zeal and quickened his conscience—" a very blessed revival of my own soul through some words which she spoke to me "— she had, nevertheless, an influence over him which was, on the whole, opposed to the stern and fanatic tendency of his own native temperament. Her mind was a singularly gay and cheerful one, and no one could distinguish more clearly than she did between piety and misanthropy. She was also liberal in her mental judgments, ardent and curious in her reception of new ideas ; without pretending to enter into the details of physiological speculation, she was inclined to welcome novelty, rather than to reject it. The volumes which my father published during the last five years of her life show, unless I am greatly mistaken, how wholesome was her influence upon his mind in these two directions. Nothing could be more cheerful than the *Devonshire Coast*, while *Tenby* is positively playful. Nor in any of these books, or in the monographs of a more technical nature which accompanied them, is there betrayed any want of sympathy with the progress of zoological thought, or suspicion of its tendency, although the principles of Biblical theology are boldly and frequently maintained. With Edward Forbes and Charles Darwin he was in correspondence, and was exchanging with them memoranda which more and more directly tended to strengthen evolutionary ideas. In some of the monographs on the class of zoophytes which Philip Gosse issued in 1855 and 1856, passages are to be found which show the author to

have grasped, or rather, perhaps, to have been prepared
to grasp, the doctrine of biological development.

But it has to be confessed that such evolutionism as he
accepted was timid and unphilosophical, and that sooner
or later he would certainly have been brought to a halt by
the definite theory of Darwin. The belief in a direct
creative act from without, peopling the world with a sudden
full-blown efflorescence of fauna and flora, was a part of
my father's very being, and he would have abandoned the
entire study of science sooner than relinquish it. He was
aware of his limitations as a thinker ; he knew his mind to
be one which observed closely and minutely, and failed to
take in a wide horizon. He once, in later years, referring
to his isolation as a zoologist, said to me that he felt himself to be a disciple of Cuvier, born into an age of successors
of Lamarck ; and his position could scarcely be defined more
exactly. Yet it seems to me possible that if my mother
had lived, he might have been prevented from putting
himself so fatally and prominently into opposition to the
new ideas. He might probably have been content to
leave others to fight out the question on a philosophical
basis, and might himself have quietly continued observing
facts, and noting his observations with his early elegance
and accuracy.

That his mind was morbid, and his nerves unstrung, is
clearly enough to be discovered from reading the singularly
painful little *Memorial of the Last Days on Earth of Emily
Gosse*, which he published in April, 1857. In this volume,
written with distressing ability, he gives a picture of the
illness and death of his wife which it is exceedingly difficult
to describe, so harsh, so minute, so vivid are the lines, so
little are the customary conventions of a memoir preserved.
This little book, which was addressed, of course, to an
extremely limited circle, was received with great displeasure

T

by its readers, few of whom were well enough versed either in literature or life to understand the tenderness and melancholy which were concealed beneath this acrid and positive manner of writing. The reception of the *Memorial* by his wife's friends and many of his own shut him still further up within himself, and he became almost as silent and reserved as he had been before his marriage.

He was roused, however, during the spring and summer of this year, by a good deal of lecturing, in Scotland, in the North, in the midland counties. London became inexpressibly disagreeable to him, and he began to look about for a home in the country. In March he was approached by the committee of an educational scheme which was then occupying a good deal of public attention, a certain Gnoll College, which was to form the nucleus of a university for Wales, and was to be founded on a romantic acclivity in the Vale of Neath, in Glamorganshire. It was hoped that this institution would be richly endowed, and the committee was endeavouring to secure the best men in every branch as its professors. This Gnoll project gratified my father's dislike to London, and when, in June, it proceeded so far as the offer to him of the chair of Natural History, with a residence, he received the proposition with delight. But there was a worm at the root of this tree, and Gnoll never opened its academic halls. On September 1, having satisfied himself that the Welsh project would come to nothing, Philip Gosse went down to his old haunt, the village of St. Marychurch, in South Devon. This place had just been seized with a building craze, and new villas, each in its separate garden, were rising on all hands. Philip Gosse hired a horse, and rode round the neighbourhood to see what he could find to suit him, and at last he discovered, near the top of the Torquay Road, what he thought was the exact place.

It was not an attractive object to a romantic eye. It is impossible to conceive anything much more dispiriting than this brand-new little house, unpapered, undried, standing in ghastly whiteness in the middle of a square enclosure of raw "garden," that is to say of ploughed field, laid out with gravel walks, beds without a flower or leaf, and a "lawn" of fat red loam guiltless of one blade of grass. Two great rough pollard elms, originally part of a hedge which had run across the site of the lawn, were the only objects that relieved the monotony of the inchoate place, which spread out, vague and uncomely, "like the red outline of beginning Adam." By taking the house in this condition, however, it was a cheap purchase, and my father felt that it would be a pleasure to discipline all this formlessness into beauty and fertility. He never repented of his choice, nor ever expressed, through more than thirty years, the wish that he had gone elsewhere. The Devonshire red loam is wonderfully stubborn, and for many seasons the place retained the obloquy of its newness. But at length the grass became velvety on the lawn, trees grew up and hid the unmossed limestone walls in which no vegetation can force a footing, and the little place grew bowery and secluded. It was on September 23, 1857, that the family settled in this house—named Sandhurst, by the builder, in mere wantonness of nomenclature—and this became their home. Philip Gosse's restless wanderings were over.

Before going down into Devonshire he had completed two pieces of literary work, which, so far as his scientific credit was concerned, he might very well have left undone. They represent a mental condition of exhaustion and of irritation. The first of these, a volume of collected essays which had appeared in the magazine called *Excelsior*, was published in the summer of 1857. The author gave it the title of *Life in its Lower, Intermediate, and Higher Forms*, and was startled on the day of publication by seeing it ticketed in the bookshops " Gosse's Life," as though some one had obliged the town with a premature biography of him. These essays were slight, and the religious element was quite unduly prominent, as if vague forebodings of the coming theory of evolution had determined the writer to insist with peculiar intensity on the need of rejecting all views inconsistent with the notion of a creative design. This book entirely failed to please the public, who had now for so many years been such faithful clients to him ; with the scientific class it passed almost unnoticed.

No such gentle oblivion attended the other unlucky venture of the year 1857. My attempt in writing this life has been to present a faithful picture of my father's career, and I dare not omit to chronicle the disappointments and annoyances which attended the publication of his *Omphalos: An Attempt to untie the Geological Knot.* Philip Gosse was so profoundly unambitious, so entirely careless of what was thought about his doings and writings, that he can hardly be said to have made a mistake, in the ordinary sense of the phrase, in composing a book which was fatal to the advance of his reputation as a man of science. But others, to whom his fame is dearer than it was to himself, may bitterly regret that he left his own field of research, that field in which he was gathering such thick and clustering laurels, to adventure in a province of scientific philosophy which lay outside his sphere, and for which he was fitted neither by training, nor by native aptitude, nor by the possession of a mind clear from prejudice. Thoroughly sincere as he was, and devoted to truth as he believed himself to be, he lacked that deeper modesty, that nobler candour, which inspired the genius of Darwin. The current interpretation of the Bible lay upon his judgment with a weight that he could never throw off, and his scientific work was of value only in those matters of detail which remained beyond the jurisdiction of the canon. But, as I have said before, if he could have been content to rest in detail, and to have let the ephemeral theories of man spin themselves out in gossamer and disappear ; if he could have persuaded himself to endure with indifference what he regarded with disdain, all might yet have been well. In 1857 evolutionism was crude and vague ; a positive naturalist might well have been permitted to ignore it. But, unhappily, my father's conscience tortured him into protest, and he must needs break a lance with the windmills of the geologists.

The theory around which the illustrative chapters of *Omphalos* were embroidered may briefly be described. The pet craze of the moment was the reconciliation of Genesis with geology. Most men of science at that date advocated, or thought it decent to seem to advocate, some scheme or other for preventing the phenomena of geological investigation from clashing with the Mosaic record. Many of them, with Adam Sedgwick, thought that "we must consider the old strata of the earth as monuments of a date long anterior to the existence of man, and to the times contemplated in the moral records of his creation." Very few were, in 1857, prepared to part company altogether with the cosmogony of Genesis. They preferred to evade the actual language, to escape into such generalities as " the six ages of creation," "an antecedent state of the earth prior to the recorded Mosaical epoch." It was to a generation not as yet revolutionized or emboldened by Darwin and Colenso that my father addressed his *Omphalos ;* he took for granted that his readers were sure of the fact of creation. He undertook to show them that the contents of the fossiliferous strata did not prove any process of cosmic formation which the six literal days of

Genesis might not have covered. He proposed to reconcile geology not merely to the Mosaic record, but to an exact and inelastic interpretation of it.

His theory is briefly this. Life is a circle, no one stage of which more than any other affords a natural commencing-point. Every living object has an omphalos, or an egg, or a seed, which points irresistibly to the existence of a previous living object of the same kind. Creation, therefore, must mean the sudden bursting into the circle, and its phenomena, produced full grown by the arbitrary will of God, would certainly present the stigmata of a pre-existent existence. Each created tree would display the marks of sloughed bark and fallen leaves, though it had never borne those leaves or that bark. The teeth of each brute would be worn away with exercise which it had never taken. By innumerable examples he shows that this must have been the case with all living forms. If so, then why may not the fossils themselves be part of this breaking into the circle ? Why may not the strata, with their buried fauna and flora, belong to the general scheme of the prochronic development of the plan of the life-history of this globe? The ingenuity of this idea is great, and if once we believe in the literal act of creation, it is very hard to escape from the reasoning that leads up to it. It was an example of the looseness of thought habitual to the majority of readers that those who desired to hold the orthodox view were unable to see that they were on the horns of a dilemma in rejecting my father's theory. What *Omphalos* really proved was the absolute necessity for some other definite hypothesis of the mode in which the world came into existence than any which assumed the traditional idea of a sudden creative act.

It was the notion that the world was created with fossil skeletons in its crust which met with most ridicule from readers. Philip Gosse was charged with supposing that God had formed these objects on purpose to deceive—in order, in fact, to set a trap for naughty geologists. The reply was obvious, and had occurred to him already. " Were the concentric timber-rings of a created tree formed merely to deceive ? " he had asked. " Were the growth-lines of a created shell intended to deceive ? Was the navel of the created man intended to deceive him into the persuasion that he had had a parent ? " The book, nevertheless, in spite of the beauty and ingenuity of its literary illustration, was received with scorn by the world of science and with neglect by the general public. The moment was a transitional one ; the world had just been led captive by that picturesque piece of amateur evolutionism, *The Vestiges of Creation.* It was whispered here and there that something stronger and more convincing was on the road. Hooker was murmuring in the ear of Lyell that Darwin was in possession of some "ugly facts." The human mind was preparing for a great crisis of emancipation, of relief from a fettering order of ideas no longer tenable or endurable, and no one was concerned to give even fair play to a piece of reasoning, such as *Omphalos*, whose whole purpose was to bind again those very cords out of which the world was painfully struggling. The reception of *Omphalos*, especially by the orthodox party, was an extreme disappointment to my father. So certain had he been that the whole camp of faith would rally around him, and that all Christians would accept his solution of the problem with rapture, that he had ordered the printing of an immense edition, the greater part of which was left upon his hands.

It may be interesting to print here the candid and characteristic letter which he received on this occasion from Charles Kingsley :—

"Eversley, May 4, 1858.

"MY DEAR MR. GOSSE,

"I have found time to read *Omphalos* carefully,
"and will now write you my whole heart about it.

"For twenty-five years I have read no book which has
"so staggered and puzzled me. Don't fancy that I pooh-
"pooh it. Such an idea, having once entered a man's
"head, ought to be worked out; and you have done so
"bravely and honestly.

"Your distinction between diachronism and pro-
"chronism, instead of being nonsense, as it is in the eyes
"of the Locke-beridden Nominalist public, is to me, as a
"Platonist and realist, an indubitable and venerable
"truth. For many years have I believed in that in-
"tellectualic, of which neither time nor space can be
"predicated, wherein God abides eternally, descending
"into time and space only by the Logos, the creative
"Word, Jesus Christ our Lord. Therefore with me the
"great stumbling-block to your book does not exist.

"Nothing can be fairer than the way in which you
"state the evidence for the microchronology. That at
"once bound me to listen respectfully to all you had to
"say after. And, much as I kicked and winced at first,
"nothing, I find, can be sounder than your parallels and
"precedents. The one case of the coccus-mother
"(though every conceivable instance goes to prove your
"argument) would be enough for me, assuming the
"act of absolute creation. Assuming that—which I
"have always assumed, as fully as you—shall I tell you
"the truth? It is best. Your book is the first that ever
"made me doubt it, and I fear it will make hundreds do
"so. Your book tends to prove this—that if we accept
"the fact of absolute creation, God becomes a *Deus
"quidam deceptor*. I do not mean merely in the case

"of fossils which *pretend* to be the bones of dead
"animals; but in the one single case of your newly
"created scars on the pandanus trunk, and your newly
"created Adam's navel, you make God tell a lie. It is
"not my reason, but my *conscience* which revolts here;
"which makes me say, 'Come what will, disbelieve what
"'I may, I cannot believe this of a God of truth, of Him
"'who is Light and no darkness at all, of Him who
"'formed the intellectual man after His own image, that
"'he might understand and glory in His Father's works.'
"I ought to feel this, I say, of the single Adam's
"navel, but I can hush up my conscience at the single
"instance; at the great sum total, the worthlessness
"of all geologic instruction, I cannot. I cannot give up
"the painful and slow conclusion of five and twenty
"years' study of geology, and believe that God has
"written on the rocks one enormous and superfluous lie
"for all mankind.

"To this painful dilemma you have brought me, and
"will, I fear, bring hundreds. It will not make me throw
"away my Bible. I trust and hope. I know in whom I
"have believed, and can trust Him to bring my faith
"safe through this puzzle, as He has through others; but
"for the young I do fear. I would not for a thousand
"pounds put your book into my children's hands. They
"would use the argument of the early Reformers about
"transubstantiation (which you mention, but to which
"you do not give sufficient weight), 'My senses tell
"'me that this is bread, not God's body. You may burn
"'me alive, but I must believe my senses.' Your
"demand on implicit faith is just as great as that
"required for transubstantiation, and, believe me, many
"of your arguments, especially in the opening chapter,
"are strangely like those of the old Jesuits, and those

"one used to hear from John Henry Newman fifteen
"years ago, when he, copying the Jesuits, was trying to
"undermine the grounds of all rational belief and human
"science, in order that, having made his victims (among
"whom were some of my dearest friends) believe nothing,
"he might get them by a 'Nemesis of faith' to believe
"anything, and rush blindfold into superstition. Poor
"wretch, he was caught in his own snare. I do not fear
"you will be ; for you have set no snare, but spoken
"like an honest Christian man ; but this I *do* fear, with
"the editor of this month's *Geologist*, that you have given
"the 'vestiges of creation theory' the best shove for-
"ward which it has ever had. I have a special dislike
"to that book ; but, honestly, I felt my heart melting
"towards it as I read *Omphalos*, and especially on
"reading one page where I think your argument
"weakest, not from fallacy, but from being too hastily
"slurred over. You must rewrite and enlarge these in
"some future edition—I mean pp. 343, 344. What you
"say there I think true, but I always have explained it
"to myself in this way—that God's imagining one
"species to Himself, before creation, necessitated the
"imagining of another, either to take its place in
"physical uses, or to fill up 'artistically,' if I may so
"speak, the cycle of possible forms. *This* was *my*
"prochronism ; but I don't see how *yours* differs from
"the transmutation of species theory, which your
"argument, if filled out fairly, would, I think, be.

"This shell would ·have been its ancient analogue
"of the Pleistocene, if creation had taken place at the
"Pleistocene era, and that, again, would have been the
"Eocene analogue, if creation had happened an æon
"earlier again ; and in that case the Eocene shell would
'have been afterward *transmuted* into the Pleistocene

"one, and the Pleistocene one by this time into the
"recent : but creation having occurred *after* the
"Pleistocene era, fossils representing those (and the
"early) links of the cycle have been inserted into their
"proper beds.

"Now, I wish you would look over this thought, for
"it is what you really seem to me to lead to. I am not
"frightened if it be true. Known unto God are all His
'works, and that is enough for me ; but it does trouble
"me, as a disliker of the *Vestiges*, to find you advocating
"a cyclic theory of species, which, if it is to bear any
"analogy to the cycle of individual growth, must surely
"consist in physical transformation.

"If you will set me right on this matter, you will do
"me a moral good, as well as justice to yourself.

"Pray take all I say in good part, as the speech of
"one earnest man to another. All I want is God's
"truth, and if I can get that I will welcome it, however
"much it upsets my pride and my theories. And I am
"sure, from the tone of your book, you want nothing
"else either.

"I promised to review your book. I pay you a high
"compliment when I say that I shall *not* do so, and
"solely for this reason—that I am not going to mount
"the reviewer's chair, and pretend to pass judgment,
"where I am so utterly puzzled as to confess myself
"only a learner and an inquirer writing for light.

"Believe me, yours more faithfully than ever,

"C. KINGSLEY."

By the time, however, that *Omphalos* was published, in
November, 1857, the change from London to Devonshire
had wrought its good work upon Gosse's mental health and
spirits. He lost his morbid depression ; he resumed his

own proper work of observation with enthusiasm ; and he started what is admitted to be the most serious and the most durable of his contributions to scientific literature. Since his first visit to Devonshire in 1852 the British sea-anemones and corals had attracted his constantly repeated attention. These curious and beautiful creatures had hitherto been almost entirely neglected. The sea-anemones had possessed but one historian, Dr. George Johnston, who had given them a place in his *History of British Zoophytes.* Johnston had been a good naturalist in his day, but the number of varieties with which he was acquainted was very small, and he was not by any means careful enough in discriminating species. He lived on the north-eastern coast of England, where these creatures are rare, and the consequence was that for purposes of specific characterization his work was utterly worthless. Johnston, even in his latest edition, had been aware of the existence of only twenty-four British species. Gosse increased this number to between seventy and eighty, and no fewer than thirty-four species were added to the British fauna by his own personal investigation. But even more important, perhaps, than this addition to the record of known forms, was the creation of a complete systematic analysis of the order Actinoidea, a feat which Philip Gosse performed unaided. His system of classification was accepted in all parts of the scientific world, and is still in force, with but very slight modification.

The great work in which he embodied these investigations was entitled *Actinologia Britannica,* and professed to be " A History of the British Sea-anemones and Corals." It was begun in the autumn of 1857, and concluded in the spring of 1860, having been published in twelve bi-monthly parts, the first of which was issued on March 1, 1858. During these two years, the collection and collation of facts connected with this inquiry formed the main occupation of my father's time. In 1852 he had enjoyed his first experience of marine-collecting on the shores of Oddicombe and Petit Tor, and he now returned to the same pools and coves with a fuller experience. He found the coast but little interfered with, although the aquarium mania and the prestige of his previous visit had to some degree invaded his hunting-grounds. In carrying through the great task which he had set before him, a task in which no predecessor had laid down the lines along which he was to proceed, he found it absolutely necessary to base every single observation on personal examination. In order to do this, he was obliged to provide himself with a wide variety of specimens, and to appeal to local naturalists in all parts of the British Islands for help. He printed a circular inviting the co-operation of strangers, in which he described, with minute care, what he wanted and did not want, how specimens should be packed and forwarded, and all other needful particulars. The consequence was that he stimulated the zeal of fellow-labourers in all parts of Britain, from the Shetlands to Jersey, and the morning post commonly laid upon the breakfast-table at Sandhurst one, if not more, little box of a salt and oozy character, containing living anemones or corals carefully wrapped up in wet seaweed. In those days, fortunately, the Post Office had not yet wakened up to the inconvenience to other people's correspondence which such dribbling packages might cause.

But it was to his own exertions that Philip Gosse mainly looked for the necessary specimens. Several times a week, if the weather and the tide were at all favourable, he would clamber down to the shore at Anstice Cove, at Oddicombe, at Petit Tor, or take longer excursions, to Maidencombe northwards, or to Livermead southwards on Tor Bay. In these excursions I was his constant, and generally his only, companion. He was in the habit of carrying a large wicker basket, so divided into compartments as to hold two stone jars of considerable, capacity, and two smaller glass jars. The former were for seaweeds, crabs, large fishes— the rougher customers generally ; while the latter were dedicated to rare anemones, nudibranchs, small crustaceans, and the other fairy people of the pools. To me was generally entrusted an additional glass jar, in a wicker case, and sometimes a green gauze net, such as the capturers of butterflies carry, which was to be used for surface-fishing, and for gently shaking into its folds the delicate forms that might be hiding in the seaweed curtains of large still tidal pools.

One important portion of our work on the shore consisted in turning over the large flat stones in sequestered places. Great discretion was needed in selecting the right stones. Those which were too heavily set would contain nothing, resting too deeply to admit the sea to their lower surface. Those which were balanced too lightly would be found deserted, because too frequently disturbed. But the stone sagaciously chosen as being flat enough, and heavy enough, and yet not too heavy, would often display on its upturned under surface a marvellous store of beautiful minute rarities—nudibranchs that looked like tiny animated amethysts and topazes ; unique little sea-anemones in the fissures ; odd crabs, as flat as farthings, scuttling away in agitation ; fringed worms, like bronzed cords, or strings dipped in verdigris, serpentining in and out of decrepit tufts of coralline.

When our backs ached with the strain of stone-turning, we used to proceed further into the broken rockwork of the promontory or miniature archipelago, and the more serious labour of collecting in tidal pools, or on the retreating seaward surface of mimic cliffs, would begin. Protected by his tall boots, my father would step into mid-seas, and, stooping under a dripping wall of seaweeds, would search beneath the *algæ* for such little glossy points of colour as revealed interesting forms to his practised eye. If these would not come away under the persuasion of the fingers, he would shout to me, as guardian of the basket, to hand over to him the hammer and the cold chisel, and a few skilful blows would bring away the fragment of rock, with its atoms of animated jelly adhering to it, uninjured and almost unruffled, to be popped immediately into one or other of the jars, according to his decision. This would go on until, with splashings from below, the result of eager pursuit of objects seen almost out of reach, and drippings from above, caused by the briny rain from the shaken curtains of the seaweeds, he would be drenched almost to the skin; and then, by a violent revulsion, he would seize the net, and sally forth, wading, on to the shallow waters of the sands, skimming the surface for medusæ, small fishes, and such other tender flotsam as might come within his reach. Two or three hours of all this fatigue were commonly as much as he could bear, and so much energy did he throw into the business that he would often turn away at last, not satisfied, but exhausted almost to extinction.

Even as a little child I was conscious that my father's appearance on these excursions was eccentric. He had a penchant for an enormous felt hat, which had once been black, but was now grey and rusty with age and salt. For some reason or other, he seldom could be persuaded to wear clothes of such a light colour and material as other sportsmen affect. Black broadcloth, reduced to an extreme seediness, and cut in ancient forms, was the favourite attire for the shore, and after being soaked many times, and dried in the sun on his somewhat portly person, it grew to look as if it might have been bequeathed to him by some ancient missionary long marooned, with no other garments, upon a coral island. His ample boots, reaching to mid-thigh, completed his professional garb, and when he was seen, in full sunlight, skimming the rising tide upon the sands, he might have been easily mistaken for a superannuated working shrimper.

Our excursions were usually made to points a little beyond the reach of the amateur, but sometimes we crossed parties of collectors, in dainty costumes, such as Leech depicted, with pails or baskets, and we would smile and nudge each other at the reflection that they little suspected that the author of *The Aquarium* was so near them. On one occasion, I recollect, at Livermead, we came across a party of ladies, who were cackling so joyously over a rarity they had secured that our curiosity overcame our shyness, and we asked them what they had found. They named a very scarce species, and held it up to us to examine. My father, at once, civilly set them right; it was so-and-so, something much more commonplace. The ladies drew themselves up with dignity, and sarcastically remarked that they could only repeat that it *was* the rarity, and that "Gosse is our authority."

My father was at his very best on these delightful excursions. His blood was healthily stirred by the exercise, by the eager instinct of the hunt. Extremely serious all the time, with his brows a little knitted, he was nevertheless not at all formidable here, as he so often was at home. His broad face, blanched with emotion, as he arranged his little lens to bear in proper focus on a peopled eminence of wet rock, had no such terrors for me as it sometimes had when it rose, burdened with prophecy, from the pages of some book of exhortation. The excitement in the former case was one which I could share, and we were happy so long as no stranger intermeddled with our joy. But the discovery of some other collector installed on our hunting-field, or the advent of anybody to disturb us, was sufficient to throw a cloud over everything. If we could not escape, if we pushed on in vain into a district of wilder and more slippery rocks and deeper pools, if the unconscious enemy persisted in dogging our footsteps, then the spell was broken, and home we trudged with empty jars, or with a harvest but half garnered.

Most interesting of all were the dredging excursions in Tor Bay, but my memories of them are much more fragmentary. These were frequent through the course of 1858, but after that year my father scarcely ever ventured on the water. During that last season, Charles Kingsley was several times our companion. The naturalists would hire a small trawler, and work up and down, generally in the southern part of the bay, just outside a line drawn north and south, between Hope's Nose and Berry Head. I think that Kingsley was a good sailor; my father was a very indifferent one, and so was I; but when the trawl came up, and the multitudinous population of the bottom of the bay was tossed in confusion before our eyes, we forgot our qualms in our excitement. I still see the hawk's eyes of Kingsley peering into the trawl on one side, my father's wide face and long set mouth bent upon the other. I well recollect the occasion (my father's diary gives me the date, August 11, 1858) when, in about twenty fathoms outside Berry Head, we hauled up the first specimen ever observed of that exquisite creature, the diadem anemone, *Bunodes coronata;* its orange-scarlet body clasping the whorls of a living *Turritella* shell, while it held in the air its purple parapet crowned with snow-white spiky tentacles.

When the bi-monthly parts were bound up, the *Acti-*

nologia Britannica formed a large and handsome volume, copiously illustrated with coloured plates of all the known British species and most of the varieties. The text is constructed on the lucid and elaborated system consecrated to exact manuals of this kind by the tradition of Yarrell's *British Birds.* The figures of the various sea-anemones are extremely accurate in form, size, and colour, and have but one artistic fault, namely, the want of natural grouping in the plate. In order to secure perfect exactitude, my father drew and coloured each specimen separately, and cut out his figure and gummed it on to its place in the compound illustration. Some of the individual figures suffer from the hard line which surrounds them, the result of this composite treatment of the full-page plates. The introduction, a minute description of the organization of the sea-anemones, and in particular of their unique and extraordinary "teliferous" system, has been regarded as the most sustained piece of original writing of a technically scientific character which Philip Gosse has left behind him. His anatomical statements in this preface are exceedingly minute, and are given almost wholly on the authority of his own dissections and observations, but they have never been superseded.

While this important work was slowly drawn to a conclusion, Philip Gosse occupied his leisure with a volume of a more ephemeral nature, *Evenings at the Microscope,* which appeared in 1859. This was a popular introduction to the study of microscopy. The text of the *Actinologia* was finished in June, 1859, although it did not appear in final book form until January of the next year. But almost as soon as the letterpress was off his hands, my father turned to the composition of a book which had long occupied his thoughts, a volume dealing exclusively with the æsthetic aspects of zoology. "In my many years' wanderings through the wide field of natural history," he wrote in March, 1860, "I have always felt toward it something of a poet's heart, though destitute of a poet's genius. As Wordsworth says :—

> "'To me the meanest flower that blows can give
> Thoughts that do often lie too deep for tears.'"

In *The Poetry of Natural History* (a title afterwards changed to *The Romance*) he sought to paint a series of pictures, the reflection of scenes and aspects in nature, selecting those which had peculiarly the power of awakening admiration, terror, curiosity, and pleasure in his own breast. To the composition of this volume he gave unusual care, and it remains, perhaps, the nearest approach to an English classic of any of Philip Gosse's writings. When the author repeats the experiences of others, the style is sometimes a little otiose ; but where he dwells on what has personally pleased or moved him, where he narrates his own experiences and chronicles his personal emotions, the pages of this first series of *The Romance of Natural History* preserve a charm which may never wholly evaporate. The editions of this book have been very numerous, and after a lapse of thirty years I believe that it is still in print, and enjoys a steady sale.

One chapter of this book, the final one, attracted more notice than all the rest put together, and excited, indeed, a positive furore. This was the chapter entitled "The Great Unknown," in which Philip Gosse started the suggestion that the semi-mythic marine monster, whose name was always cropping up in the newspapers, the famous sea-serpent, was perhaps a surviving species allied to the gigantic fossil *Enaliosauria* of the lias, and, in short, a marine reptile of large size, of sauroid figure, with turtle-like paddles. He judged it to be a sort of plesiosaurus, some twelve or fifteen feet in length ; and one of the illustrations of *The Romance of Natural History* was a conjectural drawing of the living "sea-serpent," constructed on the Enaliosaurian hypothesis. In the body of the book he gave a searching analysis of the more or less vague reports made by unscientific, but apparently honest persons, who had seen "the sea-serpent" from ship-board, and he strove to show that all these stories, taken in combination, tended to point conclusively to the existence of such a survival as he suggested.

The theory was worked out with great fullness, and the ingenuity of a special pleader.   The naturalists followed it with amusement and interest. Darwin was by no means inclined to reject it, as a very possible hypothesis, but Professor Owen hotly contested it in favour of a theory of his own, that the "sea-serpent" would really prove to be a very large seal. It is rather odd that after thirty years the question should still be left wholly unanswered, especially as vague reports of a monster seen in mid-ocean continue occasionally to reach the papers. I am not aware that any suggestion more tenable than my father's has yet been propounded, and more extraordinary things have been laughed at when they were first foreshadowed and have ultimately proved to be true. Considering the stir that was made about this "sea-serpent" disquisition when it was originally published, it is not a little surprising that fifteen or twenty years later a popular writer on science should have had the effrontery to steal the whole thing, *plesiosaurus* hypothesis, examination of evidence, and even the very words of Philip Gosse's arguments, and to put it forth as a little theory of his own. The perpetrator survived my father, by a strange coincidence, only a few days, and as he is dead, I need not mention his name.

The Romance of Natural History was not published

until Christmas, 1860, but it was finished in the preceding March. My father had now for three years been settled in the west, and he was growing more and more, as he expressed it himself, a "troglodyte," a dweller in a cave. The composition of the *Actinologia Britannica* had forced him into correspondence with a large circle of strangers, and had kept his human sympathies alive. But after the publication of that work, a kind of inertia began to creep over him, and he dropped his correspondents one by one. Even Charles Kingsley, with whom he had enjoyed so long and close communion of interests, seemed to lose hold over him. His household consisted, at this time, of his aged mother, whom he had brought down into Devonshire in March, 1858 ; his little son ; and Miss Andrews, a lady who undertook the housekeeping for the trio.

On February 28 old Mrs. Gosse died, at the age of eighty. She had been bodily transplanted, with all her furniture, pictures, and knick-knacks, to an apartment fitted up as closely as possible to resemble her own old room in the Poole house half a century before. She remained, until near the last, in full possession of her intelligence, rugged, vehement, slightly bewildered, filled with respect for her son, and recognisant of his kindness, yet pathetically remote from all his interests. While she was still able, on his arm, to creep out a little in the sunshine, she visited his new tropical fern-house, lately fitted up in the Sandhurst garden. The little conservatory was a great success ; in the moist hot air the transparent traceries of the delicate fronds formed an exquisite feathery vault, on either side and above the visitor. "I wonder," she said, after gazing round, "that you care to keep a parcel of fern ;" and she turned away. To her the fairy *adiantums* and *aspleniums* were no more than specimens of that wide waste of "fern," of bracken, which the open moors of Dorsetshire presented in such abundance. I remember that I was conscious of these blunt traits in my grandmother, and conscious, too, of my father's grave and unaltering attitude of respectful consideration to her. But we were a solitary family. For hours and hours, my grandmother would be sitting at her patchwork, silent, in her padded chair ; my father, almost motionless, in his study below her; and I, equally silent, though not equally still, free to wander whither I would in house and garden, so that I disturbed none of the penates of the cloister and the hearth.

In the autumn of 1860 a very happy and wholesome change was made in the tenour of our existence. My father became acquainted with a lady from the eastern counties, who was staying at Torquay. This was Miss Eliza Brightwen, whom he married at Frome, in Somerset, on December 18 of that same year. This lady happily survives, and it would not be becoming for me to dwell here on the circumstances which attended her married life. But, when her eye reaches this page in the biography of one so dear to us both, she will forgive me if I record, on behalf of the dead, as on my own behalf, our deep sense of gratitude, and our tender recognition of her tact and gentleness and devotion through no less than thirty years. It is of my step-mother, of that good genius of our house, of whom I think every time I turn the pages of *Adonais—*

> "What softer voice is hushed over the dead ?
> Athwart what brow is that dark mantle thrown ?
> *   *   *   *   *
> If it be she, who, gentlest of the wise,
> Taught, soothed, loved, honoured, the departed one ;
> Let me not vex with inharmonious sighs
> The silence of that heart's accepted sacrifice."

The year 1861 was the last in which my father retained his old intellectual habits and interests unimpaired. There was, even, a revival of the scientific spirit, a fresh response to the instinct of the observer. His principal literary work was a second series of *The Romance of Natural History*, carried forth, rather too hastily, in consequence of the extraordinary popularity of the first. It was issued in November, and sold well, but not nearly so well as its predecessor. The book suffers from the usual fate of continuations. We feel that the first series was produced because the author had something which he must say, the second because he must say something. The most interesting and important chapter was that on " The Extinct," in which the author dwells on the death of species, on the disappearance of the mylodon, the Irish elk, the æpyornis, the dodo, and the great auk. In the section on " Mermaids," he tried to repeat the success of his sensational chapter on the " Sea-Serpent," and suggested the possibility that the northern seas may yet hold some form of mammal, uncatalogued by science, which, if guiltless of green hair and a looking-glass, may yet ultimately prove to be the prototype of the mermaid. He had, however, no such definite hypothesis to produce as the old *plesiosaurus* one, and the public imagination declined to be greatly stirred about mermaids.

In the autumn of 1861 Philip Gosse returned with one of his spasmodic bursts of zeal to the accurate study of the rotifera. His successive monographs on Stephanoceros, on the Floscularidæ, and on the Melicertidæ appeared in the *Popular Science Review* in the course of 1862, and supplemented the discoveries he had made and reported twelve years before. In these papers he began a general account of the whole class of the *Rotifera*, arranged according to a classification of his own ; but the *Popular Science Review* came to an end, and the work was never completed. This important fragment of a history of the *Rotifera* is constantly referred to in the great work published by Hudson and Gosse a quarter of a century later. It only includes the three great families of the Floscularidæ, the Melicertidæ, and the Notommatina ; but it is almost a classic as regards those sections of the class.

The next year was the first for twenty years in which Philip Gosse was not actively employed in literary work. It was a season of sudden transition ; his tastes, his intellectual habits, underwent a complete change. He ceased, almost entirely, to concentrate his attention on marine forms. He abandoned his long-loved mistress, zoology, and in exchange he began to devote himself to astronomy and to botany. Both of these new interests were awakened in April, 1862—the former in consequence of the publication in the *Times* of some observations regarding coloured stars which greatly excited his imagination ; the latter through seeing Lord Sinclair's collection of tropical orchids. He began, with his accustomed energy, to devote himself to these novel interests, and he built an orchid-house, in which he presently collected and arranged a very valuable collection of these singular and fascinating plants. He imported them from the tropics on his own account, and in October, 1862, the first of many consignments arrived, in the shape of a rough assortment of orchids from the forests of Brazil.

Once more he was persuaded to take up the pen in 1863. As a popular illustrated magazine of quite a new class, *Good Words* was just then at the height of a well-deserved popularity. Dr. Norman Macleod had frequently invited Philip Gosse to contribute, but without avail ; until in the first days of 1863, being in South Devon, he called at Sandhurst, and did not leave until my father had undertaken to write a serial for the magazine, a series of consecutive papers, to cover a whole year, describing month by month, in a sort of sea-shepherd's calendar, what work a naturalist could undertake at each season on the shore. These papers were to be illustrated by at least three plates in each number, engraved in black and white in the pages of *Good Words*, but originally executed in Philip Gosse's most exquisite style, in water-colours. This serial was entitled *A Year at the Shore*, and the first instalment appeared in the magazine in January, 1864, running through the entire year. These papers were very happily written, quite in the old enchanting style of the *Devonshire Coast* and *The Aquarium*, with the freshness of that contented and wholesome period. They were full of practical advice to persons engaged in zoological collection ; and they proved, so he was constantly assured, very stimulating to the readers of the magazine.

His orchids largely occupied Philip Gosse's spare moments in the course of 1863, and in the autumn he was corresponding a good deal with Charles Darwin, to whom he had communicated in June some observations he had made on the strange and morbid-looking blossoms of the *Stanhopea*. From this correspondence I select his two earliest letters, and the replies received from the eminent biologist. They will be of interest, perhaps, to others than botanists, and are now for the first time published.

P. H. GOSSE to CHARLES DARWIN.

" Sandhurst, May 30, 1863.

" MY DEAR SIR,

" Will you kindly vouchsafe me a little word " of help ? With your charming book before me, I have " been trying to fertilize the orchids of my little collec- " tion, as they flower. With some I succeed, with others " there is difficulty. Let me tell you of the present ' fix.'

" *Stanhopea oculata* opened four great blooms on " Thursday ; to-day they begin to flag, and I delay no

"longer to impregnate. I reach down your book, turn
"to your figure at p. 179, and recognize the parts well
"enough.   Then, with a toothpick, I lift the anther
"and out come the pollinia, very well depicted by you
"at p. 185, Fig. C, except that in this my species the
"pollinia masses are much larger in proportion to the
"viscid disc.   The disc is viscid enough, and I carry the
"whole on a toothpick.   Now I want to find where to
"deposit it.   I take for granted that it is in the hollow
"(marked *a* in my sketch), which is the stigma.   But
"there is no viscosity there, nor anywhere near, up or
"down, not the slightest ; and I cannot get the pollen
"to adhere.   How can this plant be fertilized ?   And how
"would any insect do it ?   And what would an insect
"be about to touch the tip of this isolated projecting
"column ?   Supposing the great bee, or *Scolia*, or what
"not, wants to get at the hollow hypochil (though I
"don't find any honey there), he would alight on the
"epichil (whose surface is already three-quarters of an
"inch from the rostellum, and which, being movable,
"would bend away still further), and creep between the
"horns of the mesochil ; how thus could he touch the
"anther? and if he did, how could he lodge the pollen
"on the stigma ? And if he did, how could it stick, seeing
"the place is not sticky ?

"Do resolve me these doubts ; and believe me,

"My dear sir,

"Ever yours truly,

"P. H. GOSSE.

"The disc at the end of the caudicle adheres to the
"stigma, but the *pollen masses* project, and won't touch
"it, though pressed against it with force."

C. DARWIN *to* P. H. GOSSE.

"Down, June 2, 1863.

"MY DEAR SIR,

"It would give me real pleasure to resolve your
"doubts, but I cannot. I can give only suspicions and
"my grounds for them. I should think the non-viscidity
"of the stigmatic hollow was due to the plant not living
"under its natural conditions. Please see what I have
"said on *Acropera*. An excellent observer, Mr. J. Scott,
"of the Botanical Gardens, Edinburgh, finds all that I
"say accurate, but nothing daunted, he with the knife
"enlarged the orifice, and forced in pollen-masses; or
"he simply stuck them into the contracted orifice
"*without coming into contact with the stigmatic surface*,
"which is hardly at all viscid; when, lo and behold,
"pollen tubes were emitted and fine seed capsules
"obtained. This was effected with *Acropera Loddigesii ;*
"but I have no doubt that I have blundered badly about
"*A. luteola.* I mention all this because, as Mr. Scott
"remarks, as the plant is in our hot-houses, it is quite
"incredible it ever could be fertilized in its native land.
"The whole case is an utter enigma to me. Probably
"you are aware that there are cases (and it is one of the
"oddest facts in physiology) of plants which under
"culture have their sexual functions in so strange a
"condition, that though their pollen and ovules are
"in a sound state and can fertilize and be fertilized
"by distinct but allied species, they cannot fertilize
"themselves. Now, Mr. Scott has found this the case
"with certain orchids, which again shows sexual dis-
"turbance. He had read a paper at the Botanical
"Society of Edinburgh, and I dare say an abstract which
"I have seen will appear in the *Gardener's Chronicle ;* but
"blunders have crept in in copying, and parts are barely

"intelligible.   How insects act with your *Stanhopea* I
"will not pretend to conjecture.   In many cases I believe
"the acutest man could not conjecture without seeing the
"insect at work.   I could name common English plants
"in this predicament.   But the musk orchis is a case in
"point.   Since publishing, my son and myself have
"watched the plant and seen the pollinia removed, and
"where do you think they *invariably* adhere in dozens
"of specimens?—always to the joint of the femur with
"the trochanter of the first pair of legs, and nowhere
"else.   When one sees such adaptation as this, it would
"be helpless to conjecture on the *Stanhopea* till we
"know what insect visits it.   I have fully proved that
"my strong suspicion was correct that with many of our
"English orchids no nectar is excreted, but that insects
"penetrate the tissues for it.   So I expect it must be
"with many foreign species.   I forgot to say that if you
"find that you cannot fertilize any of your exotics, take
"pollen from some allied form, and it is quite probable
"that will succeed.   Will you have the kindness to look
"occasionally at your bee ophrys near Torquay, and
"see whether pollinia are ever removed.   It is my
"greatest puzzle.   Please read what I have said on it,
"and on *O. arachnites.*   I have since proved that the
"account of the latter is correct.   I wish I could have
"given you better information.

"My dear sir,

"Yours sincerely,

"CHARLES DARWIN.

"P.S.—If the flowers of the *Stanhopea* are not too
"old, remove pollen masses from their pedicels, and
"stick them with a little liquid pure gum to the stigmatic
"cavity.   After the case of the *Acropera*, no one can
"dare positively say that they would not act."

P. H. GOSSE *to* C. DARWIN.

"Sandhurst, June 4, 1863.

"MY DEAR SIR,

"I am exceedingly obliged for your kind and
"full reply. Will the following additional facts throw
"any light on the matter?

"The four flowers of *Stanhopea oculata* became
"thoroughly withered and flaccid by 1st inst., the 4th
"day after opening; yet I allowed them to remain till
"this morning, when I cut off the raceme just before I
"received your letter. As one of the germens (and this
"one of those that I had tried to impregnate) came away
"with a touch, I took it as certain that no impregnation
"had taken place; and so threw the whole on the rubbish
"heap without further examination. But, on reading
"your remarks, I thought I would examine them again;
"chiefly to see if, by piercing the stigmatic surface, which
"had been so perfectly dry, I could find any viscosity
"within. Looking first at one of those to which I had
"affixed the pollen masses by means of their viscid disk,
"I was surprised to see they were half imbedded in a
"mass of viscous fluid. The other which I had treated
"was in precisely the same condition; the viscum having
"exuded copiously, and oozing in a great globule, when
"I used pressure with my thumb and finger lower down
"the column. Let this, then, be fact the first, that though
"no viscum be visible at first on the stigma, it issues
"copiously *after the flower has faded,* from the interior,
"at the extreme point of the rostellum.

"But secondly: A day or two after my attempt at
"impregnation (which affected only *two* of the four
"flowers), I was surprised to see the pollinia of one of the
"*untouched* flowers adhering to the point of one of the

"ivory-like horns of the mesochil. I wondered, but
"could not account for it, as I felt sure I had not acci-
"dentally detached and attached them in such a manner,
"while operating on the others. But, just now, in my
"examination of the faded spike, I observed, not only
"that the pollinia of *that* flower remained still on the tip
"of the horn, but that *one of the horns* of the other un-
"touched flower has lifted its own anther, and carries
"the pollinia in triumph on its point. If this is acci-
"dental, it is surely a remarkable coincidence. But it
"suggests to me the following hypothesis :—That the
"movable lip of this curious flower, agitated by the
"wind, brings the tips of the horns now and then into
"contact with the rostellum, so as to lift the anther, and
"carry away the pollinia by touching the viscid disk.
"That as soon as the viscum exudes from the stigmatic
"cavity and spreads over its surface, similar agitations
"of the lip would cause the pollinia to swing across the
"stigma, and brushing the exuded globule of viscum, to
"adhere. If this is tenable, here is a use for these extra-
"ordinary horns. Tell me what you think of the thought.
"I regret that I was so hasty in cutting away the faded
"spike ; possibly, with a little more obstetric manipula-
"tion, or even an agitation of the flowers with my breath,
"I might have succeeded in impregnating, and in settling
"the point.

"If my hypothesis should be correct, will it not show
"that *Stanhopea* affords another example of self-fertiliza-
"tion ? For the horns of any blossom can rifle *only* its
"*own* anther, and can deposit on *only its own stigma.*
"But what an unexpected mode of proceeding! I enclose
"you one of the pollinia carried on the horn.

"Yours faithfully,

"P. H. GOSSE."

"C. DARWIN *to* P. H. GOSSE.

"Down, June 5, 1863.

" MY DEAR SIR,

" If you would prove the truth of your hypo-
"thesis, it would be extremely curious and quite new.
"It certainly seems very suspicious you having found
"the pollinium attached to the horns of the labellum so
"often. I am prepared to believe anything of these
"wonderful productions. But if I were in your place, I
"would wait till I could observe another spike, and then
"you would, I have no doubt, definitely prove the case.
"Why I should act so is because I have so often noticed
"the pollinia removed in an unexpected manner. Dr.
"Hooker published in *Phil. Transactions* that *Listera*
"ejected its pollinia to a distance, which is an entire
"mistake. The conjecture (and it was founded on
" nothing but despair) occurred to me that the vibrating
"labellum in *Acropera* might remove the pollinia ; but
" Dr. Hooker tried on a living plant and failed to make
" it act.

" Nevertheless your case may prove quite true ; the
" dried labellum seems very thin, as if it had been flexible.
" It is really a very curious case. I have some Stan-
"hopes in my stove (I know not what species), but I fear
" they will not flower this summer : should they do so, I
" will observe them and communicate the result to you.
" If you thought fit to communicate your facts now to
" any periodical, it might induce others to observe ; but
" many persons are such bad observers that I doubt
" whether you would profit by it.

" I would suggest to you to get to know (if you do
" not already do so) the appearance of the viscid matter
" from the stigma which abounds with isolated elongated

"cells, called by Brown utriculi : these I find never
"present in viscid matter of rostellum ; and when these
"parts are close, it is important to distinguish them.
"You could have then probably told whether the fluid
"which exuded from your decaying flowers was a true
"stigmatic secretion. I heartily hope your pretty little
"discovery will prove good and true.

> "My dear sir,
>
> "Yours very sincerely,
>
> "C. DARWIN."

A month later my father notes that he has been busy
"examining bee orchis for Darwin at Petit Tor," and sending him notes and drawings on *Cyanæa.* Another interesting correspondence this autumn was with Lady Dorothy
Nevill, who supplied him with ailanthus plants, and with
a brood of caterpillars of *Bombyx Cynthia*, the exquisite
Indian silkworm moth, whose sickle-shaped wings of clear
apple-green, marked with pink moons and scimitars,
emerged in due time, to our infinite delight, from cocoons
of the pale Tussore silk. But in the next chapter I shall
dwell more at length on the amateur pleasures which now
began to absorb my father's extended leisure.

In the course of 1864 my father collected some old
papers and revised them, destining them to form a volume
which he presently published under the title of *Land and
Sea*. Of this book the first hundred pages were well
worthy of preservation ; they contained the record of the
author's stay twelve years previously on the picturesque
island of Lundy, in the Bristol Channel. But some of the
other sketches were rather trivial and diffusely told, besides
possessing the disadvantage that they seemed like discarded
chapters from other books, which indeed they were—*The
Ocean, A Naturalist's Sojourn in Jamaica*, and *A Year*

at the Shore, all having supplied, from rejected or super-fluous sections, matter for chapters in *Land and Sea*. The fact cannot be shirked that the author was becoming languid, inattentive to the form of what he published, and interested in matters outside the range of his professional work. By a curious coincidence, *A Year at the Shore* and *Land and Sea* were published in book form on the same day, January 24, 1865, and this may be taken as the date when Philip Gosse ceased to be a professional author.

CHAPTER XI.

LAST YEARS.

(1864–1888.)

THE remainder of Philip Gosse's life, spent in extreme retirement in his house at St. Marychurch, does not present many features which are of striking interest to the general reader. I shall not attempt to follow chronologically the events of this calm quarter of a century. To give them a history would be to disturb their peaceful sequence, and to destroy their relation with those more stirring facts which have preceded them. A reflection of the even tenour of my father's existence will be found in the narrative which my step-mother, his sole constant companion, has been so kind as to prepare in the form of an appendix to this volume. After 1866, he came but once to London, in 1873, when he spent a day or two in town on business. On this occasion he visited Lloyd's great aquaria in the Crystal Palace, but they failed to interest him to any great extent. Since 1864 he had strangely ceased to feel any curiosity in invertebrate zoology. The first breath of revival in this direction was awakened by a letter of my own to him, in which I described to him some rarities which I had observed at the south point of the Lizard. He replied (August 5, 1874):—

"Years and years have passed since I saw any "actiniæ living in profusion; the ladies and the dealers

"together have swept the whole coast within reach of
"this place (St. Marychurch) as with a besom. Even
"*Mesembryanthemum* occurs only in wretched little
"examples, few and far between. . . . From all that you
"say, I imagine that the point of Cornwall and the Scilly
"Isles, being beyond railways, would offer many a scene
"such as you have beheld, rich to profusion in marine
"zoology, and unrifled by the rude hands of man ; and,
"old as I am, I am stimulated to try. As soon as we
"had read your letter, mother suggested whether we
"might not run down ourselves for a few days; and I
"am not sure that we shall not put the *posse* in *esse*.
"Please to give me a little more detail on the practical
"aspects. . . . Could I reach the cleft knife-like point of
"rock which you found so prolific in *nivea* and *miniata ?*
"The pale-green anemone, with banded tentacles and a
"*Sagartia* habit, which you found on the rock that you
"reached by swimming—was not this *Sagartia chryso-*
"*splenium ?* This is a species which I have never seen.
"Refer to plate vi. of *Actinologia Britannica*, and tell me
"whether it was this. . . . I am all agog as I read.
"The case of the launce you found swallowed by an
"*Anthea* is not without parallel in my own experience."

It was only a flash in the pan, however ; in the next
letter I was told that " even *early* September is no time for
elderly persons to be away from home, in a wild remote
country." The real zoological awakening had not come.

These years were not, however, in any sense quiescent.
They were amply filled with amateur occupations—the
cultivation of orchids and the study of astronomy being
the most prominent. When Philip Gosse had passed sixty
years of age, his health became settled, and he enjoyed
life to a higher degree than perhaps ever before. On
February 18, 1875, he wrote :—

"Old age creeps sensibly upon me, and makes
"its advance perceptible in many little ways ; yet,
"though I have occasional reminders that I must be
"cautious of overwork, I am remarkably free from
"pains, and life is full of enjoyment to me. In many
"things—in enthusiasm, in the zest with which I enter
"into pursuits, in the interest which I feel in them, even
"in the delight of mere animal existence, and the sense
"of the beautiful around me—I feel almost a youth
"still."

This sense of health and capacity for enjoyment increased as time went on, and the intellectual vigour was
gradually turned back into the old professional channels. In
November, 1875, after having wholly neglected the marine
aquarium for fifteen years, he began to collect and keep sea-
beasts in captivity once more. He commenced with nothing
more ambitious than an old shallow flat-bottomed pan of
brown earthenware, and for some time he was content to
buy specimens from the men who made it their business to
sell seaweeds and anemones to winter visitors at Torquay.
But in February, 1876, he ceased to be satisfied with
pleasures so tame to an old sportsman, and, armed with
a new collecting-belt and his ancient water-proof boots, he
sallied down to Petit Tor at the low spring tide, and began
to search for himself in the fearless old fashion. This
was the beginning of a revival in zoological enthusiasm,
which steadily increased, and was sustained almost to the
close of his life, culminating in his remarkable aftermath
of scientific publications. He determined to establish at
Sandhurst an aquarium of large size and on modern
principles, and he was finally moved to undertake this
project from the disappointment he experienced in failing
to keep alive some specimens of the scarlet and yellow
Balanophyllia in his earthen jars. On June 23 Mr. W. A.

Lloyd and Mr. J. T. Carrington, whom he had summoned to his aid, came down to St. Marychurch to make suggestions and plans for the tank, the main characteristic of which was to be that it should have a constant current, like those in the Crystal Palace. As it was spring tide, my father took his old friend from Oddicombe beach in a boat to the Bell Rock and to Maidencombe; but, though they were out three hours, there was a tiresome swell, and they worked in the lovely gardens of red seaweed with but little success.

Lloyd's visit had, however, its direct results. His eye was quick and his engineering sense prompt and astute. By his recommendation, Philip Gosse had a slate reservoir sunk to the level of the earth, in a coal-shed in his back garden. In this he stored two hundred and ten gallons of brilliant sea-water dipped at Oddicombe beach. In the roof over the kitchen was fixed another slate cistern of a hundred and twenty gallons, and an unused lumber-room was devoted to the reception of the show-tank, to hold fifty gallons, made of slate, with a half-inch plate-glass front. A glass pump and vulcanite pipes completed the establishment, which was fitted up under Lloyd's supervision. When all was put together, an hour's pumping, once a week, was sufficient to lift the hundred and twenty gallons of sea-water from the reservoir into the cistern, whence it flowed by a pipe with a fine jet into the tank, at the regulated rate of about seventeen gallons a day, while a similar quantity flowed from the bottom of the tank into the reservoir, thus securing a constant circulation.

The construction of this tank, which, after one or two slight hitches, worked in a most satisfactory manner, greatly revived Philip Gosse's interest in zoology. He began, once again, to haunt the shore, undeterred by the laborious exertion required, or by the exhausting climb up and down the cliffs which each visit to the beach entailed. Roundham Head, in the centre of Tor Bay, and Maidencombe, half-way between Hope's Nose and the estuary of the Teign, were at this time his favourite hunting-grounds ; but he went even further afield, running down by boat to Prawle Point and Berry Head, or to the rocks that front the black creeks at the mouth of the Dart. Regardless of his sixty-seven summers, he would strip, on occasion, and work like a youth in the cold pools of the slate, balanced carefully on a slippery foothold of oar-weed or tulse. Here are some extracts taken at random from his journal of 1876 :—

"*August 7.*—I went to Dartmouth by earliest train, "intending to hire a sailing-boat to run down to the "Prawle. Old Jones, however, declared it to be im- "practicable, from wind and swell ; I therefore made him "pull me out to Black Rock, and thence to Combe Point. "Near this latter I obtained a group of the loveliest "*Corynactis* I ever saw; the whole body and disc of "the richest emerald, the colour very positive and (so "to say) opaque, tentacles rich lilac-rose. Returning, "I examined some overhanging rocks near Compass "Cove. On one ledge of a yard square, I saw nearly "a dozen of white daisy-like anemones ; but eighteen "inches below the surface, and thus beyond reach, "though easily procurable if the tide had been good, "but it was very poor. Near the same place I saw "others, and tried to get some, but failed. At length I "obtained two noble specimens of *Sagartia sphyrodeta,* "with bright orange disc. From a pool of fuci I had "dipped a rare prawn, which I would not keep, and a "number of *Hippolyte varians.*

"*November 3.*—I wrote Harris yesterday to meet me "with a boat this morning at 10.50. But on my arrival

"at the beach, there was no one; and so I scrambled
"across to Babbicombe.   There I found Thomas just
"come in from fishing, who had been delegated by
"Harris to take me.   So he pulled me along shore to
"Hope's Nose, and proved a very agreeable and service-
"able young fellow, entering heartily into my wishes.
"There were some good crevices just below the rifle
"targets, and some at Black Head.   Yet I got but little,
"till Thomas suggested some little pools which he knew
"to be rich on the islet called Flat Rock, about a mile
"off Hope's Nose.   I accordingly climbed the rock, and
"soon found the rough leprous-barnacled surface hol-
"lowed in dozens of little shallow pools, overspread
"with fucus.   The bottoms of these were studded with
"numbers of the pretty *Sagartia nivea*, which I have not
"seen for years.   They were all burrowed in the honey-
"combed limestone, and hard to chisel out; however, I
"obtained seven.   In one pool there was a colony of
"*Bunodes gemmacea*, unusually large; I took three of
"these.   Many pools were still unexplored.   I had pre-
"viously taken a nice mass of the emerald variety of
"*Corynactis viridis*, and many good masses of fine
"algæ.   The weather was mild, and fairly fine; very
"calm; the sea smooth, and brilliantly clear.   I enjoyed
"the trip greatly."

He made no pause through the depth of this winter, but
collected on the shore during every fine day.   December
29 saw him stalking "an immense-disked [*Sagartia*] *bellis
versicolor*" under Oddicombe Point, and January 1 found
him turning stones on the beach at Livermead.   The re-
fluent tide of his zoological ardour was at its height, nor
can it be said to have slackened through the greater part
of 1877.   When he worked on the shore, Mrs. Gosse, as
she will relate, was commonly his companion; when he

took sailing excursions, he often had the advantage of the company of Mr. Arthur Hunt, of Torquay, a young naturalist of knowledge and enthusiasm, who then possessed a yacht, the *Gannet*, in which the friends undertook frequent scientific excursions, especially over the sandy Zostera-beds in Torbay, among the little archipelago which lies off Hope's Nose, at the mouth of Brixham Harbour, and off Berry Head. His letters of this period usually contain some pleasant reference to his beautiful tank and its inmates. For example (June 11, 1877), he writes :—

"Have I told you of a young lobster, which, about "two months ago, I caught in Petit Tor great pool with "my fingers, after more than an hour's effort? He was "a beautiful fellow then, just six inches long, without "reckoning his claws; but after a week or two he "sloughed one night, to my dismay next morning, for I "supposed the slough to be my pet dead, so perfect was "it in every member; but presently I saw the gentleman "in duplicate, safe ensconced in a dark corner, and at "least one-third longer. He is now very saucy and "fierce; quite cock of the walk; does me some damage "by killing and gnawing now and then one of his fellow-"captives; but this I put up with, for he is such a beauty.

"I have been out dredging several times lately again "with Arthur Hunt, who is very kind to me, urging me "to go out frequently, and putting his boat and two "dredges, and himself, and a boatman, at my entire "command, and then, forsooth, taking all as if *I* had "done *him* a great favour! The worst of it is, I can't "stand any toss—old sailor as I am—without a rebellion "within. But the bottom of Torbay is so rich in zoology, "that it is worth the scraping; and Hunt is himself a "naturalist."

In the course of 1878 a new hobby began to interfere a little with the exclusive interest in the marine aquarium. It was, more strictly speaking, his earliest hobby resuscitated. He met with a French gentleman, resident in London, who made it his business to import fine exotic *Lepidoptera* in the pupa condition. It was nearly twenty years since, in response to a suggestion from Lady Dorothy Nevill, Philip Gosse had made a brief attempt to breed the great Indian moths. He first purchased a few chrysalids of continental butterflies, amongst others *Papilio Podalirius*, *Thais Polyxena*, and *Lycæna Iolas ;* but he soon became chiefly interested in the great moths of America and India, the *Saturniadæ* and their allies. He writes (May 14, 1878) :—

"You will perhaps recollect the great atlas moth in "the midst of the box of Chinese insects on the wall of "our breakfast-room. Well, I have a living cocoon of "this species, and of a number of others akin to it. "Two noble specimens have already been evolved, and "are preserved. Then I have *eggs* of several of the "species, from one set of which (*Attacus Yamma-maï* of "Japan) I am now rearing beautiful caterpillars, on oak. "Some of these insects are North American, and were "objects of my desire and delight when I collected in "Canada and in Alabama ; and this casts an extra halo "around them. But their size and beauty make them "all very charming. '*Naturam expelles, tamen usque* "'*recurret.*' I am most thankful to say that God con-"tinues to me such health and buoyancy of spirits that I "enter into all these recreations with as much enthusiasm "as I felt forty years ago. And so does my beloved wife, "who adds tenfold to my enjoyment, both of work and "play, by her hearty sharing of both, and an enjoyment as "keen as my own. Thus are we two happy old fogies."

And again (June 26, 1878) :—

" This purchase of a cocoon or two of *Saturniadæ* has
"grown into a much greater enterprise than I antici-
"pated. I am at last gratifying the desire of more than
"five and forty years, namely, the rearing of some of
"the very *élite* of the *Lepidoptera*. Yesterday I had the
"beautiful male Purple Emperor evolved from a chrysalis,
"reared from the caterpillar. Another will probably be
"out to-night, a distinct species, closely allied. I have
"now around me the *larvæ*, attaining vast size and great
"beauty, of many of the very *principes* of the moths ;
"and several I have evolved from cocoon. One of the
"very finest I ever saw was produced in great perfection
"a few days ago ; I inclose you an accurately measured
"paper-cutting of it. It is of exquisite delicacy ; the
"wings of the tenderest pea-green, merging into snow-
"white at the body, and the front edge chocolate-purple.
"It is the noble *Tropæa selene* of the Himalayan slopes.
"These are samples which ought to make your mouth
"water, if you retain any of your boyish enthusiasm."
And again (April 7, 1879) :—

" If you are still entomologist enough to know the
"splendid *Morphos*, most lustrous, dazzling blue, great
"butterflies of South America, you will like to know
"that I have recently been accumulating a fine collection
"of these and other tropical *Lepidoptera ;* including the
"great *Ornithopteræ* of Malasia, a large number of fine
"*Papiliones*, and half a dozen species or more of the
"noblest of these *Morphos*, enough already nearly to
"fill a cabinet of twenty-four drawers. They afford me
"great delight, gratifying the yearnings of my earlier
"years, which I never expected to gratify."
During all this time, however, and in spite of all the
incentives to intellectual labour which his pursuits gave

him, Philip Gosse showed no inclination to take up the pen which had slipped from his fingers fifteen years before. It seemed now wholly improbable that he would ever resume authorship, but with the approach of his seventieth year this instinct also was reawakened. In March, 1879, he published as a separate brochure a memoir on *The Great Atlas Moth of India* (*Attacus Atlas*), with a coloured plate of its transformations. In October of the same year he became a member of the Entomological Society, and in June, 1880, he printed a monograph on the velvet-black butterfly, with emerald bands and crimson spots, which swarms in the forests of Jamaica, *Urania sloanus*. This again was followed by a pamphlet on *The Butterflies of Paraguay*.

These small memoirs were but the preliminaries to an entomological work of wide extent, demanding the expenditure of a great deal of leisure and laborious research. For a considerable time past the attention of Philip Gosse had been increasingly drawn to the singular forms and the variety of function of the prehensile apparatus employed in reproduction by the large butterflies which he had reared under his close personal observation. The only authority on this subject of the genital armature of the butterflies had been Dr. Buchanan White, who had expressed regret that he had been unable to examine any but European species. He had added : " It is much to be desired that some one, who has at his command a large collection of the butterflies of all regions, should investigate, more extensively than I have been able to do, the structure of the genital armature." My father had followed this recommendation, and in examining his great tropical specimens had discovered so much that was singular, and wholly new to science, that he became anxious to give publicity to his observations. He carried, moreover, his investigations to a length which no one who preceded him, not even Dr. White, had attempted to reach.

Among the younger zoologists of the day, few of whom were personally known to my father, there was not one in whose discoveries and career he took a livelier interest than in those of Professor E. Ray Lankester, for whom, from his earliest publications, he had predicted a course of high distinction. For the judgment of this distinguished observer Philip Gosse entertained an unusual respect, and it was owing to his advice that the elder naturalist, in his seventy-second year, started upon a course of laborious investigations, which were not terminated until two years later. In April, 1881, on the very evening of a day which had been marked in white to the recluse by a visit from Professor Lankester, Gosse noted that, "encouraged by E. R. L., I have begun my monograph on the *Prehensores.*" In October of the same year he forwarded to Professor Huxley, for the consideration of the council of the Royal Society, the manuscript of his volume on *The Clasping Organs ancillary to Generation in Certain Groups of the Lepidoptera,* accompanied by nearly two hundred figures, exquisitely drawn under the microscope, illustrating these recondite organs with such an accuracy and delicate fullness, that I have been assured that a query was raised on the council of the society as to the authorship of the drawings, which it was hardly possible to conceive had been made by a man of between seventy and eighty. An abstract of the memoir was presently read at the Royal Society by Professor Huxley, in the absence of the author. There arose, however, a difficulty regarding its being published in full in the *Proceedings* of the Royal Society, the subject being excessively remote from general interest, even to *savants,* and the illustrations, which my father considered essential to the intelligibility of the monograph, threatening to be very expensive to reproduce. My father, however, met with great kindness on this occasion from his younger *confrères*. The manuscript was finally, in March, 1882, submitted by Professor Michael Foster to the council of the Linnæan Society for publication, the Royal Society offering £50 towards the expense of printing and engraving. The Linnæan Society, thereupon, waiving their usage of not publishing papers which had been read elsewhere, undertook to bring it out, and, to my father's extreme gratification, this child of his old age was finally issued in May, 1883, as a handsome quarto, in the form of the *Transactions* of the Linnæan Society, and with all his plates carefully reproduced in lithography.

Philip Gosse had made it an invariable practice, in advancing life, to qualify every public expression of his views on natural phenomena by an attribution of the beautiful or wonderful condition to the wisdom of the Divine Creator. He had done so in his monograph on *The Clasping Organs ancillary to Generation*, appending to that memoir a paragraph embodying those pious reflections which his conscience conceived to be absolutely *de rigueur*. Rightly or wrongly, these sentiments appeared to the council of the Linnæan Society to be out of place in a very abstruse description of certain organs, which are curious, but neither beautiful nor calculated to inspire ideas of a particularly elevating nature. In sending to him the proof of his memoir, the secretary was directed to ask the author, in making some other trifling excisions, to be kind enough to put his pen through this little passage also. To the surprise of every one concerned, he absolutely declined to do this. The council was then placed in a most embarrassing position. A great deal of money had already been spent, and here was a paragraph which could not be issued, by the rules of the society, that forbid all contentious matter on the subject of religion, and which yet the author was prepared to sacrifice the whole volume rather than resign. The knot was cleverly untied by Professor E. Ray Lankester, who suggested that it should be represented to Mr. Gosse that if an atheist should wish, in future, to defend his atheism in the *Transactions* of the society, the council could scarcely forbid him to do so, if it had yielded to a Christian writer the privilege of defending his faith in Christianity. My father saw the force of the argument, and gave way, though with great unwillingness.

Meanwhile, he had for some years been engaged in a course of studies highly gratifying to his earliest instincts, and absorbing in its demands upon his attention. In an earlier chapter of this biography I have described the manner in which the observation of the *Rotifera*, or wheel-animalcules, became a passion with my father. On the whole this may, perhaps, be considered as having been the branch of zoological study which had fascinated him longest and absorbed him most. In spite, however, of the importance of the discoveries which he had made, in the course of his life, in this neglected province of zoology, he had never found an opportunity of publishing them, except partially and obscurely. He retained, in his portfolios, the buried treasures of half a century in the form of unpublished text and plates. Since Philip Gosse had corresponded with Dr. Arlidge, and had lent his help to the publication of the latest (1861) edition of Pritchard's *History of the Infusoria*, hardly any use whatever had been made of his vast storehouse of information.

Since 1867 Dr. C. T. Hudson had been at work on the same subject, independently collecting materials towards a final work on the little known and yet charming *Rotifera*. In 1879 Dr. Hudson was advised by Professor E. Ray Lankcster, who was aware of the great mass of data collected by my father, to place himself in relation with the latter. He did so, and the elder naturalist, with complete unselfishness, hastened to lay all that he possessed at the disposal of the younger. It was, indeed, a singular gratification to Philip Gosse, at this the close of his career, to find his work appreciated, and to be able to help one who was progressing along the same little-trodden path as himself. Dr. Hudson was the latest and one of the warmest of my father's friends, and the compilation of his share of the two splendid volumes on *The Rotifera*, which have their combined names on the title-page, became the principal, as it was the most delightful, occupation of my father from 1879 until the publication in 1886. The issue of the final periodical part of this work was greeted with a melancholy satisfaction by my father, who recognized very clearly that the real labour of his lifetime was closed. He was in his seventy-seventh year, and he was thoroughly conscious that he could never again hope to start another undertaking of this serious nature. Yet he was delighted to handle these volumes, the children of his old age, and to realize that he had lived to complete the publication of all his main discoveries. In reply to the objections of a member of his family, who cavilled at the fact that more prominence was given on the title-page of *The Rotifera* to the younger than to the elder naturalist, the latter replied as follows :—

"Your judgment will probably be modified, when you "are better acquainted with the facts. My position on the "title-page was the subject of much discussion between "Dr. Hudson and me ; and I chose decisively that "'assisted by P. H. Gosse' should be the mode, *contrary* "*to his wish.* He has, throughout, been most lovingly "considerate of my wishes, and only too ready to put

"me into prominence and honour. The labour, the
"plan, the publication, all the drudgery, have been his;
"so that to put his name prominent is only the merest
"justice. We have worked all through in the fullest
"harmony. Every line that he has written has been
"subjected. to my severe criticism ; and, with hardly an
" exception, all my amendments he has implicitly adopted.
" I must say I admire very warmly the introduction."

During the years in which the volumes on *The Rotifera*
were being prepared, my father exerted himself in an intellectual direction with the zeal of a young professional
man at the height of his career. He was up at five or
six in the morning, and often spent eight or nine hours in
uninterrupted work at the microscope, merely breaking
through it so far as to come down from his study with
knitted and abstracted brows, to swallow a hasty meal in
silence, and then rush up again. This excess of intellectual
work, combined with his neglect of exercise, seemed, in the
face of it, to be extremely imprudent in a man approaching
eighty. But we could not, at that time, very distinctly
observe any harm done to his health, and in some ways
the ardent occupation seemed to keep him well. As soon
as the manuscript had finally gone to the printers, however, early in 1886, he suffered from a nervous attack of an
alarming nature, which appeared to point to overwork.
Nevertheless, his great elasticity of constitution enabled
him, as it seemed, entirely to recover ; and Dr. Hudson,
like a housewife in a fairy story, who finds fresh labour for
her giant to perform, set his colleague on the mitigated
work of helping to prepare a *Supplement.* This was eventually published, in 1889, by Dr. Hudson, and contained
the description of one hundred and fifty additional species,
sixty of these being new British forms discovered by Philip
Gosse. It completed the great work, by describing every

known foreign rotifer, as well as all the British species which had been discovered since the original work went to press in 1885. This *Supplement* my father did not live to see published, and Dr. Hudson alludes to that fact, in his preface, in these graceful and generous terms :—

"The natural pleasure, with which I see -the observa-
"tions and studies of thirty-five years thus brought to a
"successful conclusion, has been indeed marred by the
"sad loss of my deeply lamented friend. His great
"knowledge and experience, his keen powers of observa-
"tion, his artistic skill, and his rare gift of description
"are known to all, and have made him *facile princeps*
"among the writers on the rotifera ; but it is only those
"who, like myself, were privileged to know him inti-
"mately, that are aware how much more he was than an
"enthusiastic naturalist. I shall never forget the hearty
"welcome (when I first met him) that the veteran gave
"to the comparatively unknown student, or the gracious
"kindness with which he subsequently placed at my
"disposal his beautiful unpublished drawings and his
"ample notes.

"A happy chance had led our observations to differing
"parts of the same subject, and our united labours have
"produced, in consequence, the now completed work ;
"but I shall ever count it a still happier chance that gave
"me not only such a colleague, but also such a friend."

So late as the last autumn of his life my father continued his occasional rambles on the shore with hammer and collecting basket. September 19, 1887, will long be memorable to his family as the latest of these delightful excursions. He spent several hours of that day upon the rocks in the centre of Goodrington Sands, surrounded by his wife, his son and son's wife, and his three grandchildren—a compact family party. No one on that brilliant afternoon would have guessed that the portly man with a grizzled beard, who stood ankle-deep in the salt pools, bending over the treasuries of the folded seaweeds, lustily shouting for a chisel or a jar as he needed it, and striding resolutely over the slippery rocks, was in his seventy-eighth year, and still less that his vitality was so soon to decline. To the rest of the family, who remained at Paignton, he wrote the next day from his own house :—

"Many thanks for making yesterday so happy a day "to me, though I felt somewhat unwell last night, pos- "sibly from exhaustion. It was delightful to see around "me your dear selves and the sweet eager children "engaged in diligent and successful search for my grati- "fication. When you all come over again, you will "think the tank a busy scene worth looking at. For, "in addition to our captures of yesterday, there have "arrived four new sea-horses and several very fine and "large *troglodytes* and *bellis*, all in capital condition. "The *Hippocampi* I poured into the tank in a moment; "the *Sagartiæ* carefully *seriatim* this morning. And, "as I say, the *tout ensemble* is worth looking at.

"Of our Goodrington lot of yesterday, the crabs are "climbing about the stone, the long pipe-fish glides like "a slender brown cord through the water, the little "black-and-white *cottus* scuttles about, and I just now "saw the goby creep out from under one of the stones ; "while the crimson weeds and the green ulva give "brilliant colour to the picture. The scarlet and blue "*Galathea* lobster I don't see this morning, but no doubt "he's all right. The children will be interested in these "details."

In October my father and mother, under the stimulus of a visit from the Rev. F. Howlett, Rector of Tisted, resumed their astronomical researches on clear nights,

" We are busy," he writes on the 22nd, "among the fixed stars, as we were more than twenty years ago, especially hunting for the charming double stars. There are no planets visible in the evenings now." No definite apprehensions crossed our minds, although he was occasionally more feeble and notably more silent than of old. But near the close of the year 1887, while he was examining the heavens late one very cold night, a newly purchased portion of the telescope apparatus became dislodged and fell into the garden ; the agitation produced by this little accident, and some exposure in leaning out to see where the lens had fallen, brought on an attack of bronchitis, and although this particular complaint was overcome, he was never well again.

Yet, through the months of December and January, there seemed nothing alarming in his condition. He was kept indoors, but not in bed, and he was as busy as ever, writing, drawing, and reading. One of the last books which he read with unabated interest was the *Life of Darwin.* All went on much in the old style until March, 1888, when a disease of the heart, which must for a long while past have been latent, rather suddenly made itself apparent. Under the repeated attacks of this complaint, his brain, his spirits, his manifold resources of body and mind, sank lower and lower, and the five months which followed were a period of great weariness and almost unbroken gloom. After a long and slow decay, the sadness of which was happily not embittered by actual pain, he ceased to breathe, in his sleep, without a struggle, at a few minutes before one o'clock on the morning of August 23, 1888. He had lived seventy-eight years, four months, and seventeen days. He was buried, near his mother, in the Torquay Cemetery, attended to the grave by a large congregation of those who had known and respected him during his thirty years' residence in the neighbourhood.

CHAPTER XII.

GENERAL CHARACTERISTICS.

IN the preceding chapters I have not, I trust, so completely failed as to have left upon the reader's mind no image of what manner of man my father was. But the portrait is still a very imperfect one, and must be completed by some touches which it is exceedingly difficult to give with justice. I have hitherto dwelt as slightly as possible upon the religious features of his character, that I might not disturb the thread of a narrative which is mainly intended for the general public. But no portrait of his mind would be recognizable by those who knew Philip Gosse best, which should relegate to a second place his religious convictions and habits of thought. They were peculiar to himself, they were subject throughout his life to practically no modifications, and they were remarkable for their logical precision and independence. I have never met with a man, of any creed, of any school of religious speculation, who was so invulnerably cased in fully developed conviction upon every side. His faith was an intellectual system of mental armour in which he was clothed, *cap-à-pie*, without a joint or an aperture discoverable anywhere. He never avoided argument ; on the contrary, he eagerly accepted every challenge ; and his accuracy of mind, working with extreme precision within a narrow channel, was such that it was not possible to controvert him on his own ground. What his own ground was it may be well to state in his own words, and those for whom these nice points of theology have no attraction may be invited to pass on to a subsequent page : I cannot, as a biographer, omit so essential a portion of my task, because it is abstruse. This, then, is my father's confession of faith, taken from a letter written in 1878 :—

" The whole of my theology rests on, and centres in, " the Resurrection of Christ. That Jesus was raised from " the dead, is an historical fact, the evidence for which is, " in my judgment, impregnable. I ask no more than " this ; everything else follows inevitably. A suffering, " dying Christ, and yet an ever-reigning Christ, was the " great theme of the Old Testament ; and Jesus did, on " numerous occasions, during His life, predict His own " death and resurrection, in order 'That the Scripture " ' might be fulfilled, that thus it must be.'

" That He was raised from the dead was distinctly the " act of God the Father ; ' but God raised Him from the " 'dead.' It was the solemn witness borne by God to " His mission. It did not prove Him to be God ; but " it proved Him to have been the Sent One of the " Father ; it was the Father's seal to Him.

" Now, then, every act and word of His comes with the " authority of God ; for He is God's accredited delegate " and spokesman. I must not pick and choose which " of His sayings I will receive ; I dare refuse none ; for " He never ceases to present the credentials of the Father. " All the wondrous scenes through which He passed, the " Temptation, the Transfiguration, the Agony, the Cross ; " His transactions with a personal devil, and with personal " demons ; His revelations concerning His own pre- " existence, His unity with the Father, the covenant of " election, the perseverance of His saints, His advent and

"judgment, the kingdom of heaven, the unquenchable
"fire of hell;—all these come to me with all the force
"of dogmas, not one of which I have the option of
"refusing, unless I refuse God; for they have the authority
"of Him whom God has sealed.

"THE OLD TESTAMENT.

"The Lord Jesus constantly cites the numerous books
"of the Old Testament as a unit—'the Scriptures,' and
"He constantly appeals to it as an ultimate authority;
"'the Scripture cannot be broken,' etc. He cites the
"words of Moses, of Isaiah, of David, but, withal, as
"spoken 'by God' (Matt. xxii. 31), by 'the Holy Ghost'
"(Mark xii. 36). He refers to the ancient narratives, as
"indubitable verities; to the marriage of Adam and
"Eve (Matt. xix. 4); to Sodom and Gomorrha (xi. 23,
"24); to the manna, to the brazen serpent; to Noah,
"to Lot, to Lot's wife, to Elijah, to Elisha. He taught
"His disciples that 'all things in Moses, the Prophets,
"'and the Psalms' were about Him, and must be fulfilled
"(Luke xxiv. 27, 44–47). Now, since the Lord Jesus
"thus honours the Old Scriptures, and never gives the
"least hint that there is any exception to this honour;
"never speaks of them as *containing*, but always as *being*,
"the authoritative Word of God; I must so receive them,
"every word.

"THE NEW TESTAMENT.

"But how can I be sure that the Gospels, the Acts,
"the Epistles, the Apocalypse, are true? are wholly
"true, wholly trustworthy; free from admixture of
"human error? A question, this, of vast importance;
"since it is in the Epistles that the great scheme of

"Christian doctrine is unfolded to faith, with dogmatic
"completeness. One may confidently say, *à priori*,
"that these could not be left to the indefinite admixture
"of human opinion, without frustrating the very purpose
"for which the Father sent the Son ; it would be to
"undermine that edifice for which He had hitherto laid
"the most solid and stable foundation.

"But we are not left to conjecture here. The Lord
"Jesus, engaging to build His Church upon the Rock,
"and conferring on Peter the privilege of the keys to
"unlock the kingdom (Acts ii. and x.), promised first
"to him (Matt. xvi. 19), and then to all the Apostles
"(xviii. 18), that whatsoever they should bind or loose,
"He would ratify from heaven. For this end He pro-
"mised them the Holy Ghost, to *abide* with them ; to
"guide them into all [the] truth ; to take of His, and
"the Father's, and show to them ; to bring all Jesus's
"words to their remembrance ; to show them things to
"come ; to enable them to be witnesses for Him (John
"xiv.–xvi., *passim*). He sent them into the world,
"exactly as the Father had sent *Him* (xvii. 18).

"The Holy Ghost in due time was given, the witness
"of Jesus-Messiah's ascension to the Divine Throne ;
"and they, thus endowed, and distinctly accredited
"(Acts i. 8), went forth 'witnesses to Him, . . . to the
"'uttermost part of the earth.'

"Here, again, my confidence finds an impregnable
"fortress. Whatever I read in the Evangels, or the
"Epistles, is no longer the utterance of a mere man,
"however pious ; it is not Luke or John, or Peter or
"Paul, that I hear ; it is God the Holy Ghost from
"heaven, bearing witness to the Sent of the Father, now
"that the Sent Son has gone up in resurrection life and
"power to the Father's Throne.

"Thus, in *The Mysteries of God*, I do not ask if this
"dogma is probable or improbable ; if *this* is worthy or
"unworthy of God, as I fashion Him in my imagination :
"I simply ask, How is it written? What saith the
"Scripture? Assured that God has not raised Christ
"from the dead, in order to tell us lies !"

Put in a nutshell, then, his code was the Bible, and the
Bible only, without any modern modification whatever ;
without allowance for any difference between the old world
and the new, without any distinction of value in parts,
without the smallest concession to the critical spirit upon
any point ; an absolute, uncompromising, unquestioning
reliance on the Hebrew and Greek texts as inspired by the
mouth of God and uncorrupted by the hand of man. The
Bible, however, is full of dark sayings, and needs, as he
admitted, an interpreter. But my father did not doubt his
own competence to interpret. He had some reason to
hold this view. His knowledge of the Bible can hardly
have been excelled. His verbal memory of the Authorized
Version included the whole New Testament, all the Psalms,
most of the Prophets, and all the lyrical portions of the
Historical Books. The condition of his memory fluctuated,
of course, and was being daily refreshed at various points ;
but I have his own repeated assurance that, practically
speaking, he knew the Bible by heart. Nor was this in
any sense a parrot-feat or trick of memory. He knew the
text of Scripture in this extraordinary way, partly because
his mind had an unusual power of verbal retention ; partly
because, for nearly sixty years, whatever other occupations
might have been in hand, no day passed in which he did
not read and meditate upon some portion of the Bible. I
have called his creed invulnerable ; and when it is considered that he could not be assailed on the side of
sensibility or sentiment, which he tossed to the winds, nor

on that of scholastic or accepted interpretation, which he never preferred to his own where the two differed, that his memory could promptly supply him with an appropriate text at every turn of the argument, and that he never accepted the most alluring temptation to fight on theoretic ground outside the protecting shadow of the *ipsissima verba* of the Bible, it will perhaps be understood that he was an antagonist whom it was easy to disagree with, but uncommonly difficult to defeat.

This being the foundation upon which Philip Gosse's religious edifice was based, it is not difficult to perceive how certain radical peculiarities of his character, to which the reader's attention has already been drawn, flourished under its shelter. His temper was unbending, and yet singularly wanting in initiative, and this was a system which provided his mind with the fully developed osseous skeleton it demanded. Revelation had to be accepted as a whole, and so as to leave no margin for scepticism. At the same time, the detail of Biblical interpretation opened up a field of minute investigation which was absolutely boundless, and which my father's near-sighted intellect, so helpless in sweeping a large philosophical horizon, so amazingly alert and vigorous in analyzing a minute area, could explore, without exhaustion, to an infinite degree. Hence what fascinated him more than any other mental exercise, especially of late years, was to take a passage of Scripture (in the Greek, for he never mastered Hebrew), and to dissect it, as if under the microscope, word by word, particle by particle, passing at length into subtleties where, undoubtedly, few could follow him.

Protected by his ample shield, the text of Scripture, he was quite calm under the charge of heterodoxy which sometimes reached him in his retreat. It is not a matter for surprise that with his remarkable temperament, his isolated and self-contained habit of mind, he found it impossible to throw in his lot with the system of any existing Christian Church. In middle life he had connected himself with the Plymouth Brethren, principally, no doubt, because of their lack of systematic organization, their repudiation of all traditional authority, their belief that the Bible is the infallible and sufficient guide. But he soon lost confidence in the Plymouth Brethren also, and for the last thirty years of his life he was really unconnected with any Christian body whatever. What was very curious was that, with his intense persistence in the study of religious questions, he should feel no curiosity to know the views of others. In those thirty years he scarcely heard any preacher of his own reputed sect; I am confident that he never once attended the services of any unaffiliated minister.

He had gathered round him at St. Marychurch a cluster of friends, mostly of a simple and rustic order, to whom he preached and expounded, and amongst whom he officiated as minister and head. This little body he called "The Church of Christ in this Parish," ignoring, with a sublime serenity, the claims of all the other religious institutions with which St. Marychurch might be supplied. His attitude, without the least intentional arrogance or unfriendliness, was exactly that which some first apostle of the Christian faith in Ceylon or Sumatra might have adopted, to whom his own converts were "the Church," and the surrounding Asiatics, of whatever civilization, of whatever variety of ancient and divergent creed, merely "the world." He made no attempt, however, to proselytize; he alternated his expositions to the flock under his care by addresses, of an explanatory and hortatory character, to outsiders, in "the Room," as his little chapel was with severe modesty styled. But his view was that the light was kept burning in the small community, and that on those in the darkness around lay the solemn responsibility if they were not attracted into its circle of radiance.

Over such a mind, so earnestly and deeply convinced, external considerations could have little sway. "My mind to me a kingdom is," my father used often to repeat, but not at all in the sense of the poet. Society had no court of appeal against any course of action which my father's conscience prompted, and it was rather a subject of congratulation that, having chosen to lead a retired and meditative life, he really did not come into collision with the world. He belonged to the race from which passive martyrs are taken. He had no desire to go out with a trumpet and a sword, but in his own quieter way he was as stubborn as any of the victims of Bloody Mary. If he had happened to object to any of the modes in which government, as at present constituted, operates in social discipline; if, for instance, he had formed conscientious scruples against paying rates, or being vaccinated, he would have offered the absolute maximum of resistance. Fortunately for his domestic peace, he did not come into collision with the law on any of these points. But he had peculiarities which showed the iron rigidity of his conscience. He had a very singular objection to the feast of Christmas, conceiving this festival to be a heathen survival to which the name of Christ had been affixed in hideous profanity. This objection showed itself in amusing and bewildering ways. He regarded plum-pudding and roast turkey as innocent and acceptable, if the fatal word had not been pronounced in connection with them ; but if once they were spoken of as " Christmas turkey," or a " Christmas pudding," they became abominable, " food offered to idols." Biblical students will observe the source of this idea—a most ingenious adaptation to modern life of an injunction to the Corinthians. Friends who knew this singular prejudice were particular to send gifts for New Year's Day; and I well recollect my father's taking off the dish-cover and revealing a magnificent goose at dinner, while he paused to remark to the guests (none of whom, by the way, shared this particular conviction), "I need not assure you, dear friends, that this bird has not been offered to the idol."

This was a case in which, we may all admit, the delicate scruples of Philip Gosse's conscience were strained in a somewhat trivial direction. A graver question may be raised, though I will not be so impertinent as to attempt an answer, by my father's rigid attitude toward those who were not at one with him on essential points of religion. "I could never divide myself from any man upon the difference of an opinion," said Sir Thomas Browne, and modern feeling has been inclined to applaud him. But my father was not modern, and it would not merely be absurd, it would be unjust, if I were to pretend that he was liberal, or would have thought it godly to be liberal. Towards those who differed from him on essential points of religion, his attitude was as severe as his masculine nature knew how to make it. He was not sympathetic; he had no intuition of what might be passing through the mind of one who held views utterly at variance with what seemed to himself to be inevitable. He could be indulgent to ignorance, but when there was no longer this excuse, when the revealed will of God on a certain point had been lucidly stated and explained to the erring mind, if then it were still rejected, no matter on what grounds, there was no further appeal. To that kind question of Fuller's, "Is there no way to bring home a wandering sheep but by worrying him to death?" my father would have answered by a mournful shake of the head. The fold was open, the shepherd was calling, the dog was hurrying and barking, and the wickedness of the sheep in refusing to return seemed almost inconceivable.

The reader cannot but have already observed how few and how ephemeral were my father's intimate friendships with those whose station, tastes, and acquirements might have been supposed to tally with his own. In the world of literature and science he scarcely kept up a single close acquaintanceship. Of friendship as a cardinal virtue, as one of the great elements in a happy life, he had no conception. He could make none of those concessions, those mutual acceptances of the inevitable, without which this, the most spiritual of the passions, cannot exist. Even those who were most strongly attracted to him, fell off at last from the unyielding surface of his conscience; this was the secret of his brief and truncated intimacy with Edward Forbes, whom he had seemed to love so well. The ardent patience and sympathy of Charles Kingsley, the friend from the outer world whom he preserved longest, wearied at length of an intercourse in which principles were ever preferred to persons. In later years one example may suffice. Dora Greenwell precipitated herself on the friendship of Philip Gosse with an impetuosity which at first bore everything before it, and in a copious correspondence laid open to him her spiritual ardours and aspirations. He was gratified, he was touched, but to respond was impossible to him; he had the same purely didactic touch, the same logic, the same inelasticity for every one, and friendship soon expired in such a vacuum. A phrase in a letter to myself gives its own key to the social isolation of his life. " I am impatient and intolerant," he writes, " of all resistance to what I see to be the will of God, and if that resistance is sustained, I have no choice but to turn away from him who resists."

His extraordinary severity towards those who occupy the extremes of Christian dogma, towards the Church of Rome and towards the Unitarians, was a result of this idiosyncrasy pushed to its extreme. In 1859, when he was lecturing in Birmingham, before the Midland Institute, he was invited to meet some of the principal personages of the town at dinner, and, in particular, a well-known gentleman, who is now dead. Philip Gosse accepted the invitation with pleasure ; but shortly before the party met, the host received a note saying that it had just been mentioned to Mr. Gosse that Mr. —— was a Socinian. Had Mr. Gosse been unaware of this, he should have desired to ask no questions, but, the information having been volunteered, he had no alternative but, with extreme regret and even distress, to explain that he could not " sit at meat with one whom I know to deny the Divinity of the blessed Lord." To realize what this sacrifice to conscience involved, it must be recollected that my father was a man of elaborate and punctilious courtesy, and extremely timid. I could multiply examples, but it is needless to do so.

It will perhaps be assumed from this sketch of my father's religious views, that he was gloomy and saturnine in manner. It is true that, at the very end of his life, wrapped up as he grew to be more and more in metaphysical lucubrations, his extreme self-absorption took a stern complexion. But it had not always been so in earlier years. He was subject to long fits of depression, the result in great measure of dyspepsia, but when these passed away he would be cheerful and even gay for weeks at a time. Never lonely, never bored, he was contented with small excitements and monotonous amusements, and asked no more than to be left alone among his orchids, his cats, and his butterflies, happy from morning till night. On the first day of his seventy-eighth year, he wrote to me in these terms :—

"My health is fair and my vigour considerable. I am "free from pains and infirmities. My zest and delight "in my microscopical studies is unabated yet, so that "every day is an unflagging holiday."

This description of his feelings, at a time when the shadow of death had almost crossed his path, is significant, and might be taken to characterize his inward feeling, if not always his outward aspect, through the main part of the last thirty years of his life. He could even, on occasion, be merry, with a playfulness that was almost pathetic, because it seemed to be the expression of a human sympathy buried too far down in his being to reveal itself except in this dumb way. I cannot exactly describe what it was that made this powerfully built and admirably equipped man sometimes strike one as having the immatureness and touching incompleteness of the nature of a child. It was partly that he was innocent of observing any but the most obvious and least complex working of the mind in others. But it was mainly that he had nothing in common with his age. He was a Covenanter come into the world a couple of centuries after his time, to find society grown too soft for his scruples and too ingenious for his severe simplicity. He could never learn to speak the ethical language of the nineteenth century ; he was seventeenth century in spirit and manner to the last.

No question is more often put to me regarding my father than this—How did he reconcile his religious to his scientific views? The case of Faraday may throw some light, but not very much, upon the problem. The word "reconcile" is scarcely the right one, because the idea of reconciliation was hardly entertained by my father. He had no notion of striking a happy mean between his impressions of nature and his convictions of religion. If the former offered any opposition to the latter, they were swept away. The rising tide is " reconciled " in the same fashion to a child's battlements of sand along the shore. Awe, an element almost eliminated from the modern mind, was strongly developed in Philip Gosse's character. He speaks of himself, in one of his letters, as having been under " the subjugation of spiritual awe to a decidedly morbid degree " during the whole of his life. He meant by this, I feel no doubt, that he was conscious of an ever-present bias towards the relinquishing of any idea presumably unpalatable to his inward counsellor. It was under the pressure of this sense of awe that, when his intellect was still fresh, he deliberately refused to give a proper examination to the theory of evolution which his own experiments and observations had helped to supply with arguments. It was certainly not through vagueness of mind or lack of a logical habit that he took up this strange position, as of an intellectual ostrich with his head in a bush, since his intelligence, if narrow, was as clear as crystal, and his mind eminently logical. It was because a " spiritual awe " overshadowed his conscience, and he could not venture to take the first step in a downward course of scepticism. He was not one who could accept half-truths or see in the twilight. It must be high noon or else utter midnight with a character so positive as his.

It followed, then, that his abundant and varied scientific labours were undertaken, whenever they were fruitful, in fields where there was no possibility of contest between experimental knowledge and revelation. Where his work was technical, not popular, it was exclusively concerned with the habits, or the forms, or the structure of animals, not observed in the service of any theory or philosophical principle, but for their own sake. In the two departments where he accomplished the greatest amount of original work, in the *Actinozoa* and the *Rotifera*, it was impossible for hypothesis of an anti-scriptural tendency to intrude, and if the observations which he made were used by others to support a theory inconsistent with the record of creation, he was not obliged to be cognizant of any such perversion of his work. He used, very modestly, to describe himself as "a hewer of wood and a drawer of water" in the house of science, but no biologist will on that account under-rate what he has done. His extreme care in diagnosis, the clearness of his eye, the marvellous exactitude of his memory, his recognition of what was salient in the characteristics of each species, his unsurpassed skill in defining those characteristics by word and by pencil, his great activity and pertinacity, all these combined to make Philip Gosse a technical observer of unusually high rank. In the article which the *Saturday Review* dedicated to my father at the time of his death, a passage was quoted from the preface to his *Actinologia Britannica* (1859), as giving in excellent terms the principles upon which his analytical labours in zoology were performed :—

"Having often painfully felt," he there said, "in studying "works similar to the present, the evil of the vagueness "and confusion that too frequently mark the descriptive "portions, I have endeavoured to draw up the characters "of the animals which I describe, with distinctive pre-"cision, and with order. It is reported of Montagu that, "in describing animals, he constantly wrote as if he had "expected that the next day would bring to light some "new species closely resembling the one before him ; and "therefore his diagnosis can rarely be amended. Some "writers mistake for precision an excessive minuteness, "which only distracts the student, and is, after all, but the "portrait of an individual. Others describe so loosely

"that half of the characters would serve as well for half
"a dozen other species. I have sought to avoid both
"errors : to make the diagnosis as brief as possible, and
"yet clear, by seizing on such characters, in each case, as
"are truly distinctive and discriminative."

As early as 1831 Philip Gosse began to be a minute and
systematic zoologist. I have attempted to describe how,
in the remote wilds of Newfoundland, with no help whatever towards identification, except "the brief, highly condensed, and technical generic characters of Linnæus's
Systema Naturæ," he attacked the vast class of insects, and
struck out for himself, specimens in hand, a road through
that trackless wilderness. The experience he gained in
this early enterprise could not be overestimated. Long
afterwards, when complimented on the fullness and precision of his characterization, he wrote of his struggles with
the Linnæan *Genera Insectorum,* and added that it was then
that he "acquired the habit of comparing structure with
structure, of marking minute differences of form, and
became in some measure accustomed to that precision of
language, without which descriptive natural history could
not exist." If I may point to one publication of my
father's in particular, the acumen and accuracy of which in
technical characterization have been helpful to hundreds
of students, I will select the two volumes of the *Manual of
Marine Zoology,* which so many an investigator has paused
to take out of his pocket and consult when puzzled by
some many-legged or strangely valved object underneath
the seaweed curtain of a tidal pool.

As a zoological artist, Philip Gosse claims high consideration. His books were almost always illustrated, and
often very copiously and brilliantly illustrated, by his own
pencil. It was his custom from his earliest childhood to
make drawings and paintings of objects which came under

his notice. In Newfoundland he had seriously begun to make a collection of designs. In July, 1855, he stated (in the preface to the *Manual of Marine Zoology*) that he had up to that date accumulated in his portfolios more than three thousand figures of animals or parts of animals, of which about two thousand five hundred were of the invertebrate classes, and about half of these latter done under the microscope. During the remainder of his life he added perhaps two thousand more drawings to his collections. The remarkable feature about these careful works of art was that, in the majority of cases, they were drawn from the living animal.

His zeal as a draughtsman was extraordinary. I have often known him return, exhausted, from collecting on the shore, with some delicate and unique creature secured in a phial. The nature of the little rarity would be such as to threaten it with death within an hour or two, even under the gentlest form of captivity. Anxiously eyeing it, my father would march off with it to his study, and, not waiting to change his uncomfortable clothes, soaked perhaps in sea-water, but adroitly mounting the captive on a glass plate under the microscope, would immediately prepare an elaborate coloured drawing, careless of the claims of dinner or the need of rest. His touch with the pencil was rapid, fine, and exquisitely accurate. His eyesight was exceedingly powerful, and though he used spectacles for many years, and occasionally had to resign for a while the use of the microscope, his eyes never wore out, and showed extraordinary recuperative power. He was drawing microscopic rotifers, with very little less than his old exactitude and brilliancy, after he had entered his seventy-eighth year.

In *A Naturalist's Rambles on the Devonshire Coast* (1853) he first began to adorn his books with those beautiful and exceedingly accurate coloured plates of marine objects which became so popular a part of his successive works. These were drawn on the stone by himself, and printed in colours by the well-known firm of Hullmandel and Walton with very considerable success. The plates of sea-anemones in this volume, though surpassed several years later by those in the *Actinologia*, were at that time a revelation. So little did people know of the variety and loveliness of the denizens of the seashore, that, although these plates fell far short of the splendid hues of the originals, and moreover depicted forms that should not have been unfamiliar, several of the reviewers refused altogether to believe in them, classing them with travellers' tales about hills of sugar and rivers of rum. Philip Gosse himself was disgusted with the tameness of the colours, to which the imperfect lithography gave a general dusty grayness, and he determined to try and dazzle the indolent reviewers. Consequently, in 1854, in publishing *The Aquarium*, he gave immense pains to the plates, and succeeded in producing specimens of unprecedented beauty. Certain full-page illustrations in this volume, the scarlet Ancient Wrasse floating in front of his dark seaweed cavern ; the Parasitic Anemone, with the transparent pink curtain of *delesseria* fronds behind it, the black and orange brittle-star at its base ; and, above all perhaps, the plate of star-fishes, made a positive sensation, and marked an epoch in the annals of English book illustration. In spite of the ingenuity and abundance of the "processes" which have since been invented, the art of printing in colours can scarcely be said to have advanced beyond some of these plates to *The Aquarium*. Philip Gosse was never again quite so fortunate. Even the much-admired illustrations to the *Actinologia*, in 1860, though executed with great care and profusion of tints, were not so harmonious, so delicate, or so distinguished as those of 1854. To compare the author's originals with the most successful of the chromo-lithographs is to realize how much was lost by the mechanical art of production.

Philip Gosse as a draughtsman was trained in the school of the miniature painters. When a child he had been accustomed to see his father inscribe the outline of a portrait on the tiny area of the ivory, and then fill it in with stipplings of pure body-colour. He possessed to the last the limitations of the miniaturist. He had no distance, no breadth of tone, no perspective ; but a miraculous ex-actitude in rendering shades of colour and minute peculiari-ties of form and marking. In late years he was accustomed to make a kind of patchwork quilt of each full-page illus-tration, collecting as many individual forms as he wished to present, each separately coloured and cut out, and then gummed into its place on the general plate, upon which a background of rocks, sand, and seaweeds was then washed in. This secured extreme accuracy, no doubt, but did not improve the artistic effect, and therefore, to non-scientific observers, his earlier groups of coloured illustrations give more pleasure than the later. The copious plates in *A Year on the Shore*, though they were much admired at the time, were a source of acute disappointment to the artist. There exists a copy of this book into which the original water-colour drawings have been inserted, and the difference in freshness, brilliancy, and justice of the tone between these and the published reproductions is striking enough. The submarine landscapes in many of these last examples were put in by Mrs. Gosse, who had been in early life a pupil of Cotman.

Between 1853 and 1860 my father lectured on several occasions in various parts of England and Scotland, with marked success. He was perhaps the earliest of those who, in public lecturing, combined a popular method with exact scientific information. He was accustomed to use freehand drawing on the black-board, in a mode which was novel when he first began, but which soon became common enough. He gave up lecturing mainly because of the extreme shyness which he never ceased to feel in addressing a strange audience. Had he not expressed this sense of suffering, no one would have guessed it from his serene and dignified manner of speaking on these occasions. His fondness for romantic poetry, and his habit of reciting it at home with a loud, impressive utterance, naturally produced an effect upon his manner in public speaking and lecturing.

It was a subject of constant regret to us in later years that he would not cultivate, for the general advantage, his natural gift of elocution. He needed, however, what he certainly would not have accepted, some training in the conduct of his voice, which he threw out with too monotonous a roll, a rapture too undeviatingly prophetic. But his enunciation was so clear and just, his voice so resonant, and his cadences so pure and distinguished, that he might easily have become, had he chosen to interest himself in human affairs, unusually successful as an orator. But it would doubtless always have been difficult for him to have stirred the enthusiasm, though he would easily have been secure of the admiration and attention, of an audience. Of late years, as long as his health permitted, he preached every Sunday in his chapel, always with the same earnest impressiveness, the same scrupulous elegance of language; but apt a little too much, perhaps, for so simple an audience, to be occupied with what may be called the metaphysics of religion.

His public speaking, however, was highly characteristic of himself, which is more than can justly be said of his letters. These were usually very disappointing. This did not arise from lack, but from excess of care; the consequence being that his letters, even to the members of his own family, were often so stiff and sesquipedalian as to produce a repellent effect, which was the very last thing that he intended. Letters, to be delightful, must be chatty, artless, irregular; anything of obvious design in their composition is fatal to their charm. My father had a theory of correspondence. He arranged the materials of which he wished to compose his letter according to a precise system, and he clothed them in language which reminded one of *The Rambler*. Hence it was rarely indeed that any one received from him one of those chatty, confidential epistles which reveal the soul, and touch the very springs of human nature. Letters should seem to have been written in dressing-gown and slippers; my father's brought up a vision of black kid gloves and a close-fitting frock-coat. The absence of anything like picturesque detail in them is very extraordinary when it is contrasted with the easy and romantic style of his best books. In his public works he takes his readers into his familiarity; in his private letters he seemed to hold them at arm's length.

The fullest expression of Philip Gosse's mind, indeed, is to be found in his books, and some general estimate of the character of these may at this point be attempted. Viewed as a whole, his abundant literary work is of very irregular character. Much of it bears the stamp of having been produced, against the grain, by the pressure of professional requirements. A great many of his numerous volumes may be dismissed as entirely ephemeral, as conscientious and capable pieces of occasional work, effective enough at the time of their publication, but no longer of any real importance. Another considerable section of his popular work consists of hand-books, which are not to be treated as literature. Yet another section consists of books in which the religious teacher is pre-eminent, in which the design is not to please, but to convict, admonish, or persuade. When these three divisions of his vast library of publications are dismissed as valuable each after its kind, but distinctly unliterary, there remains a residuum of about eight or nine volumes, which are books in the literary sense, which are not liable to extinction from the nature of their subject, and which constitute his claim to an enduring memory as a writer. Of these *The Canadian Naturalist* of 1840 is the earliest, *A Year at the Shore* of 1865 the latest. Charles Kingsley's criticism of these volumes, expressed thirty-five years ago, may still be quoted. Surveying the literature of natural history, Kingsley wrote, in *Glaucus* :—

"First and foremost, certainly, come Mr. Gosse's
"books. There is a playful and genial spirit in them,
"a brilliant power of word-painting, combined with deep
"and earnest religious feeling, which makes them as
"morally valuable as they are intellectually interesting.
"Since White's *History of Selborne* few or no writers on
"natural history, save Mr. Gosse and poor Mr. Edward
"Forbes, have had the power of bringing out the human
"side of science, and giving to seemingly dry disquisi-
"tions and animals of the lowest type, by little touches
"of pathos and humour, that living and personal interest,
"to bestow which is generally the special function of
"the poet. Not that Waterton and Jesse are not excellent
"in this respect, and authors who should be in every
"boy's library : but they are rather anecdotists than
"systematic or scientific inquirers ; while Mr. Gosse, in
"his *Naturalist on the Shores of Devon*, his *Tour in*
"*Jamaica*, and his *Canadian Naturalist*, has done for
"those three places what White did for Selborne, with

"all the improved appliances of a science which has
"widened and deepened tenfold since White's time."

The style of Philip Gosse was scarcely affected by any
other external influences than those which had come
across his path in his early youth in Newfoundland. The
manner of writing of the most striking authors of his own
generation, such as Carlyle and Macaulay, did not leave
any trace upon him, since he was mature before he met
with their works. The only masters under whom he
studied prose were romance-writers of a class now wholly
neglected and almost forgotten. Fenimore Cooper, whose
novels were appearing in quick succession between 1820
and 1840, introduced into these stories of Indian life
elaborate studies of landscape and seascape which had a
real merit of their own. *The Canadian Naturalist* shows
evident signs of an enthusiastic study of these descriptive
parts of Cooper. John Banim, the Irish novelist, whose
O'Hara Tales captivated him so long, left a mark on the
minute and graphic style of Philip Gosse, and there can be
little doubt that the latter owed something of the gorgeous-
ness and redundancy of his more purple passages to the
inordinate admiration he had felt for the apocalyptic
romances of the Rev. George Croly, whose once-famous
Salathiel he almost knew by heart. After the year 1838
he ceased to read new prose books for enjoyment of their
manner, and his style underwent but little further modification.

The most characteristic of my father's books, as types
of which *A Naturalist's Sojourn in Jamaica* and the
Devonshire Coast may be taken, consisted of an amalgam
of picturesque description, exact zoological statement,
topographical gossip, and easy reflection, combined after a
fashion wholly his own, and unlike anything attempted
before his day. White's *Selborne*, alone, may be supposed

to have in some measure anticipated the form of these books, in which the reader is hurried so pleasantly from subject to subject, that he has no time to notice that he is acquiring a great quantity of positive and even technical information. A single chapter of the *Devonshire Coast* opens with a picture of the receding tide on the north shore at the approach of evening ; proceeds to a particular account of two remarkable species, the one a polyp, the other the rare sipunculid Harvey's Syrinx, each so described that a mere tyro ought to be able to identify a specimen for himself ; describes the Capstone Hill and its attractions, like a sort of glorified hand-book ; tells a thrilling story of the loss of a child by drowning ; gives a close analysis of the physiological characteristics of a fine sea-anemone, *gemmacea*, of a singular marine spider, and of an uncouth sand-worm ; recounts an entertaining adventure with a soft crab ; carefully depicts the scenery of the hamlet of Lee ; and ends up with an elaborate account of the habitat, manners, and anatomy of the worm pipe-fish (*Syngnathus lumbriciformis*).

So much is pressed into one short chapter, and the others are built up on the same plan, in a mode apparently artless, but really carefully designed to mingle entertainment with instruction. The landscape framework in which the zoology is set will be found to bear examination with remarkable success. Every touch is painted from nature ; not one is rhetorical, not one introduced to give colour to the composition, but each is the result of a series of extremely delicate apprehensions retained successively in the memory with great distinctness, and transferred to paper with fine exactitude. I know of no writer who has described the phenomena of the falling tide on a rocky coast with as much accuracy, or with more grace of style, than Philip Gosse in the passage which I have alluded to above in my accidental synopsis of a chapter taken at random from the *Devonshire Coast.* I quote it here as a good, yet not exceptional example of his style :—

"How rapidly the sea leaves the beach! Yonder is
"an area distinguished from the rest by its unruffled
"smoothness on the recess of the wave; presently a
"black speck appears on it, now two or three more; we
"fix our eyes on it, and presently the specks thicken,
"they have become a patch, a patch of gravel; the
"waves hide it as they come up, but in an instant or two
"we predict that it will be covered no more. Mean-
"while the dark patch grows on every side; it is now
"connected with the beach above, first by a little
"isthmus at one end, enclosing a pool of clear per-
"fectly smooth water, a miniature lagoon in which the
"young crescent moon is sharply reflected with in-
"verted horns; the isthmus widens as we watch it;
"we can see it grow, and now the water is running out
"of the lakelet in a rapid; the ridges of black rock
"shoot across it, they unite;—the pool is gone, and the
"water's edge that was just now washing the foot of the
"causeway on which we are sitting, is now stretched
"from yonder points, with a great breadth of shingle
"beach between it and us. And now the ruddy sea is
"bristling with points and ledges of rock, that are
"almost filling the foreground of what was just now a
"smooth expanse; and what were little scattered islets
"now look like the mountain-peaks and ridges of a con-
"tinent. The glow of the sky is fading to a ruddy
"chestnut hue; the moon and Venus are glittering
'bright; the little bats are out, and are flitting, on
'giddy wing, to and fro along the edge of the cause-
"way, ever and anon wheeling around close to our feet.
"The dorrs, too, with humdrum flight, come one after
"another, and passing before our faces, are visible for

"a moment against the sky, as they shoot out to seaward.
" The moths are playing round the tops of the budding
"trees ; the screaming swifts begin to disappear ; the
"stars are coming out all over the sky, and the moon,
" that a short time before looked like a thread of silver,
"now resembles a bright and golden bow, and night
"shuts up for the present the book of nature."

In the obituary notice of my father published, in 1889,
in the *Proceedings of the Royal Society*, it is remarked by
the author, Mr. H. B. Brady, that he was "not only a
many-sided and experienced naturalist, but one who did
more than all his scientific contemporaries to popularize
the study of natural objects." Until his day very little
indeed was generally known on the subject of marine
zoology. The existing works on these lower forms, exceedingly limited and imperfect as they were, gave little
or no impression of the living condition of these creatures
in their native waters. It was Philip Gosse's function to
take the public to the edge of the great tidal pools, and
bid them gaze down for themselves upon all the miraculous
animal and vegetable beauty that waved and fluttered there.
In doing this, he was immensely aided by his own invention of the aquarium, which was instantly accepted by
naturalists and amateurs alike, and became to the one a
portable studio of biology, to the others a charming and
fashionable toy.

The volumes of *Punch* for thirty-five years ago reflect
the sudden popularity of this invention ; and, in addition
to the innumerable private vivaria, large public tanks,
fitted up in accordance with Philip Gosse's prescriptions,
were started all over Europe. The late Mr. W. Alford
Lloyd, whose affectionate devotion to my father deserves
the warmest recognition, was the agent in whose hands
the practical development of the scheme spread to the

construction of great public aquaria. These institutions achieved, perhaps, their highest success at Naples, under the admirable superintendence of Dr. Anton Dohrn ; but it is to the initiative step taken by Philip Gosse in 1852 that science owes the elaborate marine biological stations now established at various points along the European coast. He would not be equally proud to witness the most modern expression of the aquarium philosophy. When he was eagerly proposing the preservation of marine animals alive in mimic seas, he certainly did not anticipate that within forty years an aquarium would come to mean a place devoted to parachute monkeys, performing bears, and aerial queens of the tight-rope.

His interest in natural objects was mainly æsthetic and poetical, depending on the beauty and ingenuity of their forms. He regarded man rather as a blot upon the face of nature, than as its highest and most dignified development. His attention, indeed, was scarcely directed to humanity, even in those artistic amusements to which he dedicated a large part of his leisure. His second wife's predilection for landscape painting led him, about 1870, to learn the rudiments of that art, and he amused himself by taking a variety of studies in the open air, on Dartmoor, in the valley of the Teign, and by the shore, always selecting a point of view from which nothing which suggested human life was visible. These landscapes, if they were not very artistic, were often marked by his keenness of observation and originality of aspect. It is curious and highly characteristic that, notwithstanding all his familiarity with animal shapes, and his extraordinary skill in imitating them, he was absolutely unable to copy a human face or figure. When I was a child, I was for ever begging him to draw me "a man," but he could never be tempted to do it. "No!" he would say, "a humming-bird is much nicer, or a shark, or a zebra. I will draw you a zebra." And among the five thousand illustrations which he painted, I do not think that there is one to be found in which an attempt is made to depict the human form. Man was the animal he studied less than any other, understood most imperfectly, and, on the whole, was least interested in. At any moment he would have cheerfully given a wilderness of strangers for a new rotifer.

His appreciation of the plastic arts, notwithstanding his training and his skill, was very limited. He was positively blind to sculpture and architecture, to the presence of which his attention had to be forcibly drawn, if it was to be drawn at all. After lecturing in some of the cathedral cities of England, he has been found not to have noticed that there was a minster in the place ; much less could he describe such a church or appreciate it. He occasionally visited the Royal Academy, and exhibited considerable interest, but invariably in the direction of detecting errors or the reverse in the drawing or placing of natural phenomena, such as plants, animals, or heavenly bodies. Of the drama he disapproved with a vehemence which would have done credit to Jeremy Collier or William Law, and he would have swept it out of existence had he possessed the power to do so. With all his passion for poetry, he would never consent to read Shakespeare. He was inside a theatre but once; in 1853, on the first night of the revival of Byron's *Sardanapalus* at Drury Lane, he was present in the pit. Faraday—as little of a playgoer as himself, I suppose—was a spectator on the same occasion. To my father, the attraction was the careful antiquarian reproduction of an Assyrian court, founded upon the then recent discoveries made at Nineveh by Botta and Layard. In after years I asked him what effect this solitary visit to a theatre had produced upon him. He answered, with his usual severe candour, that he had observed nothing in the slightest degree objectionable, but that one such adventure would satisfy him for a lifetime.

The one art by which he was vividly affected was poetry. The magic of romantic verse, which had taken him captive in early boyhood, when he found it first in the pages of *Lara*, never entirely lost its spell over him. Milton (though with occasional qualms, because *Paradise Lost* was "tainted with the Arian heresy"), Wordsworth, Gray, Cowper, and Southey, were at his fingers' ends, and he had certain favourite passages of each of these which he was never weary of intoning. He liked Southey, because he was, as he put it, "the best naturalist among the English poets," and had described sea-anemones like a zoologist in *Thalaba*. He was much more interested, towards the end, in portions of Swinburne and Rossetti, than he had ever been in Tennyson and Browning, for neither of whom he had the slightest tolerance. Almost the latest conscious exercise of my father's brain was connected with his love for poetry. During his fatal illness, in July, 1888, when the gloom of decay was creeping over his intellect, he was carried out for a drive, the last which he would ever take, on an afternoon of unusual beauty. We passed through the bright street of Torquay, along the strand of Torbay, with its thin screen of tamarisks between the roadway and the bay, up through the lanes of Torre and Cockington. My father, with the pathetic look in his eyes, the mortal pallor on his cheeks, scarcely spoke, and seemed to observe nothing. But, as we turned to drive back down a steep lane of over-hanging branches, the pale vista of the sea burst upon us, silvery blue in the yellow light of afternoon. Something in the beauty of the scene raised the sunken brain, and with a little of the old declamatory animation in head

and hand, he began to recite the well-known passage in
the fourth book of *Paradise Lost*—

> " Now came still evening on, and twilight grey
> Had in her sober livery all things clad."

He pursued the quotation through three or four lines,
and then, in the middle of a sentence, the music broke, his
head fell once more upon his breast, and for him the
splendid memory, the self-sustaining intellect which had
guided the body so long, were to be its companions upon
earth no more.

APPENDIX I.

My step-mother has been so kind as to contribute some notes of that constant companionship with the subject of this memoir which she enjoyed through nearly thirty years. I think her intimate recollections will be appreciated by all readers of this book; they certainly will be prized by that narrower circle for whom they were primarily intended.

Reminiscences of My Husband from 1860 to 1888.

My first acquaintance with Philip Henry Gosse was made early in March, 1860. My sister and I had come from the eastern counties to spend the winter in Torquay. We came in February as strangers, never having been in this part before. We were recommended to Upton Cottage, in the suburbs of Torquay, where some kind friends, Mr. and Mrs. Henry Curtis, were living, who made us very happy for some months. One morning in March, the late Mr. Leonard Strong came into the Cottage and said, "I am just come from the Cemetery, where I have been conducting the funeral service over Mr. Gosse's mother, who had lived with him ever since he left London about two years ago." I at once asked, "What Mr. Gosse? Is he the noted naturalist?" "Yes," said Mr. Strong; "and he lives in St. Marychurch, close by you. The name 'Sandhurst,' in plain letters, is on his gate. He is the minister of a small church at the east end of that village." I knew him to be an eminent naturalist, but had formed no idea where he lived. Our curiosity was awakened, and we agreed that, when some opportunity occurred, we would go to this chapel, which proved to be, more properly speaking, a public room for meetings, in order to see and hear him. The friends with whom we were living were equally interested.

After two or three weeks we planned to go on a Sunday evening to this public room, where a section of the Christians called " Plymouth Brethren " were meeting, according to the simplicity of the New Testament Scripture principles, without ritual, choral adjunct, or outward adornment.   Here we found Philip Henry Gosse addressing the meeting from a high desk in the corner of the room next the window.   There were about thirty or forty people present.   It was a gospel address from a part of the story of Boaz and Ruth, which history he was going through on successive Sunday evenings.   It is a singularly beautiful type of Christ and His Church.   I found, afterwards, it was a favourite method with Mr. Gosse to illustrate the New through the characters of the Old Testament.   He would say, " There is but one key, whereby we are able to unlock the hidden treasures contained in the Bible, and this one key—which is Christ—aided by that spiritual discernment of sacred things, which the Holy Spirit alone can give, will enable us to unfold and open many hidden truths, lying far beneath the surface of apparently simple narrative, but which will be found to be highly typical of our Saviour, the Redeemer of His Church, of His person, and of His work."

After the meeting was over, my friend and I walked with Mr. Gosse and his little son as far as Sandhurst gate.   Before we parted, he told Mr. Curtis that there were Scripture-reading meetings held at his house, and that he would be pleased to see him and any friends who liked to accompany him.   We returned to the cottage, well pleased with the minister and his courteous and kind manner to us as strangers.   At this time, he was deeply engaged in literary work, bringing out his *Romance of Natural History* and completing his *Actinologia Britannica.*   He was in the full vigour and swing of his useful life, ardent and enthusiastic in every movement.   Two or three times a week he and his son, who was always with him—"the little naturalist," as he had been called in one of his father's books—would go, when the tide was fittest, with a basket, filled with many bottles and jars of various size, chisel, hammer, and other implements, to the shores far and near. They might often be seen, running and jumping down the declivities of the rocks, till they reached the pebbly shores at Oddicombe or Babbicombe.

His study, which I was permitted to look into on a later visit, was the largest sitting-room on the lower floor of his house, and was his workshop. Shelves surrounded the walls, filled with books ready for reference on each branch of his many literary studies; a large glass-fronted bookcase stood against the wall, opposite to the chair in which he sat always, during the winter, with his back to the fire, at a large table covered with books, papers, and implements. On his left hand, close to the window, was a long narrow table, upon which were shallow aquaria of various sizes, round, long, and square; one with three tall glass sides and a slate at the back to keep out the strong light from the window looking south-east—the first sea-anemone tank made for private use. These tanks were all filled with salt water, which, being kept mechanically in agitation, did not need frequent renewal, but strict attention to take out the dying animals. The clearness of the water was aided by seaweeds of brilliant hues. Into these tanks he brought the sea-anemones, small fish, and divers curious things, whose habits he closely watched, and whose forms he examined and drew faithfully.

He was an accomplished and most delicate draughtsman. His rapid eye would discover the various and minutest characteristics, and then classify them, ready to write their future history in his attractive manner. Some of his books he lent us to read, which formed an interesting topic of conversation during his increasingly frequent visits to the Cottage.

Mr. Gosse's most intimate friend at this time was Dr. J. E. Gladstone, cousin of the late Premier, who was the clergyman of the Furrough Cross Church, a free church built a few years before by Sir Culling Eardley Smith and others, in consequence of the very High Church doctrines then held in the parish of St. Marychurch. Mr. Gladstone and Mr. Gosse together instituted Bible readings, at which many intelligent Christians from Torquay and St. Marychurch met to read and have conversation over the Word of God. These were held at Sandhurst once a week, and continued, with but few intermissions, until my husband's last illness.

He manifested the same eager and enthusiastic spirit in his study of Divine things, as in his scientific pursuits. He studied the Bible as he would study a science. He must know what each separate portion was about, who the inspired writer was, what he was wishing to say, and for what purpose it was written; also how it was connected by prophecy or quotation with the New Testament, either in the Gospels or in the Epistles. He was microscopic in his readings, and in his interpretations of the Word of God, for he most implicitly believed every word of the original languages to be Divine, and dictated and written, through the writers, by the Holy Ghost. These languages, through their antiquity, are necessarily obscure; thus he was content to leave many passages and even chapters unexplained, satisfied that they never contradicted each other. Where two sides of a doctrine or subject are decidedly stated, he would reverently stand, and say, "There they are! I cannot put them together, but God can. I leave it to Him and am silent. Only through the Holy Spirit can it be received into the heart." This mode of thought was characteristic of Philip Henry Gosse. He had a wide grasp of the Holy Scriptures. He spoke of them as if the key had been given to us, and he sought to unlock their stores. He was familiar with the letter from a child, and, having been brought up in the old Puritan school, he was thoroughly sound in all the cardinal points of Evangelical doctrine.

On July 9, 1860, I see noted in his diary, "There was a large meeting at the new room in Fore Street, St. Marychurch." This chapel, which he had built, being now finished, the Church and congregation removed to it; and henceforward the meetings were continued there. The routine was the "breaking of bread," prayer, singing hymns, and a discourse by Mr. Gosse as the pastor of the Church. In the evenings, a gospel sermon by him.

During this summer he occasionally brought up to the Cottage his microscope or some natural history objects, and gave a familiar lecture on them. Some young friends were staying with us, and we all benefited by his interesting and cheerful remarks. These occasional visits were looked forward to by us all with great pleasure. The party sometimes accompanied him to the beach at Oddicombe or Babbicombe, when he always took great pains to show his mode of collecting, and sometimes brought out new and curious and lovely creatures, when we gathered around and exclaimed, in our ignorance of such matters, "How beautiful! how wonderful!" and at the end agreed that we had spent a delightful morning.

My sister, in July, left Torquay, and I remained at Upton Cottage the rest of the summer, as we had let our house at

Saffron Walden for two years. I resolved in my mind that for the remaining Sundays, I would go with my friends to the little meeting in Fore Street, St. Marychurch. Many years before, whilst paying a visit at Clifton to an old friend, we had together attended the Church led by Mr. George Müller, of the Orphanage, Bristol, whose principles were those of "Brethren;" and on another occasion I had been the guest of Sir Alexander Campbell at Exeter. Their views had taken considerable hold on my own mind, and made a strong and lasting impression. Thus, I was prepared, even after the lapse of many years, to attend like meetings with pleasure and profit; especially as they were led by one so able, so intelligent, and so spiritually minded, as was Mr. Gosse.

On September 3, 1860, I left Torquay, as I supposed finally, and returned to the house of an uncle and aunt at Frome, as to a temporary home. I took leave of my friends at the Cottage, and of Mr. Gosse and his son at Sandhurst, after a most pleasant stay of eight months. However, as God had planned it, on September 6 I had a letter from Mr. Gosse, proposing and urging, in strong terms, that I should become his wife. This certainly was no little surprise to me. However, after a week or two of consideration and consulting my friends, I accepted the offer of his hand.

On the 21st he came to Frome to visit me. We were married at Frome on December 18, 1860, and came direct to Sandhurst. I see our marriage noted in his diary, date December 18: "I was married at Zion Chapel, Frome, by the Rev. D. Anthony, to my beloved Eliza Brightwen; and after refection, we left by train and got to Sandhurst about nine." It had been fine in the morning, but by the time we arrived at Sandhurst a deep snow had fallen; and the next morning, geraniums and other plants, carefully stored, were all drooping their heads and almost killed. So ends this memorable time. I had a hearty welcome from my dear little stepson, of whom I had already seen a good deal, and who was warmly attached to me. My beloved husband and he made me quite at home, telling me many of their old traditions and amusing family stories, with much fun, and we had quite a merry breakfast. I soon found out that Mr. Gosse had a good deal of humour and fun when quite in the intimacy of his home, notwithstanding that to his circle of friends and neighbours he

was grave and somewhat stern, as became one who had taken
the position of pastor.

It was his custom to call the servants in for reading the Scriptures, and for prayer, every morning after breakfast. We all had
our Bibles, to follow him in the reading; he made many remarks
illustrating the subject in hand, which rendered it a very interesting and instructive Bible lesson. The same routine was carried
on every evening, before supper, at about nine o'clock. His
manner with the servants was kindly, but always firm; and
I soon learned that he *bore rule* in his family. He always had
a "good night" for the servants and "God bless you," and a
greeting in the morning. He kept early hours, breakfasting at
7.30 even all through the winter months, which hour we kept
up to the end. He was a most industrious man, generally in
his study between five and six o'clock. I found no difficulty in
falling in with his habits of early hours, or with his punctuality
throughout the day, having been brought up in somewhat homely
and orderly habits; so that after we got settled together, I soon
fell into his ways. When the weather was fine, we used to walk
together, and when the tides were suitable, we made expeditions
to the rocks to collect the sea-animals.

In the mornings I used to sit with him in his study, copying or
rendering some necessary help. After a time, he began to take
me round to the cottages of the sick and poor of his congregation.
We had thus an insight into the life of the Devonshire people,
which was very interesting to us both. He was a great favourite
among his people, and a visit from Mr. Gosse was always considered an honour, and a profit too, as he would discuss some
instructive (generally Bible) subject, and thus place himself on
easy terms with them. This practice he kept up for a few years,
until, the numbers of his flock having become more numerous, he
found visiting too fatiguing. He had few friends of his own rank,
but there were some with whom we exchanged visits, and who
came to the Scripture-reading meetings at Sandhurst one morning
in each week.

He never opened out to general visitors. He always spoke of
himself as a *shy* man. Some might think him stern and unsocial;
he was a recluse, and a thorough student in all his ways, and a
true "home bird." Often when, in after years, I remonstrated

with him on his isolation, and urged him to go out more among his friends, he would say, " My darling, 'my mind to me a kingdom is,' " which might seem a trifle selfish, if selfishness could be considered at all a constituent in the heart of my beloved husband. He was of a remarkably even disposition. I never saw him give way to those frailties or minor faults that are so often exhibited in the lives of less exalted, or of uncontrolled characters. His life was given to studies of a grave and more or less religious nature, or else to closely thought-out scientific studies, especially those of natural objects. His mind being habitually occupied with this higher order of thoughts, he seemed to find it impossible to unbend to the lighter topics of everyday conversation. He was wont to excuse himself by saying, " I have no small talk."

In 1864, when he was writing *A Year at the Shore* in the spring, we three had great pleasure in walking or driving, as the case might be, to the various bays and rocky shores of the Devonshire coast. My dear husband and son would rush down, with strong india-rubber boots or sea-shoes, and work hard, with hammer and chisel, carefully taking off the anemones and other sea-animals from the rocks, or fishing in the pools for wrasse, blennies, pipe-fish, or other sea-creatures, while I would sit on a camp stool, either watching them, sometimes with a field-glass, or reading, or drawing some of the lovely sea-views in my sketch-book. Then, when we got home, there was the eager looking over the haul, and putting the creatures in large basins to be watched and drawn, till they could finally be placed in the tanks. Thus, subjects were prepared for each month in the year, and this gave us much occupation before *A Year at the Shore* was completed.

That year, 1864, I had a considerable accession of property, which was valuable as giving my husband more rest and enabling him to have more leisure; so that he did not need any longer to work, either in writing or in lecturing. In 1866 he began to take a great interest in some of the rarer kind of plants, especially orchids, which he had always greatly admired, and had collected to hang in his house, when he was in Jamaica twenty years earlier. This remembrance brought afresh the interest before him. He had built a small plant-house against the westerly side of our dwelling-house. The boiler for heating the pipes was put on the

foundation of the cellar under the drawing-room; this had the
additional value of warming our house, which before was a very
cold one. This he afterwards enlarged, and eventually our
garden contained no fewer than five hothouses or conservatories.

After the first small importation of orchids, which was not, by
the way, very successful, though of great interest to us, and helpful
in teaching the gardener the management and culture of these
difficult and rare plants, he continued to make additions, partly
through sales at plant auctions, and partly through orchid
gardeners; buying small plants and growing them on, till they
are now become good specimens, and interesting objects of
instruction and pleasure. His gardener was specially facile in
reception of his instructions, and in a few years learned the
treatment, and was so successful, both in growing the orchids, as
well as other rare plants, that his master left them very much to
his knowledge of the treatment and care.

In 1867 Captain Bulger, an Indian officer, who afterwards
went to the Cape, repeatedly sent a small cargo of valuable
plants; one plant among them especially, which we have kept
until the present time, greatly interested my husband, but it was
not until 1889 that it flowered for the first time. The bulb above
ground is a very large onion-shaped one; the long narrow and
stiff leaves from it are of a peculiarly wavy and fan-shaped growth.
The flowers, which are bright pink and small, come upon a wide
flat stem, about twelve inches high, in a bunch spreading out to
fourteen inches in diameter, and over one hundred in number,
and are of the Hexandria order. It is extremely rare in England,
and has been named by the Horticultural Society *Brunswigia
Josephine.* Captain Bulger, whom my husband had never seen,
was greatly attached to him through his books, and entered into
correspondence, which lasted until the captain's death in Canada.

In 1866 my dear husband went to London—the first time since
our marriage that he had left me for more than a day. He took
his son to enter the British Museum, and to settle him in
London.

In 1868 my husband and I paid an interesting visit to Poole,
in Dorsetshire—the place where he had been brought up by
his parents from two years old. We walked around to see all
the familiar places—the home of his parents, in Skinner Street,

which was a narrow cul-de-sac, with the Independent Chapel on the opposite side of this little street, where the family attended. He and his brother had been in the choir, William having played the violin. We obtained leave to go inside his old dwelling; and there he searched all the rooms, and endeavoured to see if any traces existed of sentences and aphorisms, which he and his brothers used to write under the chimney-slab or other places. At length, he found, in a corner of the ceiling, some lines of his own writing, fifty years old, but still unobliterated by cleaning or whitewash. The old familiar water-butt in the corner of the little back-yard, and other reminiscences, brought back many of his youthful thoughts, occupations, and amusements; the harbour and quay, from whence, as a boy, leaving the parental roof, he went out to Newfoundland.

We walked to see the old oak tree in a field outside the town, in which he used to sit on Saturday afternoons and half-holidays, with his great friend and favourite school-fellow, John Brown, reading and discussing their histories and their little empires and infant zoological studies, thus sowing the seeds of that incipient life, which afterwards developed into his great, extended, and accomplished mind. He made a sketch of the fine Poole Harbour and Brownsea Island, sand rocks, Old Harry Cliff, from Parkstone, where we walked several times to visit our kind friend, Walter Gill, who kept a large school there. This view we painted together in water colours, and finished when we got back to Sandhurst; it is framed and hangs in the dining-room to this day, with many other landscapes, which his skilful hand drew from the spots.

A little later, when the interest of the orchids wore off, and his gardener had attained sufficient skill to cultivate them independently, he began to form a collection of foreign butterflies, for which he had considerable facilities. Through his scientific knowledge, he had large acquaintance with men who, in this line, were able to help to secure valuable and choice specimens. These he obtained chiefly from the tropics, by writing to persons and collectors named to him, who would send considerable numbers of butterflies, their wings folded when life was just extinct; being put in three-cornered envelopes, they would travel well, being packed together in cigar and similar boxes. He would make his selection of half a dozen or so, and send the remainder to London, or to dealers in other places, who would make their principal remuneration out of them. He would frequently write to missionaries and others, desiring them to collect for him at their leisure, liberally refunding them for time and labour.

A very interesting and intimate intercourse of this kind was thus opened up with a family of young brothers in the Argentine Republic; four young men, the Messrs. Perrens, relations of some dear friends of ours in Torquay, with whom we have for many years kept up a bright and happy friendship.

The relaxing these butterflies and fixing them in the cabinets was an occupation of deep interest to us. The strict order and arrangement, with the name of every insect and its habitat, written in his beautiful handwriting, makes these cabinets most valuable. Many an hour has been spent in looking them over with our friends; his eagerness in opening the drawers of the cabinets, with his valuable remarks, information, and the incidents attaching to individual specimens, made these visits most instructive as well as interesting. He was always willing to impart amusement and information when he saw that it was valued.

My husband could very rarely be induced to leave home, but in 1869, at the end of September, we decided to make a short outing, and we started in a carriage for Haytor, on Dartmoor. We stayed at the Rock Inn, and took several excursions; and Mr. Gosse made drawings of various scenes. The Haytor Rock he sketched most enthusiastically after his usual manner. The weather changed to wet and very misty, but he was very desirous of getting several sacks full of *sphagnum* moss for his orchids. The squeezing of the water out of this moss gave him cold, and produced violent pain in his hands. He became so unwell that we were obliged to return home at the end of a fortnight. After a few days his physician, Dr. Finch, pronounced him suffering from rheumatic gout in his hands; it also attacked his knees. Several treatments were applied, and he kept his room some weeks, but gradually got worse. In November he went to Torquay to try the Turkish baths. He took them twice a week, and continued them to the end of the year. He gave up the Bible-reading meetings, and also all the chapel services for a while; but he found at length that his limbs became easier, and by the end of the year he resumed his work.

In 1874 he had attacks of what seemed to be a form of aphasia, and though they were not alarming, he was prevailed upon to make another excursion. A trip to Derbyshire was selected; though it was rather late in the year, we started for Matlock Bath. We left home November 12, 1874, slept at Gloucester, and went on the next morning to Matlock, where we got lodgings on a very high point overlooking the winding river, the Dove, and with a charming view on to the hanging woods the other side. Though these trees were leafless, the branches were often so covered by the light and white frost, that on several of the November mornings they looked like fairyland. We made some very interesting excursions in the neighbourhood, which all tended to re-establish health. One of my sisters made us a visit here on her way home to Manchester, which greatly heightened our pleasure. We returned home in the early part of December.

In 1875 the diary shows that my husband had become interested in a variety of evangelical missions. Many letters were written, and donations given to colonial objects and others. We were made acquainted with Miss Walker Arnott's work in Jaffa. In the diary notice is made of Katrina Abou Sitte, a Mahomedan orphan and Syrian child, ten years old, selected by Miss W. Arnott as our *protégée* for ten pounds per annum, to be given by us for her board and schooling at Jaffa. This was continued for several years, till she left; she has since been married to a Christian Jew. We have frequently had very sweet and grateful letters from her, calling us her "English parents," often with small presents made of products of the country and from Jerusalem, where they were living. Mr. Gosse also took up with considerable eagerness Mr. Pascoe's mission-work in Toluca, Mexico, and carried on a pleasant correspondence with that gentleman, helping him to continue his printing work in that place. He became a liberal contributor to the China Island Mission. Mr. Guinness's work and institute had also a large share of his help and interest.

At this time we engaged a Bible woman of our own to visit in St. Marychurch. My husband took up once more, for a while, the consecutive and orderly visiting of the poor and sick of his flock, to all of whom he was kind and liberal. He was the sole pastor and conductor of all the meetings, both at the Table of the Lord, in worship, and in the preaching. His discourses were mainly expository. He was accustomed to take a whole chapter or chapters of a Gospel or an Epistle, focussing all the salient points, and then turning to other portions of Scripture which would shed light, or to quotations that would explain the subject in hand. In the Old Testament he would take a character, bringing out the important features, or it might be those prophetical of the future, thus making a Biblical figure stand out, with all the motives that actuated him, either for good or evil, as the case might be. These discourses were most attractive and enjoyable. He always kept very close to Scripture, knowing a good deal of the Greek and something of the Hebrew language.

All this labour, besides his scientific work, collecting at the shores, his tanks, his cabinets, his plant-houses, are minutely tabulated in folios and diaries; histories of many specimens written in full; contributions to scientific societies, which occupied his mornings in examinations in the microscope and other work. All this tells what an industrious man he was. In a letter to a friend, who sent him a manuscript to look over and criticize, he says, " I am sorry to have kept your manuscript so long, but I could read it only at caught intervals, for my time is most pressingly occupied. I am generally in my study soon after five a.m. ; and, what with the work of the Lord and some scientific investigations, which, I hope, will bring glory to Him, I know not what leisure means." And this letter was written in June, 1881, when he was in his seventy-second year.

My son has described the manner in which, in 1876, his father returned to the study of marine animals. This led him once more to take frequent excursions to the sea-shore, in which I was his constant companion. The living objects which he discovered were brought home and placed in the large show-tank, which about this time he fitted up in a small room at the back of our dwelling-house. When he went out dredging, or collecting on the rocks which he had to approach in a boat, I was not so commonly his companion. The filling of the tank and the watching of the animals as they made themselves at home in its corners and crevices was an unceasing source of pleasure to us both. In

1878 I recollect that an octopus was offered to us by the son of a Babbicombe fisherman, who had taken it in a trammel-net. We hesitated, but at last decided to buy it for the large sum of fifteen-pence. In the afternoon the boy brought it up, and my husband turned it into the lobster's corner of the large tank. It was indeed a hideous beast, the body about the size of a large lemon. It was very vigorous and active, yet not wild. After an hour or two, while I was present, it pushed up into the further angle of the glass partition, and managed to squeeze its body through into the area of the tank, and presently found a place for itself near the bottom of the middle of the glass tank, clinging with coiled arms to the glass. A month later, the best tide of the whole year, my husband and I drove to Goodrington Sands, where, at the central ledges, he made a good collecting. A young lady who was catching prawns gave us some, and our driver-boy found a hole in which my husband took a wonderful number of fine large prawns, squat lobsters, with others, and a large plant of *Tridœa edulis.* All the above were lodged in the tank in good condition. A crab we gave to the octopus, who instantly seized and devoured it, together with the head of a large fish and a dead giant prawn. In November the octopus became languid for a few days, hiding in the remotest corners—we thought shrinking from the severe cold that had set in. It died on the 8th, after having lived with us nearly ten weeks.

All these recreations were a great rest to Philip Gosse's active brain, as the exercises and air were healthful to his body, and to me they were a source of very great enjoyment. My husband was a true naturalist, and the fact that for many years he got his livelihood by writing books on natural history, wandering among the rocks and pools, mingling all his thoughts and sympathies with the God who formed these wonderful varieties of creation, gave a zest to his life which sedentary reading or authorship in his study could never have realized.

As Kingsley has said, " Happy truly is the naturalist ! He has no time for melancholy dreams. The earth becomes transparent ; everywhere he sees significance, harmonies, laws, chains of cause and effect endlessly interlinked, which draw him out of the narrow sphere of self into a pure and wholesome region of joy and wonder." My dear husband was essentially a religious man.

The attitude of his mind was heavenly; and only in the face of God, as a Father in Christ, could he enjoy the marvels of nature. The psalm was often on his lips, "Thy works are great, sought out of all them that have pleasure therein."

About this time (May, 1877), I was paying a visit to a relative in Somersetshire, and in an evening walk found a spot in a lane where were a number of glow-worms, some of which I sent home. He put them on some grass in the garden, and in his next letter he asks me to send him some more. He says, "Can you not persuade your cousin or some gentleman to go with you a night walk, and get some more glow-worms, for I think I can keep them luminous for some while? You ask what they are? Glow-worms are beetles; but the female sex has neither wings nor wing-sheaths, and it is the female alone that is luminous. They belong to a family of the great class Beetles (Coleoptera), which are remarkably soft-bodied all their life. The cantharides or blister-flies belong to the same family. There is scarcely any visible difference in form between the grub and the perfected female; the male, however, has large, but flexible, parchment-like wing-cases. In most of the foreign species (there are many in Jamaica, for example) both sexes are luminous." Having lived in Jamaica so long begat in him the love for animal and insect life, as also vegetable life in the tropics.

Before he went to Jamaica he met with some dear friends, in intercourse with whom, as previously related in the former part of this life, his religious views underwent an entire change. He speaks of them in a late letter to Mr. George Pearce, now engaged with his wife in missionary labour in the north of Africa : " It is always pleasant to receive a letter from you, and with you to go back along the memories of more than forty years, to those happy days, so loaded with blessing for my whole life since, when we met, a loving and happy band, around the table of dear W. Berger and his wife M. Berger in Wells Street night after night, while the Holy Ghost poured into our receptive hearts 'the testimony of Jesus,' and began at last to make 'the word of the Christ to dwell in us richly in all wisdom.' A few weeks ago our beloved and bereaved brother, W. Berger, kindly came down on purpose to stay a few days with us, to renew that happy intercourse which is ever vivid with myself."

In another letter to the same friend, he recurs to that happy period of his younger life : " How sweet the assurance of your undying love, and how sweet the recollection of that happy early time, when God gave me the precious gift of personal acquaintance with you and other dear brethren. What a *punctum saliens* was that in my life ! I had been reared by godly parents (*Independents*). About a year before I knew you, my friend Matthew Habershon had lent me his two volumes on prophecy, which first opened my eyes to the pre-millennial Advent of our Lord. The first volume I began after closing my school on a summer evening (June, 1842) ; and before I went to bed, I had read it right through. I possessed a very full knowledge of the letter of Scripture from childhood, so that the proofs of the doctrine commended themselves to me as I read without cavil. It was a glorious truth to me. I hailed the coming Jesus with all my heart. So absorbed was I, that when at length I finished the book, I could not, for some considerable time, realize where I was ; it seemed another world ! From that time I began to pray that I might be privileged to wait till my Lord should come, and go up to Him without having been unclothed. Forty long years have passed. I am now a man of grey hairs ; but I never cease to ask this privilege of my loving God (Luke xxi. 36), and every day I ask it still. Of course, I have no assurance that so it will be. I have no such revelation as Simeon had (see Luke ii. 26) ; but I wait, I hope, I pray." This hope of being caught up before death continued to the last, and its non-fulfilment was an acute disappointment to him. It undoubtedly was connected with the deep dejection of his latest hours on earth.

In another letter he wrote to this same friend in North Africa, 1881, he says, " Within a few years back, when the sole ministry in Marychurch and the pastorate there had become somewhat too much for my advancing years (I am now in my seventy-second year), a loving Christian gentleman, Mr. William King Perrens, who had had experience in the same work, came to reside in our neighbourhood, and he has now, with my wishes, become a sharer with me in the oversight, and we labour together in fullest harmony. There are now about one hundred and twenty in fellowship and in 'the breaking of bread,' mostly poor and working people in the midst of much worldliness and Popery, and we wait for our

Lord's promised return in those views of Divine prophecy which you knew I held diverse from those held usually by ' Brethren ' so called fifty years ago."

Mr. Perrens, though looking for the return of the Lord Jesus, did not accept the " year-day " system or the historical fulfilment throughout the age, or dispensation, of the prophecies, either of the Book of Daniel or the Revelation; but this divergence of opinion did not hinder their mutual regard and united labour for the Lord.   My husband followed the old-fashioned Protestant scheme held by Scott the commentator, Bishop Newton, Elliott, Bosanquet, and, lastly, H. Grattan Guinness, who has so ably written *The Approaching End of the Age*, viewed in the light of history, prophecy, and science.   This mode looks on "the times of the Gentiles" as starting from Nebuchadnezzar, into whose hands God gave the kingdoms of the earth, after He had taken the kingdom from Israel, "who shall be led away captive into all nations, and Jerusalem shall be trodden down of the Gentiles until the times of the Gentiles shall be fulfilled."

These subjects of prophecy from the Scriptures were, in detail, under the constant study of my dear husband in some form or other.   He had a large number of books in his library, both ancient and modern, dealing with these prophecies.   He was a daily reader of the *Times* newspaper; he used to say the great object of his reading this paper was to see " the decadence of the nations, both Eastern and Western, in their downward progress." He always kept his Polyglot Bible on the chimney-piece at his right hand, and that was continually brought down on any new event—war or collision among the nations—to see if it could be possible to glean any fresh light from the Prophets on the occasion of this fresh outbreak ; especially the Eastern Question would give eager aspirations towards the break up of the Turkish empire, and the setting Palestine free for the return of Israel.

This year, 1884, he brought out a new edition of his *Evenings at the Microscope*, correcting and enlarging some portions of the book.   This was not his own property, as he had written it some twenty years earlier for the Society for Promoting Christian Knowledge.

This year also he began to write expositions of Scripture ; some were from notes of his Sunday morning discourses taken by a friend at the time, afterwards published in a small volume as *The Mysteries of God*. This was to him a deeply interesting work for God, and written with much prayer that it might be blessed to His children. He had so often been requested by members of his congregation, and others, to write and publish his discourses, that at length he consented. As he went on with these expositions, they were of the deepest interest to us both, unfolding so much of Scripture that had not, in its fullest depth, been previously discovered to us, especially in the three chapters on "The Psalms." He says at the commencement: "An effort is here made, in the fear of God, to search for heavenly wisdom as for hid treasure beneath the surface of the Word; to examine the lively oracles as with a microscope, persuaded they will be found well worthy of the closest research. Some of the essays may seem to some abstruse, and may be thought to be mere idle speculation. But, if carefully weighed, I hope they will be found to rest on the revealed mind of God in every particular. I have advanced nothing. I have anticipated nothing on mere speculation. For every statement that I have made I have aimed to rest on the inspired Word. I have desired strictly to limit myself to the elucidation of what is written in the Book. The constant reference to the very words of the Holy Ghost will, I trust, plead my apology for what may seem a dogmatic tone. As His trumpet gives no uncertain sound, so, as the whole tenour of Scripture shows, believers are expected to *know* with confidence the things which are freely given them of God. We have the mind of Christ."

My dear husband was especially scriptural on the atoning sacrifice of Christ, who suffered, "the just for the unjust;" also on the supernatural humanity and sinlessness of the Son of Man. He expressly states, "I hold that, under the righteous government of God, suffering of any kind or degree is impossible, save as the just wages of sin. But since the holy Child Jesus suffered as soon as He came into the world, as He was made under the Law, and since in Him was no sin, of what was this suffering the wages, but of that iniquity of us all, laid on Him, exacted, and for which He became answerable? (Isa. liii. 6, 7).

"The Psalms reveal to us that the Holy One was vicariously bearing throughout His life the iniquity and reproach of man, and various pains of body, though all of these in varying measures, and probably with longer or shorter intermission. The Father's personal complacency in Him, and His loving confidence in the Father, were in no sense inconsistent with vicarious enduring. All suffering He ever bore, He bore as our vicarious Substitute, as second Adam, with culmination of pressure at the garden and the Cross; but he never lost sight of the love of the Father. All, all helped to pay the ' ten thousand talents ' of our debt to God. In Him is no sin ! "

In 1884 my dear husband had the first symptoms of diabetes. He was sometimes much depressed, but the doctor's good care and a prescribed diet strengthened him, and he recovered. Notwithstanding depression, I see by the diary of that year that his great energy of mind enabled him to get through much general reading. In the autumn and winter months he subscribed to Mudie's Library, as had been his habit for some years. He was a rapid reader, and got through a large number of books of various interest, chiefly in the evenings—travels of naturalists ; histories of all parts of the world ; missionary exploits largely. He watched with great interest the development and opening of that wonderful quarter of the world, the " Dark Continent." By these means his general depression wore off, and he grew more cheerful. He was more indoors than usual, being afraid of the inclemency of the weather, until the summer of 1885 came, when he resumed his usual outdoor exercise.

It was always a great delight to him to watch the signs of spring and early summer. He was up early in the morning, with his study window open for the fresh air, listening for the first voice of the cuckoo, or for the songs of the many birds which used to congregate in the trees around. There was one which we called " the cuckoo tree " in a near meadow, which we could see from the upper windows of our house. He always tried to be the first who heard or saw this bird, which for many years came there. In the diary I see frequently, " I walked round by (or through) the cuckoo meadow and sat under the tree, the bird voicing over my head." Of late years there were so many inhabited houses that this bird almost ceased to appear : quite a disappointment to him.

I find by the end of this year *The Mysteries of God* was

published. It was received very favourably by the religious press, and there were many interesting letters from those who appreciated the book.

The following years, from 1885 to 1887, saw him returning to the old occupation and study of the *Rotifera*, or "wheel-animalcules." He became acquainted with Dr. Hudson, of Clifton, and with him brought out the two volumes of *The Rotifera, or Wheel-Animalcules.* His ardour and persistency in the microscopical study of these minute animals at his advanced age were remarkable. He was whole days with the microscope before him in his study, interrupted only by correspondence with various students over England, Europe, and America.

In our frequent drives, when this study could be intermitted, we would, with bottles in baskets, search the dirty ditches, and sundry ponds and puddles, for these tiny, almost invisible, animalcules. Three young ladies, daughters of some intimate friends about three miles distant, were enlisted into the work of procuring "ditch-water" to be examined, and it was a great amusement in their various walks to bottle up the water.

I must not omit to say that, during parts of these years, he was occupied in the study of the heavenly bodies. We had a good telescope, through which, on clear and starry nights in the autumn, we obtained a very fair idea of the principal constellations, double stars, and nebulæ. An accident happened to this telescope, and it was rendered useless; but through *The Bazaar* he obtained, from a clergyman in Worcester, a more powerful one, which gave us further vision into the wonderful space of these far-off worlds. The sequel of this deeply interesting study towards the end of 1887 brings me to the close of this valuable life. The winter nights became cold, and his ardour to stand adjusting the instrument at open windows brought on an attack of bronchitis, which at the beginning of 1888 settled into a serious illness. Mischief at the heart was discovered by the doctor, and although we still took short walks and drives together into the country for some little time, his health soon proved to be broken.

January 8 was the last time he was able to expound the Scriptures at the chapel. He gradually gave up all study, and, indeed, all reading. It seemed that his brain was entirely unable to receive mental impressions. He was obliged to spend nearly the whole night sitting in his chair by the fireside, his breathing being so difficult that he could not lie down in his bed. He became unable to walk upstairs, and therefore two of our good carriage-drivers always came in about eight o'clock, and carried him up to his room. Friends frequently dropped in to see him in the morning; it seemed to give him some satisfaction to receive them, though he was not able to converse much. His son's wife came down to us from London, and we had the comfort of her help and company every day. In his calmer and more lucid moments he described himself as still expecting the personal coming of the Lord. Even within the last fortnight, seeing me distressed, he said, "Oh, darling, don't trouble. It is not too late; even now the Blessed Lord may come and take us both up together." I believe he was buoyed up almost to the last with this strong hope.

I was often surprised to find how entirely he had lost interest in all his beloved studies. For the last two months he entered his study but twice—once to glance at his accustomed Greek New Testament, which he left open at the Gospel of John xvii.; and again, for the last time, to look cursorily round. The last evening it happened that he was carried upstairs by our kind and diligent Bible reader for the villagers. This was a week before he died. He never came downstairs again, but remained, with but little intelligent expression, until August 23, 1888, at one o'clock in the morning, when he passed in his sleep to be with his expected Lord. He was very restless nearly the whole of that night, but towards midnight he became quiet. To the nurse who was with him he said, "It is all over. The Lord is near! I am going to my reward!" Early in this evening, a kind neighbour, Mr. Bullock, had come to his bedside and asked to pray. At the end of his prayer the precious sick one seemed to respond distinctly, in prayer for all the dear members of his Church, that "I may present each of them perfect in Christ Jesus."

I will insert a slight notice of my husband's character which was written by one who knew him well in the latter part of his life, published in the *Christian*. "'To every man his work.' A question arises—Is it possible to separate man's work into two parts, and to say this is secular and scientific, and this is religious? We think not. Philip Henry Gosse proved that a man might live all his life in the service of God, and, in doing so, serve his own generation in the best possible way. His chief glory, indeed, is that he so combined science with religion, that we cannot detect where the one ends and the other begins, so beautifully are they woven together in his works. It is as a *truster* in, and a revealer of God, that he stands forth prominently; not only God as revealed in His Word, but God as declared in His works. To him this God was one God, and he was perfectly persuaded that the written and the unwritten books could not contradict each other. First anchoring himself to God and His Word, he was able safely and profitably to explore the wonderful works of the Creator, without drifting away into unknown wastes, and losing his way altogether.

" He had learned to distrust his own intellect, and to rely on the intellect of God. As a describer of what men call 'natural objects,' which are really manifestations of God, Mr. Gosse had few equals. His vivid pictures, fitly framed in graceful and sparkling language, captivate the mind at once, while his reverent spirit cannot but make his readers feel that he is describing what he loves as the handiwork of his Father in heaven.

" Equally happy was his method of expounding the Word of God. His sentences were terse, vigorous, and pointed; his illustrations apt and unstrained; while his knowledge of the Scriptures, both of the Old and New Covenants, was astonishing.

" To say that he never erred in his interpretations of the Word would be to say that he was not human. His impulsive, eager spirit, combined with the warmth of his imagination, sometimes led him, perhaps, into an untenable position, and carried him beyond what is written.

" It is not possible to over-estimate the value of the testimony which he has left behind him. Gifted with an extraordinary intellect, admired as an author, looked up to as an authority on all subjects connected with natural science, having admirable conversational powers, Mr. Gosse might, if he had so chosen, have occupied a very high and distinguished position in worldly society. But he did not so choose. 'Esteeming the reproach of Christ greater riches than the treasures of Egypt,' he preferred to bury himself in a little country village, and quietly and unobtrusively to serve the Lord Christ.   All that he was, and all that he had, he laid at the feet of Jesus.

"Another testimony, most valuable in these days, is the living proof which he has afforded that it is possible to be a man of science and yet to be a devout believer in the inspired Word of God.

"He believed ' *all* that the prophets have spoken,' and could not tolerate any departure therefrom, either in himself or others. This made his utterances sometimes seem stern and dogmatic. Having formed an opinion on any matter, he clung to it tenaciously, almost to the point of being unyielding, and even combative.   The inflexibility of his submission to God and His Word has, in some quarters, earned for him the epithets of 'Puritan,' 'ascetic,' 'recluse,' and so on.   But how refreshing and invigorating is such a decided form of godliness, compared with that flaccid, flavourless Christianity and monkish agnosticism that is so fashionable in these days.   The Lord keep us from being neither 'cold nor hot.'   As to the influence of his life and teaching on earlier, present, or future generations, 'the day' alone will declare it.   If 'salt,' 'light,' and 'living water' have any preservative, beneficial, and fructifying influence on the sons of men, then, surely, when the day comes, many will rise up and call him blessed."

ELIZA GOSSE.

July, 1890.

APPENDIX II.

An account of the religious experiences of my father in the year 1842 and onwards I have thought it proper to give here, in his own words and without comment. The following passage, written in February, 1888, it may be interesting to note, was only just concluded when his fatal illness attacked him, and is the latest of his compositions :—

A great crisis in my spiritual life was approaching ; for the Holy Ghost was about to unfold to me the hope of the personal Advent of the Lord Jesus, of which hitherto I had not the slightest conception. Two of the most valued of my pupils were Edward and Theodore Habershon ; the elder of whom, Edward, a thoughtful and very amiable youth of fifteen, had already secured a large place in my affections. He had occasionally spoken to me of his father, Matthew Habershon, as an author, and had suggested that I might feel interested in his works on sacred prophecy. But I had never heard of them or him ; and Edward's words met with little response. One day, however, Mr. Habershon sent for my acceptance his *Dissertation on the Prophetic Scriptures*, second edition. It was in June, 1842, when days were at the longest. I began to read it after my pupils were dismissed in the afternoon, sat in the garden eagerly devouring the pages, and actually finishing the work (of four hundred octavo pages) before darkness set in. When I closed the book, I knew not where I was ; I had become so wholly absorbed in the great subjects, that some minutes elapsed before I could recall my surroundings, before the new world of my consciousness did " fade into the light of common day."

Of the Restoration of the Jews, I had received some dim inkling already, perhaps from Croly's *Salathiel;* but of the destruction of the Papacy, the end of Gentilism, the kingdom of God, the resurrection and rapture of the Church at the personal descent of the Lord, and the imminency of this,—all came on me that evening like a flash of lightning. My heart drank it in with joy; I found no shrinking from the nearness of Jesus. It was indeed a revelation to a spirit prepared to accept it. I immediately began a practice, which I have pursued uninterruptedly for forty-six years, of constantly praying that I may be one of the favoured saints who shall never taste of death, but be alive and remain until the coming of the Lord, to be "clothed upon with my house which is from heaven."

Subsequently, Mr. Habershon gave me his *Historical Exposition of the Apocalypse*, two volumes. This also is a work of great value, though, as increasing study made me more critical, I found numerous matters of detail to which exception might be taken; and though his confidently anticipated dates were not realized, as, indeed, those of none others are yet, the grand outline of interpretation of Divine prophecy given is beyond dispute. But to me, who had known nothing higher than the narrow and bald lines of Wesleyanism, it was, as I have said, a glorious unveiling. Its immediate effect was to deliver me from Arminianism, on behalf of which I had hotly disputed with my father, only a few months before.

The enlargement of mind and heart thus effected was, doubtless operative in the preparation for another important spiritual change,—the perception, and then the reception, of what are known as "Brethren's principles."   And this though there was no definite or sensible connection between the two movements in my mind.   There was living in Hackney a young gentleman, a classleader in the Methodist society, with whom I was on visiting terms.   His wife was preparing a little brochure for publication, and they requested me to give her, professionally, some literary assistance in the work.   Thus I was thrown much into their society; and as they were both earnest believers and both of engaging manners and of amiable disposition, the acquaintance became unrestrained and very agreeable.   One day, Mr. Berger observed, "I wish you could know my brother Will; you would be much interested in each other!"   And soon after he managed that his brother should be present on one of my evenings.   I was charmed with William Thomas Berger : his meekness and gentleness, his exceeding love and grace—the manifest image of Christ in him—drew to him my whole heart ; and then began a mutual esteem and friendship, which no cloud has ever shadowed from that day to this.

It was about the beginning of the year 1843 ; and presently William Berger told me that he was on the eve of marriage, and was then just about starting on a wedding tour, but that on his return he would be pleased to welcome me to their house.   Accordingly he and his bride (who had been Miss Van Sommer) renewed the invitation in the following May, and I became immediately a welcome visitant.   She was a very sweet, simple Christian lady, very lowly and very loving ; they were indeed true yoke-fellows, of one heart and soul, constantly overflowing in kindness towards me.   Both of them had been for some time prominent in the little band in Hackney who, discerning the evil of sectarian division in the Church of God, had associated together in the Name of Jesus only, refusing any distinctive title but that one common to all believers, of "Brethren," and including under this appellation all who, in every place, love the Lord Jesus Christ, whatever their measure of light or scripturalness of practice.   That the Church of God, and every believer in particular, was called to separation from the world, they perceived ; and hence, the connection of the Church with the State was totally repudiated.   The energy of the Holy Spirit in the assembly of the Church was acknowledged, and maintained to exist now in the same amplitude as in the Apostolic age ; and it was inferred that the liberty of ministry in the Church at the present age is exactly that seen in 1 Cor. xiv. In this I judge they were in error ; for this supposes that the miraculous gifts ($\chi\alpha\rho\acute{\iota}o\mu\alpha\tau\alpha$) are still extant, of which there is no evidence.

All this, however, became known to me only by degrees.   Until I knew the dear Bergers, I was not aware that a movement of this character was in existence ; nor had I so much as heard, during my three years' residence in Hackney, that in a little retired building, called Ellis's Room, a body of Christians holding these views met every Lord's day.

Quite early my new friends invited me to take part in a meeting held weekly at their house, for studying the Holy Word.* Of such a "Scripture reading," now so common, I had never heard. I found, sitting round a large table in their dining-room, each with a Bible before him, about ten persons—William and Mary Berger, George Pearse, Capel Berger, Edward Spencer, Edward Hanson, James Van Sommer, and perhaps one or two more; and I took my place in the little company. They were engaged on Rom. i., and the seventeenth verse occupied the whole evening. Such a close and minute digging for hid treasures was a novelty to me; as was also the deference and subjection to the Word of God, and the comparing of Scripture with Scripture. The company present were pretty uniform in mental power and education; almost all could refer to the Greek original; and there was unrestrained freedom of discussion, and perfect loving confidence. Many points were examined; for the converse was necessarily somewhat desultory. Only one prominent topic has fixed itself in my memory, viz. the heavenly citizenship. This so amazed me that I exclaimed, "Because I am a Christian, surely I am not less an Englishman!" Hanson, at whom I looked as I spoke, only shook his head, and I was silent; till, just before the meeting closed, I emphatically said, "I have learned a great truth to-night!"

I had already formally severed my connection with the Wesleyan society, and now took my place on Lord's day mornings with the little company (some forty or fifty lowly believers) who met to break bread at Ellis's Room :—a change for which I have ever since had reason to thank God.

---

* My father's memory fails him when he says "quite early." It was in pril, 1847, that he began to take part in these meetings.—E. G.

INDEX.

A

Abaco, Bahamas, 118
Abraham and his Children, Mrs. Emily Gosse's, 256
Academy of Natural Science, Philadelphia, 113
Actinia. See Sea-Anemones
Actinologia Britannica, ib.
Alabama, life and scenery in, 124–148
Alder, Joshua, 243, 266
American ideas of British, 140, 141
Andrews, Miss, 293
Aquarium. *See* Marine Aquarium
——, Gosse's *The*, 246, 251, 252, 261, 288, 297, 340
Arlidge, Dr., 318
Asplanchna, 226
Assyria; her Manners and Customs, Arts and Arms, Gosse's, 231

B

Babbicombe in 1852, 237
Baird, Dr. William, 172
Balanophyllia, 241
Banim's *O'Hara* tales, 55, 345
Bate, C. Spence, 252
Battersby, Robert, 266
Battle of Hastings, No. 1, Chatterton's, 17
Bear, curious case of shooting a, 134
Beavers, 65, 66, 108
Bell, Mrs. Susan, "Aunt Bell," 12.
——, Thomas, F.R.S., their son, 12, 156–158, 170, 250
Berger, Mr. William Thomas, 212, 376–

Bermuda, 205
Best, Hannah, afterwards Mrs. Thomas Gosse, 3, 4; marriage, 5; gives birth to PHILIP HENRY, *ib.*; contributes to family maintenance, 6; loneliness in Poole, 9; care and solicitude, 13; strength of character, 16; visits her parents, 18, 19; in Wimborne, 153; keeps house in Hackney for Philip, 167; removes to Kentish Town, 172; return to Hackney, 179; association with daughter-in-law, 221; quits son's residence, 234; rejoins her son at St. Marychurch, 293; her death, *ib.*
——, Philip, grandfather of P. H. Gosse, 4
Bethune, Rev. G. W., 114
Bible, knowledge of the, 328, 329
Birch, Dr. Samuel, 211
Birds, Gosse's, 219, 221
—— *of Jamaica*, Gosse's, 211; *Illustrations to*, 218, 219
Blandford school, Gosse enters, 21
Bluefields, Jamaica, 185, 186, 188, 201
Bohanan, Mr., of Jamaica, 126, 129, 131
Botta, at Nimroud, 231
Bowerbank, James Scott, 223, 230, 243, 245, 253, 257
Bowes, Emily, afterwards Mrs. Philip Gosse, 215; ancestry, *ib.*; education, 216; meets Philip Gosse, 217; personal appearance, *ib.*; portrait painted by G. F. Joseph, A.R.A., *ib.*; marriage with PHILIP HENRY, 218; temperament, 221; married life, *ib.*, 261, 262; assists in translating Ehrenberg's *Die Infusionsthierschen*, 224; death of her aunt, 225; death of her mother, 227; literary assistance to husband, 242; feeble

health, 251 ; benefited by Tenby, 254 ;
publishes *Abraham and his Children*,
256 ; issue and great success of her
Gospel Tracts, 260 ; distressing illness,
262–264 ; sympathy with others, 265 ;
final illness and death, 270 ; traits of
character, 272 ; *Memorial*, 273, 274

Bowes, Hannah *neé* Troutbeck, mother
of preceding, 215, 227

——, Nicholas, of Boston, U.S., 215

——, Lucy *neé* Hancock, his wife, 215

——, William, father of Emily, 215, 227

Brady, Mr. H. B., 348

Brightwen, Eliza, afterwards Mrs. P. H.
Gosse, her marriage at Frome, 294 ; on
sea-shore expeditions, 311 ; pupil of
Cotman, 341 ; *Reminiscences of my
Husband*, App. I.

Bristol, Thomas Gosse at, 5

British Birds, Yarrell's, 290

—— Museum, 170, 172, 226, 231, 233 ;
collections for, 178, 210

British Quadrupeds, Bell's, 156

Brixham, 239

Brook Farm, co-operation at, 87

Brown, Mr., of Poole, 11

——, John Hammond, 17, 22, 26, 35,
54

Burlington, U.S.A., Gosse at, 111, 112

Bus, Vicomte du, 211

Butler, Bishop, 14

Butterflies, Camberwell beauty in Newfoundland, 71 ; in Alabama, 129, 130 ;
swallow-tail in Newfoundland, 89 ;
English, 167 ; *Heliconia* in Jamaica,
183 ; velvet-black (*Urania Sloanus*),

—— *of Paraguay*, Gosse's, 315

Byrne, Old Joe, a trapper, 65–68

Byron's *Tales*, 15, 25, 351

C

Cahawba, Alabama, 132

Camden Town, lodgings in, 243

Campbell, Sam, Gosse's negro assistant,
187, 190, 197, 201

Campbell's *Last Man*, 28

Canada, 89–109, 130 ; voyage to, 89, 90 ;
autumn scenery in, 98 ; description of
a winter tempest, 161, 162 ; Gosse's
emigrant life at Compton, 91–104, 110

Canadian Naturalist, Gosse's, 96, 102,

151, 155, 171, 177, 194, 344, 345 ; successful sale of MS., 157 ; publication
and style, 159–162 ; its success, 162

Carbonear, Newfoundland, Gosse at, 31,
33, 73, 75, 81, 83, 101, 113 ; book club,
38, 39 ; winter in, 44 ; Gosse leaves,
89

Carrington, Mr. J. T., 309

Cayo Boca, West Indies, 119

Centipede, Note on an Electric, 171

Claiborne, Alabama, 114

Clarke of Liverpool, William, 151

Clement, Father, its effect on Gosse, 19

Colemans, the, of Bluefields, 185, 186,
201, 208

Compton. *See* Canada

——, Captain, 73

Comptoniensa, Lepidoptera, 100

Conception Bay Mercury, The, 76

Conrad, Timothy A., conchologist, 114

Content, Jamaica, visit to, 192

Cooper, Fennimore, works of, 55, 345

——, Dr. Samuel, of Boston, 215

Creation, The Vestiges of, 279, 282, 283

Croly, Rev. George, 76, 345, 376

Crystal Palace Aquarium, collects for,
250

——, Lloyd's aquaria, 306, 309

Cuming, Hugh, of Gower Street, 178

Cuvier, 273

Cyclopædia Pantologia, 11

D

Dallas, Alabama, 123, 125, 146

Dalston, residence in, 209

Darwin, Charles, 150, 161, 230, 256, 272,
276, 277, 279, 292, 297, 323 ; characteristic letters, 266–269 ; fertilization of
orchids, 299, 300, 303, 304

Davy's *Salmonia*, Sir Humphrey, 102

Devonshire, visits to, 236–243, 257–259 ;
settles in, 272–323. *See* also St. Marychurch

—— cup coral (*Caryophyllia Smithii*),
240

—— *Coast, Naturalist's Ramble on the*,
240–242, 249, 250, 259, 261, 272, 297,
339, 344, 345 ; profits on publication,
245 ; synopsis of a chapter, 346 ; specimen of its style, 347

Dohrn, Dr. Anton, 349

Dolphin (*Coryphæna psittacus*), capture, and changeable colour in dying of, 121
Doubleday, Edward, 171, 178, 233
——, Henry, 171
Drew, Mrs., of Poole, 17
Dujardin's *Systolides*, 231
Dyson, David, 179
Dyster, Frederick, 254

E

Egypt, Monuments of Ancient, 211
Ehrenberg's *Die Infusionsthierchen*, 224, 226, 255
Elson, Mr., merchant of Carbonear, 34, 37, 38, 43, 57, 61, 68, 71, 75, 79, 88 ; decline of his firm, 105
Emigrant life in Canada, 92–96
Encyclopædia Perthensis, earliest study, 11
Entomologia Alabamensis, an unpublished work, 130
—— *Terræ-novæ*, 79–80
Entomological Journal, 71, 80, 96 ; extracts from, 100, 101, 106–109
—— Society, 315
Entomologist, The, Edward Newman's, 171
Entomologist's Text Book, Westwood's, 172
Entomology of Newfoundland, 102
Epping Forest, 167, 171
Epps, Dr. John, 270
Essays of Elia, 38
Evolutionism, position towards, 273, 276, 277, 336
Excelsior Magazine, 275

F

Fairbank, Dr., 202
Faraday, 335, 350
Fishes, Gosse's, 225, 227
Florida Reef, 118, 119
Floscularidæ, the, 295
Fog-bow or circle off Newfoundland, 62
Forbes, Edward, 243, 252, 255, 268, 272, 333, 344
Foster, Prof. Michael, 317
Fourierism, 87

G

Gamble, T., of Carbonear, 47
Garland and Co., Messrs. George, of Poole, 24, 29
Geology and Genesis, 277
Glaucus, or the Wonders of the Shore, Kingsley's, 253, 257 ; projects of Gosse noticed in, 344
Glimpses of the Wonderful, 178, 179
Good Words, contributes to, 296, 297
Goodrington sands, 321, 322
GOSSE family, 2
——, Elizabeth, afterwards Mrs. Green, sister of Philip Henry, 71–73, 103, 156, 162 ; her death, 163
——, Etienne, author of *Le Médisant*, 2
——, Mrs. Emily. *See* Bowes, Emily
——, Mrs. Hannah. *See* Best, Hannah
——, PHILIP HENRY, ancestors, 2 ; birth, 5 ; earliest recollection, 6, 7 ; first illness, 10 ; attends dame's school, 10 ; first impression of natural objects, 10, 11 ; love of natural history aroused, 11, 12 ; rebuffs, 13 ; strength of memory, 16, 17 ; attends Sells' school, 17 ; love of books, 18 ; enters Blandford school, 21 ; thinking powers, 21 ; rambles and zoological studies, 22, 23 ; appearance at age of fifteen, 24 ; enters mercantile house, 24 ; leisure hours, 26, 27 ; love of *lepidoptera*, 27 ; appears in print, 28 ; escape from drowning, 28 ; accepts a clerkship in Newfoundland, 29 ; friendship with W. C. St. John, 34–37, 39–42 ; life in Newfoundland, 37, 38, 42, 43 ; attachment to Miss Jane Elson, 45 ; clerical work, 48, 51, 57–59 ; remuneration, 51, 52 ; change from boy to man, 54 ; attempts novel writing, 57 ; keeps a journal, 59 ; gains information on seals and seal-fishing, 57–60 ; susceptibility to ghostly fears, 60 ; moved from Carbonear to St. Mary, 61, 62 ; life at St. Mary's, 62–64 ; return to Carbonear, 65 ; attempts poetry, 69 ; commences serious study of natural history, 70 ; becomes a Christian, 70 ; visits England, 70 ; sister's illness develops religious feelings, 72, 73 ; return to Newfoundland, 76 ; letters exhibiting eagerness of natural history observations,

76-79 ; " collection," 79 ; amateur instruments, 80 ; first insect cabinet, 82, 110, 112, 148 ; religious fervour and rigidness of thought, 83, 149, 150, 214, 276-283, 324-332 ; buoyant Canadian anticipations, 86, 87 ; quits Newfoundland, 89 ; becomes Canadian settler at Compton, 91 ; farm, 92-95, 97, 103 ; his *Canadian Naturalist*, 96 ; teacher in a township school, 99, 100 ; recognized by Canadian Scientific Societies, 100 ; temporary ill-health, 103, 104, 197, 212, 233, 234, 256, 259 ; tired of Canada, what prospect for a school at Poole? 104 ; change of intention, resolves for Southern States, *ib.* ; sells farm, 105 ; position at age of twenty-eight, 105 ; journey from Canada to United States, 111, 112 ; welcome by scientific men of Philadelphia, 113-115 ; voyage to Mobile, 115-121 ; reflections, 121-123 ; passage to King's Landing, 123 ; engaged by Judge Saffold, *ib.* ; up-country experience, 124, 125 ; school-house, Mount Pleasant, 126, 127 ; daily routine, 127-129 ; entomological activity, 129-132 ; skill as a zoological artist, 130 ; subjected to social peculiarities, 140, 141 ; morbidity of mind, 144, 145 ; farewell to Dallas and the Saffolds, 146 ; quits America and arrives at Liverpool, 148 ; sale of entomological collection, *ib.* ; Atlantic voyage, 150, 151 ; refuses a museum curatorship, 151-153 ; attachment to Miss Button, 155 ; seeks fortune in London, 155, 156 ; unexpected good fortune in sale of *Canadian Naturalist* MS. to Van Voorst, 157 ; gives instruction in flower-painting, 158, 162 ; pursuits in 1839, 159 ; sketches of Sherborne, 163 ; sister's death, 163, 164 ; ill fortune, 164 ; starts an academy in Hackney, *ib.* ; process of self-education, 167-169 ; opening up of a literary career, 169, 170, 177, 178 ; gains valuable friends, 171, 172 ; removes to Kentish Town, 172 ; nocturnal pursuits leads to arrest, 173 ; suggested visit to Jamaica for British Museum, 178 ; voyage, 179-182 ; occupation in Jamaica, 183-202 ; father's death, 189 ; bitten by a scorpion, 202 ; homeward voyage, 202-205 ; appearance in 1846, 206, 207 ; accidental portrait, 207 ; example of his severity of reproof, 208, 209 ; slow growth of means, 210 ; thoughts of visit to Azores, *ib.* ; literary activity, 211, 212, 218, 219, 227, 231, 232 ; courtship and marriage to Miss E. Bowes, 217, 218 ; residence in De Beauvoir Square, 219 ; seclusion of home life, 221 ; buys a microscope, 222 ; its effect, *ib.* ; starts study of *Rotifera*, 222, 223 ; birth of his son, 223 ; daily division of studies, 224 ; member of Linnæan and Microscopical Societies, 225 ; improved fortune, *ib.* ; inaugurates new method of natural history observation, 228, 229 ; archæological studies, 231 ; social life, 232, 233 ; marine researches on shores of Devonshire, 238-243 ; return to London, 243 ; experiments towards, and establishment of, marine aquariums, 243, 244 ; agrees to collect for Zoological Society's aquarium, 244 ; becomes a popular lecturer, 245 ; visits Weymouth, *ib.* ; dredging and collecting expeditions, 244-249 ; returns to London (Islington), 252 ; visit to Tenby, new friends, 253, 254 ; conducts classes on sea-shore at Ilfracombe, 257-259 ; and at Tenby, 264 ; activity in 1855, 259 ; elected F.R.S., 261 ; wedded life, 261, 262 ; correspondence with Darwin, 266-269 ; death of first wife, 270 ; its effect, 270-274 ; position as a zoologist, 273 ; premature hopes of an abortive Welsh professorship, 274 ; finally quits London for South Devon, 275 ; study of sea-anemones, 284-290 ; working garb, 287, 288 ; literary work, 284, 289-293 ; household at St. Marychurch, 293 ; second marriage, 294 ; abandons zoology, 296 ; cultivates orchids, *ib.* ; correspondence with Darwin, 297-304 ; ceases professional authorship, 305 ; marine zoological enthusiasm revived, 307-309 ; excursions described, 310-312 ; study of astronomy, 307, 322, 323 ; resuscitation of *Lepidoptera* studies, 313-317 ; publication of *Rotifera*, the joy of his old age, 319, 320 ; final family ramble on sea-shore, 321 ; bronchial attack, coupled with heart disease, proves fatal, 323; burial at Torquay, *ib.*; social isolation, 333; contradictions of temperament, 334, 335; scope of scientific labours, 336, 337; claim as a zoological artist, 338–341; characteristics as a lecturer and public speaker, 342; as a letter writer, 343; criticism of his books, 343–348; unable to depict human figure, 349, 350; solitary visit to a theatre, 350; love of poetry, 351, 352

Gosse, Thomas, miniature painter, 1; father of PHILIP HENRY, 2; birth and training, *ib.*; courtship and marriage, 3–5; wanderings, 5, 6; located at Poole, 7; voluminous writer of unpublished works, 14, 189, 190; love of reading, 15; joins his son in Kentish Town, 172; removal to Hackney, 179; his death, 189

——, William, of Ringwood, 2; his daughter Susan, 12

——, William, brother of PHILIP HENRY, 5, 24, 43, 84, 163; sails for Newfoundland, 20; welcomes his brother on arrival, 33

Gould, John, 211

Gray, George Richard, 172

——, John Edward, *ib.*

Green, Mr. and Mrs., of Worcester, 3

——, Mrs. Elizabeth. *See* Gosse, Elizabeth

Greenwell, Dora, 333

Griffen's *The Collegians*, 56

H

Hackney, residence at, 158, 164, 165, 167, 172, 213, 234

Haffenden, Mr., of Jamaica, 184

Hamburg insect cabinet, 82, 110

Hampton, Captain, 79, 82

Hancock, Governor John, 216

Hankey, John A., 210

Harbour Grace, residence of St. John family, 34, 55, 68, 81

Harrison, Samuel, 75, 76

——, Slade and Co., of Poole, 29, 47

Hayti seen from the sea, 203

Hill, Richard, Jamaica naturalist, 194–198, 202, 212, 267, 269

Home Friend, The, 242

Hooker, Sir William, 178, 303

Howard, Mrs. Robert, 218

Howlett, Rev. F., 322

Hudson, Dr. C. T., 255, 296, 318, 371

Hunt, Mr. Arthur, of Torquay, 312

Huron Lake region, 91, 97

Huxley, Professor, 254, 316

Hyena, South African, 23

I

Ilfracombe, 239, 257

Infusionsthierchen, Ehrenberg's *Die*, 224, 255

Infusoria, Pritchard's *History of the*, 222, 318

Insect cabinet, 82, 110, 112, 148

Islington, residence in, 252

Israel, The Restoration of, unpublished poem, 76

Jamaica, 180–205; starts for, 178; ornithology, 180; approach to, 181, 182; scenery, 186, 199, 200; natural history observations by R. Hill, 194–196

——, *Birds of*, 211, 212; *Illustrations to*, 219

——, *Naturalist's Sojourn in*, 193, 196, 225, 227–229, 344, 345

—— Society, the, 198, 200

Jaques, G. E. and Mrs., of Carbonear, 43, 83, 85, 87, 88, 151; remove to Canada, 89; their farm, 95, 105, 110, 111

Jardine, Sir William, 211

Jews, History of the, 219, 220

Johnston, Dr. George, 243, 284

Joseph Andrews, 26

Joseph, G. F., A.R.A., portrait of Mrs. Gosse, 217

K

Kendrick, Major, 135

Kentish Town, residence in, 172, 173

Kew Gardens, 178, 233

——, *Guide to*, 259

Kingfisher's nest, discovery of a, 19

Kingsley, Rev. Charles, 151, 251, 252, 255, 256, 293, 333; germ of *Glaucus*, 253; letter on Gosse's *Omphalos*, 280–283; dredging for specimens, 289; criticisms of Gosse's works, 344, 345

Knight, Rev. Richard, Wesleyan minister, 70

L

Labrador fleet, 33, 44
Lacerta viridis at Poole, 13
Lamarck, 273
Land and Sea, Gosse's, 304
Lankester, Prof. E. Ray, 261, 316, 318, 319
Lara, Byron's, 25, 351
Lar sabellarum, paper on, 266
Layard at Nimroud, 231
Leamington, 225
Leidy, Dr. Joseph, zoologist, 113
Lepidoptera, Comptoniensa, 100. *See also* Butterflies
——, Gosse on *The Clasping Organs ancillary to Generation of certain*, 316, 317
Lester, Mr., M.P. for Poole, 28
Lever's exhibition, Sir Aston, 27
Lewin, Mr. and Mrs. J. L., 197
Life in its Lower, Intermediate and Higher Forms, Gosse's, 276
Lightning, description of effect on a house struck by, 53
Lighton, Sir Charles, 259
Liguanea Mountains, Jamaica, 199
Linnæan Society, 225, 232, 256, 259, 266, 317
Linnæus's *Systema Naturæ*, 82, 338
—— *Genera Insectorum*, 338
Lisby, Edward, 24
Livermead, Tor Bay, 285, 288
Liverpool, Gosse at, 151, 153
Lloyd, W. Alford, 306, 348
Loader, parish clerk of Carbonear, 84, 85
Loddiges, George, florist, 158
London district, Lake Huron, 91, 97
Longicorns, 204
Longmans, Messrs., 225, 229
Low, Hugh, 179
Lundy Island, 242, 304
Lush, W. F., 44, 113

M

Macleod, Dr. Norman, 296
Mammalia, Gosse's, 212, 220
March, Mary, of Newfoundland, 60
Marine Aquarium, first germ, 235; natural one, 237; first serious attempt to create, 243; its inventor, 244; first private, 250; its popularization, 252, 348, 349; at St. Marychurch, 309, 312, 320
Marine Aquarium, Handbook to the, 259
—— biological stations, 349
Martin of Poole, 62
——, John W., of St. Mary's, Newfoundland, 62–65
Melicertidæ, 295
·Melly, Mr., insect buyer, 148
Memory, training of the, 165, 166
Methodism, Gosse and, 153, 154, 375
Microscope, Adams's *Essays on the*, 70
——, Gosse's *Evenings at the*, 290
Microscopical Society, 223, 224, 230, 232, 243, 259
Mitchell, D. W., 211, 244
Mobile, voyage from Philadelphia to, 115–121; visit to, 148, 149
Molloy, Dr., of Carbonear, 81
——, Dr. P. E., of Montreal, 92
Montego Bay, Jamaica, 197
Montreal museum, 100
Moravians, 186, 191, 192
Morgan, Mrs., of Clifton, 270
Mount Pleasant, Alabama, Gosse's school at, 126
Murray, John, 225
Museum. *See* British, Montreal, Philadelphia

N

Natural History, Annals and Magazine of, 226, 248, 252, 259
——, Gosse's *Romance* (or *Poetry of*), 291, 292; second series, 295
——, views on study·of, 227, 228
Naturalist's Sojourn in Jamaica, Gosse's, 196, 225, 227–229, 304, 344, 345
Nevill, Lady Dorothy, 304, 313
Newell, Mr., of Carbonear, 43, 46, 54, 57
Newfoundland, 30–88; voyage to, 30, 31; scenery, 33, 107, 163; Irish element, 42, 81, 86; planters and their course of business, 47, 48; fisheries and fishing population, 48–50; "North Shore," 49; winter, 56, 57, 66; overland winter journey, 66–68; contrast to Dorsetshire, 74; meteorological notes issued in, 76; landscape, 78, 79; entomology, 81, 86; party spirit and outrage (1833), 81;

Gosse its first naturalist, 82, 338 ; papers
  on temperature, 100 ; state of its society
  (1838), 105
Newfoundland, *Entomology of*, 101, 102
Newman, Edward, 171
New York, Gosse at, 112
Nineveh, winged bull of, 226, 231
Noseworthy, Brother, 145, 146
Notommatina, 296
Nuttall, Thomas, botanist, 113

O

Ocean, The, Gosse's, 173–178, 304
Oddicombe, 237, 285
O'Hara Family tales, Banim's, 55
Omphalos, Gosse's, 276–283
Opossum hunt in Alabama, 135–140
Orchids, Jamaica, 184, 187 ; fertilization
  of, 297–304
Ornithology, Gosse's *Popular British*,
  220, 221
——, Wilson's *American*, 160
Osborne, Mr., of Jamaica, 198
Otter slides, 66, 67
Owen, Sir Richard, 230, 292

P

Paget, Dr. Sir James, 262
Parkstone, 73, 74
Parnell, Dr., 195
Peachia. See Sea-anemones
Peale, T. R., zoologist artist, 113
Pennant, 159
Penny, R.A., Edward, 3
Philadelphia, 104, 113, 114
Phippard, sailmaker, 30
——, J.P., William, of St. Mary's, 62,
  63
Pimlico, Mrs. Gosse in, 265
Plessing, Mr. and Mrs., 186
Plymouth Brethren, theology of, 213, 214,
  330
Poole in 1812, 8 ; Gosse family in, 6, 7,
  20, 26 ; Philip Henry leaves, 29 ; re-
  visited, 71, 73–75, 103
Popular Science Review, 295
Prickly pear, 122
Pritchard's *History of Infusoria*, 222, 318

Public Ledger of Newfoundland, 81
Puerto Rico, coast scenery, 203
——, San Juan, 203, 204
Punch and the Marine Aquarium, 348

Q

Quebec, its approach described, 90, 94
Quekett, John, 223

R

Racoon, chasing the, 138, 139
Religious feelings, 31, 32, 169, 213, 324–
  334, Appendix II.
Remingtons of Massachusetts, 216
Remoras, or sucking fish, described, 120,
  121
Renouard, Rev. G. C., 211
Reporter, Royal Agricultural Society's, 195
Reptiles, Gosse's, 221
Reynolds, Sir Joshua, 2
Ringwood, Gosse family at, 2
Robinson's drawings of birds, etc., Dr.
  Anthony, 198, 200, 202
Rocky River, Newfoundland, 66
Ross, Sir James, 173
Rossetti, Dante G., 226
Rotifers, Gosse's studies of, 222–224,
  226, 235, 252, 255, 256, 295, 318, 337,
  350
Rotifera found in Britain, Gosse's *Cata-
  logue of*, 231
——, Gosse's *Diœcious Character of the*,
  261
——, Gosse's *On the Structure, etc., of*,
  255
——, Hudson and Gosse's, *The*, 318–321 ;
  Supplement, 321
Royal Society, Proceedings of, 171, 255,
  259, 316
——, Gosse's election, 261, 263 ; obituary
  notice of Gosse, 348

S

Sacred Streams, Gosse's, 224, 227
Saffold, Hon. Chief Justice Rueben, 122,
  123, 146
——, Rueben, junr., 125

Salmonia, or Days of Fly Fishing, Sir Humphrey Davy's, 102

Salter, Dr. Hyde, 262

——, Tom, Gosse's cousin, 11, 75

Saturday Review on Gosse's death, 337

Saunders, W. W., letter to, 209, 210

Savannah-le-Mar, Jamaica, 184, 185, 188, 189

Saw-whetter, Sound of the, 111

Scarron's *Roman Comique,* 26

School Seventy Years ago, A Country Day, 17

Scorpion on ship in North Atlantic, 77 ; and off Kingston, 202

Scott, J., of Edinburgh, 299

——, Sir Walter, works of, 55

Sculpen (*Cottus*), 114

Sea and Land, 242

Sea-anemones (*Actinia*), 241 ; *rosea* and *nivea,* 239, 253 ; *bunodes coronata,* 289 ; *Sagartia,* 241 ; *bunodes, ib.,* gastronomic test of *crassicornis,* 241, 242 ; *peachia,* 256

—— and Corals, Gosse's *History of the British* (*Actinologia Britannica*), 284, 290, 307, 337, 340

Sea-serpent, theory of the, 291, 292, 295

Sea-side Pleasures, Gosse's, 242

Seal fishery, departure from and return to, Newfoundland, 48

Seal pelts delivered, method of checking, 57, 58

Sedgwick, Adam, 277

Sells, Charles, of Poole, 17, 39

Selma, Alabama, 146

Serpentine, *Asplanchna* in, 226

Sherborne, 157, 163

Shore, A Year at the, 296, 305, 341

Sinclair, Lord, 296

Slade, Elson and Co., 47, 93 ; decline of the firm, 105

Slavery in Southern States (1838), 142, 143

Sly, Mrs., 10

Smith, Anker, A.R.A., 2

Society for Promoting Christian Knowledge, Gosse writes for, 169, 170, 173, 211, 219, 231, 242

Southey's *Thalaba,* 351

Sparrow, America, 115

Sprague, Mr., 79

Squirrels in Alabama, 133

St. John, William Charles, 34, 54-57, 76 ; his father, Oliver, 34 ; portrayed, 34-36 ;

warm friendship for Gosse, 36, 37 ; death, 37 ; letter recounting early walks, 39, 40 ; burlesque poem on Gosse, 41, 42 ; marriage, 68

St. John, Hannah and Charlotte, 55

St. Mary's, Newfoundland, Gosse a clerk in, 61 ; described, 62, 63

St. Marychurch, Devon, visit to, 236, 239 ; buys a house and settles at, 275 ; life in, 306, 307, Appendix I.

St. Thomas, West Indies, visit to, 204

Stacey, Miss Mary, 262

Stanley, Bishop, 250

Star crane fly of Newfoundland, 101

Stephanoceros, 222, 295

Stoddards of Massachusetts, 216

Sucking fish. *See* Remoras

Surrey Zoological Gardens, collects for Aquarium of, 250

Swallow, Jamaica green, 223

Swanage, at, 20

Systema Naturæ of Linnæus, 82, 338

T

Tarrant Monkton, 22

Tegg's *London Encyclopædia,* 82

Tenby, its attractions, 253, 254 ; revisited, 264

——, Gosse's, 254, 256, 259, 272 ; profits of, 261

Thomas, Luke, 30, 32

Thoreau, Henry, 161

Titton Brook, early recollections of, 6

Tom Cringle's Log, Michael Scott's, 185

Toole, Ned, and the Ghost, 63, 64

Tor Bay, Kingsley and Gosse on, 289

Torquay, 351 ; Gosse's burial place, 324

Tramp, anecdote of a, 15

Troutbeck, Hannah, 215

——, Rev. John, 215

Trumpet Major, Hardy's *The,* 22

Twohig, Mr., 69

V

Van Voorst, John, purchases MS. of *Canadian Naturalist,* 157 ; friendship to Gosse, 158, 170, 211, 245

Vivarium, its inventor, 243, 244

W

Walsh's *Brazil*, 151
Ward, William, A.R.A., 2
Warington, Robert, 243
Waterton, Charles, *Wanderings*, 160
Wesleyan Society, joins the, 83, 84;
 thoughts of the ministry, 153, 154;
 local preacher, 169; severs connection
 with, *ib.*
West Indies, visit to, 180–205; revisit
 contemplated, 227
Westwood, John Obadiah, Prof., 172
Weymouth, marine researches at, 246,
 247, 251, 257
Whale, *Beluga* or white, 73; toothless of
 Havre (*Delphinorhynchus micropterus*),
 181
White, Adam, 172, 233
——, Dr. Buchanan, 315, 316
——, Gilbert, of Selborne, 106, 160, 180,
 344, 345
—— *Oak*, passage to Mobile in the, 115
Whymper, J. W., 172, 173, 177, 212
Whitneys of Massachusetts, 216
Wight, visit to Isle of, 234
Wilberforce, Bishop of Oxford, 254
Wilkes, Lieut. Charles, 113
Wilson, Alexander, ornithologist, 114,
 115, 160, 229

Wimborne, Philip Henry and mother at,
 153
Winthrop, Governor, 215
Winton, Henry, outrage on, 81
Wombwell's menagerie, 22, 23
Wood, Mr., of St. John's, 47
Woodpeckers (*Picus principalis* and
 Picus auratus), 131
Worcester, Thomas Gosse at, 1, 3–5; his
 marriage, and birthplace of PHILIP
 HENRY, 5

Y

Yarrell, William, 20, 290
Youth's Magazine, contributes to, 28

Z

Zoology, views on study of, 228, 229
—— *for Schools*, Text-book of, 221, 222,
 224, 227
——, *Introduction to*, 48, 169, 170
——, *Manual of Marine*, 256, 257, 259,
 263, 338
Zoological artist, Gosse as a, 338, 339
—— Gardens Aquarium, 244; Gosse
 collects for, 246; dispute re-conditions,
 248, 249

THE END.